INFINITE MAGIC

THE HIDDEN PROPHECY TRILOGY BOOK 3

LILY SKYY

Infinite Magic
Copyright © 2022 by Lily Skyy
www.LilySkyy.com

First Edition: July 2022

ISBN 978-1-956525-90-8 (ebook)
ISBN 978-1-957989-38-9 (paperback)

Published by Books to Hook Publishing, LLC.
www.BooksToHook.com

CONTENTS

CHAPTER I
A NEW DAY

Kinza watched the hundreds of flowers float up on the wind, rising high above the smoke of the pyre.

Many of the blooms she recognized, but many she did not. It seemed a rather apt representation of her time in Rhapta. Many things were familiar, like the path the sun takes or a mother's love. But many were not, like the Anunnaki she watched now as they coaxed the fire higher and the smoke and wind away from the eyes of the dancing crowd with nothing more than magic.

She supposed she could add funerals to the list of things that were different for her. She remembered attending her own parents' funeral, and it was a somber affair, with the usual black clothing and tears. Anunnaki reacted differently, though, when their loved ones passed. She had discovered this over the last two days as this city mourned the loss of their kin in the attack. Today's funeral was the largest; thousands of people made their way out of the city, past the outskirts, into the field beyond—still within the barrier, though.

Instead of the dark mourning clothes she was used to, they

wore bright patterns, painted their faces, and wore beads and feathers in their hair and on their arms. Ekaja had helped Kinza this morning to dress appropriately. She gave her a bright orange dress that clasped over one shoulder and braided part of her curls back, adding tiny lapis beads in the design. Her face was painted simply with marks of red and yellow, and a feathered cuff added to her bare arm.

Looking at the mass of people now, dancing and chanting through their tears, she thought that this might've been what they needed. They had cried enough over the past few days, over their destroyed city and lost loved ones. Zaid had translated some of the chanting for her, explaining that they were celebrating the life of the dead, and the bigger the celebrations, the better the life they had.

Hakim must have had one heck of a life, Kinza thought to herself. They had come out at dawn, temporarily setting aside their work rebuilding to celebrate the passing of their Grand Elder. He had died peacefully in his sleep the night after Tahir's attack on Rhapta. Even the magical healing from Kinza's newfound Aura had not been enough to stop the slow marching of time. Anunnaki didn't live forever, and Hakim's time had come.

Kinza watched the dancing, mesmerized by the rhythm and the sound of the beads, until a woman danced over and pressed a cup into her palm. She smiled and urged her to drink before dancing off. Kinza looked at the suspicious brown liquid, but it smelled sweet, so she took a sip. It was surprisingly bitter and had her puckering her face.

Zaid's chuckle rumbled next to her. "It's a type of mango beer," he said, looking at the cup like it was a worthy adversary. "Careful. It's stronger than you think."

"I think I'll continue to get my daily fruits and vegetables the old-fashioned way," she said, setting it down.

"That's probably best," he said, turning back to watch the dancing. He looked regal standing there next to her, his clothing as vibrant as hers. It had felt like the moon had fallen out of the sky when he showed up to walk her to the funeral that morning. Instead of his usual black attire, he wore a pair of flowing bright orange and yellow pants, and instead of a shirt, his chest was painted in a series of intricate designs in red, yellow, and black paint, making his tattoo stand out. She wasn't ashamed to say she liked it. The bright colors, the hundreds of flowers in the wind, the dancing. It made death seem less scary and more like a part of the natural cycle of life, something worth celebrating.

True to his word, Zaid had hardly left her side in the last two days. They had entered into a different kind of chaos, one of rebuilding and restructuring, and Kinza was at the center of it, but somehow still an outsider. She and many others didn't know where she would fit into the puzzle that was the new Rhapta. A few of the Elders had left with Tahir and still had not been found, leaving a gaping hole where leadership had been in many parts of the city. Not to mention, Hakim had dropped two bombs on them. The first, when he revealed Kinza was the descendant of Rhapta's long-lost prince, and, therefore, the current heir. And the second when he passed, leaving an empty seat where the Grand Elder had sat and guided his people for nearly two hundred years.

Needless to say, everything was in shambles.

Zaid had done his best to explain things where her knowledge of the Anunnaki was lacking, but he was honestly most helpful when he was just present. It was nice to have someone to stand next to when the weight of the Anunnaki's eyes were getting to be too much. Slowly, word had spread about who Kinza was. First, she had been the outsider from the prophecy, then she was their enemy, but now she was their princess?

She wasn't surprised by the mixed looks she got or the telepathic whispers as she went by. It was just so *tiring*. Some came up to her, begging for a blessing or just to touch her face or her hands, smiling through tears of relief. Others shot her scathing glances and moved away when she came near, cursing her footsteps. And others were just innocently curious, asking where she was from, what her abilities were, and if it truly had been her who had caused the Aurastones to light up like they did. She didn't know where she would fit into all of this, but Zaid had stayed beside her.

It couldn't go on forever, though.

Zaid looked up at the sun that sat high and bright above them, signaling midday. "I have to go now. Savar will be angry if I'm late," he said.

He had been putting off meeting with the leader of the venari, hoping to avoid another assignment at a time like this. Apparently, the attack on Rhapta did nothing to slow the ubir that ran free out in the world, harming humans and causing destruction. A few venari had returned over the last few days to a shocking discovery, but had merely been sent out on another assignment. The only reason Zaid hadn't been sent yet was that he had flat out just avoided Savar, but a message had come that morning—given to Zaid by a young boy who demanded money and ran off—that included a time Zaid was to meet with Savar. He couldn't avoid his responsibilities anymore, and Kinza didn't have the authority to stop it.

She nodded reluctantly. "Okay, I'll see you later then, hopefully?" She desperately hoped he wasn't sent out immediately.

"Hope so," he said and was gone, his tall form striding back through the grass to the city walls.

Kinza sighed. *And now I'm alone.* She continued to watch the dancing and smiled at those who looked friendly, but she quickly felt out of place. Looking down at the cup of mango beer on the ground, she debated picking it up and wondered if it would help the feeling in her chest. But before she could really think about it, someone filled the empty spot in the grass next to her.

"Feeling overwhelmed yet?" Mikah asked, giving her a teasing smile.

"You have no idea," she said. "Will they do this all day then?" she asked, gesturing to the funeral.

"Some will stay all night as well, but most will leave fairly soon. It's usually when the guakal wine runs out," he said with a wink.

His clothing wasn't terribly different from hers. He had a long bright red wrap that wound around his body and was thrown over one shoulder and a cuff on his bare arm. He didn't have any face paint, though, allowing his handsome face to bask in the sun as he watched the festivities. Kinza had the distinct impression of a preening peacock—albeit a good-looking peacock.

They watched for a few more minutes before he turned to her. "Would you like me to walk you back to the city?" he asked. She was about to say no when he held out his elbow to her, a playful smile on his face.

She chuckled and took it, and they started making their way back among a few others. The path they took wound through the outskirts, which had been hit the hardest the first night of the attack. Some of the ramshackle homes were now leveled or burned to the ground. Many of the poorer inhabitants were picking through the ashes and trying to collect scraps of wood and other materials to rebuild.

The fact that she, an outsider, had been clothed and fed regardless of whether she was a princess or an enemy, but these people lived in such conditions, appalled her. But she also didn't know what to do for them either. She didn't have any say as to what resources went where.

She turned her face away and tried to pay attention to what Mikah was saying.

"—and that street would be the best path in autumn for the fieldworkers to carry supplies out, just not back in," he was saying. She honestly had no idea what he was talking about but nodded politely.

She laughed a little. "Mikah, are you giving me a rundown of a travelers' guide to Rhapta?" she asked.

He looked at her with raised eyebrows. "Has no one given you a tour yet?"

"Of course not. We've been a little busy," she said before realizing he was partially teasing again.

"Well then, it's my duty as—as, well... I don't know what my position is anymore now that my mentor turned out to be an enemy of the state, but I would be glad to give you a tour of Rhapta. That is if Her Highness isn't too busy?"

She rolled her eyes, still uncomfortable with the moniker. "Lead the way. I dub you official tour guide of Rhapta."

He grinned and led her through the open gate into the city. "This is the grand eastern entrance of the city," he said as they walked past a pile of rubble, "that has stood for thousands of years... well, it *did*. If you look to your right, you'll see the old residential district"—he swept an arm to the right—"and just a few plazas up that way, you'll find the Consort's Plaza where the wives of old Rhaptan kings used to live and spend their time away from their boring husbands."

Kinza laughed. "They didn't like their husbands?"

Mikah shrugged. "Apparently, the monarchy had a lot of tedious duties with minimal time for fun."

"Hmm." She hummed. They walked on for a little while, Mikah telling her seemingly random facts about each district of the city. As she listened to him talk, she realized she was feeling a bit better.

Throughout the day, people went back to work repairing the broken pieces of the city. Rubble was slowly swept away, repairs were made, and people hauled goods back and forth. While the Anunnaki didn't need to eat very often, they couldn't go forever without food. Food production and distribution had stopped during the attacks, but people quickly worked together to tend to the fields and harvest the ever-growing crops.

What still amazed Kinza the most were the abilities. People moved loads of rock through the air simply with their minds. A woman wove streams of water across a cleared boulevard to wash away the grime. Children were tended to in large gaggles by teachers who twinkled sparkling lights in the air to keep their attention. They were perpetually on a "field trip" as the schoolhouses had been demolished, and teachers were doing the best they could.

Kinza marveled at how well the Anunnaki worked together in near harmony when only days ago they were at each other's throats. The Unfettered that had been captured were currently being held in one of the many empty buildings across the city under heavy guard and more than enough laqueus, but this was a side of the Anunnaki that Kinza hadn't seen yet.

"And this plaza is one of the many business sectors. You will find high-fashion vendors, the best metal workers, and several accounting services here," Mikah was saying as they entered a particularly large plaza near the center of the city.

As they strolled over the white limestone streets, eyes followed Kinza wherever she went. It truly was a relief to see people in every corner of the city now, as opposed to when she, Zaid, and Khalil felt as if they had been wandering through a ghost town. But she felt like she was an animal in a zoo. People gasped and whispered as she passed.

This time, two young girls ran up to her, saying something in Rhaptan before handing her two little flowers.

Kinza smiled but looked at Mikah hesitantly.

"They said, 'For you, princess,'" he translated for her.

Kinza smiled and just said, "Thank you," as she took the flowers. She tucked them into the top hem of her dress, and the girls seemed particularly happy about that. They squealed as they ran back to their mothers. As Kinza watched them run off, she caught two people in white robes across the plaza, eyeing her and whispering animatedly. The looks they were giving her were less than friendly.

"Old men will always bicker at the ascension of younger men," Mikah said, his proud nose in the air. She wondered if he had ever been humble in his life.

"Who said that?" she asked as they resumed their walk.

"I did," he said, affronted. "Don't worry about them. Of course they would be upset when someone younger and prettier than them comes along with a claim to the Rhaptan throne. But it won't matter. Those two have very minor positions in the city."

Kinza hadn't met all of the Elders yet, but their reactions to her were the same as the rest of the Anunnaki. Some adored her, some were merely curious, and some saw her as a threat and treated her with near hostility. She didn't think they would harm her, but it made her nervous. Some of the kinder Elders were a bit more cautious than her, though.

She looked behind her and Mikah, and sure enough, her two shadows were lurking far behind her—but not too far. She had been assigned two guards to be with her at all times since her initial welcome into the city was anything but welcoming. They tended to stay out of the way, but their presence was guaranteed. She did feel safer with them around, not as safe as she did with Zaid, but it was better than nothing.

"Don't I need them on my side, though? I thought how they feel about me is reflected on the people?" she said.

"True, but that was before," he said. "Now that you are Kinza Solace, The Outsider from the Prophecy and Heir to the Rhaptan Throne, and not Mitra of Rhapta, it's different." He gave her a pointed look at the end.

Kinza chuckled. "You aren't going to ever let that go, are you?" The sun shone down on the fountain in the center of the plaza. Just then, two men seemed to finish the repairs, and water started spurting out in a great gush, more forceful than it should have been. Children ran screaming in laughter at the spray.

"Not a chance," he said with a smile. "I will admit that I was absolutely fooled." He sighed. "Such are the charms of women."

Kinza snorted. "Such is the blindness of men, you mean." Even though they laughed, she was eternally thankful for the image of Mikah standing over her, an unusual coldness in his eyes as he defied his mentor and stopped Tahir from cleaving her in two. Even after realizing she had lied to him about her identity. She had expected him to be angry, but if anything, he was impressed.

"You haven't had any official meetings about the, you know, queenship, have you?" he asked.

Kinza inwardly groaned. "I do tomorrow morning," she said. "I'm supposed to meet all the Elders at the Grand Hall to talk about... that." It was the last thing she wanted to do, but she acknowledged that it *might* be a teensy bit important. Would she be queen, or would she just go home?

Mikah nodded. "Do you need any company? I mean, I'll probably be there anyway, but..."

"Zaid said he would take me," she replied. She didn't mention that there was a chance he could be sent on another assignment before then, but she pretended it was otherwise.

Mikah's eyes rolled so hard it looked like he was trying to look into his brain, and Kinza couldn't hold back her laugh. "Ah, yes, your guard dog," Mikah said. "You know, if you are feeling particularly unsafe, I'm happy to assign you two additional guards. Then you wouldn't have the smell of wet canine following you around." He spoke as if it was a perfectly plausible solution to an atrocious situation.

It was Kinza's turn to roll her eyes. "I like having him around. But I'm sure I'll see you there."

Mikah sighed. "Fine, whatever Her Highness wishes. Come, let me show you the swiftest way back to your humble abode," he said, seamlessly falling back into his teasing manner.

They made their way across the city, cutting through the central plaza that was packed with people going about their daily business. They passed into the abandoned eastern quarter that was no longer so abandoned. Since many homes had been destroyed, many citizens had set up temporary housing within the forgotten homes in the eastern and southern quarters. They pushed aside the overgrown vines and flowers and cleared away a few plazas to set up camp for the time being.

Kinza was given her own home in a small plaza not too far from the city center. Just like many others, this plaza was a dead end with buildings on three sides and the entrance to the street on the fourth. The white limestone walls and roof were still intact—which was saying something—and a door was eventually added. The central fountain was dried up and overgrown, but she still thought it was pretty.

As Kinza and Mikah entered her plaza, Mikah's eyebrows rose high. "I see you have a few fans," he said. All around the front door were flowers and tiny trinkets. They were gifts from Rhaptans who thanked her for saving them or from those who knew she was the heir.

"Wait here." One of Kinza's guards moved in front of them and entered the house. They did this every time to make sure no one was lying in wait, and when he came out, he gave her the all-clear.

Kinza turned to Mikah. "Well, thank you for the much-needed tour. I'll see you tomorrow at the Grand Hall, then?"

"Yes, Your Highness," he said with a slight bow of his head.

Kinza laughed as she walked toward the door. "Careful," she said over her shoulder. "I might just start acting like a queen." She heard Mikah's laugh as she stepped inside.

Kinza ascended the steps out of the bathtub. Truly, it was more of a pool, but she was told it was used as a bathing chamber back when people still lived in this area of the city. The water had been a sweet relief from the baking heat of the morning, and she mused over the extravagance in such a simple dwelling as she got dressed.

She didn't think she had been placed in a very large home, but she kept finding little luxuries like this one. There were five or six empty rooms in the house, most of which she hadn't figured out what they were for, but she had selected the one with a high window looking out onto an inner courtyard as her bedroom. There was a bedroll with a mound of blankets, furs, and pillows, all gifts on one side. On the other side of the room were sets of clothes Ekaja had tailored for her, all in the Rhaptan styles.

She found a bright green set that she slipped on. It was a

cropped, one-shoulder shirt and a wrap skirt with yellow and red detailing along the edges. She had noticed that all Rhaptan clothing tended to be bright and flowy, helping cool bodies down under the African sun.

It had only been a few days since all the chaos, but she could already feel herself moving into a routine, and the idea of even having a routine was mindboggling after days of near-death experiences. She almost felt guilty for enjoying a nice bath or an afternoon nap until she reminded herself that fighting for one's life day in and day out was not what life was supposed to be, even if there was still work to do. Grams would tell her there was no point in being anxious over something meant to make you feel better.

Moving out into the main room, she noticed the sun was starting to set and cast a deep orange color on the far walls. There was very little furniture, and the few things she did have were more gifts from people around town or were scrounged up by Zaid. There was a low, square table that she kept the food on, but as she looked at it, she noticed a note had been left for her.

Her name was written on it in English, and the inside was written in English as well.

My lovely Kinza, come have dinner with the girls and me? Ekaja

Kinza smiled broadly. Ekaja had gone into full motherhood mode apparently now that Zaid was home *and* Kinza was here without family. Ekaja had been one of those who had believed in the old prophecy that an outsider would come to either save Rhapta or bring it to the ground. She was also part of a small group that had believed that she would save it and truly believed in her and the good she could do. The group had helped her temporarily when she had needed advice, as well as over the past couple of days, and had shown her nothing but kindness and hospitality.

Judging by the sun, she guessed it was dinner time and decided to head over there. As soon as she stepped outside, she stopped and realized she had no idea where she was going.

"Umm," she said, pulling the note back out. She flipped it over, and there was an address written on the back. Smiling, she ran over to one of her guards that were stationed at the entrance to the plaza. "Excuse me, I need to go here. Do you know where this is?" she asked.

This guard was short and had a huge beard, looking something like a gnome to her. He glanced at the note and nodded abruptly before marching off.

"Thank you!" she piped. The other guard took the rear, and the three of them strolled through the evening city. The air was still warm, and people went about their work as if the time of day didn't matter. She supposed it didn't when your home was shattered and you had nowhere to sleep.

It was a decently long walk to Ekaja's neighborhood, and Kinza was pleasantly surprised to see how full of life it was. The last time she had been here was with Zaid and Khalil when they were looking for Ekaja. But this entire neighborhood had been deserted, and they only found destroyed homes and shattered doors. Now people congregated at their neighbors' doors, chatting about this or that, yelling at their children, and smiling for the first time in days.

Kinza took the little staircase that wound up in-between two buildings. Ekaja's home sat on top of the stacks of little houses overlooking the city. Before she reached the top, Kinza could hear a cacophony of voices. The door was open, so she nervously peeked inside.

"Hello?" she said, looking around.

She was met with nearly ten faces that beamed at the sight of her. "Kinza!" they shouted, clearly already laughing due to some joke.

Ekaja came up to her and pulled her into a hug. *Kinza, I'm glad you got my note,* she said into her mind. Kinza was slowly getting used to the voiceless speech that the Anunnaki used. Many of them spoke aloud for her benefit, but the majority of the citizens still spoke telepathically.

Me too, Kinza replied. *I wasn't sure what time dinner was, so I left right away.*

It's perfect! Ekaja said and ushered her into the room. Ekaja's home consisted of only one main room and a few bedrooms at the back of the house, making Kinza's gifted home look like a palace. But it was clear this place was filled with love by the decorations that adorned the walls, the well-worn books on the shelves, and painted shutters on the window that sat open to let the evening breeze in.

Kinza was starting to recognize a few faces, including Aisha's, the secret double assassin that helped her escape after Tahir's men had tried to kill her. Kinza also recognized Tiamat, Ekaja's friend with the invisibility trick. Kinza waved to Aisha and sat down next to Tiamat.

There was food spread out on a low table that made Kinza's mouth water from the smell alone. Spiced meats, seasoned vegetables, and fresh fruit took up every inch of space. The group welcomed Kinza, and they all laughed and joked over the course of the meal. It almost felt like just a group of friends having an easy meal on a beautiful night in their easy lives. Almost like the city wasn't broken around them, and they weren't a hidden species with magical powers, and Kinza wasn't the heir to a throne she hadn't known existed. The thought of dealing with that last part had the food turning in her stomach.

Did I tell you what Berati said last night when she came home? one of the women said conspiratorially. Kinza thought her name was Imit.

No, tell us! the others said.

She was sent to work on the southern wall, you know, near the quarries? She said that the other side of the barrier flickered! Imit exclaimed.

The women seemed shocked, and some covered their mouths with their hands.

Aisha nodded. *I saw it myself, but near the lower east quarter. It looked like it rippled almost just yesterday afternoon.*

Many of the women spoke in hushed whispers for a minute about what it could mean.

Ach! said a woman whose name Kinza didn't know. She was by far the oldest in the group and somehow also the feistiest. *You all know exactly why it does that. That's why* she's *here, remember?* she said, jabbing a finger at Kinza.

Me? Kinza squawked.

Ekaja said. *Yes, dear. Keeping the barrier up is a tenuous business at best. Not everyone knows this, but the barrier has not been doing well for a while. Amir used to talk about it,* she said, looking down at her hands in her lap. Kinza remembered hearing the brutal story of what happened to Zaid's older brother before he died.

Tenuous? the old woman said. *Blech! It's failing, Ekaja! The barrier has been failing for decades. I'm not surprised it's starting to collapse now after all the death in the city.*

The group started chittering at the word "collapse." Many of them looked scared at the mere mention of it.

Kinza placed a piece of fruit into her mouth and savored

the ripeness before swallowing. *I did hear a little about that, but what does that have to do with me?*

Ekaja looked like she was about to explain, but the old woman interjected. *Hush! All of you. I will tell you newborn babes the story of the barrier. I'm almost old enough to remember.* A few women chuckled at that.

The old woman settled in and cleared her throat. *Thousands of years ago, when Rhapta was still known to humans and open to the world, the current Rhaptan king saw that humans were becoming frightened of the Anunnaki. We all know that fear breeds hatred, and... and you can see where this is going.*

The king decided it was time for the Anunnaki to leave the societies of men, so with the magic of the Aurastone and his own will, he raised the barrier over the city—all on his own, with nothing but his love for his people.

The women whispered in awe at the king, and the old woman continued.

Over the millennia, the weight of the barrier was passed down from king to king. That was the strength of the Rhaptan monarchy's lineage. They weren't just royalty because they were elected; they were stronger. *Rhapta thrived for many thousands of years that way, but as we know, over time, people started to get restless, wanting to leave the city.*

Wait, Kinza said. *What about the barrier? There hasn't been a king in two hundred years, but the barrier is still here.*

Shh! the old woman said. *I'm getting to that. So, over time people started escaping—becoming ubir—and the population started dwindling, but slowly. Then, two hundred years ago, our old king died, and Prince Malik disappeared into the night, yet the barrier stayed. The Elders took over and quickly tasked their best scholars to study the barrier. After much research, they realized the barrier was held up by psychic energy, or our Auras. Since the monarchy has always had larger Auras, they were able to hold the barrier up alone. But with them gone, a large enough population would be able to do it as well. But the population was still dwindling. Now with that damned Tahir causing all this ruckus and death, the barrier is probably near collapsing!*

The mood in the room had turned somber, the whispers more hushed as people looked at one another.

What happens if it does collapse? Kinza asked.

Everyone went silent at that, and not a single voice answered her. What would happen if Rhapta was revealed to the world? Was she supposed to hold the barrier on her own? It had taken every ounce of her being to do what she had done with the Aurastones the other night, and it had only lasted a minute. But hold the entire barrier? Forever?

Kinza spent the rest of the night back in her bed, tossing and turning over the thought. Her dreams were filled with angry humans with torches and pitchforks coming up through the forest and into the city.

CHAPTER 2
NOT ENOUGH TIME

Kinza woke to the sound of birds tweeting. On any other day, she might have enjoyed the innocent sound, but she had slept fitfully last night and wished she could block out the sound with noise-canceling headphones or something.

She groaned into the pillow before deciding to get up. The sun wasn't quite over the horizon yet, so she took the time to quickly bathe, hoping it would invigorate her before she needed to meet with the Elders. She had no idea what she was going to say to them or what they would say to her. They hadn't had another meeting with all of them since the morning after the attack.

She went about her morning routine, washing and dressing in a turquoise outfit with indigo and gold stitching. The entire time, though, she was thinking about Zaid instead of the Elders. Had he been sent away in the middle of the night? Was the last image she would have of him be him walking back to the city after the funeral? She tried to quell her anxiety by focusing more on getting ready. There were more gifts left last night, and she now had pots of oils and jars of what looked like hand-made makeup and perfumes.

There was only so much she could do though, so eventually, she headed out into the main room. She needed to be at the Grand Hall just a little after sunrise, and it wasn't too far of a walk. The sky was just starting to lighten, so she sat at her little table, eating fruit and sweetbread, her knee bouncing with nervousness. Not about her meeting, but about whether or not Zaid would show up this morning to walk her there.

When the knock sounded at her door, she practically sprinted to open it. She was breathless when she yanked it open, and immediately her face filled with a smile at seeing the tall storm cloud of a man before her.

"Since when are you a morning person?" Zaid said, eyeing her skeptically.

Realizing how ridiculous she probably looked, she cleared her throat and tried to relax her stance. "I—uh, slept really good."

Zaid raised an eyebrow.

"I had dinner at your mother's last night, so I was out like a light," she said with an awkward laugh.

"Ah," Zaid said, as if that made sense. "Are you ready?"

"Yep!" she said and stepped outside, her breakfast forgotten on the table. They started heading in the direction of the Grand Hall, Kinza's two guards following behind.

Zaid was back to his usual black clothing today, and Kinza found it comfortingly familiar, so within minutes she had relaxed from her morning anxiety.

"So... no new assignment yet?" she asked casually.

"Not yet," Zaid said. "I more or less got a verbal lashing for avoiding Savar, but I have to go back after the meeting." He heaved a sigh. "There are a ton of ubir in South America right now, near Sao Paulo, and only one venari there at the moment."

"Ah," Kinza said. "That's not good." She thought for a moment. "Last night at dinner, the other women were saying that the barrier might collapse soon."

"Yeah, I heard that from a few people too." They were walking along one of the wide boulevards, birds filling the baobab trees that lined the street. A few early morning workers were already out and setting up for the day. There were always vendors out this early with hot rolls or sweetbreads ready for when the rest of the city woke up. Kinza liked the smell of the food mixed with the morning dew.

"What happens if it does?" she asked, fiddling with a curl.

"That... would be bad," he said hesitantly. "Humans would be able to see and just wander in. Since human governments pretty much monitor everything by satellite now, they'd probably see it right away. The fight we had the other night would be a cakewalk compared to what we would have to deal with."

Despite the dark thought, Kinza giggled a little. "Cakewalk? Since when do you use such blatantly human terms?" she teased.

Zaid snorted. "I spend almost as much time out there as you do," he said, gesturing vaguely to the edge of the barrier outside the city. They finally reached the central plaza, where scholars and workers were already going about their day.

On the other side of the plaza stood the library that held the headquarters of the Apostles of Truth under the building. The structure was still being rebuilt, but after the fight, the Elders and the Apostles had come to some sort of tenuous truce. The Apostles had fought bravely to defend the city, losing many, including their leader Sa'id. Kinza was not ashamed to say she had cried when she learned he had died after saving her in battle, and she was one of the people who stayed the longest at his funeral. Nim had been there as well, as he was the new de facto leader of the Apostles, and they had sat in silence most of the time.

The Elders had realized how much information the Apostles truly had acquired and were interested in what else they had. Kinza watched several Apostles now hurrying in and out of the Grand Hall as if scholastic pursuits were a death-defying race. She supposed it was for them.

Kinza and Zaid were content to walk in silence across the plaza. Kinza caught sight of the left wing of the Grand Hall, which still had a gaping hole in the side from when she collapsed it with her explosion. They went up the front steps instead and entered the shadowy hall that was just starting to fill with the morning sun that was peeking over the tops of the buildings.

Zaid led her down the main hallway and turned right at the main intersection. From there were sets of large doors on either side. None of them were labeled, so he probably was leading them based on his perception of heartbeats. He stopped at one of the doors on the left.

"This is it, ready?" he asked.

"Sure..." she said, feeling anything but.

Zaid paused with his hand on the handle and looked over her face. "You sure? We *could* just ditch and take a vacation in Cabo. Well... it would probably have to be Sao Paulo, but—"

Kinza laughed. "I'm sure," she said, meaning it now. "Open the door," she urged. He grinned and did as she asked.

Inside was something of an auditorium. They entered on the main floor, which led to the circular speaking area in the middle. Around that, in a semicircle, were raised tiers of seats that were already filling with Elders and apprentices and even a few scholars. The man Kinza recognized as Elder Ishar was standing on the main floor and noticed them as they walked in.

Ah, Kinza. Good, you are just in time, he said, walking over to her. When he noticed Zaid behind her, he said, *Hatem, what are you doing here? Shouldn't you be with Savar... or on assignment?*

Before Zaid could respond, Kinza said, *I asked him to be here, if that's okay?*

Ishar's face looked like it wasn't, but he nodded and indicated for them to take a seat. They chose two seats on the end of the lowest tier and watched the rest of the room fill in. One of the seats was more decorated than the others but was purposely left empty—in honor of their Grand Elder who had passed. In the seat next to it sat a tiny woman with very short hair who looked roughly Kinza's age. She wore pale gray robes and sat in absolute stillness with her eyes closed.

Kinza recognized a few other faces that started to trickle in, but most of them she did not. There were supposed to be fifty Elders, but with one having passed and four others off with Tahir, the forty-four remained here with their apprentices. The only apprentice without a mentor was Mikah, who still walked in as if they were waiting on him.

"Morning, Kinza," he said and smiled as he went to take a seat across the room.

Kinza just smiled back. They waited a few more minutes before Kinza caught Zaid looking at her oddly. "What?" she said.

"Nothing," he said, turning back to watch the room.

An Elder, whose name Kinza found out was Ekbal, banged a gavel and said, *Let's get started!* It seemed as if he was going to lead as he sat on the other side of the decorated chair. *Everyone, take your seats!*

An Elder Kinza didn't know called out, *Ekbal, shouldn't Eta be leading? Is she not the next Grand Elder?* Some of the others in the room shouted in agreement, and some took the opposite stance, saying neither of them should be leading. Kinza didn't think it really mattered, but who was she to say?

We haven't spoken yet on the matter of the new Grand Elder. Let the dead rest a day, would you? Either way, Eta has expressed that she would prefer I lead today, at least until the Grand Elder matter is spoken about. That shut everyone up for the time being. Kinza glanced at the woman sitting on the other side of the decorated chair and wondered if that was Eta.

Eta was Hakim's apprentice and the only other seer in Rhapta, Zaid said in her mind directly. *She most likely will be the next Grand Elder, but...* he shrugged. Kinza thought she looked so young to be in such a high position of responsibility, but then again, Kinza was the one who was supposed to be queen. There was probably some irony in that.

Ekbal started again. *Today we are here to talk about Kinza Solace, the apparent heir to the Rhaptan throne.* Some people had a few comments about that, but Ekbal actually looked at Kinza reassuringly. She had found some of the Elders to be somewhat understanding of the position she was in, Ekbal included.

Can I interject for a moment, another Elder asked, *to ask why a venari is here?* Some others echoed his sentiment. Clearly it was a political faux pas for someone who *wasn't* in a political position to be here. Even the guards had been stationed outside.

Zaid looked up at that, and even Ekbal looked at him questioningly.

I asked him to be here, Kinza said, speaking up for the second time. She didn't give an explanation and hoped they wouldn't ask for one. Ekbal pursed his lips but nodded, and no one said anything else, but she could feel the annoyance in the room from a few people.

Back to the agenda at hand, we have a couple of matters to decide, and I will list them as such. One: are we changing our governmental structure back to a monarchy after two hundred years without them? And two: how do we know when and if Kinza can truly be queen? Let's start with the first. Any opinions? Ekbal asked.

That opened a floodgate of voices that Kinza could hardly keep up with. Some thought there was no need for a monarchy since they had been doing fine without one. Others pointed out that they were, in fact, not doing fine. Many suggested that Kinza was not fit for the role as she didn't grow up here and was never trained to be a leader like Rhaptan kings had been in the past.

She couldn't disagree with the last part. She just wanted to do what was most helpful for them, but didn't know what that was. Based on the first few minutes of this conversation, she was surprised they had gotten anything done in the last two hundred years.

There was one thread among the arguments that stood out. Many people wondered if it was even possible if she could be queen. What did that mean? Wasn't she the heir? She honestly wanted to throw up at the thought of being the leader of a civilization, but she had decided she wanted to help these people somehow. She had made that decision kneeling on the floor of the Grand Hall just a few days ago and would stick with it. But still, why *couldn't* she be queen?

Excuse me, she dared to say. Slowly the voices died down, realizing she had spoken. *But what do you mean* can I *be queen? Not to sound forward, but didn't Grand Elder Hakim say I was the last prince's descendant?*

Many faces turned to Ekbal to explain. *This brings us to the second point then,* he said with a sigh and looked at her as he explained, but it was clear many of the apprentices did not know this either. *The inauguration of Rhaptan royalty is fairly simple, just a little ceremony. But we are in an unprecedented situa-*

tion that makes it not so simple. The ceremony is short and usually takes place in the largest temple in the city, but that's not what actually makes the heir the king—sorry, queen.

The room was quiet, so he continued. *Historically, the sitting king would just know when the heir was ready to take over. A lot of it had to do with whether or not the heir could hold the barrier, but honestly, it was something the monarchy was in control of. And none of us here were part of that. So we could very well just name you Queen of Rhapta, Kinza, but that doesn't mean that you are the queen. It's more than that. This isn't like human monarchies where someone just decides to be the king or queen and that's that. The Anunnaki race is connected psychically, in similar ways bees are connected to their queen in a colony.* Ekbal shrugged. *This is something we've never dealt with before.*

Ah, was all Kinza replied. How was she supposed to know if she was the queen or not? She didn't understand what any of that had truly meant. She already could speak telepathically and had all of her abilities. Couldn't they just give her the crown? It was fair to say that she had not the slightest inkling of how she would deal with the barrier, but she figured she could figure that out as she went along.

Does anyone have any idea on how to tell if she is ready? Ekbal asked the room. *Any knowledge from the scholars?*

A few people shrugged or offered unhelpful comments. The scholars didn't seem to know much about the process either. So far, this queen business was not going well. If they never found out if Kinza could be queen or not, what was her purpose? It seemed more like they would just revert back to the Council of Elders again.

A very old, wrinkled woman with long white hair cleared her throat. Those in the room who had been speaking quieted quickly. It seemed she had a modicum of respect.

Elder Hija, do you have an idea? Ekbal asked.

Hija gave a non-committal shrug. *I don't know if this would tell us if she is the queen or not, but I am happy to offer my services.* Many in the room whispered at that and nodded in agreement.

Kinza looked at Zaid questioningly.

Hija is the only Anunnaki with almost as many abilities as you, he said. *I think she has four. But one of them is that she can detect exactly what your abilities are and how many you have.*

I could have used her weeks ago, Kinza mentally grumbled. The Elders in the room talked over this and if it would have any weight on Kinza's queenship or not. The conversation drifted back to whether or not they even needed Kinza, and another argument broke out. Kinza had a hard time not becoming frustrated at the lack of progress and the bickering. She knew she probably looked like a petulant child slouching in her chair with her arms crossed and brows lowered.

She caught sight of Mikah across the room, looking at her. He had a slight smirk on his face, and Kinza couldn't contain her own grin and sat back up, *trying* to look like she enjoyed this. At least to keep her and Mikah from laughing.

Kinza turned back at the conversation between Ekbal, Hija, and a scholar when she caught Zaid looking at her weirdly again. And he didn't look happy.

Can I help you? she teased.

A funny look crossed his face, but before he could respond, Ekbal addressed her again. *It's a decided first step, then. Kinza, you will meet with Hija tomorrow morning to decipher exactly how many and what abilities you have. If anything new comes to light, we will go from there. For now, we will work with what we have to rebuild the city and hopefully keep the barrier from falling. We'll reconvene tomorrow evening.* He banged his gavel, signifying the end of the meeting.

Everyone stood and started filing out of the room. Kinza

and Zaid made their way out into the hall. "You have to go back to Savar now?" Kinza asked.

Zaid nodded reluctantly and placed a hand on her shoulder. "Don't worry; I'll get you a t-shirt from Brazil if he sends me out right away."

Kinza grinned and tried very hard to focus with his hand on her bare shoulder.

"Another eventful meeting," Mikah said with a sigh, coming up to Kinza. "Hello, Your Highness," he said before turning to Zaid. "I didn't know they let dogs into governmental meetings."

Kinza felt the warmth leave her shoulder as Zaid's hand dropped. "I was invited," Zaid said, crossing his arms.

"I don't know why," Mikah said. "Your Magnificence, should we resume our tour?" he said, holding an elbow out to Kinza.

She laughed and took his arm. "I'll see you later, hopefully?" she said to Zaid.

"Hopefully," he said and stalked off.

"Now," Mikah said. "Should we stroll the avenue of warriors that smells like sour armpit or the richly perfumed central markets? And can I say, you smell divine today?"

Kinza let Mikah lead her out of the Grand Hall and into the city with the same anxiety she had that morning.

ZAID STRODE ACROSS THE PLAZA, people moving away from him as usual. They moved a bit quicker today, probably because he was in a foul mood. He had tried to hide it as best he could with Kinza, but his mask had slowly been slipping throughout the meeting.

He almost crumpled at her smiling face when she answered the door, but what hit him in the chest was watching her smile or laugh every time Mikah looked at her. Zaid knew he had no right whatsoever to expect her to be like that with him, especially not after how he had treated her after they arrived in the city. But it still hurt to watch.

She had proposed that they start over, and she had kept her promise and seemed to have forgiven him entirely for his behavior. He just couldn't help feeling like he still hadn't done enough. He spent as long as he could avoiding Savar just to spend more time with her. He had used the time to help her get a few pieces of furniture into her temporary housing. She had said that was enough, but he had other thoughts.

At night after she slept, he collected little things around town he thought she would like. He really didn't know what her tastes were, so he just grabbed everything. Blankets and pots and jars of makeup that he had left with the other things sitting outside her door. She had even worn the little jar of perfume he had left for her this morning, and he felt proud he had done something right.

Yet she still laughed with Mikah and still walked off with him.

He entered a small side street on the other side of the plaza that led to the next boulevard. There were many large buildings here, most of which were being rebuilt. Zaid entered the front doors of one of them. There was no sign out front and no one there to greet him, but he knew it was being watched at all times. The home of the venari wasn't exactly hidden, but it wasn't advertised either.

He stepped inside and through a short hallway that led to a large inner training ring filled with a light coating of sand. The training ring had no ceiling above it, being exposed to the elements. The two floors of the building that surrounded it were the only shelter. There were only a couple of people here in the ring and walking along the upper balcony. Doors and hallways lined both floors. Most of them were supposed to be bedrooms, but with so few venari, many of them were used for storage or other types of training.

The tall, wiry form of Savar stepped out from the shadows of the lower floor. *You're late,* he said.

The meeting ran long, Zaid replied.

The meeting you weren't invited to? Savar said. Zaid didn't bother replying.

He and Savar had always had a tense relationship. It had always seemed like Savar's only purpose in life was to rip Zaid apart both physically and mentally. He knew that it was only to make him stronger. The life of the venari was hard, harder than they let people think. The isolation of being away from the Anunnaki while going on assignment after assignment capturing people that were trying to kill you. Only to be greeted by hatred and mistrust upon his return to the city he was trying to save each time.

Savar had tapped Zaid to be venari when he was eleven, saying he would end up being a great hunter, and he had been right. But Savar had never relented, even when Zaid was wounded or tired over the years. He would push and push like he was doing now, poking at wounds Zaid would rather leave alone.

To say that Savar had been scathing yesterday when Zaid finally met with him was an understatement. Savar knew Zaid's thoughts inside and out, and it had taken him all of five minutes to realize why Zaid had been avoiding him.

Venari cannot be consorts, Savar had said, like throwing a javelin straight into his heart. Zaid hadn't even thought that far into his own life, and here Savar was, telling him about a future he couldn't have.

Walk with me, Savar said now, and Zaid followed dutifully. He was usually good at that, doing his duty. They took the sheltered path around the lower floor, watching the two venari spar in the ring.

Just give me a couple more days, Zaid said finally.

And what about the people the ubir kill on a regular basis? Savar asked. *Should I give them a few more days?*

Zaid was silent at that.

There has been an increase in ubir over the past few weeks, I would assume due to this mess we're in. But soon, things are going to change, Savar said. *We need to deal with the ubir we know about now.*

What do you mean? Zaid asked. The venari had done the same thing the same way for centuries.

Hakim is dead, Savar reminded him.

Then who are we getting the assignments from? Zaid asked. Hakim had always foreseen glimpses of ubir out in the world and would give that information to Savar to distribute to the venari. Without Hakim to see where they were, it was like walking out there blind. Before Hakim's time, there hadn't been that many ubir, and the seers were more common. Now the only seer was Eta.

I've already met with Eta, and it's apparent she isn't up to Hakim's level, meaning that we've got nothing, Savar said, confirming Zaid's thoughts. *Very soon the world is going to have a terrifying problem if the ubir keep getting out and we can't find them. I've tried to bring this up with Ishar and the other Elders, but they're preoccupied with the barrier issue.*

He stopped to watch the training ring. The two venari fought like their lives depended on it. One moved like mist in the air, but the other always seemed to know where he would be. *I already sent Tejas out, and he's almost as good as you. Meaning I should have sent you already.*

Savar...

Savar looked at him. *We need to deal with the ubir that we know about now, so when the hoard starts piling up out there, we're ready.*

Please, just a few more days. Zaid was pleading now.

Savar turned back to the training grounds. The one like mist suddenly found himself with a knife at his throat, a drop of scarlet blood trickling down.

You are a fool, Hatem. You leave in two days.

Zaid knew he was right; he always was. But as he walked out of the building, all he could think about was telling Kinza they had more time.

CHAPTER 3
REVELATIONS

Kinza was up before dawn the next morning. She got dressed in her usual routine and sat waiting in the main room of her little house until it was time to leave. She brought in the little gifts that were left for her, flowers, a silk robe, and a box of candies.

Mikah had taken her around more of the city yesterday, and she wasn't sure of the last time she had laughed that hard. The jokes and charm that poured out of him were like a tap that never turned off. It didn't make her stop thinking about the meeting with the Elders, though.

She hadn't realized the Rhaptan monarchy—really the entire Rhaptan culture—was so complicated. When Zaid and his friend Haris had originally told her about the city and its people, she had imagined a primitive group of magical people that lived in the woods. But with every question she had answered, three more sprung up in its place. Would anything ever be simple again?

When the knock came at her door this morning, she did a better job of acting nonchalant. "No assignment yet?" she asked him.

"Nope," Zaid said with a slight grin. He looked happier than when he had left yesterday.

"Good," she said, closing the door behind her. "I won't look a gift horse in the mouth."

"What?" Zaid asked, his face contorting.

She laughed and said, "Grams says to never look a gift horse in the mouth. I think it means when you receive a gift, you're not supposed to question it."

They started toward the central plaza, the ever-present guards filling in far behind them.

"Have you talked to your grandma again?" he asked. Zaid had let her keep his cell phone in case Grams called her again.

"Not yet. She told me to just do what I needed to do, and she would be there when I got back, whenever that is."

"Does she still hate me?" Zaid asked.

"Probably," Kinza said with a laugh, and Zaid's eyes crinkled at the corners with his grin. "Have you heard from Khalil at all? I feel like I haven't seen him."

"Yeah, he's over in the outskirts where he feels most useful. He was working on rebuilding his workshop so he could start taking patients again. A few people out there still have injuries. In fact, the moment I walked in the door, he told me to get out unless I was there to do something useful," Zaid said.

Both of them laughed at that as it sounded just like Khalil. They got to the Grand Hall in no time, and Zaid led her back up and into the cool interior. It was going to be sweltering today, judging by how warm it was already. They didn't go far and ended up in a smaller room than the day before. It was fairly simple with just a few tables and chairs, looking more like a large office than anything.

Ah, you're early, said a voice from behind them. They turned to find Elder Hija entering, using a cane to help her walk. Kinza thought she would probably benefit from a wheelchair but chose not to say anything.

All right, I suppose we can get started, she said as she sat in one of the chairs. She looked Kinza up and down as if analyzing her and then said, *Huh!*

That's it? Kinza said, looking at Zaid, who shrugged.

What? No, no, no, Hija said. *I'm just having a look at ya. I'm surprised a little thing like you scared an entire city, but eh, what do I know?* she said with a shrug. *Now, bring a chair and pull it closer. My name is Elder Hija, and I don't do that much for the government. There, now you know about me.*

Kinza restrained a chuckle but pulled a chair closer. Zaid leaned against the wall and watched them. *Nice to meet you,* Kinza said. *So, you are going to tell me my abilities? I think I know them all by now...*

Do you? Hija asked. *Tell me.*

Well, there's the teleportation and speaking and understanding Rhaptan...

Uh-huh, keep going, Hija said.

And I'm able to control my Aura, and I usually end up just making it explode. And I have the normal Anunnaki things like the healing and tele—

Hija waved a hand. *Anything else?*

I think I might have another one where the back of my neck starts tingling when danger is close by. Zaid's eyebrows went up at that one, and she remembered she hadn't told him about it. *And then there is the fire, but I think that's part of the Aura thing. And yeah, that's it.*

Hija grabbed her hand then and held it for a minute before dropping it again. *You missed one,* she said abruptly.

I—I did? What else is there? Kinza asked.

You have a stronger connection to Rhapta than most, probably due to your royal blood. You've had dreams of Rhapta before, right?

Even before you knew it was here? Hija asked, leaning both hands on her cane.

Yes! Kinza said. *I had them for a week straight before I got by other abilities.*

Hija nodded as if that made sense. *So you technically only have five, but the ability to control your own Aura could mean a thousand things in itself. You may have only done 'explosions' as you say, or fire or making Aurastones glow, but I'm sure there are other things you could do with it. The other four are fairly simple; dreams that connect you to Rhapta, the ability to know when danger is near, the Rhaptan language, and the teleportation.*

Kinza nodded, thinking them over. She didn't like the sound of the Aura situation. Did that mean that at any time, she could magically do something else like levitate cars or turn someone into a fish? She would probably have to talk to Jabari again. The Apostle scholar turned Kinza's personal trainer had been busy with repairs the past few days, but he would know how to help her control them better.

It was interesting how just *knowing* what her abilities were made her feel better. Back before she had arrived in the city, she had been terrified because she didn't know what was happening to her. And when abilities kept popping up, the other Anunnaki hadn't known what to think. Now that she could see the problem, she felt a little more in control and could at least make a plan to deal with it.

You have four abilities, right? Kinza asked curiously.

Hija chuckled. *Oh yes, but nothing like yours.*

Kinza smiled. *Tell me anyway?*

Well, you know the first. I can see exactly what abilities people have. I can also see in the dark; I remember any song I've ever heard down to the note. Oh, and I always win at cards.

Zaid barked a laugh. *Are you sure the last one is an ability?*

Oh, yes, she said with a satisfied smile, leaning back in her chair. *Before my husband died many years ago, he used to tell his friends I only had three abilities. He would invite me to play cards with them some nights, and of course, I always won, and we'd split the money. Of course, his friends found out eventually, and we tried to make me lose.* She shook her head. *Never happened. I'm just good at gambling. Nothing like exploding a hole in the Grand Hall,* she said to Kinza with a wink and laughed. *That one will go down in the history books.*

Thank you for sharing, Kinza said. *And for the record, I'm a firm believer that the fourth is an ability.* Kinza had a distinct impression that Hija and Grams would get along almost too well. The three of them headed back out into the hall. *So I suppose this means there was nothing new or surprising, right?* Kinza asked.

Well, I'm not so sure, Hija said, stopping to look at her. *Knowing that you are psychically connected to Rhapta enough that you would get dreams while on the other side of the planet... that's only something Anunnaki royalty would have.* She shrugged. *It may just be another nail in the coffin that you are, in fact, Malik's heir, but I don't know...*

Hija trailed off as they saw a man coming sprinting up the steps of the Grand Hall as if the hounds of hell were at his heels. Without stopping, he shot down the main hall and nearly skidded into the wall as he veered to the right and down one wing of the building and out of sight.

Hija heaved a sigh. *I'm sure the meeting tonight will be eventful. Best enjoy yourselves until then.* She gave one last smile and hobbled off down the hall.

"That was odd, right?" Kinza asked Zaid, who was still looking down the hall toward where the man had run.

"Yeah, he's venari too," Zaid said.

"Do you think he just got back?" she asked. "Could something have happened?" She thought about Grams again and wondered if she should call her. She didn't think Tahir or any of the Elders would go after her grandmother, but it still made her nervous. Either way, Grams had told her no when Kinza suggested she come home immediately to take care of her.

Besides finding out that she was Anunnaki, one of the biggest revelations of the past few weeks was that Grams was Ummanu, one of the human sentinels that knew about the Anunnaki and existed in the world as their allies. Most of them watched over the portals, but a very few did not, like Grams. Kinza had gone her whole life not knowing about the Anunnaki when Grams had known everything the entire time. Had Kinza's mom known? Had she been Anunnaki as well? Kinza looked forward to one day having the conversation with Grams.

There were so many things in Kinza's "human" life that hadn't been dealt with. Mainly because she didn't know whether or not she would be going back. As far as she knew, she had been removed from her community college roster by default. And Mitra. Kinza mentally cringed at the thought of her best friend. Grams had said she would tell Mitra she was alive but wouldn't tell her any details. Kinza couldn't imagine the absolute fit Mitra would throw when she found out Kinza was alive and well but just not calling her. She would need to deal with that at some point.

"We don't have to be back until this evening," Zaid said as they strolled down the Grand Hall steps. "What do you want to do all day?"

Kinza squinted into the morning sun. "I don't know. I think I want to do something useful today. I just don't know what."

"Okay, come on," Zaid said, nearly jogging down the steps now.

"Wait, what?" Kinza said, running after him. Thankfully,

he slowed when he got to the bottom of the steps. "What's your idea?"

"You'll see," was all he said. She huffed and decided to just follow him. They walked across the plaza and then the entire eastern quarter. She noticed the looks they got, the wariness and fear at Zaid, and the mixed emotions at her. She understood why they were looking at her like that, but Zaid didn't deserve any of their attitudes. If she did ever become queen, she would need to find a way to change people's perception of venari.

They got to the wall. Zaid stepped through and kept going down through the ramshackle homes of the outskirts on a semi-familiar path. They finally got to a half-built building. Calling it a "building" would have been a stretch, though; it was hardly bigger than a bus.

"What are we doing here?" Kinza asked as a tall man with soft curly hair stepped out of the structure.

"Something useful," Zaid said with a grin.

"Khalil!" Kinza said with a smile and went to hug the man. He merely allowed the hug to happen but patted her on the head.

"Hello, Kinza. I see you are doing well," he said.

"Well enough," she said, stepping back. It had only been a few days, but it felt like forever. She hadn't known Khalil long but had quickly decided she liked him, and they were, therefore, friends.

Khalil looked at Zaid. "What are you doing here? Aren't you supposed to be on an assignment?"

Zaid rolled his eyes. "Everyone keeps saying that," he muttered. "We're here to help."

"Really?" Khalil asked, looking at Kinza, who nodded. "Perfect, I need a roof!" he said with a clap of his hands. Only then did Kinza realize she wore the wrong footwear.

The three of them started on the roof and quickly gained help from others. Soon enough, there were nearly twenty people helping Khalil to rebuild his workshop. They scavenged for wood and supplies, and when there were none, they went out into the forest to chop down trees and gather what they could. Kinza had a few choice words to say when Khalil told her the people inside the city had more than enough supplies, but many wouldn't share with the outsiders.

"Why don't the people that live out here just move into one of the million homes in the abandoned areas of the city?" she asked as they worked. Kinza had collected dust and a few leaves in her hair; she would have to have Ekaja redo it.

"Most don't agree with the Elder's rule," Khalil said, grunting under the weight of a board Zaid tossed him. "If you hadn't noticed, no one out here opposes the idea of you being queen."

Kinza looked around at the people that had gathered to help and realized she hadn't received one bad look the entire time they had been out here. Most of them either joked with her or offered to help. One man had even offered to give her his boots, but she declined as politely as she could, based on the state of his feet.

"So, hypothetically, if I did become queen, they would move back in?" she asked, hammering nails into a wall. They weren't exactly in a straight line, but it would do.

"Maybe," Khalil said. "There are still people like the Unfettered who want nothing to do with Rhapta."

"Did we find anything else out about the Unfettered, by the way?" Kinza asked Zaid. The Unfettered had a pretty extensive list of claims about Kinza, and she was desperately curious about how they knew what they did about her.

"I'm surprised Mikah didn't tell you already," Zaid said. Kinza thought he almost sounded bitter.

"Tell me what?" Kinza asked. She knew Mikah was one of the people who had been involved in questioning the Unfettered. It was probably due to his ability; being able to see people's recent memories and remove them entirely would come in handy in those situations.

Zaid tossed Khalil another board. "One of the first men he inspected ended up having an odd but dangerous ability. It's actually the exact *opposite* of Mikah's; he could implant memories into someone's mind, but they didn't last very long."

Kinza gasped and dropped the hammer. "So when Phil said all those things about me, it was because someone made him think those things were *real*?!"

Zaid nodded, looking grim. Probably because he was one of the many people who actually believed Phil. "I guess, yeah. Makes sense why it was so convincing."

"I told you I forgave you already," Kinza said, looking at him.

He looked back at her a moment and smiled. "Yeah, I know," he said softly.

Khalil gagged, breaking the moment. "Enough of that! And hurry up, I don't have a home still," he said, gesturing to Zaid for another board.

They worked until the sun started on its downward arc, and Zaid and Kinza needed to head back. Khalil thanked them, and they waved as they left, their new friends saying goodbye. It was still boiling outside, and Kinza's clothes stuck to her skin with the dirt and grime she had acquired.

"Ugh, gross. Do I have time to bathe?" she asked.

Zaid nodded and looked almost as bad as she did. He walked her back to her house and said he would be back soon. She watched him zip off at ridiculous speeds back to wherever he stayed. She didn't know why he didn't stay closer to her. There were plenty of empty houses, and she knew he didn't live with Ekaja. Maybe the venari were required to live in the same place.

Kinza spent a solid twenty minutes in the bath, languishing and enjoying the scented water before she decided to get out. Realizing how late it got, she dressed quickly and headed outside to meet Zaid.

"I thought you died," Zaid said, startling her. He was leaning against the wall waiting for her.

She laughed, closing the door. "No, you didn't, unless you suddenly lost your ability."

He just rolled his eyes.

They went back to the Grand Hall, but the moment they stepped inside, everything felt tense for some reason. "I think something happened," Kinza said, remembering the man who had run in earlier.

"If something really bad happened, they would have alerted the city. So at least we aren't in imminent danger... again," Zaid said.

They went back to the same auditorium-like room as the day before, and, indeed, as soon as they stepped inside, they were met with a flurry of arguing voices. Some Elders were practically in a shouting match while others shook their heads in disgust and others sat wide-eyed. It looked like everyone was already there, including Mikah, who was arguing with Eta.

Upon seeing Kinza, Elder Ekbal called for quiet. Mikah went to take his seat, shaking his head in irritation. Eta sat in the same seat, looking as if nothing had happened. Most of the Elders and apprentices took their seats. It took several bangs of Ekbal's gavel to bring everyone to silence.

Kinza and Zaid took their seat, with no one questioning Zaid's presence this time. *Let's get started,* Ekbal said. *As many of you have heard, we received new intelligence this morning on former Elder Tahir's whereabouts, and they are not good.*

Kinza suddenly felt tense and clenched her fists in her lap.

We had a few venari out in the world looking for evidence of Tahir and the other Elders. Ekbal heaved a sigh as if what he was going to say was too heavy to hold. *We've located him, and it looks like he's in China right now. We found this out because of a video that went viral on human social media. I wasn't able to watch it myself, but the venari explained that it looked like Tahir had purposely got into a public place and displayed his abilities to the humans, covering an entire town square in ice.*

Many of the Elders gasped, and Kinza felt her heart turn to stone in her chest. Had Tahir truly outed himself to the humans? She had thought the idea of the barrier failing was bad, but if Tahir was out there flaunting his abilities, who knew if the humans wouldn't come running?

Arguments had broken out again, many asking why he would do such a thing or if he had turned into ubir. Kinza remembered Zaid telling her that a very select few of the Elders—probably Tahir and his cronies—had access to the venari tattoo techniques that allowed them to leave the city safely if needed. It was very possible that Tahir had done it to himself and the other Elders before leaving, but it wouldn't last forever.

From what a few of us have decided, Ekbal started again, *it looks like Tahir is still sane. Well—as sane as we consider him to be. So this wasn't a wild attack of an ubir. No, we believe he did this on purpose. Tahir has a very limited time out in the human world before he either becomes human and loses his abilities or chooses to become ubir.*

Now, from what we all know about Tahir, having worked with him for decades, he is a sore loser. I'm willing to bet he would see this city burn to the ground at the hands of the humans rather than give up control. Many Elders nodded in agreement and shouted out angry sentiments.

We've also received additional intelligence from Mikah and the others who have questioned the Unfettered about Tahir's orders, Ekbal said. *We learned that among the Unfettered, many of them have abilities that would explain the near mind control tactics that they deployed against the rest of the city. It was also confirmed a very select few of them had orders directly from Tahir, so we can finally confirm that the army of Unfettered was indeed Tahir's and not Kinza's.*

Many people looked at her then, and despite the eyes on her, she felt a massive weight leave her shoulders. She knew that most people no longer believed she was the one behind the attack, but it had never been proven. Now that it had, it felt a little easier to breathe. She figured that would go away soon, depending on if they were able to deal with Tahir or not.

We've also been working with the Apostles of Truth, Ekbal said, nodding toward Nimatullah, who sat across the room. *And we have discovered that Tahir is behind a staggering number of atrocities in this city going back decades. To be frank, there are even some suspicions that Tahir's own father had something to do with the death of the last king and the disappearance of Prince Malik.*

The room exploded into arguments again at the mention of the long-lost prince. Kinza had no doubt that a relative of Tahir had hurt her ancestors. Tahir had ordered the death of her own parents ten years ago. Kinza felt dread worm in her gut, and as if sensing her discomfort Zaid scooted a little closer to her so that her shoulder was practically touching his arm.

Ekbal heaved another sigh, and Kinza wondered if he would even sleep tonight. He looked so on edge. *I know that many of these revelations are shocking, but we need to deal with the present issues at hand. They are as such, one: the barrier is still failing. Two: Tahir is letting humans know he has abilities, and we don't yet know what his aim is. And three: we still have the matter of the queenship to attend to. Let's go back to the third. Elder Hija, did we learn anything helpful about Kinza's abilities?*

Hija sat with her cane a few tiers up and shrugged. *The only thing new that we learned was that she has a psychic connection to Rhapta that allowed her to have something like prophetic dreams of the city while she was on the other side of the planet. But that's all.*

Several jaws dropped at that, swiveling their heads to look at Kinza. She didn't know if she should say anything but Ekbal just continued.

All right, we'll come back to that later. Does anyone have any ideas on the barrier? Ekbal asked the room.

Where is Elder Balasi? someone asked. The room was quiet at that as people looked around for the Elder. Kinza had met the quiet Elder with calculating eyes. She was told he was the representative of human relations—whatever that meant. It seemed that many people, other Elders included, didn't truly know what he actually did.

Balasi is working at the moment, trying to find out more about what Tahir is doing, Ekbal said. *He felt as though his work was more important than this meeting at the moment, and I agreed with him, so he will let us know when he learns more.*

The Elders nodded, temporarily pacified.

At the moment, Ekbal said, *our main concern has now shifted to what to do about Tahir. If the barrier falls, we may have a window of time before the humans realize we are here, but if they learn through anything Tahir does and says that we exist... I don't know.*

The conversations went on for another half an hour, people going back and forth on what to do. The first choice was to send venari out to capture Tahir, but there was a good chance that would only incite Tahir to act out more. Others suggest letting him be until his tattoo extension wore off and he became human within the next few weeks. Others suggested they go back to the camp, but that was shut down quickly.

In the end, they decided to wait to see if Elder Balasi came up with any additional information. Another meeting was set for the following morning, and Ekbal banged his gavel, releasing everyone. Kinza and Zaid were silent as they walked out of the Grand Hall and into the now dark plaza. A few Aurastone lamps lit the area though, allowing those going to and from home to get there safely.

"This is bad," Kinza said as they walked in the vague direction of her house.

"Yeah," was all Zaid said. He walked with his hands in his pockets, staring at the ground. Kinza kept forgetting that Tahir had been as much of a mentor to Zaid as he was to Mikah. While Zaid hadn't said anything about how it affected him, Kinza also hadn't asked Zaid how he was doing either, but she always assumed he was fine with his perpetual stoicism.

"You okay?" she asked as they turned onto her street.

He tilted his head to look at her and gave her a small smile. "Yeah," he said. Her face must have belied her belief in his statement, so he bumped her shoulder with his own for good measure.

That was probably the best she was going to get. At least she had more time to talk to him in the coming weeks.

CHAPTER 4
LOVE LOST

I'm starting to hate these meetings, Kinza said to Zaid as they sat in the same meeting room the following morning. He only grunted in response, but she knew he was concentrating on not throttling the attendees as much as she was.

The meeting hadn't even started yet, and arguments had begun in full force. Elder Ekbal and Eta were in hushed conversation, and on the other side of Ekbal sat Elder Balasi, who was notably missing last time. He sat quietly analyzing the room, not talking to anyone unless it was necessary. Kinza had the distinct impression of an alligator waiting in the water for the perfect moment to strike.

Ekbal banged on his gavel. *Let's all quiet down now and make this meeting a fraction less tedious than it needs to be,* he said. The Elders and apprentices slowly took their seats and hushed their private conversations.

*As you all can see, Elder Balasi is here with us today having gathered a significant amount of intelligence while you all slept soundly in your beds. I'm going to—*Ekbal sighed and dropped his officious tone, his shoulders sagging—*I'm just going to let him explain. Do try to keep your heads on.* He gestured toward Balasi to take the floor.

Kinza glanced across the room at Mikah, who looked particularly annoyed today, which wasn't in itself unusual; she just noticed that he didn't usually show it. *This is going to be interesting,* Kinza thought to herself.

Balasi cleared his throat, but everyone was already listening. *I will start by saying what the venari from yesterday said was true. It has been confirmed that Tahir was found in a Chinese town, displaying his abilities. From what we know, he has not been captured by human authorities, nor has there been a second display.*

He paused before continuing.

As many of you know, my role as an Elder is to oversee the Anunnaki relationship with humanity. For thousands of years, it has been our purpose to guide humanity as an older sibling would guide the younger ones.

Someone interjected; one of the apprentices by the annoyance of the surrounding Elders' faces. *But we haven't been in true contact with humanity in thousands of years, have we not?* the young man asked. *We guide them from the shadows now.*

Balasi looked immensely more patient than Kinza would have expected from him. But she had the same line of thought the apprentice did.

Not entirely, Balasi said, causing a wave of surprise to ripple throughout the room. Balasi and Ekbal exchanged a glance before he continued.

About a hundred or so years ago, during the time of the Industrial Revolution, my predecessor realized it was becoming immensely difficult to hold sway in human society while we were stuck here in the city. So we sent three people out into the world, and with our guidance, we were able to help them into positions of power. CEOs, presidents, finance moguls, celebrities; we helped them to become an influence on humanity.

The hushed whispering was getting louder, and Zaid started drumming his fingers on the table next to Kinza.

If you sent them out, wouldn't that have just made them human, lose their abilities, and forget about us? an Elder asked.

Yes, Balasi said. *This is why we were with them when it happened to remind them of their people and their mission. All three ended up living long lives, but as soon as any of them passed, we would just replace them. This is how we still have some sway on humanity.* Balasi leaned back in his chair, content to let the now chaotic arguments take over. He looked like a man who had been resigned to the fact the storm would come and knew he just needed to wait for it to blow over. Kinza wasn't so sure it would.

Elders shouted in astonishment. How had they not known that three Anunnaki were basically sacrificing their magic every generation to have some measure of control over humanity? Kinza was starting to realize how Tahir had gotten away with as much as he did. She was learning to respect many of the Elders, but the majority of them were blind to the world. Only a very few were smart enough to question the workings of their own society, and even fewer were fit to lead it.

A headache started to throb above Kinza's eyes as Ekbal pounded his gavel, calling for quiet. She wanted to suggest a megaphone, but she wasn't sure that would actually help.

What does this have to do with Tahir? an Elder asked.

Balasi nodded and leaned forward now that the worst of the verbal storm had gone by. *What we believe is that Tahir is trying to sway the three human-Anunnaki to his side. I believe it is true that he would rather see Rhapta burn than let someone else rule. He is a power-hungry lunatic, if I may be frank. If he does sway them to his side, we can assume all of humanity will be against us if and when the barrier falls.*

The room was eerily quiet now, the gravity of the situation slowly sinking in.

Would they do that? Would the three human-Anunnaki really listen to him? someone asked.

Possibly, Balasi said hesitantly. *Keep in mind we don't communicate with them often, and it's very difficult without going to them physically. They have lived nearly their whole lives as humans, and none of them know about what has happened here recently. All I know is he is getting their attention first with this stunt of his. He went for the Anunnaki in Asia, but there are two more; one in North America and one in Europe at the moment.*

We must get to them first! an Elder cried, many more following his sentiment. *We must have them on our side!*

The conversation continued longer than it should have, but Kinza couldn't stop thinking about how big of a mess this was. Tahir was out in the world, causing havoc, trying to turn everyone against them, the barrier was failing, and she didn't even know if she was the queen or not. The mood in the room ranged from irritation at the lack of common knowledge on the situation to outright fear. She agreed that they would need these human-Anunnaki on their side. Three mega-powerful people under the influence of Tahir? No. Nope. No way. Kinza had decided to help these people, and now she knew how.

Yes, you are all correct, Ekbal was saying. *It is apparent that we need to reach back out to these human-Anunnaki before Tahir does. Balasi, are you able to connect with the other two before he does?* Ekbal asked, turning to Balasi.

Balasi bobbed his head back and forth. *Yes, as long as Tahir didn't send the Elders he took with him on his behalf. Generally, the only way we contact them is by sending out venari once or twice a year with orders on how to adjust human relations. I could send someone out, but if Tahir has already reached them, I'm not sure how well our venari will be able to convince them. Tahir is known for being persuasive.*

Almost everyone glanced in Zaid's direction as the only venari in the room, one who shouldn't have even been there in the first place. Some of the looks were tinged with the usual wariness or disdain toward venari, and it made Kinza's blood boil. Thankfully, she was about to take the attention off him.

Excuse me, she said and quickly found over fifty pairs of eyes on her. *I have a suggestion.*

Ekbal nodded. *Go on.*

Why don't I go? We clearly aren't getting anywhere on my queenship, and Tahir needs to be dealt with. And I am the heir... wouldn't that have some clout at least? She was proud of herself for speaking up, but they still needed to agree.

You think you can convince someone like that? one of the younger Elders sneered. It was clear what they thought of her being here.

Well, yes, Kinza said. *Need I remind you that I am actually in a more similar position to the human-Anunnaki than any of you. I grew up in human society and know it well even though I am Anunnaki.* She turned to Ekbal. *Where exactly are the other two?*

Ekbal looked to Balasi, who settled a calculating gaze on her. It wasn't malicious, but she made a mental note not to try to lie to him ever. He looked like the type of person to find out everything eventually.

One is in Paris, and the other is in Chicago.

A wide grin split Kinza's face. *I'm from Chicago, actually.*

She could tell that many of them were considering her suggestion. *You would go by yourself?* Ekbal asked.

Oh! No, I'd take Zaid, of course, Kinza said, and suddenly all eyes were back on Zaid, who sat rigid in his chair. Several Elder's all but expressed their utmost distaste, but Balasi had just said he would have sent a venari anyway. Ironically, he was the first to speak.

I think it could work, he said, nodding. *It would definitely be better than just one venari going alone.*

What does everyone think? Ekbal asked.

Of course that prompted another twenty minutes of arguing, but in the end, it was decided that this was the best course of action. Kinza and Zaid would leave in the morning and go to the human-Anunnaki in Chicago and make sure they didn't side with Tahir. If possible, they would also attempt to go to the one in Paris as well. In the meantime, the Elders here would try to deal with the barrier and would hopefully come up with some way to keep the city from revealing itself to the world.

Zaid stood as soon as Ekbal banged his gavel and strode out of the room with Kinza on his heels. She didn't catch up to him until they were on the steps of the Grand Hall.

"Zaid, hold up. You didn't like my idea?" she asked.

"No, it was fine," he said, still walking, looking like a horse ready to bolt.

"Zaid!" she said, grabbing his arm and forcing him to face her. He relented and looked down at her. "Why do you seem angry then?" she asked. "It's not like you have to go ubir-hunting at the moment, so both of us are just sitting here anyway."

He sighed. "I'm not mad. But if we are going to leave in the morning, I need to prepare a few things." He paused. "I'll see you in a little bit. I think my mother wanted to have dinner tonight if you want to come."

She released his arm and nodded. "Okay, yeah, that sounds good. See you in a bit then." She watched him turn into a blur as he ran off and wondered if something more had been bothering him.

"Well, aren't you the brave little queen," came a voice from behind her. She already had a wry smile on her face before she turned.

"Gee, thanks for your support, Mikah," she said. He was striding down the steps behind her, and Kinza saw that the woman, Eta, was hurrying down as well, looking as if she were going to throw up. But before Kinza had a chance to go over to her, she had hurried off into the crowd of people that were almost always present in the plaza.

"I meant it," Mikah said. "Truly. Even though I find it unnecessarily dangerous, and it makes me nervous that you'll be out there with Tahir, I thought it was a good plan."

"Hmm, okay," Kinza said. "Do you think you all will be able to fix the barrier? I haven't been much help in that department."

Mikah looked up at the sky as if it held the answers. "I'm not sure, but we'll figure it out. And what does Her Highness have planned for the remainder of the day?" he asked with a sly grin.

Kinza already knew where this was going and said, "I don't know, walk around a bit, find someone to help."

Mikah rolled his eyes. "Your planning skills are mediocre at best. I think you need my more experienced and superior skills at time-wasting. Come, apprentice. I will show you the way." He grabbed her wrist and looped her arm through his.

"Apprentice? I think I outrank you, actually," she pointed out.

"Whatever Her Majesty wants to believe," he said and steered her south through the plaza and toward the southern quarter. For the rest of the morning and afternoon, they walked down through the southern quarters by the quarries that were now abandoned. She was pretty sure she had seen the city three times over now, but she didn't care. It was a good distraction.

Tahir had been the Elder representing that section of the city, and the overseer Walid died in battle. There had been a lot of Aurastone research happening, and one of the apprentices was looking into it, but it was low on the priority list right now.

Mikah didn't talk to her about the stones themselves, though. Instead, he told her stories about children who would sneak into the quarries and steal pieces of Aurastone without the guards seeing them. She had a feeling that he was the child in question, but she didn't say anything, not wanting to burst his storytelling bubble.

As they walked, Mikah would snag one of the wildflowers that grew over everything down here. When Kinza had been on the run through the city with Zaid and Khalil, they had hidden in the abandoned sectors several times. Kinza had always thought it was beautiful. It seemed as if Mother Nature was slowly taking back what belonged to her. She didn't care if you were human or Anunnaki, magic or not; she would win in the end. Kinza thought there was a certain beauty to that.

They walked for hours, stopping here and there to talk with people. Mikah was very familiar to people being that he was an apprentice, and Tahir had been a well-known mentor as well. Old ladies and young women would swoon at Mikah's smile. Some of the younger women Kinza's age gave her jealous looks, but she didn't care. Kinza realized she liked Mikah. He was charming, kind, and handsome—

Kinza Solace, she berated herself. *If you don't stop that right now...*

They had started on their way back north when the barrier rippled. Mikah had plucked another one of the wildflowers when they both snapped their heads to the sky. They watched as the clear blue sky rippled like a mirage. Suddenly she felt the psychic presence of the barrier in her mind *stop*. She waited for one, two heartbeats before the barrier snapped back into place. The blue sky rippled like a stone splashing in a pond before settling.

"It's not supposed to do that, is it?" she said.

"No," Mikah said, still looking up. "But it's fine now. Shall I walk Her Royal Majesty back to her house?"

Kinza rolled her eyes and started walking on.

"I see the lady likes to take the lead," he said with a smile. "Worry not; I can follow." Mikah walked her all the way back home, coming up with increasingly ridiculous titles for her along the way. By the time they got there, she had achieved the moniker "Her Most Majesticness, our Lady of the White Star" in reference to her Aura that the entire city had seen.

Her stomach hurt from laughing, but Mikah had been dubbed her Official Distractor from her queenly stressors. As she turned to enter the house, Mikah cleared his throat from behind her.

She turned to find him standing much closer with arms behind his back. He had lost almost all of his playfulness as he looked at her intently. She had to admit, he did look a lot like Prince Charming, standing there in the late afternoon sun.

Kinza felt a blush creep up her cheeks at the intensity of his expression. "Yes?" she said, raising her eyebrows.

She thought he was about to move closer when he pulled one arm out from behind his back, presenting a bouquet of wildflowers that he had collected. "For you, lady mine," he said with a slight smile.

"Thank you," Kinza said quietly, and she took the bouquet, their fingers brushing in the process.

Mikah took a half step closer, and she dared to look up. Her breath hitched at the look on his face as if he had been bewitched. Her heart started galloping as he leaned closer, playfulness entirely gone now.

The sound of boots on stone came from the entrance of the plaza, breaking their reverie.

Kinza whipped around to find Zaid standing there with an unreadable expression.

Zaid hurried across the central plaza to the small side street that led to the boulevard on the other side. He wanted to get to the house of the venari before Savar found out about the trip to Chicago in the morning.

He pushed open one of the double wooden doors and stepped inside. Thankfully, it looked empty. Maybe he had been fast enough. He wanted to be the one to tell Savar about the change in plans; it would be a thousand times worse if he found out from someone else. And the leader of the venari was a man that found everything out eventually.

Zaid took the rickety wooden staircase to the second level and followed the balcony around, past the empty bedroom doors. He stopped before the one on the opposite side that looked over the training grounds. This room was reserved for Savar's office as Zaid had dreaded standing here a hundred times before.

The beginning of his venari training had been a bad time in his life. His brother had started spiraling down with the Apostles and the Unfettered, and Zaid had started training for a job he had never wanted, a job that people hated him for. He tried to run away or abandon his duties on several occasions, but they always found him and brought him back to drop him at this door.

The punishments were simple. He would always be asked to hold out his hands, palms up. A reed would come out of the air to land stinging on his hands. The reed wasn't the real punishment, though. It would be Savar's words that hurt the most. He would tell you exactly why the venari were needed.

"Every moment you shirk your duty is another moment an ubir has to kill a human," he would say. "You ran away today, and another person died." His words were harsh and unkind, but they were true. There were more ubir than venari, and ubir needed to kill to keep their abilities.

After what happened with Amir, the concept of death was more vivid in Zaid's mind. He never ran away again, never skipped out on an assignment. He became good at doing his duty.

Zaid knocked on the door now and waited.

Come, the voice came. Zaid stepped inside and looked around the familiar room. It was almost spartan with a single desk, chair, and bookshelf. No mementos or weapons or even a rug. On the bookshelf were stacks of papers and record books of venari, their abilities, and their assignments. Zaid knew that one of the thickest books there was his, having done more assignments than any other venari his age. But none of that would matter now.

Savar sat at the desk scribbling in another record book.

Savar, I wanted to speak with you. I needed to tell you something before—

If this is about your upcoming excursion to the United States, then there is no need, Savar said without looking up.

No punishment. No reed.

How had he found out so fast? The meeting only ended minutes ago. Zaid hesitated before turning to leave but paused again with his hand on the door handle. The smart thing to do would be to leave. But Zaid didn't feel like being smart today.

Why? he asked, turning back around. *Why aren't you angry with me?*

Savar finally glanced up. *Because anger would be pointless. You don't learn from anger; you learn from pain. And this—*he waved a hand vaguely toward the door, but Zaid had a feeling he meant Kinza—*will only cause you pain in the end. The best course of action is just to let you continue on this path you have chosen and let you find the consequences yourself.* Without another word, he went back to his scribbling.

No anger. No stinging palms.

Zaid left then, walking back across the second floor, down the rickety staircase, and out the front door.

Savar was wrong. It was *already* painful, but Zaid could handle it. He had told Kinza he would stay by her side, and he wouldn't go back on that promise now. He wouldn't abandon her again. Somehow everything would turn out okay. He knew he would need to go back to his duty eventually, but what he was doing now was important. He was helping the heir to the Rhaptan throne save the city. How was that a bad thing?

He went back to the central plaza. It was afternoon now, and he still had a little while before going to his mother's for dinner. She always demanded he did so when he was home between assignments. He felt bad leaving her alone so much; his father had died when Zaid was young, and Zaid was already a venari when Amir died. Now she had no one. Hopefully, when Zaid finally did go back to work, she would dote on Kinza instead. She practically did already, seeing as she'd been inviting her over without Zaid.

He smiled and headed over to the markets and vendors along the main boulevard that bisected the city. He hadn't lied when he told Kinza he needed to run a few errands before they left the next day. He should have gotten his mark touched up while he was still at the house of the venari, but that ship had sailed. He needed to have additional lines added to the tattoo that stretched over the left side of his chest every three weeks or so; otherwise, he would quickly turn human out in the world. Kinza wouldn't need to do that since she had the mark of the Rhaptan monarchy.

He gathered the needed supplies they would require to get to Mochi, the little town at the base of Mount Kilimanjaro. They would probably want food on the way there but would have to get other items in town. It would take time to get there, back to the portal, and then back down to Chicago from northern Michigan, and he wouldn't be able to run since it would be daylight and someone would surely see him and Kinza.

Once he was done gathering supplies, he headed toward the inner eastern district where Kinza's house was. He didn't know if she was home, but it would be a good place to start. She had said she wanted to go to dinner at his mother's. He had also thought about telling her about the mission he had been avoiding and his argument with Savar, but she was already stressed enough with literally being handed an entire civilization on a platter. She was always so feisty and confident. He sometimes forgot she was so young and practically all alone here. He still had the residual guilt of being the one who had brought her here in the first place, and he felt it was his duty to help her through the aftermath.

He couldn't lie to himself, though. It was no longer a duty to him.

It didn't take long for him to get there. He was thinking about how it would be nice to spend some time alone with Kinza again when he turned the corner into her little plaza.

The sight of the two people standing outside of her door made him stop dead in the middle of the plaza.

Savar had been right.

"I—uh—" Kinza stuttered as Zaid stalked across the plaza toward them.

His face was as closed off as it had ever been. He didn't look at her as he dropped a bag by her door and said, "Supplies for tomorrow," before turning around and walking away.

"Wait!" Kinza said, watching him walk away. She turned to Mikah and said, "Sorry, Mikah. There's this dinner—"

"Not to worry, Your Highness," he said. "I'll see you tomorrow before you leave." He was perfectly polite, but his lips were pursed as he gave her one of his short bows and left, striding the opposite way.

Kinza immediately ran off to catch up with Zaid, who had managed to get halfway down the street already.

"Wait!" she called again. Why was he upset? And more importantly, why was she embarrassed? There was nothing that she should be ashamed of. She finally caught up to him and said, "Geez, hold up. Some of us don't have freakishly long legs. Where are you going?"

"To my mother's for dinner." His eyes were kept firmly ahead of him as he walked.

"Why didn't you wait for me?" she asked. She hoped that if he heard her wild heartbeat, he would assume it was from running to catch up to him. Thankfully, he wouldn't be able to see the blush that was heating her cheeks either.

"I didn't realize you were going," he said.

"I said I would."

"Ah, my mistake. You looked a little busy." His words made her feel guilty, but they shouldn't have. She was well within her rights to like a guy or even kiss one if she wanted to. He had no reason to be this upset—and she had no business feeling guilty about it.

"Well, I wasn't," she replied. She was more confused than anything right now. He had acted oddly after the meeting that morning, and now he was even weirder. Zaid wasn't the type to talk about anything, especially how he was feeling, but she would kill to have a mind-reading ability right now.

They walked the rest of the way to Ekaja's in silence. There were still people milling about, and the sound of hammering filled the neighborhoods still. The evening light caught the tops of the building, making them look like they were on fire. Zaid took the steps two at a time up to Ekaja's home and knocked on the door as Kinza was struggling up the steps behind him.

Ekaja answered the door in a flurry of silks and beads. "My dears!" she said, pulling them both in for a hug.

"Hello, Mother," Zaid said, pulling away almost immediately and heading into the house.

Ekaja gave Kinza a confused look, and she returned it with an apologetic one. "I will just hug you today then," Ekaja said with a smile and pulled her back into her arms. She smelled like jasmine, and Kinza sagged into her a bit. She then ushered them to the table where she had practically cooked a feast. There was hardly any empty space left for them.

"Kinza, how are you finding the Elders?" Ekaja asked Kinza after a few minutes of eating.

"Well, um, to be honest, I'm not sure how they've ever gotten anything done with all the bickering they do," she said, putting another bite of food in her mouth.

Ekaja had a small smile at that, and they sat in silence for a few minutes. "Are you two leaving right away tomorrow?"

"No."

"Yes."

Kinza turned to Zaid with a curious look. "We have a few more errands to run before we go, and we need to meet with Balasi about the exact location of the person we need to find." He said it without looking at her and went right back to shoveling food into his mouth.

"Ah, okay."

They ate the rest of their dinner with Ekaja's eyes glancing back and forth between them suspiciously. When they were done, Zaid thanked his mother and walked out into the night. Kinza caught sight of Ekaja's worried eyes. She knew Zaid's mother worried about him every time he left the city, but there was nothing any of them would do about it. Thankfully, Zaid wasn't on any type of dangerous ubir-hunting activities this time.

"Thanks again for dinner," Kinza said as Ekaja hugged her goodbye.

As she did so, she said, "It'll all turn out all right." Kinza had a feeling she wasn't referring to the trip to Chicago. She left and went to try and catch up with Zaid.

Just like before, he was well on his way down the street. "Will you wait?" she called to him, breaking into a jog. He didn't turn around, so she had to run faster to catch up to him. She realized that it was a bad time to be running after an enormous meal. She kneaded the stitch in her side and said, "You didn't want to walk me home?" She had almost caught up to him, but he didn't slow.

"I figured you knew your way around with all the touring you've been doing."

Kinza stopped dead in the middle of the road. "Why are you mad?" she said and crossed her arms. She was starting to get fed up with his attitude. She hated that she felt guilty over Zaid showing up at her house when she and Mikah were having a moment. But he shouldn't have been so upset about it in the first place.

Zaid kept walking, but she knew he was fully aware she had stopped because eventually, he did too. Exhaling a sharp breath and rolling his shoulders, he turned and walked back to where she was standing. "I'm not mad," he said.

Kinza didn't buy it for one second, and her face must have shown it because he placed both hands on the side of her face, forcing her to look at him, and said, "I'm. Not. Mad."

"Right... sure. Totally believe that," she replied, arms still crossed. "You're mad that I'm hanging out with Mikah, and you shouldn't be. You two have some weird childhood feud, and somehow, I'm in the middle of it."

He sighed and dropped his hands. "I mean it. You can like Mikah all you want. I wish you many fat healthy babies. I literally couldn't care less, okay?" He raised his eyebrows at her as he waited for an answer.

Kinza felt like she had been doused with a bucket of cold water. How was this night getting progressively worse? She had felt guilty over him seeing her with Mikah, so shouldn't she feel better hearing that he didn't care? She should've, but she didn't. Instead, her stomach twisted at his words.

"Fine," was all she said.

They started walking again, this time with him going slower. He walked her all the way back to her house before turning and heading toward the central plaza. Kinza went inside and flopped, fully clothed, onto her bed.

She was upset with herself, and she didn't know why. She hated this whole situation, but if she were being honest with herself, she had been avoiding the thought of her and Zaid's relationship for quite a while now. He had, in such a short time in her life, played several different roles. He had been her kidnapper and enemy first, and then her protector and maybe friend, and then a stranger to her when he thought she was *his* enemy. He had promised to stay by her side, but what had that meant? Just as her glorified bodyguard? She considered him far more than that, but now she wasn't sure he felt the same about her.

She covered her face with her pillow before groaning into it. It was at times like these that she missed her mother acutely. Boy problems would be something Sadia could have helped her with. In fact, there were a lot of things Sadia would've had advice on. Whether it was about what to wear to how to respond to a text. Sadia would always have an answer and would give it with absolute conviction. Over time Kinza realized she must've viewed her mother through the eyes of a child because she had thought her mother had known everything. Now, as a sort-of adult, Kinza knew Sadia couldn't have known the answers to *everything*, but must have always projected confidence for her daughter's sake.

It didn't stop Kinza from missing her, though. Just to have someone there to tell you everything would be all right—even if it was a lie—was one of those things you didn't realize you counted on until it was gone.

Even though it was getting late, Kinza didn't feel tired. She went into the bathroom, which was quickly becoming her favorite room in the house, and drew a bath. A few bottles of soap and bath oil had been left outside in the pile of gifts, and she dumped some of them in. When the sweet scent of blood orange and something dark and woodsy filled the room, she placed the bottles in a pile of her favorite gifts with the perfume and makeup.

Then she spent an absurdly long time lounging in the warm water, thinking about nothing and everything. She didn't let herself feel guilty about how long she lounged there and reminded herself of how much she had done over the past few weeks. She tried to remember all the people she had helped, the justice she got on her parents' killers, and the friends she had made and told herself the stress she was going through now would pass. Zaid was never truly far from her thoughts, but she didn't let herself stop enjoying the moment she was in.

She had let her eyes drift closed, and when she opened them, she was pleased to see the room was glowing faintly from the light of her Aura refracting out of the bubbles. It faded quickly, but that was okay. She went to bed feeling a little better and slept soundly, dreaming about a city full of faceless lights sleeping under the moon. In her dream, Kinza lay down with them and slipped into the darkness of deep slumber.

CHAPTER 5

PREPARATIONS

The pounding door woke Kinza from a quickly fading dream. She had sudden flashbacks of the night of the battle in Rhapta when she had been woken similarly.

Launching out of bed, still tangled in the sheets, she looked around. It was still dark out and silent in her house. Had she dreamed of the pounding on the door?

The pounding came again, followed by Zaid's annoyed voice. "Are you awake or dead?"

Kinza groaned and went to answer the door. Pulling it open, she saw the sun hadn't even started its ascent, and stars still twinkled in the sky. The only break in the starlight was Zaid's dark form looking her over.

"Not dead then. Just lazy."

Kinza mustered an annoyed grunt and waved him in. "Give me five minutes. I didn't know we were leaving this early."

"I told you we were leaving just before dawn," he said, stepping in and looking around.

Kinza hurried to dress, pulling on the simplest outfit she could find. A pair of loose green pants and a cream-colored graphic tee someone had given her. The venari occasionally brought back human things to sell, and she was thankful because she wouldn't stand out when she got to Moshi. She loved the silkiness of Anunnaki clothing, but the familiarity of the t-shirt reminded her of home, and she found herself getting excited to see Chicago again.

"Are we just going to use the portals to get back again?" she asked when she stepped out into the main living area. Zaid was lounging at her table, picking off a few grapes from the bowl that sat there.

"Yes," he said, popping one into his mouth.

"Do you think—" she started.

"Yes, I figured you'd want to see your grandmother," he said while glancing at her. "You can call her when we get to Moshi if you want."

Kinza exhaled a sigh of relief. She didn't know if they would have time to see Grams, and the thought of not seeing her when they would be so close weighed on her. "Thank you."

Zaid didn't get up and instead said, "So you aren't going back for good then?"

"I've decided that would be too much like running away from my problems," she replied. "I would feel too guilty if I just went home knowing that an entire civilization might fall when I could've done something."

Zaid nodded as if that settled something. "Let's get going then," he said and went outside. He still had hardly looked at her since he arrived, and she was hesitant to broach the topic of the night before. She didn't want the whole trip to be of them arguing again.

"You said we had a few more things to do before we left?" she asked, closing the front door behind her as she followed him out.

"Yep. I need to get my tattoo touched up, so we'll go to the house of the venari first," he said.

"Where's that?" she asked. It was so early that it was almost chilly without the sun, and Kinza rubbed her bare arms.

"You'll see."

Back to no talking then, she thought with a mental roll of her eyes. This was going to be a long trip.

ZAID LED Kinza through the city to his home of close to eight years. It was a secret location, but very rarely did anyone who wasn't venari enter inside. So it felt odd when he held the door open for Kinza as she stepped inside.

He almost felt self-conscious as she looked around at the empty training grounds and hallways that wrapped around the building. It was plain and unadorned like everything else about the venari life. There were no pretty gifts left at the door, no sweet-smelling flowers or perfumes, and no smiling faces to greet them. Her expression didn't give any hint of disappointment, though.

"Where's your room?" she asked.

"It's upstairs, but there's not much to see," he said, heading up the rickety staircase.

"Can I see it anyway?" she asked, following him. "I bet you have some weird collectibles, painted rocks or something."

"Maybe later," he said. He knew she was only trying to lighten the mood. The air had felt... tense since he had arrived at her house. The memory of the day before still stung, but he was resigned to not making it worse. And bringing her into his personal space like that would definitely not help.

When they got to the upper floor, they were met by the

stern figure of Savar, and Zaid stopped up short. His expression would be unreadable to Kinza, but Zaid knew that the head of the venari was looking at him with pity and disdain. Zaid was determined not to shrink under that gaze and prayed that Savar wouldn't say anything about his disapproval of the situation.

"Oh, hi!" Kinza said, looking between them.

"Kinza, this is Savar, the head of the venari and our trainer," Zaid said, still looking at him. "He's the one who helps us with the tattoos." At that thought, he hoped that Savar *would* help him. Zaid only had a vague understanding of the ink and didn't particularly want to mess up.

Savar finally looked at Kinza and gave a slight bow of his head in respect. "It's a pleasure to meet you, Your Highness." He gave one last look at Zaid, seemingly imposing his displeasure into his gaze before gesturing to his office without another word.

They followed him silently down the hall to one of the empty bedrooms near his office that was used for tattooing. Along one wall was a bedroll and on the opposite was a shelf filled with jars of plants, ointments, and needles next to ripped-up stacks of linen. Zaid already knew what to do and slipped his shirt off and lay down while Savar got to work.

Kinza hovered in the doorway, looking around with interest. "So, how do you know when you need to touch it up?" she asked.

"The outside will start to fade, and you don't want to let it get too light like this," Zaid said, gesturing to his tattoo. It was the same palm-sized mandala with two smaller circles inside that every Anunnaki had. There was also a network of swirling lines that spread across his chest and shoulder that were much lighter than the middle. Kinza glanced at it and then immediately away.

Savar was quiet, getting the ink ready with practiced precision. Zaid had watched the process a thousand times, but he still didn't feel confident he could produce the same results if he had tried. Savar took out a few dark leaves from a jar and placed them in a mortar with several different oils and other roots before starting to grind them with the pestle. The mixing wasn't the hard part; it was selecting the right leaves.

Kinza's eyes followed Savar, and she seemed to be thinking along the same lines. "Why exactly does this work?" she asked suddenly.

Savar looked up from his grinding with a puzzled expression.

"I mean, why does a plant allow you to leave the city temporarily?" she clarified.

"We don't really know," Savar said, focusing again on the ink. "The process had been an Anunnaki tradition for thousands of years, and we no longer know who discovered it; only that it works."

"What is it exactly?" Kinza asked, leaning against the doorjamb.

Savar emptied the contents of the mortar into a small dish and started preparing the needle, wrapping the end in a stiff cloth. "They're just the leaves of African violets. They grow along the outer edge of the quarry near the forest."

"Really?" she asked, eyebrows raising. "Just violets? Would any violets work?"

"No," Savar said, moving over to Zaid to start the process. "The hardest part of creating the ink is getting the right leaves from the right plant. Sometimes we pick them, and the ink does nothing, or the tattoo fades quickly. Other times the ink will last for over a month. All we really know is the closer to the quarry, the better."

Zaid had to restrain himself from yelling at Savar. Why was

he being so helpful to her when he was the one who thought Zaid shouldn't get involved with her?

"Hmm, interesting," Kinza muttered to herself. Zaid was inclined to agree. He had always thought the idea odd that a small commonplace flower would have such profound properties. He thought about Tahir, who had spent so much time in the quarries with Walid, the old overseer, studying the Aurastone. Tahir was out there in the world now with a few other Elders and apprentices who hadn't turned human. Had Tahir discovered which violets were the best and would allow the tattoo to stay permanent? He must have, but the idea was astonishing. If the Rhaptan public got their hands on something like that, there would be more chaos than ever. The ability to come and go was something the Anunnaki had thought was no more than a lofty dream for their entire existence.

Savar had started by dipping the tiny needle in the ink before he got to work darkening the faint lines in Zaid's skin. There seemed to be an unspoken agreement that neither of them would speak about Savar's displeasure as long as Kinza was here.

Kinza was tilting her head, trying to get a better look from her spot in the doorway, curls swaying with the effort.

"You can come to watch if you want," Zaid said.

Kinza came closer and sat at the end of the bedroll, eyes fixed on the needle. "So no one knows why the monarchs have the full tattoo then?" she asked, touching her abdomen. Zaid had seen her tattoo on several occasions. The center was the same as everyone else's, but instead of swirling lines, hers had delicate chains and gems extending across both sides of the mandala to stretch across her upper abdomen, never needing to be touched up as his did if she wanted to leave.

"Not that I'm aware of," Zaid said, looking at Savar.

Savar shrugged. "Just like the African violets, there are many things we don't understand about the magic that happens here."

Kinza's face twisted in thought, and Zaid could see the gears working behind her eyes. It was the face she made any time he told her details about Anunnaki life that would seem preposterous or outlandish to humans. He imagined it was her way of processing the information before accepting it. He had to hand it to her; she had taken in mountains of such information in the last few weeks. She had fought him tooth and nail—literally—up until the point she had been given proof of the Anunnaki magic. But since then, she had taken most things in stride, accepting them after a time.

They sat in silence for the next twenty minutes as Savar worked through the tattoo, depositing the dark ink into Zaid's skin. The slight pain was so familiar that he could have fallen asleep but was instead acutely aware of Kinza staring at his chest the entire time with the same expression on her face.

"Does everyone know how to make the ink?" she asked as Savar was finishing up the last line.

"No," he said, thinking. "It is myself, Hakim before he passed, Ekbal, Ishar, and Tahir. The venari all know the process since it is mostly used for them, but none of them have been really taught which plants to pick."

"Hmm," she said, scowling at the mention of Tahir.

"Done," Savar said, pulling back and letting Zaid sit up. The Anunnaki healing was already working to knit the skin together to prevent any infection. He put his shirt back on and nodded in thanks. Savar only started cleaning up, so Zaid went out into the hall with Kinza.

She still had that expression as she looked around at the empty bedrooms. "Where to next?" she asked.

"The Grand Hall," he replied, grabbing the duffel bag he

had left outside the door. Halfway down the hall, he stopped at an empty room and turned the handle, stepping inside.

"What are you doing?" Kinza asked.

He just held the door open and indicated to the contents of the room. It was only slightly less empty than Savar's office, with a bedroll, a few chests, and a rack of weapons along one wall. "See? Boring."

"This is your room?" she asked, fully stepping inside and looking around. She walked over to one of the large chests and started to open it. "You're right, it looks boring, but—"

Zaid slammed the chest shut. "No prying." If she found the stacks of books that had been Amir's, they would be here for hours.

"Fine, fine..." she said with a slight grin. "Be all mysterious if you want."

Zaid just shook his head. "Come on. I want to be on our way before noon. And Balasi should be waiting for us now in the Grand Hall."

Kinza and Zaid took the short walk over to the central plaza. The light of morning was starting to creep across the sky, pushing the stars back. Kinza couldn't stop thinking about the ink, though. She wasn't sure why this of all things stuck with her after witnessing the magic of the Anunnaki lives, but something about the African violets, the ink, and Tahir kept swirling around in her mind. Like a puzzle she needed to put together, but she was missing a few pieces. It was important even though she didn't know why.

The early morning vendors were setting up, and a few waived to Kinza. She couldn't have eaten if she tried, though.

The dinner she had at Ekaja's would last her days. She wondered how Grams would take it when she turned down the lasagna she made almost weekly. The thought of seeing her only family had her thrumming with anticipation and nervousness. They had talked on the phone, but would Grams be angry with her? Was *she* angry with Grams? She had been Ummanu her whole life; had she known she married the heir to the Anunnaki throne? Or did she find out about all of that later? There were so many questions she had, and she knew that the time she would have in Chicago would be limited. Hopefully, they would be able to convince this human-Anunnaki person to side with them quickly so they could go back to saving the city from collapse.

They took the steps up into the hall and onto the marble floors. Kinza followed Zaid through the hallways to a decent-sized office toward the back of the building with a wall of windows looking out onto the north quarter of the city. Zaid knocked on the open door as they stepped inside.

"Zaid, Kinza," Balasi said, looking up from the papers on his desk. Kinza was surprised to see several human books sitting on the extensive bookshelves that lined one side of the room. They were in a variety of languages but clearly had the glossy pages of a modern printing press and university-issued textbooks. Was this how they kept up to date on human affairs?

"Hello, Elder Balasi," Kinza said. "We are here to talk about the…"

"Yes, of course. You need to know who you are looking for," he said, gesturing to two chairs before his desk. "Please, have a seat, and I'll tell you what I can."

Kinza and Zaid sat, and Balasi set aside the stack of papers he had been reading. "So, as we discussed in the meeting, you are going to the Chicago location, correct?"

"Yes, I figured that made sense since it's my home," Kinza said.

Balasi nodded as if that made sense. He was perfectly polite, but something about him made Kinza nervous. Not in a malicious way, but as if she was truly being *seen*. The way Elder Balasi's eyes tracked around the room and over her made it seem like he was analyzing every piece of information he picked up, no matter how small. She had a feeling nothing would escape this man's notice.

"So, the man we have in Chicago goes by the name of Edmund Clark—"

"The billionaire?!" Kinza burst out.

Both men turned to her. "You know him?" Balasi asked.

"I'm mean, yes—well, no," Kinza stuttered. "He's one of the richest people in America, let alone Chicago. I used to clean in his office building downtown. Super fancy. He's Anunnaki?"

"Used to be," Balasi corrected. "Remember, all of our plants in human society have allowed themselves to become human before we remind them of their pasts. Mr. Clark has been human for about fifty years now and has risen through human society over the last thirty. It takes time to acquire wealth and power. As you may know then, he started out in the financial industry but had branched out into real estate and commerce. He owns properties around the world, and his company is the holder of many smaller subsidiaries. So when I say that he is a busy man, I mean it."

Balasi rifled through a few of his papers before finding the one he was looking for. "He is mostly autonomous like the other human-Anunnaki, but they meet with us once every few years routinely so we can provide advice on how to sway human society. Other than that, he would have had very little contact with Anunnaki over the last fifty years. I know he had hired an Ummanu into his company, but I have no idea who.

The hardest part with be getting a meeting with him. Here is his work and home address," he said, sliding a piece of paper across the desk.

"I don't have a phone number since that would be useless for us, and he changes it frequently. You'll have to do your best to get in contact with him, but you can tell him I sent you. Not that it'll mean much since there is no way to prove it. He's free to come back here if he wants proof, but I doubt he will be able to leave his work. Here is a relatively current photo as well." He handed over a magazine clipping of a man who looked like he was in his early fifties in a crisp suit jacket. He had short, graying hair and a wide smile with artificially white teeth.

"How old is he actually?" Kinza asked.

"About eighty-two if I remember correctly," Balasi said. "He is the youngest of the human-Anunnaki."

"And the others?" Zaid asked.

Balasi pulled out some more papers. "Wang Hàorán is the chair of a family-run conglomerate from Sichuan, China. I don't believe his family knows he is—or was—Anunnaki, but he has kept in contact with us until recently. He did spend some time as a politician in the eighties and nineties, so he holds some sway there as well." He handed them a newspaper clipping of another man who looked to be in his seventies or even eighties, surrounded by a large number of people Kinza assumed were his family. They all wore expensively tailored clothing and stood outside of a glass building.

"And the last is Vivienne Moreau, a French fashion icon of past generations. She has connections *everywhere,* so don't let her lowly millionaire status fool you if you do get the chance to go there. She has her hands in several high-end labels and runs a few smaller businesses herself. Her business office is in Paris, but her main residence is in the Bordeaux countryside." He handed over another photo of an elegantly dressed woman in her sixties, posing in front of a massive window that looked out into extensive gardens. It looked like it was from a Vogue interview, and Kinza thought she might've seen her name before in a few other magazines.

Balasi took a breath and continued. "Obviously, these are not the names they were born with, but they have adopted these identities and have lived them for many, many years. I would focus on Mr. Clark for now and if you have time, see if you can sway Madam Moreau as well. My connections have all but confirmed that Wang has sided with Tahir, so I cannot express how important it is to at least get Mr. Clark on our side." His eyes bore deep into Kinza's own, imploring her to understand. "Even if we find a way to keep the barrier from collapsing, it won't matter if Tahir brings the human-Anunnaki into whatever vile plans he has. The three of them, led by him, could bring destruction across the globe. And worst-case scenario, the barrier does fall, and Tahir brings them to our doorstep."

"Do you really think he would do that?" Kinza asked, holding the papers.

"I have known him for longer than you have been alive, and many, including myself, have fallen for his words in the past. He is charming and manipulating, and *convincing*. One thing I know for sure is that Tahir believes in himself to a fault. He thinks that it would be better for things to happen his way, or not at all. I believe he would rather watch Rhapta and the rest of the planet burn instead of allowing someone else to rule the Anunnaki—whether it's the Elders or you."

Kinza hadn't been given any more information on what she needed to do to become queen. Apparently, the scholars were doing more research, but that hadn't produced any results so far. For now, the imminent danger was Tahir, followed closely by the collapsing barrier.

"Great," she said. "No pressure."

Balasi grimaced but said, "Actually, yes. A lot of pressure. I'd rather not watch the world burn, so be convincing when you talk with Mr. Clark."

"Anything else that could help us?" Zaid asked, leaning forward.

Balasi shook his head and placed his hands on the desk before him, thinking. "If I were you, I would try to get in contact with the Ummanu he employed. Maybe he'll be able to help you get in contact with Mr. Clark. We'll do our best to stay in contact, but realistically it's difficult at best, especially with the preoccupation of the barrier."

"Do you have a cellphone?" Zaid asked.

Balasi looked taken off guard for a moment. "I suppose, yes. But it doesn't work here. It's just a backup in case we need to send someone down the mountain to use it."

"Keep it on hand just in case," Zaid said. "One of the other venari out there has a technology ability and made my phone work here last week."

"Ah, that's right. Okay," Balasi said and wrote down the number for him. "Either way, expect little to no communication from us. Just do the job and come back as quickly as possible."

Kinza and Zaid thanked the Elder and said their goodbyes before heading back out into the hallway. They could see the sun coming up over the horizon now, and the light was spilling into the Hall, outlining a figure walking toward them. Zaid audibly exhaled.

"Mikah," Kinza said, hoping she sounded more pleasant than awkward. "You're here early."

He sketched a bow and smiled at her. "Good morning, Your Excellency," he said, completely ignoring Zaid. "I have much work to do today, and I did say I would see you before you left. Are you leaving now then?"

"We are, yes. Hey, I wanted to talk to you about something—"

Zaid left, walking toward the plaza.

"—But I don't have time before I leave. Let's catch up when I get back, okay?"

"Yes, of course," he replied. "We'll be plenty busy as well trying to figure out what to do in regard to the barrier."

"Hopefully, the scholars and Elders will figure out this queenship thing as well. Maybe I can help with the barrier if they figure out how," she said.

"Good point. I'll mention it to them again," he said.

"Thanks, Mikah," she said, placing a hand on his arm. She hoped he understood what she meant. She didn't know where their relationship stood or how he even felt about her after yesterday. But it wasn't the most pressing issue, so it would need to wait.

He gave her a genuine smile and took her hand, placing his lips on the back. "Anytime. Do be careful."

"I will," she said with a blush and went to catch up to Zaid.

The plaza was just starting to get busy with apprentices, Elders, and scholars all heading to work early. Imminent doom didn't slow for beauty rest, so many of them had bags under their eyes and weary expressions. Zaid was waiting for her in the center.

"I forgot I needed to grab one more thing before we go," he said, not mentioning Mikah. "It'll be faster if I run. Mind waiting here a minute?"

"No, that's fine. I'll be here," she replied.

"I'll be right back," he said and darted off, already out of the plaza.

Kinza watched the white and blue robes fluttering in the

breeze as the Rhaptans went about their work. Construction was already starting again this early, filling the plaza with the sound of hammering and shouting. She turned to find a small, gray-robed woman coming toward her. Kinza recognized Eta's dainty face as she came closer, looking ever serene. She wondered how she could always stay so calm and collected in the midst of the chaos of Rhaptan life over the last few weeks. She had the ability of sight, though, so maybe as a seer, she saw everything coming anyway.

"Your Highness," Eta said aloud, stopping before her. Her voice was quiet but methodical and not unpleasant to listen to.

"Hello, Eta," Kinza said. "Call me Kinza, please."

Eta gave her a slight nod. "As you wish. I haven't had the opportunity to introduce myself yet and wanted to make sure you knew I was here for you if you need it."

"Oh!" Kinza said, slightly taken aback. "Thank you, that means a lot... although I'm not sure what..." she trailed off, not entirely sure how to respond. She had a few people offer her their services, but she had no experience in managing people. "You are a seer, right?"

Eta gave her an understanding smile, and Kinza found that she was starting to like the young woman. "Yes, although I'm not nearly as helpful as Hakim would be. I know that there is still some... pushback in regard to your queenship, but I want you to know I will support you in any way that I can."

Kinza suddenly realized what she meant. If the Elders overturned Kinza's claim to the throne and reverted back to the Elder Council as the form of government, it would most likely be Eta who would lead in the position of Grand Elder. It hadn't been officially stated, but the council—and all of Rhapta—had relied heavily on Hakim's visions. It would only make sense that his apprentice would follow in his footsteps, effectively making her Kinza's political opponent.

Yet here she was, making it clear that she had no intentions of being an opponent. Eta was probably one of, if not the most important supporter Kinza could have, and she was suddenly grateful.

"Thank you, it means a lot," Kinza said. "I still don't even know where I stand with that within this barrier and Tahir issue." She had a sudden thought. "Could I, maybe, ask you for a favor then?"

"Of course," Eta said, tilting her head to the side.

"I know the Elders and scholars are looking into the queen-ship thing and trying to see if there is a way for me to help with the barrier, but there is one other thing. In the Apostles of Truth, there is a man named Badr; he's a friend of mine. Would you have him look into the tattoo ink the venari use? You can let him know I sent you."

Eta's brows furrowed. "You think the ink can help us?"

"I don't know, but I think it's important to something. See if he can find Tahir's research. I know he had been studying it for years. On second thought, maybe that's something Mikah could do..."

"Not to worry," Eta said. "I can contact them both and see what we can find out. There are very few people who know much about it, but we can at least try."

"Thank you," Kinza said as she saw Zaid coming back across the plaza, parcel in hand. "I think it's time for us to go now. It was really nice meeting you."

Eta gave her a gentle smile. "You as well, Kinza. Good luck. Oh!" she said, and Kinza paused. "I almost forgot to mention, pick the red one."

"What?" Kinza said, just as Zaid was arriving.

"Come back safely," was all she said as she walked away, clasping her hands within her sleeves.

"You good?" Zaid said, looking at Eta's retreating form.

"Yeah, she just wanted to say she was on my side," Kinza said, watching her as well.

"That... actually would really help," Zaid said. "She may not look it, but Eta has a powerful gift. If it grows to anything like Hakim's was, you'll want to keep her close when you are queen."

"I realize that," she said more to herself than anything. "So, did you get what you needed?"

"Yep," he said, holding up the package.

"What is it?"

"Tennis shoes," he said, looking down at her sandaled feet. "We'll be hiking down the mountain."

"Oh," she said, looking down as well. "Right. Didn't think of that." She heaved a sigh. "Okay, let's go do this again. And maybe let's not almost die this time."

Zaid chuckled as they headed out of the city.

CHAPTER 6
THE SWEETNESS OF HOME

Kinza swatted the seventeenth branch out of her face, projecting her frustration at the leaves. It did nothing to fend off the swarm of mosquitos that were descending on her like a free buffet. She growled in annoyance as she smacked one that had landed on the side of her neck, and two more took its place.

"What did the forest ever do to you?" Zaid muttered from further down the path. Calling it a path was a stretch since Kinza was only following behind Zaid, who was wandering in seemingly random directions down the mountain.

"The abuse is mutual," she replied, pulling out another leaf from her hair. The branches practically reached out to her to snag in her hair and on her clothes, and the roots definitely were coming up from the ground at exactly the right time to trip her. How she had gone uphill in the dark was a mystery to her.

They had left the city and gone to the edge of the barrier where there was almost a doorway to the forest. The totem pole that she had first seen in her dreams was still there, planted between two trees, and as Kinza stepped through the barrier, she felt almost a sense of nostalgia. Whether it was due to missing the human lands or Rhapta, she wasn't sure yet. Everything in her life had been surreal since coming to Rhapta, and she felt like she was waking up from a vivid dream now that she was back in the forests surrounding Mount Kilimanjaro.

Unfortunately, the awkwardness between her and Zaid was the same as last time too. They had been walking for thirty minutes now and memories of their time coming here kept bouncing around. Had that only been last week? It felt like an eternity had passed, and she was no longer the same person she had been when she arrived. She knew Zaid was thinking about their trip here as well, but neither of them said anything.

"How long until we get there?" she asked, kicking at a bush. She would have to thank Zaid for the shoes at some point. On second thought, they were probably given to her so he wouldn't have to carry her down.

"A few hours," he said, adjusting the duffel bag on his shoulder. The day was already starting to get hot, and sweat dampened their necks from the exertion.

"Great," Kinza said to herself.

They walked in silence for a while, and Kinza couldn't help but remember the night Tahir's assassins had captured them. She shuddered at the memory of Jafar's voice in her head, telling her they had killed her parents. Her abilities had been so volatile then, even though they were only marginally better now. She had only had one other training session with Jabari that mostly involved her meditating and "thinking good thoughts," since that's what seemed to help her the most. She did notice how it steadied her thought.

She hadn't had any near-death experiences since the battle in Rhapta, but she had noticed how calm her Aura felt after her sessions with Jabari. The tingling at the back of her neck didn't jump at every stressor, and she didn't turn into an exploding human fireball when someone startled her. Maybe with more training, one day, she would be able to command her Aura to do other things, like heal... or hold the barrier.

She had tried sensing the barrier again like she had when it had glitched when she was with Mikah. Its presence was always there, like the faint hum of the air conditioning in Grams' house. She had tried mentally pushing or prodding at it, but it was resolute and wouldn't budge. How could it feel so strong, yet suddenly be so weak as to collapse? She knew she *technically* was supposed to be able to hold it on her own, but she was starting to doubt that. Maybe her royal blood was too diluted.

"We'll never get there at the rate you are going," Zaid called over his shoulder. She realized she had lagged behind a little while she was absorbed in her thoughts. She picked up the pace as best she could, still thinking.

"Hey," she said, and he looked over his shoulder at her. "Sorry about yesterday, I—"

He waved her off dismissively and kept walking. "Don't worry about it. I should be sorry. I was just in a bad mood."

She didn't know why she apologized when she did nothing wrong. She just wanted this awkwardness to be over with. "I know," she replied, pulling her hair out of another branch. "You and I just..." she didn't know what she was trying to say.

"Yeah, don't worry about it," he said quietly.

"Well, I do worry about it," she said. They had entered a denser part of the forest, and the branches had Kinza's hair at every step. "I just want..."

Zaid stopped and looked back at her. The weight of his gaze sent butterflies fluttering through her stomach. "You want what?" he asked even quieter.

She had stopped to detangle her hair and said, "I meant what I said after the battle. I just want you... around."

"Around?"

She sighed. They were dancing dangerously close to a topic they had refused to acknowledge before. "Yes," she said finally, not feeling brave enough to elaborate further.

Zaid looked at her a moment and nodded before walking back toward her. He came close, and Kinza found herself holding her breath as he reached up to help her with the leaves in her hair. When he was done, he fished around in the bag and pulled out a hair tie. "I also meant what I said when I said I would be there," he replied. "But I am still venari, and I'll have to go back to work after all this is taken care of. Either way, I'll be *around*."

She nodded and took the hair tie, pulling her curls into the safety of a bun. "Right. Yeah, no, you're right," she said, a little too focused on her hair and definitely not avoiding his gaze at all.

"Okay," he said finally. "Well, let's get going. I want to hitch a ride on the highway before noon."

"Hitch a—we're going to hitch a ride? With strangers?" she asked incredulously.

"It's not like the car is going to be where we left it," he said, turning to stalk back down through the trees.

"It'd be nice," she grumbled, following Zaid down the mountain.

THE WIND WHIPPED through the van, sending errant curls into Kinza's face. Despite being crammed onto a hot tour bus that had passed their way on the highway, she was enjoying the breeze and the sunlight.

The city of Moshi was coming into view as the driver turned down the radio, announcing that the bus would be stopping soon. Kinza let her hand drape out of the window and looked to find Zaid trying to fend off a conversation from an overly hyped tourist sitting next to him. She had to suppress a laugh at the annoyed expression on his face as the man showed him pictures on his phone of the view from the top of the mountain.

Ten minutes later, the bus eased into the traffic of the city, and Kinza could smell the cooking from several open-air restaurants nearby, making her mouth water. They pulled up to stop nearby a small market, and they all shuffled outside.

"Really, the view was spectacular!" the tourist said with arms waving. "You should go up if you get a chance. It's worth the cost."

"Mhmm." Zaid hummed dismissively. He grabbed Kinza's arm and steered them away quickly. "I'll be sure to do that."

"I think he wanted to be friends," Kinza said with a laugh as they crossed a street in the opposite direction. "You should have gotten his number."

Zaid's mouth quirked into an almost smile. "Not a chance." He looked around and found the way they needed to go. "Come on, let's go see Bahati," he said with a sigh. Kinza remembered the Ummanu woman in Moshi who yelled at Zaid for spontaneously appearing in her house.

It didn't take them long to get back to the slightly quieter neighborhood and to Bahati's modest home. Zaid knocked on the door this time.

"You're not just going to go in?" Kinza asked.

"I'm hoping she sees it as respectful," he replied, looking unconvinced.

The door flung open a moment later, and the woman herself was standing in the doorway with a child on her hip and a disapproving expression. She snapped at Zaid in another language, and Kinza knew Zaid wasn't getting off easy. Zaid replied, gesturing behind her, and Bahati eyed Kinza up and down before starting to shout at Zaid again.

I think she just doesn't like you, Kinza said to Zaid, who only glared back.

Eventually, Bahati waved them in and into the empty bedroom where the portal was located. Bahati went into another room and came back with no child and an armload of crystals. Kinza's stomach started to twist at the memory of the nausea she got from her first portal endeavor. Bahati placed the crystals in a line along one wall of the room, shuffling them around when she wasn't satisfied with the ordering. When the last one was placed, a mirage-like curtain rippled along the wall. Colors swirled at first and then settled, and Kinza could almost make out Haris's basement, and she smiled.

Bahati cackled a laugh. "Good, go puke in the other one's house," she said in English and waved them through. Zaid just rolled his eyes out of Bahati's view and strode through, Kinza following shortly behind.

Just like last time, her skin felt like a thousand little needles were prickling over her arms and legs, and the nausea made her stomach toss and turn. But when she stepped through, it settled again, and she was relieved to not have to mop Haris's floors.

"God, you look terrible," she heard Haris say to Zaid behind her. But when she turned, her eyes instead fell on the old woman standing by the stairs, hair wrapped up in the familiar silk scarf and a thousand wrinkles at the corners of her kind eyes.

"Baby, is that you?" Grams said, squinting into the dim light of the basement.

"Grams!" Kinza shouted, and her momentary shock left her as she ran into the older woman's arms. "I missed you," she mumbled into her shoulder while inhaling the heavy floral scent that seemed to follow her grandmother around.

Grams chuckled. "Well, don't break my back. It's flimsy enough as is." Kinza pulled away, and Grams smiled at her, wiping away the tears that had formed in Kinza's eyes. "That's enough of that.

"Yeah, what about me?" Haris said, coming up to Kinza. Even in the half-light, Kinza could see the smattering of freckles across his grinning face.

Kinza snorted. "Okay fine, you get a hug too," and pulled him in.

"I'm glad you decided not to kill this one," Haris said brightly to Zaid, earning a prompt whack from Grams on the arm.

"Upstairs, all of you," Grams said, turning to hobble up the dilapidated staircase. "I can't see a dang thing."

The house was in a much better state than when they had left it. It seemed Haris had repaired all the damage the ubir had done to his little cottage-like home. The view from the window showed a crisp early morning October in Michigan, and she could just make out the inn whose property Haris's house sat.

"You want to tell us what actually happened now?" Haris said, closing the door to the basement. Kinza had given Grams a brief rundown of what had happened in Rhapta but nothing in too much detail and without all the specifics.

Kinza had no idea where to start and found herself looking to Zaid. *How much do they know about Rhaptan politics?* she asked.

Enough to understand how they operate, but not much more

than that, he replied. He turned to Haris. "One of the Elders led an army of rebels in Kinza's name against Rhapta, and with so many deaths, the barrier is collapsing, Kinza's queenship is up in the air, and the Elder is running free in the world, exposing the Anunnaki and putting humanity on the brink of chaos."

Haris was serious for once, and Grams let out a low whistle before turning to him and saying, "You got any whiskey?"

"Here, put that in the oven," Grams said, handing Kinza a casserole dish. She decided food was in order if they were going to be talking about a worldwide threat. Grams had shooed Haris and Zaid outside to talk, leaving Kinza to help her in the kitchen. Kinza didn't miss the assessing look Grams gave Zaid as she did so.

Kinza had almost forgotten that Grams had bested Zaid the night he had abducted Kinza. She was surprised she didn't start swinging the moment she saw him, but she knew that was a conversation that would come up eventually.

For now, she told Grams everything that had happened since that night. She told her about traveling to Rhapta, the burned city, the prophecy, and Tahir, about her abilities that had manifested practically overnight, and how Kinza was the heir to the throne of a civilization that was near collapse. Grams gave no reaction as she listened, and only when Kinza told her about how Tahir's assassins had killed her parents did a single tear fall from her eye.

She nodded. "I had a feeling it was the Anunnaki that did it, but I could never prove it." She heaved a sigh and leaned on the counter. "It's good to finally know. My poor Sadia... killed because of a stupid prophecy."

Kinza gave her a look. "Grams, that prophecy is me."

"I know, sweetie, you know what I mean. Whether human or Anunnaki, it seems men resort to killing when they are faced with fear. It seems this Tahir has never known how to handle his own fear... or greed." She scowled at the mention of him. The trees outside the window were almost bare and swayed in the chilly breeze.

"So, Grams," Kinza said, picking at the edge of the counter. "Did you know this whole time then that I was Anunnaki? Did my mother?" she asked quietly. "Was *she* Anunnaki too?" The question had burned in her chest since she had realized her mother's line had descended from the escaped Rhaptan prince. The thought of her mother having not been human either made her feel closer to her.

Grams thought a moment. "My family had been Ummanu for generations, much as Haris's family has. We were from further south but moved up here at some point. I had never met an Anunnaki, but my grandfather would tell me stories of when he was younger and the keeper of a portal about the venari that would come through with extraordinary powers. He even told me a story of an Anunnaki prince that long ago had escaped in the dead of night from their secret city when one of his father's most trusted advisers turned on them and had the king killed."

Kinza gasped, but Grams continued. "Now, I believed them only to be stories, you see. My father said he hardly remembered seeing Anunnaki in his youth, and by the time I came around, we no longer watched a portal, effectively cutting us off from the circle of information. My grandfather still urged us to protect their secrets though if we ever came across them. When I was about twenty-five, I worked as a receptionist in a salon, real nice place for women. One day the most gorgeous man I had ever seen walked in and came up to the counter and asked for a haircut. I laughed and told him it was for women only; he would need to find a barber. He looked at me and winked and said, 'I know that. I just needed an excuse to come to talk to you.'"

Kinza smiled. "Grandpa Ray?" she said with a laugh. The room was starting to warm with the smells of Grams' cooking.

"You know it!" Grams said, her face brightening. "That man was slick; he would come in time and again asking for a 'haircut' until eventually, I agreed to go on a date. And you know the rest."

"Did you know who he was?" Kinza asked. "That he was a descendant of Malik?"

"Not at first," Grams said, with a shake of her head. "After we had been together a while, he told about stories his grandparents used to tell him as a child. As I listened to them, they sounded similar to mine, and I began to wonder if he was Ummanu like our family was. Over time I started to notice he had an uncanny sense of when danger was near. One night about a year after we were married, he woke me up and said we had to go outside. I'm pretty sure I cursed at him left and right—mind you, I was pregnant with your mother. He said he didn't know why but we had to go. So, I put on my house coat. The entire time, he was rushing me to move quicker. We barely made it to the street when the house exploded."

Kinza inhaled a breath. "This was your first house that burned down?"

Grams nodded. "Gas leak. He said he woke to the back of his neck tingling, the same feeling he got any other time he felt some sort of danger."

"I have that!" Kinza exclaimed, touching the back of her own neck.

"That's when I think I knew," Grams said. "I think I realized then—truly understood—that the stories our grandparents told us were true. Ray was Prince Malik's descendant. I don't think he ever knew, or if he did, we never talked about it. I also don't know why the knowledge was only passed down as a story and not a fact through his family. Maybe this prince had been in hiding from that adviser? I'm not sure."

Kinza thought for a second. "We had a meeting with the Elders and scholars the other day, and one of them mentioned that it might be a possibility that Tahir's father was involved in the old king's death. Maybe that was true, and Prince Malik was afraid that they would come after him and his family."

Grams nodded in agreement. "That makes sense. Especially if he was anything like this Tahir, who seems to have hoodwinked everyone and their mother."

"Did he have any other abilities?" Kinza asked. "Did Mom?"

"No," Grams replied. "Ray lived an otherwise human life. Nothing else was odd, and you know he died just before you were born of a heart attack. Your mother, my baby girl, came out as perfect as could be. So beautiful, just like her father and you," she said with a wink. "But I decided not to continue the stories our grandparents told us, especially when Sadia never showed any signs of abilities."

"Why not?"

Grams heaved a sigh and gave her a look. "Now, don't get angry with me. I did what I thought was best."

"Okay..." Kinza said.

"After the night of the gas leak, I did a little research without Ray's knowledge. My grandparents had passed, but my parents were still Ummanu, and they had connections to others in the network. I started asking them questions about the Anunnaki and if there were any of them that lived outside the city. They laughed at me, but I kept pushing. I contacted an

Ummanu who lived down in Louisiana—nice lady, makes a mean gumbo."

"*Grams,*" Kinza said, urging her on.

"Anyway, she told about a prophecy the Anunnaki had, about an outsider that would come to the city one day and either destroy it or save it." Kinza frowned, knowing the prophecy well. "She told me as much as she knew about them and how they viewed this prophecy. I didn't ever know for sure; mind in my heart, I knew it would be one of the prince's descendants. But as I told you before, men kill when they are afraid, and I wasn't about to put my family in harm's way. So I never mentioned it to Ray, nor Sadia, hoping that it would…"

"Just go away?" Kinza suggested with a wry grin.

"I had to get wise somehow, right?" Grams replied with a laugh. She sobered and said, "When your parents were killed, I knew I was right. The problem was, I thought they had won and that your mother had been the one in the prophecy, and they had killed her. Now, ten years later, here you are, showing us we were *all* wrong. It was always you, baby."

"Yeah," Kinza said, still frowning. "Me."

Grams ran a hand over her hair. "Don't worry; it'll be all right. Tell me, you and that hooligan are going to find who now?"

"Grams, Zaid isn't a hooligan."

"Mhmm," Grams said, peering into the oven. "Your father was a hooligan too, knocking on my door at all hours, trying to talk to your mother. Turned out to be a great father, though."

"What—are you suggesting—?" Kinza sputtered.

Grams shrugged. "Don't think I didn't see the way you were looking at him earlier. He was giving you the same googly eyes back."

Kinza shook her head "Zaid, my *friend,* and I need to convince one of the three human-Anunnaki that live around the world. Tahir already got to the one in China, and then there's one here and one in France. The one here is Edmund Clark."

"The billionaire?" Grams asked, eyebrows going straight up as she pulled the casserole dish out and set it on the stove.

"That's the one," Kinza said, grabbing plates to set the table.

"Well, how are you going to get to him?"

"I was hoping you had an idea."

"Me?" Grams said.

"Yeah, one of the Elders said that Edmund Clark hired an Ummanu into his company. I was hoping you know who it is."

"Hmm," Grams said. "I don't, but I'm sure Haris and I could find out. It might take some time, though. How fast do you need to get back to the city?"

"As soon as possible. The barrier is falling, and I also need to figure out how to hold it up. Hopefully they figure out how to officially make me queen by then."

Grams stopped what she was doing and turned to her. "You're going to do it then?" she asked. "You're going to live there and be the queen of the Anunnaki?"

Kinza hesitated, not wanting to hurt Grams' feelings. "I have to," she said. "I can't help but feel responsible. Even though it's not my fault, I still have the ability to help them, and if I don't, it'll eat away at me forever," Kinza said quietly.

Grams patted her cheek. "That's my girl."

"You're not mad?" Kinza asked tentatively.

"Heck no! The best I could have hoped for you was a good education and a satisfying career. But you snagged a kingdom all on your own. I will sleep peacefully at night knowing that you are over there being pampered head to toe."

Kinza snorted. "It's not like that. It's actually... hard."

"Oh, I know. But you'll figure it out," she said with a smile.

There was not a single doubt in her expression. "Go get those boys; dinner's ready."

THE FOUR OF them sat at Haris's dining table with only the sound of silverware clinking.

Zaid had filled Haris in on everything that was happening to give Kinza a moment alone with her grandmother. It was clear the old woman cared for her granddaughter fiercely, but Zaid kept his guard up. There were several pockets in her floral dress that could hide pouches of Deathstone, and he knew she wouldn't hesitate to use them. Haris had filled him in on what was going on within the Ummanu network. There had been chattering among them but with no real information. It probably all came from the venari that had come and gone from the city, spreading the news as they traveled the world looking for ubir.

The Ummanu had had little contact with the majority of Rhapta in the past several centuries. There were records of Ummanu coming and going within the city thousands of years ago, but as it became more and more removed from human society, there were fewer human ally visitors. Zaid always thought it was a shame that the Anunnaki and Ummanu didn't interact more. The Ummanu were proof that some humans could live alongside them without fear, as friends. They could have helped the city to say present as well. There was no reason the Ummanu—or any human—couldn't travel the portals, but it was forbidden. Not that the Elders would ever know. For now, the Ummanu were merely the keepers of their portals and patient friends hiding in human society.

"I haven't had a home-cooked meal in years," Haris said, shoveling down his second plateful.

Grams eyed him from across the table. "You had better slow down. My cooking's great, but my Heimlich not so much."

Zaid ducked his head to hide his smile.

"What are you grinning for?" Grams asked him suddenly. She pointed her fork at him. "You owe me a new cast iron pan. Nobody has a head that hard." Zaid's smile quickly turned back into a scowl at the memory of the pan swinging at him. Never in all his venari training had he been prepared for an old woman with a Deathstone in one hand and a frying pan in the other coming at him like a linebacker. He ignored her and went back to his food. Haris was right, though; she could *cook*.

Kinza cleared her throat. "Anyway... so Grams. How did you get here exactly?"

"The Buick," she said, pointing her fork at the front door.

"By yourself?!" Kinza asked. "You drove?" Zaid thought the level of concern Kinza had over her elderly grandmother was adorable. Maybe it was because Kinza did see her as an elderly woman while Zaid knew there was a grizzly bear lurking beneath.

Grams leveled her a patient look. "I am perfectly capable of driving when I need to. After this one," she said, nodding at Zaid, "decided to blow up my house, I reached out to my Ummanu contacts, looking for anything odd. I'm not in the network like I used to be, so it took a few days, but I finally reached this one"—she jerked a thumb at Haris now—"who said you two came through."

"*I* blew up your house?!" Zaid said, finally speaking. He turned to Kinza, imploring her to come clean. He felt that the majority of Grams' behavior toward him was justified, but he wouldn't be blamed for blowing up her house.

"Um, Grams, the explosion was me..." she said.

Grams gave her an impressed look. "Should've aimed for his head."

Haris was grinning, as usual. "Our little cherry bomb," he said to Kinza, who stuck her tongue out at him.

"How did you find Laiq then?" He hadn't seen the older venari in quite some time. They were always on assignment at opposite times, rarely crossing paths, but he had always been helpful when Zaid was younger. He had shown Zaid how to use a cellphone before his first assignment. He understood human technology probably better than the humans themselves, making him an excellent choice for a venari.

"It took a while," Haris said. "I had met him only once, but remembered his ability. I made a post on my Twitter account looking for him, mentioning Anunnaki and venari. He picked up on it and called us. Quick that one."

"You tweeted, and a venari came running?" Kinza asked, the beads in her hair glinting in the evening light coming in through the window.

Haris shrugged. "I deleted it after, but yeah. It was a long shot, but it worked. So what are you guys going to do now?"

"Well, we need to talk to Edmund Clark," Kinza said, looking at Zaid. "Grams said you and she could reach out to the Ummanu network. Mr. Clark apparently has one in his employ. In the meantime, I figured we could just try to go to his office?"

Zaid was going to object, but he couldn't think of a better option. They could break in and *make* Edmund Clark listen, but that seemed just about the worst way to convince him. The Ummanu might be their only ticket in, but it didn't hurt to scope out the places he frequented in the meantime.

He nodded. "Yeah, we can do that. We can do some more research too, find out what kind of person he is."

Haris snorted. "He's a billionaire. He likes money. Tell him you're an investor."

"That'll work," Grams said. "Up until he asks you one question about investing."

"Yeah, but then you're already in," Haris countered.

Zaid sighed. "We can figure it out on the way there tomorrow. I think we should sleep here tonight, though."

The others nodded, but as Grams gave him a shrewd look, he knew he would be sleeping with one eye open tonight.

CHAPTER 7

INQUISITION OF THE UNKNOWN

It wasn't even noon, and Mikah was close to losing his patience. He had arrived early for another day of going page by page through Tahir's office. The former Elder had years' worth of notes, research, memos, and records, dating back to well before Mikah was born. Most of it was routine nonsense, which was precisely why Mikah was frustrated.

If he was being honest with himself, he wasn't upset over the lack of information or even at Tahir. He was upset with himself. He had known Tahir for years and had idolized him and every move he made. What did that say about him? He had prided himself on knowing Tahir better than anyone else, yet he had probably been fooled worse than anyone. He had been with Tahir every day, following him to the quarries and in meetings with other city officials. He had prepared speeches for him and given his opinion on matters. Didn't that make Mikah no better than Tahir?

His own father had been a staunch supporter of Tahir and had engrained his own values in Tahir, so no wonder Mikah would idolize him as well. But every time Mikah's mind returned to the battle in Rhapta, his stomach soured. The bloodshed and screaming still haunted his nightmares, but it was the merciless look on Tahir's face as he was about to bring his sword down on Kinza that was burned into his mind.

He realized he had never—not once—known Tahir. But now here he was, deemed the most qualified to go through his old mentor's office to dig up any intel he could find. Elder Balasi still had his contacts out searching for Tahir after his ice display a few days ago, but so far, nothing new had turned up. Many of the Elders turned to Mikah to provide clarity on Tahir's actions. Shouldn't they be locking him up instead? Did they not suspect Mikah of assisting him? He had half a mind to throw himself into the city's dungeons, but he knew his father would only pay to have him released.

What about these, sir? an attendant asked him from the corner. He held up a stack of files Tahir had kept on the quarry's visitor logs.

Not important, Mikah said and went back to leafing through the pile on the desk. So far, this was the most interesting stack he had found. It was a collection of historical records on the Rhaptan monarchy dating back to the late Egyptian period. They had gathered that Tahir had been getting the majority of his information from Hakim over the years, at first becoming his trusted friend and eventually by force in his later years. But without Hakim, the playing field was level, and Tahir's largest opponent was Kinza.

Mikah hadn't known what to make of her at first after having thought she was merely a beautiful Anunnaki commoner caught in the war. Finding out she had been clever enough to deceive him and hide her true identity had sparked a burning interest in him. It was rare that someone could play at his level. Most people used brute force or hid behind others to get what they wanted. Kinza had been smart, though, gaining information from a vital member of the opposing side, all the while running around a city filled with people trying to kill her.

Sly little fox, he thought to himself. It was unfortunate she kept the venari dog with her at all times. Mikah had thought he was starting to move past his annoyance with Zaid; that is, until, for the second time in their lives, Zaid took something away from him.

They both knew that had Zaid not been tapped for venari, Tahir would've chosen him as his apprentice. Mikah had tried to push away his bitterness at coming in second to someone he cared about, but it all came roaring back the moment the venari had walked into the square the other night.

Kinza had looked at Mikah like he was the sun, moon, and stars, and Mikah had been elated that someone might actually *care* about him. But then, like a comet comes burning across the sky, Zaid arrived, and it was like Mikah didn't exist. Kinza only had eyes for him, nearly forgetting Mikah was there, even after Zaid left her standing by the door.

He shook his head, trying not to soil his already ruined mood. He wouldn't let an ounce of that bitterness show.

A knock came at the open door. He looked up to find the slight form of Apprentice Eta standing in his doorway and fought a losing battle to keep his composure. Since she had blatantly rebuffed his advances for an alliance—let alone friendship—while they were still in the camp, their interactions had hardly improved.

Can I help you? he couldn't help but drone out and went back to flipping through the papers.

May I speak with you? she asked. Her voice never raised nor showed much more emotion. It was almost like a hum in his head when she spoke, echoing around.

Can it wait? he said. *As you can see, we have important work going on here.*

You will speak with me, so you might as well stop delaying it, she said and walked away. Mikah sighed, and the apprentice in the corner tried to make himself invisible. Mikah liked Hakim's visions better. They were more about grand political maneuvers instead of annoying inconveniences to Mikah's day.

He got up and went out into the hall where Eta was waiting. When he reached her, she turned and kept walking toward the back of the building, where an open walkway stretched under the shade of the Grand Hall's roof.

Well? he said. *Are you going to tell me I'm going to die next Thursday?* She had been known to give cryptic messages to people, never clarifying what they meant or referred to. He wasn't entirely sure she knew what they meant either. A far cry from Hakim's prophetic dreams that spanned generations.

She didn't rise to his taunt and instead said, *Did Tahir ever talk about his knowledge of our tattoos? Or any research?*

You want to know how he's still Anunnaki?

Yes and no. I'm doing research on my own, she said vaguely.

At whose behest? he asked. There were already several scholars looking into this but gaining no headway. It seems that Tahir had told no one about how he did it. Just like how he told no one about how extensive his Aurastone research was. So much so that he created an entire camp outside of the city that allowed Anunnaki to be safe. He had done two impossible feats in a matter of days.

Kinza's, she said without looking at him. Her steps were steady and methodical, making it look like she was floating, and her gray robes dragged on the stones.

He looked at her. *You are working for Kinza now? I didn't realize you were close. Do the Elders know you are supporting her?*

That's not important right now. Kinza asked me to look into

Tahir's research on the tattoos, specifically the ink itself. She said there was a scholar within the Apostles of Truth that might be able to help as well. I was going over there after to meet with him, she said.

Mikah was confused. Everything he had ever heard about Eta was that she was the perfect apprentice, never breaking a rule and always doing as Hakim said. She kept quiet in meetings and never spoke out of turn. Yet here she was, not checking in with the Elders, doing secret research, and with a former rebel group at that.

We've studied the ink for years, and there is nothing new to learn, he said eventually. *If Tahir knew something, he didn't write it down, and he certainly didn't tell me.*

So you don't know how the venari tattoos work either? she asked. *Tahir was one of the few people who did.*

Mikah smiled at a passing group of Elders as Eta kept her eyes down. *I know that the ink comes from the African violets on the far edge of the quarries. That's probably how Tahir became interested in them in the first place. Further than that, I have no idea what's special about them or why.*

Eta's delicate brows pinched together, forming a line between them. *The violets? Why those?*

Mikah sighed, reigning in his irritation. *I don't know. Can't you just* see *why?*

She turned him a withering glare. *That's not how it works,* she said simply. *Visions are a construct of—*

Several people milling about outside the hall screamed. A moment later, Mikah felt the barrier in his mind snap, and he looked up toward the sky. There was no ripple or mirage against the fluffy white clouds.

It's not coming back, Eta said, worry bleeding into her voice.

It will, Mikah said, eyes trained on the sky. He breathed and counted in his head. *One one-thousand, two one-thousand, three one-thousand, four*— and it snapped back into place with a groan. He could hear a woman crying inside the building and people huddled together as they waited in case it fell again.

When it didn't, Mikah released a breath he hadn't realized he had been holding. Eta was still looking up, concern tinging her normally serene expression. *I'll take another look through Tahir's office today and let you know if I find anything. Just don't expect much.*

Thank you, she said, finally tearing her eyes away. *I'm meeting with that scholar shortly here, but I'll be in the hall for the remainder of the day.*

He nodded, and she left down the path, and only after she was out of sight did he realize that was their first encounter where she hadn't left out of contempt.

ETA'S MIND was a verifiable storm. Not that it was any different from most days, but some days were harder to bear than others. And the number of those days had been increasing since the loss of her mentor.

Hakim had been a steady, calming presence in her life for over ten years. She had gotten her gift early, at only eight years old, predicting a thunderstorm—not unlike the one in her mind now—that would wipe out the crops if they didn't harvest soon. When it turned out to be true, Hakim had come to the orphanage to see her, and her life had changed.

Her parents had died when she was young. People said her mother had visions as well, but it drove her to madness and eventually to seek out the Unfettered. Not long after, she was a known ubir and was caught by the venari. Her father died of grief five months later, and Eta had been handed over to her new keepers.

Hakim had become her family, though, after he came that day to ask her about her visions. She told him that she had never had a vision before. She was adamant that she had only ever received "images." Hakim had laughed and said those were visions too, like puzzle pieces but no picture.

Over the next period of her life, he taught her how to calm her body, and her mind would follow suit. He taught her how to decipher the images in her head that flashed by at alarming speeds. Sometimes they had no meaning at all. Other times they were clear as day; a knife in someone's chest, a heat wave rolling in, gold in the coffers. Hakim said that they would be clearer over time as long as she stayed calm. But how could she be calm when he was gone?

In her late teens, she had realized the gravity of her gift when someone had referred to her as the "future Grand Elder." Since then, fear had quaked her visions at the thought of basically being the leader of the Anunnaki. How was she supposed to be an idol to her people *and* focus her energies inward to decipher the visions? Hakim had managed well enough, but there were still flaws in the system.

Now, at twenty-one, she tried to separate her memories of Hakim's lessons from her visions, squeezing every last drop of wisdom from them as she navigated her new place in Rhapta. And then Kinza had come knocking like a godsend. Eta could have wept when she realized she wouldn't have to rule. If Kinza was queen, Eta could focus on her visions instead of playing the part of a brave ruler. So here she was picking her way through a destroyed library, trying to help another young woman become queen so she wouldn't have to.

The building was quickly being restored, but since it was one of the few that lined the central plaza, it had been hit the hardest in the battle. She mourned the loss of books and scrolls that held information from thousands of years ago, all neatly stacked on their shelves. Indigo-robed scholars had tied up their sleeves and were installing new shelves while young apprentices ran around trying to shelve books. At the far end of the main room, Eta could see a part of the wall that had been destroyed, and within was the broken entrance to a tunnel that led under the building.

The home of the Apostles of Truth.

Up until recently, they had been a symbol of anarchy and dissent among Rhaptans, but after the battle of Rhapta, where they had fought alongside the citizens, it was clear who they really were. Their new leader, Nimatullah, had declared on several occasions in the Elder meetings that the scholars had vital information that could be shared, and they were hoping to work in tandem with the Elders instead of against them. Since then, there had been a tenuous peace, and the Apostles had come out of hiding.

Eta was ashamed to say that she couldn't tell the difference between the Apostles and any other scholar. They all ran around with the same fervor as if the world were going to end if a scroll was not returned immediately or a page was torn.

She stopped a woman with long braids and spectacles on the end of her nose. *Excuse me, I'm looking for a scholar named Badr?*

The woman rolled her eyes and pointed toward the ceiling. *Upstairs, second door on the left. The room with all the papers.*

Papers?

You'll know when you see it, she said and went back to her work. Eta nodded her thanks and went to find the staircase. When she did, it was missing most of the railing, and she dodged workers on her way up, holding her robes so she wouldn't trip. She peered in all the open rooms, most of which looked to be large offices or conference rooms, until she found the one she was looking for.

The woman had been correct. Most of the rooms were chaotic due to the construction happening, but this one was chaotic because of the pieces of paper that stuck to nearly every surface of the walls and ceiling. Most of the furniture had been removed, leaving only a small desk and a chair, both of which were covered in piles of open books and scribbles of notes.

She knocked on the door, not seeing anyone. *Hello?*

She jumped when a head popped up in the corner. She hadn't seen that there was someone seated there, covered almost completely in papers as well, head bent into a book. Seeing his face, he looked to be no older than seventeen or eighteen. *Sorry?* he said, getting to his feet. *Did I miss another appointment? Please don't tell Jabari. He'll murder me. Well, not literal murder, but I'll be shelving scrolls like a first-year for a month.*

No, no, Eta said. *I'm sorry to bother you. My name is Eta; I'm—*

Hakim's apprentice, he said, quickly getting to his feet. *Yes, I know.* He was tall and a little too skinny, but he had the energy of an excitable squirrel. *My name is Badr, Apprentice Apostle and scholar. How can I help you?*

In Eta's mind, images of maps and stones fluttered past those of pickaxes covered in blood. African violets floated on the wind, and—she closed her eyes for a moment, commanding her thoughts to hold steady. *Sorry to bother you,* she said, opening her eyes again. *Kinza told me to seek you out about something, something I'm researching for her.*

Badr's face brightened at the mention of the young woman. *Ah, then I'm happy to help! Please come in and, oh, hold on a moment.* He emptied the stacks of books from the chair onto the floor.

Thank you, she said.

What were you and Kinza researching? Is it related to the barrier? If so, there's already a team assembled for that. He had a somewhat sour expression, as if he hadn't been invited onto the team.

Are you familiar with the venari tattooing process? she asked. *The one used so they can go out into the world for a short time?*

Ah yes! The violets used to add extensions to our biological tattoos. What of it?

Kinza believes there is something to be found in the ink. At Badr's expression, she continued. *I think it may be in regard to the fact that Tahir has discovered something that allowed him— and several others—to leave the city permanently. I've already spoken with Tahir's apprentice Mikah, and he said Tahir had years' worth of research on the quarries—right near where the violets grow. I was hoping you could help me look into it and see if we can't figure out what Tahir knows.*

Badr had the far-off expression of deep thought. *If we do figure it out, that will impact the Anunnaki more than a collapsing barrier or crazed Elder ever could. If we could walk the world...*

Eta nodded as his understanding took hold. *I'm not sure if Kinza is planning on making the information public right away— assuming we find it—but she said it was important. And I want to help her.*

Badr nodded. *As do I. What do we already know?*

Eta thought for a moment. *Only that a handful of people actually are able to make the ink, it comes from the violets on the far side of the quarry, and it's only temporary.*

Badr nodded. *We could consult the existing texts on the ink, but they are limited and inconclusive anyway. I propose we start from the beginning.* He started pacing around the room, picking up and setting down random pieces of paper. *We'll need to speak with a few people to know how they make it; that will be the first step. And we'll also need to obtain any research Tahir had on the quarries or the ink.*

Mikah said he would look into it for me, Eta said with a nod.

Great. Then let's go talk to the venari, he said, setting his papers down and heading toward the door.

What—now? Eta asked, getting up.

I assume time is of the essence? he said, ushering her out and locking the door behind her.

Yes, but if you have other work...

The queen's work is of the utmost importance in my book, he said as they headed down the stairs. Eta felt somewhat foolish, needing to hurry her steps to keep up with the young man's long strides.

Can I ask what all that was back there? she said, indicating back toward the room.

Ah, it's all my work, he said.

Not to be rude, but it's a horrid mess. They stepped out onto the street. The house of the venari wasn't far, but she also had never gone there before and looked around a moment before deciding their direction.

Yes, um, that's the nature of my gift, he said, scratching the back of his neck.

Your ability is messiness?

Not exactly, he said with a laugh. *I see patterns over time. Events that happen over weeks or even centuries that are somehow connected. I compile that information to come to conclusions that others wouldn't have ever seen. So my thoughts are chaotic, and my work tends to reflect that.*

I understand more than you know, Eta said, dampening her own visions as they walked. *Your ability would be monumentally helpful to me.*

Really?

She nodded, turning onto the correct side street. *My visions are chaotic and disjointed, and it's hard to see the meaning behind most of them. What I wouldn't give to have your ability as well...*

They had arrived at the house of the venari and strode up to the door. Eta had never been here before, had never met a venari, actually. She had only seen them in passing, or at the ubir trials when they were brought back. The venari had always felt like ghosts to her, moving in the dark recesses of the city, rarely seen but harmless to the people. She knocked on the front door now.

Badr shuffled his feet as they waited. Eta knocked again, and just before she knocked a third time, the door opened. Behind him was a short man with dyed red hair and a tired expression. *Can I help you?* he asked, looking them over.

Yes, Badr said. *We are looking to speak to the head of the venari.*

The man's eyebrows rose. *Are you now? What in the world would make you want to do that?*

Let them in, Rafael, a voice called from behind him. He stood a little straighter and opened the door wider to let them in. Eta stepped inside the nearly empty building. The only people were two men in the training ring in the middle, sparring. The younger was doing all he could to keep up with the Elder, but within moments the younger had doubled over in pain from a strike to his gut. Badr winced.

The older man stood and said something to the younger. He was tall and wiry but strode over to them with a level of control that was impressive after watching the fight. *I am Savar. You were looking for me?*

Yes, we, um... Badr started.

My name is Eta; I'm the apprentice of Grand Elder Hakim, who has now passed. I am doing research at the behest of Kinza Solace about the ink used for the venari tattoos. Are you able to answer a few questions for us?

Savar sighed. *I should have made her sit outside,* he said. At their confused expressions, he said, *I need to do rounds. We can talk as we walk.* They quickly followed him, and he gave orders to the two other venari, who scrambled off to do as they were told. Savar started walking along the hallway of rooms that lined the training ring, opening some to inspect and closing others as he went.

All the information about the ink has already been recorded. I'm not sure what else I can tell you, Savar said.

Eta and Badr exchanged a glance. *We are just starting from the top,* Eta said.

I assume this is because of Tahir?

Yes, Eta replied. *We know he must have learned something that the rest of us don't know, and we think it's important.*

Could you tell us how it's made? Badr asked.

Savar nodded. *The ink is made from the African violets that grow on the outside edge of the quarry mixed with a few different oils as a carrier. The carrier oils don't really matter and can be switched; it's the violets that are the tricky part. If you pick the wrong ones, it won't work.*

How do you know which ones are the good ones? Badr asked.

That... I would need to teach you in person, and it takes many years to understand, as it did when I was taught.

Do the violets produce the same results every time? Badr asked instead.

No, depending on the plant, some produce stronger ink than others. He shrugged. *No idea why.*

Badr nodded, thinking as Savar looked through a few more rooms on this level. Most of them were bare and non-descript, and despite the open-air training ring, it felt dark and gloomy in here. No wonder all the venari had such dour expressions;

they practically lived in the shadows of both the Anunnaki and human worlds.

What's the longest you've ever seen a tattoo last? Badr asked.

Two months, but only once. So when I say that it's astounding Tahir has managed to leave permanently, I'm somewhat skeptical that he was telling the truth.

You mean, you think he is going to turn human? Eta asked.

That's my best guess. I have never seen anyone able to leave that long other than Kinza Solace. That being said, Tahir did manage to create a satellite city of sorts with the knowledge he gained from the quarries. I'm not sure how that's related to the violets, but he was able to figure that out, and it was considered impossible.

We are looking into the quarries as well, Eta said. *Would you be able to show us which flowers you would pick? I mean, actually go out to the quarries.*

Savar closed another door and started up to the next level. *I'm a little busy today with training, but if you really are that intent, I can take you tomorrow—*

The barrier snapped, and all three of them stopped. Savar ran over to the railing and looked up, peering at the sky. Eta's visions came in rippling waves in response to her own fear, and she closed her eyes to regain some semblance of control. She couldn't help but think of what would happen if humanity discovered them. She'd had flashes of those visions too, of possible futures that gave her nightmares. Cities burned or destroyed, armies marching toward them, machines flying in the air above the city. She had seen Anunnaki taken to glass and steel facilities deep below the earth to be tested on. Poked and prodded like butterflies nailed to a board. And soon enough, all the Anunnaki would turn human, and the real humans would wonder what happened and continue to poke at them until they expired.

Eta shoved those thoughts away now, demanding

authority of her own mind as she inhaled and exhaled. She didn't know how much time had passed when she felt the barrier ease back into place.

That was a long one, Savar mused.

And they're happening more frequently, Badr said, looking at the sky. *It's all the deaths. There isn't enough of a collective Aura to keep it up.*

Let's hope those scholars of yours figure out something quick, Savar said before turning back to Eta. *I was going to say I can take you tomorrow morning if you really want to see the flowers. I need to collect more anyway.*

I would appreciate that, Eta said, looking to Badr.

I'll be there too, he said.

Savar nodded. *Then if you'll excuse me, I have another training to attend to, but I'll see you just after dawn.*

Eta and Badr thanked him and headed back out to the street and the daylight. *I'll do some more research tonight on the ink and the quarries and see what I can find.*

If Mikah gives me anything from Tahir's notes, I'll bring those as well. I need to get back to the Grand Hall, but I appreciate your help, Badr. Thank you.

Anytime! he said. *I'll see you tomorrow.*

He left to head back toward the library, and Eta went straight down the street toward the central plaza and the Grand Hall. The heat of the late afternoon made the sweat trickle down her back inside her heavy robes, but it would soon cool as the sun set. Many people were starting to make their way home to their families. Eta didn't have one of those, and the Grand Hall was the closest thing to home she ever had. It was traditional for Elders to live in the residential quarters of the hall, similar to monks who lived simplistic lives, but after the battle, the traditions had seemed to melt away like an animal shedding its winter coat in the summer. She had seen

Elders walk around the city when they never used to, and knew some moved into homes as well.

Nothing had changed for Eta, though, as she headed back to her small room on the upper floors of the hall's right wing. It was empty during this time of day, Elders and apprentices usually worked well into the evening, but she felt a headache coming on and desperately needed to rest.

As she turned onto her hallway, she was hit with a vision stronger than most.

Blue sky filled her sight, and slowly, the expanse of desert land stretched before her. She was moving, walking—no, she was in the body of someone who was walking; many someone's. They were blurry and out of focus. Suddenly they knelt down, and Eta saw a river sparkling in bright relief against the heat of the desert. She— he—dipped their hands in the cool water, lifting to drink and—

The vision stopped, and Eta found herself back in the hallway of the Grand Hall. A wave of dizziness overcame her, and she put her hand against the wall. Closing her eyes, she tried to breathe. It had been a long time since she had had such an all-consuming vision. Rarely did they take over her sight as if she were truly there. What had it meant? Just like most of her visions, she had no idea when or where that was. It could have been past, present, or future with no indication of its value.

Hakim had taught her not to try to dwell on the visions she couldn't understand but to let them happen, and either she would gain something from them, or she wouldn't. So she did just that. As soon as she regained her footing, she walked the rest of the way to her room and laid down for a long nap.

CHAPTER 8
GUILT LIKE KNIVES

After having spent time in the baking warmth of Tanzania, Kinza felt at home driving down the coast of Lake Michigan toward Chicago. Orange and yellow leaves scattered across the road as Zaid pushed the ancient Buick to its limits.

"Boy, you may live through a car crash, but I sure won't," Grams snapped at him from the back seat.

Zaid pursed his lips but let off the gas a little. All four of them were crammed in the car, Kinza in the backseat with her grandmother. They had left early that morning to be able to make it to downtown Chicago by lunch. The ride was long, but Grams had handed Kinza her phone and said, "I charged it for you. You might have a few hundred messages from Mitra."

Kinza groaned. "What did you tell her?"

"Well, she called the night after you left. She was worried, but I told her you were really sick. But then she stopped by and saw the house—try explaining that one to the police—and she was hysterical. I told her it was a gas leak, but I had sent you to a relative for a little while," Grams said.

"A relative? She knows I don't have any other relatives," Kinza said, wincing.

"Well, you could call her," Grams replied.

"And say what? Sorry, I was kidnapped and taken to a magical city, and now I'm the almost-queen?" Zaid glanced at her from the rearview mirror while Haris fiddled with the radio.

Grams patted her arms. "You'll think of something."

Kinza turned on her phone and found Grams was correct. An absurd number of messages from Mitra, along with a few from their boss Karin asking when she was coming back to work. That didn't include the emails from the school saying she had been automatically dropped from her courses for nonattendance. Looking through the messages from Mitra hurt the most, though. Many of them asked her to just reply with a yes or no, letting her know she was alive. But of course, Kinza never answered them.

She closed the messages, vowing to deal with them later, and spent the rest of the car ride going through social media. News she had missed, pictures that had been posted, and useless ads filled the screen. It all felt a little absurd in the face of her real problems. She had cared so much about these things just a few weeks ago, but now it all seemed silly with the weight of a civilization resting on her shoulders.

Turning off the phone, she mulled over how to get Edmund Clark to trust her and side with her. She could prove she was Anunnaki pretty easily; the issue would be proving that she was someone who could be trusted—or at least that Tahir was *not* to be trusted. Maybe she could show him the news footage of Tahir's little ice stunt in China, assuming he hadn't already seen it. She would just need to think of something before they got there.

"Has Basma returned at all?" Zaid asked Haris quietly, and

Kinza turned to listen. Basma was part of the pack of ubir they had taken down before leaving for Rhapta. She was the only one to get away after attempting to kill Kinza by pushing her off a roof. Kinza shivered at the memory of the lithe woman. For an ubir, her eyes had been unnervingly steady.

"No," Haris said, rubbing his forehead. "I've alerted all the other portal-watchers within a hundred miles, just in case she tries to travel. But no one has seen or heard of any disturbances. She's probably lying low still."

Zaid grunted in agreement. "But that also means she'll probably need to kill again soon. Did Laiq or anyone else say they were on her assignment?"

"No, Laiq is the only other venari I've seen in a while. Venari numbers seem to be dwindling as quickly as ubir are rising."

Zaid's knuckles tightened on the steering wheel. "I know. You still have enough Deathstone?" he asked, looking at Haris.

"Yeah, plenty."

"Oh yeah, you owe me more of that too," Grams said, nudging Zaid's seat.

Haris turned around and gave her a wide smile. "I'd be more than happy to pay my brutish friend's debt," he said. "I have a stockpile I can send you."

"All right," Grams replied. "But don't try to butter me up with that cheesy grin of yours." Haris only smiled wider and turned back around.

They were entering the city now and taking the split on the highway toward Grams' side of town. "How much of the house was damaged?" Kinza asked lightly.

"Oh honey, you did a number on that one," she said, almost proudly. "The repairmen have been out all week fixing pipes and putting up new walls. No, don't give me that look. We have more than enough money to fix it all up."

Kinza couldn't help but feel guilty. For all of Gram's confidence, Kinza knew they didn't have much money. It was the reason Kinza had to work through most of high school, and this had probably wiped their savings. Maybe she could find a way to send all the gifts and jewelry she had been given in Rhapta to Grams.

They pulled up to Grams' house, and Kinza wondered how Zaid knew where he was going before she remembered he had stalked her for a full week before the kidnapping. Grams and Haris climbed out of the car.

"I'm going to change quickly," Kinza told Zaid before following the others in. Looking at the little house as they walked up to the front door, she realized Grams had severely underestimated the damage. Nearly the entire left side of the house had been replaced with new wood and paneling. There was a temporary roofing situation going on, and a few of the windows were boarded up until new glass could be installed.

Grams went in the front door and started giving Haris a tour while demanding he takes his shoes off. The sight of the familiar living room with the cluttered bookcases and mismatched couches almost brought Kinza to tears, but she remembered Zaid was waiting in the car.

She hurried to her room and tried not to be shocked to see most of her stuff had been taken out for the repairs—assuming it hadn't been destroyed in her explosion. There were some piles of clothes, and she dug out a pair of jeans and a green jacket before slipping them on.

"We'll be back later," she called to Grams and Haris. "Call us if you find anything!" and she was out the door. She hopped back into the front seat of the car, and she and Zaid drove over to busy downtown Chicago.

"Are you happy now?" Zaid asked suddenly as they were in the midday bumper-to-bumper traffic.

"Hmm?" she said. "What do you mean?" she was on her phone looking up the address to Edmund Clark's office. He had several buildings, but she was pretty sure the main one she had worked in before.

Zaid gestured around toward the looming skyscrapers and honking of the cars. "Now that you are back in all of this? You've missed it, right?"

"Ah, well, yes, I suppose." He gave her a quizzical look, and she continued. "It does feel like home, and I *have* missed it. It's very different from Rhapta, but at the same time, it almost feels like this life belonged to someone else. To the version of me who thought she was human and not 'Anunnaki queen.'"

"Mmm," he hummed, understanding. "Is that a bad thing then? Feeling like a different person?"

Kinza thought about it for a moment, ignoring the car next to them and throwing rude gestures. "I don't think so... I guess it would seem pointless if we never changed. I couldn't imagine being the same person with the same understanding of the world for the rest of my life. It would feel too... closed off." She took a breath. "It feels odd, though, learning so much about myself in such a short amount of time. Kind of like iden-tity-whiplash."

Zaid nodded, and she could see he was lost in his own thoughts now, so she let him be. Within ten minutes, they had parked across the street from one of the taller silver and glass buildings. There were three sets of double doors, and she could make out the long reception counter inside.

"So, you got a plan or...?" Zaid said, looking at the front of the building.

"Eh, I was just going to ask for a meeting," she replied.

"We're not investors then?"

"Not all of us are as optimistic as Haris," she said. Zaid gave her a quick grin, and they hopped out. The inside of the building was spotless and airy, with sculptures hanging high above them. Two security guards stood by the doors, and employees were entering through a row of turnstiles off to the right. There was a large seating area closer to the door, but Kinza strode right up to the white counter, trying to look as important as possible in jeans and tennis shoes. Now would have been a great opportunity for some sort of illusion-based ability.

"Hello, how can I help you?" the woman behind the counter asked with a blinding smile. She was gorgeous with a slicked-back bun, not a hair out of place, and clear skin.

"Yes, I'm here to see Edmund Clark. My name is Kinza Solace."

The woman's smile faltered as she looked Kinza over. "And what time was your appointment for?"

"Well, we don't exactly have an appointment, but he said we could just show up and let the front desk know we were here."

"Mmm, I see," tapping on her computer. "Unfortunately, I don't see any availability on Mr. Clark's calendar today."

"But he said we didn't—"

"You'll need an appointment to see Mr. Clark," the woman said sharply. She reached over and took a card off the counter, and handed it to Kinza. "You are welcome to look on our website for facilities employment if you are looking for a job. Otherwise, you can direct any questions to our customer service team."

"I—"

"Have a nice day." Kinza knew when she was being dismissed.

"Let's go," she muttered to Zaid, and they left the lobby, aware of the security guard's eyes on them the whole way out.

"Did you have a plan b?" Zaid asked when they were back

on the sidewalk. The security guard was eyeing them through the glass, and Kinza had to restrain herself from making a face at him.

"No, maybe—" Zaid's phone buzzed, and he pulled it out. "It is Haris?"

"Yeah," he said. "Looks like they already found the Ummanu who works for Edmund Clark. We should head back."

She nodded, and they started down the sidewalk, passing by valet parking and worker vans. They had only made it a few feet when a familiar voice said behind them in disbelief, "You have *got* to be kidding me!" Kinza turned to find her best friend, a sack of rags in one hand and vacuum in the other, standing by one of the vans.

"Mitra!" Kinza exclaimed, a mixture of emotion welling up inside of her. She took a step forward but immediately back-paddled when Mitra stalked toward her, seething with anger.

"This is *not* happening," she said, dropping the vacuum and rags. "I am *not* seeing *my* best friend who fell off the face of the earth, with some *punk*"—the punk in question took a safe step backward—"after she *didn't answer a single one of my texts!*" Kinza had seen Mitra angry on several occasions, over dumb boys, rude people on the street, or when the gas station was out of Hot Cheetos. She claimed it was because she was an Aries, but Kinza knew that Mitra just liked to get riled up; she was rarely ever truly angry. But right now, Mitra looked like she wanted to chop her into bitty pieces and the back of Kinza's neck was confused, not quite tingling, but not entirely sure it shouldn't.

"Mitra, I'm sorry—"

"*Sorry?* No, Kinza, I'm sorry you were so sick you couldn't pick up the phone to let me know you were alive!" People were watching them as they passed, and she could see the security guard inside the building talking into his radio. "I'm sorry that your grandmother sent you away to wherever for whatever reason without a cellphone. I am *so* sorry. Gosh, how rude of me. Is this your nurse?" she said, pointing at Zaid, who was looking at Mitra like a radioactive substance.

"Kinza, we should get back," he said quietly. Kinza nodded, and he left to get the car.

"Mitra—"

"No way," she said, crossing her arms. Her long black hair was in a braid and swayed with her anger. Despite the reaction, Kinza knew she wasn't just angry, but close to tears. "You are not ditching me again. At least tell me why you don't want to be friends, because you are clearly fine. It looks like you even got your hair done and everything," she said, waving toward the half braids that Ekaja had done for her.

"Mitra, stop for a moment!" she said. "I've had a *really* long week, and I'll tell you everything but right now is not a good time. I'll call you later, and we can talk."

Mitra crossed her arms. "No. Either you tell me right now, or don't bother calling me ever again. We have talked nearly every day for years, and you suddenly cut me off like an amputated arm. I don't know what's with you right now, but either we're best friends, or we're not."

Zaid had pulled up to the curb with the Buick, and Kinza could see two security guards coming out of the building. If they didn't move, they would be asked to leave.

Kinza exhaled a growl. "Okay fine, get in the car!"

Thankfully, Mitra didn't think twice and jumped in the back seat.

What are you doing? Zaid asked Kinza.

She met his eyes in the rearview mirror as she climbed in next to Mitra. *She's my best friend. She'll find out eventually.* She just didn't know if they would still be best friends after she told her the truth.

Speechless was not a word Kinza would use to describe the usually talkative Mitra. But it applied now. She sat in the back seat, opened mouthed as Zaid pulled the car up to the curb and parked. Kinza could see his eyes were wide as he got out to let her deal with the damage.

Traitor, she said to him as he headed up to Grams' house. Kinza had told Mitra everything. Everything. She had laughed at first and started yelling again until Kinza let her Aura out, just a little. She had been getting good at it, but this time it was little more than a blip. That little blip, however, was more than enough to make Mitra's jaw snap closed. She was silent for the rest of the trip as Kinza detailed everything that had happened over the last week.

"So," Mitra said, licking her lips. "Just to clarify, Tall, Dark & Handsome over there *kidnapped* you, but we're not mad about it?"

"Not really anymore."

"And you are one of those—those Anunnaki people with magical powers?"

"Yup."

"And they all look human and could be anyone?"

"Well... kind of. Only the venari can travel—and me."

"Because you're the queen?"

"Almost."

"Oh, right. Sorry, *almost.*" Mitra sat there staring out the window for a minute before abruptly getting out. Kinza watched her round the car to the sidewalk where she stopped. "Are you coming, Your Highness?" she said, hands on her hips.

"Great," Kinza muttered to herself. "This is fun." She got out and walked up to the front door.

"And your grandmother?" Mitra asked. "Is she Anunnaki too?"

"No, Grams is Ummanu. They're human, but like watchers or human allies." She unlocked the door and stepped inside.

"Gotcha, human allies for the secret magical people around the world." Grams and Haris were sitting in the living room with Zaid leaning against the wall. "Oh right," Mitra said, seeing Haris and throwing her hands up. "Let me guess, another magic person. And what's your ability? Shooting laser beams out of your eyes?"

Haris grinned and leaned back in the armchair. "I'm exceptionally attractive."

Mitra swiveled a look to Kinza, who sighed. "All right, Mitra knows everything, so we don't need to talk in code or anything. And no," she said to Mitra. "Haris is Ummanu like Grams."

"I'm still attractive, though," he said to Mitra with a wink.

"Mitra, honey, how's your mom doing?" Grams said, and Kinza could have kissed her.

Mitra looked like she was still coming out of her shock but said, "Good, she's really good. She said you should come over for dinner sometime."

Grams smiled. "I'd love to."

Kinza could feel Zaid's impatience across the room as she kicked off her shoes. "So, you guys already found the Ummanu who works for Edmund Clark?"

"Yeah," Haris said. "I'm waiting for him to email me back again."

"You emailed the Ummanu network?" Kinza asked.

"Just the midwestern branch," Grams said, eyeing Mitra, who still hovered in the doorway, looking like she was in a dream. "Maybe I should make some tea."

Fifteen minutes later, they were all seated in the living room with Grams' lavender tea and plates of sugar cookies. At the first sip, Kinza practically melted into the couch. Grams made most of her teas herself with her garden in the back and the rows of dried flowers hanging from the kitchen ceiling.

Mitra broke the silence. "So why exactly are you trying to talk to this billionaire guy?" She sat next to Kinza with her hands wrapped around her mug.

"Basically, there are three really powerful people in the world who used to be Anunnaki. Tahir is trying to get them on his side—which would be bad—so we are trying to beat him to it," Kinza said.

"And Tahir is the lunatic who tried to get you killed?"

"Yep."

Mitra wrinkled her nose. "Well then, I don't like him."

"Neither do we," Zaid said from across the room. Kinza didn't even have to look to know where he was. Zaid's presence was becoming a permanent fixture in her mind, and she couldn't say she was mad about it.

"So who is the Ummanu then?" Kinza asked.

Haris pulled out his phone. "A guy name Louis Reddington. His family was from Wisconsin, but he relocated here for the job six years ago. I told him it was on important Anunnaki business that you needed to meet Edmund Clark about, and he said he would see what he could do about setting something up."

"I'm surprised the Anunnaki don't have a hotline for these people. Is it really this hard to get ahold of them?" Mitra asked.

"The human-Anunnaki exist pretty autonomously," Zaid said, "only checking in once every few years. Otherwise, they live mostly human lives with considerable power that the Anunnaki help them build in the first place. But once you have power, it's much easier to gain more on your own."

"What happens after you convince them?" Mitra asked. "You just go back to the city forever then?"

Kinza was aware of the others looking at her for an answer. She had tried not to think about what would happen to Grams and Mitra after Kinza left to be queen—assuming she ever figured out how. And on the flip side, if she stayed in Chicago, the thought of never seeing Zaid again was... acute. Even if Mitra now knew about the Anunnaki, she still had her family and her life here. Kinza would outlive her by a lot, and burying your friend seemed like a cruel punishment in life. But Kinza had said she would help the Anunnaki, and if she turned her back on them when she had the power to help, she would never assuage the guilt. She was the one who had to live with herself.

"Yeah, I need to go back," Kinza said finally. Mitra wilted but nodded. Kinza almost wished she would yell instead.

Haris's phone buzzed in his lap. He opened the message and his eyes tracked across the screen. It must have been long because the rest of them sat there for a full minute in silence.

"If you don't read that message sometime this year, I'm going to lose my mind," Mitra said, regaining a little of her spunk.

Haris finally raised his eyes to give her an intrigued smile. "You have a lot of pent-up rage, don't you?" Before Mitra had a chance to respond, he said, "It's from Louis. He said he could meet you over lunch tomorrow."

"Where?" Zaid asked.

"At a restaurant downtown," Haris said, looking over the message again. "You do need to go alone, though," he said, looking at Kinza.

Zaid snorted. "No, but we'll be there anyway."

Kinza leveled him a stare. "I'll be just fine at a restaurant," she said.

We don't know that Tahir hasn't already gotten to him yet, he replied in her head.

Last time we checked, Tahir wasn't in the city, Kinza said.

I'd rather not take the chance when I could be easily sitting at the table next to you. He doesn't have to know.

I'm pretty sure he'll know, Zaid. You don't look like someone to frequent a five-star restaurant.

I'm seriously offended, he said, a small smile playing across his lips.

Grams cleared her throat a little too loudly. Kinza looked to see Haris grinning into his mug as Mitra said, "Well, that was weird." Her eyes were bobbing between Kinza and Zaid.

"Zaid is going to be across the street," Kinza said pointedly.

"Outside the door," he corrected.

She sighed and waved a hand. "Fine, outside the door. So until then, we can't really do anything else." She looked to Mitra. "I can buy you the bus fare to get home."

"Absolutely not," she said, affronted. "I'm staying here."

"Why?"

"Because if after you finish this, I'll probably never see you again, so I'd like to enjoy the last day with my best friend," she replied.

Kinza didn't know what to say, but thankfully, Haris came to the rescue. "She can stay; I don't mind," he said brightly. "Gives me something to look at other than the horrid construc-tion plywood."

Grams hurtled a throw pillow at him and found herself laughing with her best friend for the first and last time in forever.

THE FIVE OF them spent the rest of the evening watching cheesy TV shows and eating Gram's leftovers. Even though Grams had said they had more than enough money for repair, she didn't fail to notice the leaky faucet in the bathroom or the draft coming from Gram's bedroom. She would need to find a way to help her pay for the additional repairs.

When it was time to sleep, the guys took the couches, and Kinza and Mitra put together a makeshift bed of blankets and pillows in her bedroom. The bed had apparently been one of the things that got destroyed.

After they turned off the lights, they lay in the dark for several minutes, but neither of them slept. "So, how long and have you and Doom & Darkness been a thing?" Mitra asked finally.

"What?!" Kinza said, turning to Mitra in the dark. "We are not a *thing*."

"Mhmm. The thing is, I don't remember the last time a guy followed you around like a bodyguard, not to mention he couldn't stop looking at you." The blankets rustled as she turned over.

"That's pretty much what he is," Kinza said, sounding more like she was trying to convince herself. "My bodyguard."

"Do I look stupid to you?" Mitra said, and they both burst out into laughter, seeing as neither of them could see each other at the moment.

Grams pounded on the wall next to them. "You girls go to sleep!" They only laughed harder into the pillows.

When they finally calmed down, Mitra said, "Kinz, I feel like none of this is real, and at the same time, I feel like crying because I'm never going to see my best friend again. But it wouldn't be so bad if I knew you were happy."

"I am happy," Kinza replied. "I'm going to be queen, remember?"

"That's a job," Mitra said. "Jobs don't make you happy; people do. And I have a feeling that Mr. I Am Darkness would make you happy."

Kinza whacked Mitra's arm with a giggle. "Stop calling him that."

"See?" Mitra said. "You defend him like he's already yours. What's wrong with being together? You don't like him?"

Kinza exhaled. "No, I do like him. I just... I'm not sure he feels the same way. And if I told him that and it was true, things would be weird, and I don't want to lose what we already have." There it was. Kinza hadn't admitted it out loud before, but getting her to talk with Mitra's specialty.

"That's a pathetic excuse not to try."

"Pfft, okay, then I'll tell him if you go on a date with Haris, because I can see that one a mile off," Kinza replied.

The sound that came out of Mitra was a cross between a snort and a scoff before she rolled over. "I'm going to sleep now."

Kinza laughed. "See?"

"*Goodnight*, Kinza," Mitra said.

Kinza lay there thinking about what would happen if she did tell Zaid how she felt, but the doubt crept back in as soon as Mitra was asleep, snoring softly. Kinza's mind rejected the thought of Zaid turning her down and leaving her alone to be queen while he got to travel the world, free as a venari.

She decided she was happy the way things were.

CHAPTER 9

LOST EFFORTS

Kinza watched the steam rise from her cup of coffee, trying to let it settle her mind as she pushed away the negative thoughts from the past few days and focused on the good things in her life.

Grams sat across from her—which did help her remember the good things—but trying to conjure her Aura was especially difficult this morning, especially with someone watching her. She huffed a breath and let her muscles relax before giving it another go. She was about to throw in the towel when Grams gasped.

"There!" she said the moment Kinza's star-white Aura rose from her skin like a sleepy cat before vanishing. Grams clapped and cheered for her like she had when Kinza had gotten second place in her third grade spelling bee. She hadn't done anything miraculous, in fact, Jabari would tell her it was a pitiful attempt, but Grams was overjoyed. She supposed Grams had never truly seen an Anunnaki display their abilities.

"That was nothing compared to what I did a few days ago,"

Kinza said, sipping at her coffee. "Sometimes it's big, sometimes it's nothing." She shrugged.

"Honey, you're doing wonderful," Grams said with a light in her eyes. "Now, what about the fire? My coffee's a little cold."

Kinza snorted. "Unless you want me to incinerate your kitchen, that's probably not the best idea."

"Hmm, probably not," Grams said, eyeing her collection of dead flowers that were strung from the ceiling, most of which she used for teas. "My hip has been acting up. What about that healing thing you mentioned?"

Kinza gave her a wry smile. "I'm not even sure that's an ability of mine. Khalil could help you if he were here, though."

"Oh well," Grams said. "You ready to meet that man today? Mr. Clark?"

Kinza exhaled. "I guess. I need to be ready, but I have no idea what I'm going to say to him."

"Think of something quick because we need to leave soon," came Zaid's deep voice from the doorway to the kitchen. She figured he had already been awake since she hadn't woken up until almost eleven anyway. He didn't seem like the type to sleep past dawn.

"Coffee's on the counter," Grams said, nodding to the pot.

"Thank you," he replied. "But I don't drink caffeine." Kinza noticed how cautious he had been around her grandmother since they arrived. Grams hadn't been overly nice to him, but to be fair, he did kidnap Kinza like a maniac. On the other hand, was he trying to make a good impression?

Grams turned to her with big eyes. "Who doesn't drink caffeine?" Turning back to Zaid, "What do you run on? The blood of your enemies?" Kinza smiled into her coffee.

A slight smile played across his lips, the first Kinza had

seen since before their fight a few days ago. "It's against venari training, only slows me down."

Grams eyed him over the rim of her mug. "Maybe that's a good thing."

"We're leaving in twenty," was all he said to Kinza before disappearing back down the hall. He had said that he wasn't angry about what happened with her and Mikah, but he still seemed off. She needed to talk to him, and they would conveniently be alone in the car on the way to her meeting with Mr. Clark. A perfect time to corner him, so he didn't get a chance to speed-walk away from her.

Kinza gulped down the rest of her coffee. "I should probably get dressed," she said, depositing the cup into the sink. She peered out the kitchen window and saw the gray clouds coming over the horizon. "Hopefully it doesn't rain," she muttered.

"Take an extra jacket, so you don't catch a cold," Grams said, kicking her feet up onto Kinza's vacant chair.

"I don't think Anunnaki catch colds," Kinza said, heading to her room.

Zaid wove in and out of traffic on the freeway, speeding toward downtown Chicago, and secretly hoped he didn't get pulled over. He never actually had driving lessons and certainly didn't have a license.

"I don't think we are going to be late if you slow down a little," Kinza said from the passenger seat. She had seemed deep in thought as she stared out the window at the darkening rain clouds. Zaid wanted to ask her what she was thinking about, but that was something a friend did, and he was trying hard to keep his distance.

The last two days with her had been hard. He had no idea how to act around her. On the one hand, he wanted to stay close and protect her and help her when she needed it. On the other hand, Savar had been right. The closer he got to her, the more it was going to hurt him in the end. She was clearly happy that she had reunited with her grandmother and her harpy of a best friend, but he could tell she was still stressed about... *everything*. He wanted to ease that stress without getting too close, lest she tramples all over his heart again without even realizing it.

"We were supposed to meet him at twelve-thirty." He eased off the gas a little.

"*We* are not supposed to be doing anything. *I* am supposed to meet Mr. Clark for lunch, and I'm sure he'll live if I'm two minutes late."

He rolled his eyes and kept his focus on the road. If she were planning on being queen, she would need to at least get used to having a security detail at all times.

Kinza shifted in her seat. "All right," she said suddenly. "I know you're not a big talker, but I feel like you are still mad at me or something."

He glanced at her and found her expressive dark eyes looking him over. "No, I told you I was never mad," he said as calmly as he could, hoping that would be the end of it. Of course he wanted to throttle Mikah, but never *her*.

"Hmm, okay," she said, turning back to the window. It lasted all of thirty seconds before she said, "We're friends, right?"

Zaid's hands involuntarily tightened on the steering wheel. This was exactly the kind of conversation he was trying to avoid. "Yeah, sure. Friends."

She seemed to brighten a little at that. "Okay, good." The rest of the ride passed in near silence, with Kinza occasionally telling him he was going the wrong way or to slow down. The restaurant was connected to a five-star hotel close to the lake. They found a spot down the street, and Zaid was surprised to see a homeless shelter on the corner, so close to the hotel. It was a low building with a nondescript sign out front, but he knew what it was based on the line of people outside. Many homeless shelters didn't open for the night until the evening and closed again in the late morning.

Zaid and Kinza got out of the car, paid the meter, and headed down the street to the restaurant. Her gaze was focused on the line of homeless, though, and a look of sorrow passed over her face.

"What is it?" he asked.

"Couldn't they at least bring those people blankets or something to drink?" she said, nodding to the shelter. "It's cold and looks like it's going to rain."

Zaid pursed his lips and wished he could help. His venari assignments had brought him all over the world, and seeing people living in unfortunate situations wasn't something new to him. Especially when he saw that the ubir liked to prey on those types of people because it was less likely that someone was going to come look for them. On his first few assignments, he tried to contact the families of the victims, but over time he learned to block it out as he did with everything else in his life. There were too many people that needed help, and he was doing as much as he could by capturing the ubir. It still felt like throwing a spoonful of water into an inferno.

"Come on," he said. "You don't want to miss your appointment."

THE VALET HELD the door open as Kinza stepped into the restaurant. The interior was dim and was a warm relief from the chilly temperatures outside. The room was relatively busy, even for a lunchtime meal. Waiters moved between tables draped with white linen. Dark leather booths filled alcoves lining the room for a more private experience.

The hostess greeted her, and she let her know she was meeting someone here. "I'm looking for Mr. Clark. I'm not sure if he's arrived yet or not..." she said, scanning the tables.

"Oh!" the hostess said, giving her a once over. "Mr. Clark is this way. He did say he was expecting... someone." Kinza didn't bother rising to the taunt and followed the woman through the room. She led her to one of the back alcoves, and Kinza caught sight of a man already seated, facing the front. The hostess left them, and Kinza ignored the simpering smile the woman gave her as she walked away. Kinza immediately saw the reason for the woman's reaction.

"You must be, Ms. Solace?" the man said. "Please, have a seat." He gestured to the other side of the booth. The pictures had not done him justice; he was very handsome, and his white teeth flashed in the low light of the alcove. Zaid wouldn't be happy that she wasn't in sight of the windows.

Despite being surprisingly handsome, Kinza wanted to run back to the hostess and ask her how old she thought Kinza was. He looked like he was in his fifties and far, far too old for Kinza. No wonder the woman in the lobby the day before was so rude.

"You can call me Kinza," she said with a smile. "You are Mr. Clark then?"

"The one and only. I hope you don't mind, I already

ordered for us. I'm on a tight schedule." Kinza wanted to point out that she did mind, but she wasn't here to eat.

"No problem. I'm just happy you agreed to meet me," she said. It wasn't lost on her that she had, in fact, gained a meeting with one of the richest people in America in under twenty-four hours without ever having met him. And now she was here, sitting across from him in a restaurant she couldn't dream of affording. The menu didn't even have prices listed, for crying out loud. He seemed in his element though, in a crisp suit tailored to his broad shoulders, and the strategic graying of his hair around his temples gave off an air of experience and wisdom.

"Anything for a distant relative," he said with a wink. "Ah! Here's our food." A waiter came by and placed several dishes on the table. Oysters, crab legs, a bowl of pale green soup, and steamed buns. "I hope you like seafood," Mr. Clark said and thanked the waiter.

"Ah, yeah," she said but couldn't remember the last time she and Grams had had any. "I've never been here before, but I worked in the hotel next door a few times. Or used to." She took a spoonful of the soup first and found it to be cold, practically chilled.

"And now you are... what? An almost-queen?" he asked, taking the meat of a crab leg with a little fork. How did he know that? Kinza glanced around at the people sitting at the surrounding tables. "Don't worry," he said. "No one can hear us in here, and the closest tables are my security. We can speak freely."

"Yes, I suppose. Not quite queen but almost." She set down the piece of bread she had ripped off. "I'm sorry, I was told you had no idea what had been going on the last few weeks?"

Mr. Clark had a small smile as he slurped down the contents of an oyster. After he swallowed, he said, "These are delicious, yes? I find myself coming here at least twice a week. The food is always fresh. And to answer your question, I do have my ways of obtaining information if needed. It's highly unusual for an Ummanu in my employ to reach out to me about a new Rhaptan monarch. So, I have done my research, and it seems you've all had a busy time."

His dismissive tone aggravated her. "Not to be rude," she said, "but you make it sound as if you are not one of us."

He slurped down another oyster and took a sip of a burgundy-colored wine. "Technically, I'm not Anunnaki anymore. I haven't been for a very long time. My contact with Balasi and even Hakim is few and far between. I am typically out of touch for long periods of time with no news as to what is happening in the city. My... appointment to this position was designed that way. So I could operate autonomously without *needing* them at all times. In a way, I am more of an ally instead of a member."

Kinza didn't know what to say to that. She wasn't sure what she expected, but she assumed he would have the same pride in the Anunnaki as everyone else did. He seemed to think recent events didn't even pertain to him. His next words only added to that.

"I was surprised to hear of Tahir's betrayal. He was always a steadying presence on the council. And the attack on the city sounded dreadful. I hope many were not hurt?" he asked, lifting his brown eyes to hers.

His words left the food in Kinza's stomach churning. She leveled him a stare. "Many died, sadly. The city was practically destroyed, and we are still working to rebuild it. Everyone is trying to repair the damage as best as they can."

"That's the spirit!" he said with an encouraging smile. "How's your food?"

Out of the corner of her eye, Kinza saw a familiar form slip down the back hall of the restaurant while glancing inconspicuously in her direction to check on her. It seemed Zaid didn't approve of her seating arrangement so far from the door.

"It's great," she said a little tersely and set down her fork. "I'm glad to hear you are caught up on events, so I want to get straight to the point. Tahir's treachery is not finished. We don't know his exact plans, but he has contacted Wang Hàorán in an attempt to sway his allegiance away from Rhapta and to Tahir himself. I'm here to ask that you do not do the same."

Mr. Clark looked thoughtful as he swirled his wine around in his glass. The waiter stopped by and refilled it for him before he spoke. "Yes, I've heard of Tahir's... decisions of late. They are a bit on the riskier side of things. And I assume that you would like me to swear allegiance to you instead?" He eyed her over the rim of his glass. She couldn't tell if he was even taking her seriously or not, but she responded as if he did.

"Calling Tahir's decisions 'risky' is a gross understatement. He staged a civil war among his own people, tried to have a complete stranger murdered just in case I was the one from the prophecy, and now he is out in the world threatening the security of Rhapta. Please tell me you've seen the video of him demonstrating his abilities in that town in China. If humans find out we exist, and from Tahir, this could end very badly. So, yes. I would rather you swear allegiance to me, or to Rhapta's government at least, instead of Tahir and his plans."

Mr. Clark nodded before responding. "All right, I can see your side of things. I agree that Tahir's demonstration was an oversight on his part. There is no reason to risk humanity's knowledge at this point. Do you have a plan once you are queen? I mean, Rhapta hasn't had a monarchy in almost two hundred years. Everything has changed now that Hakim is gone. Do you have a plan to lead the Anunnaki?"

Kinza grimaced. "I'm working on it. The Elders are still trying to figure out the coronation piece—"

"Ah, yes. The passing of the barrier."

"—but once that is settled, there are several Elders who are backing me at the moment, and many scholars are helping to create the best possible government. It's been hardly a week since the attack, so we are rebuilding, but I'm confident that we can figure something out."

Mr. Clark nodded, looking somewhat impressed, and Kinza's hopes brightened a little. The waiter came by again to see if they wanted dessert, and Kinza wanted to whack him for interrupting.

"No, thank you, we'll pass on dessert. But please tell Pierre his food was absolutely terrific once again." He smiled that mega-watt smile, and the waiter promised he would relay the message.

When the waiter left, Kinza asked, "So? It would settle the minds of the Elders to know that you won't turn humanity against us as well."

Mr. Clark removed his napkin from his lap and placed it on the table with a sigh. "I'll be straightforward with you, Kinza." He looked at her now, as if for the first time. "I think you are a great kid with a wonderful heart. I can see you want to do your part. The thing is, I'm doing my part as well. I have been for a long time, and I quite like it. I maintain a certain level of influence in human society, and Rhapta sends me messages on how to make the world a better place. Usually this is adjusting my stocks, hiring or firing someone, or merging with other companies, but it's very autonomous. And I'd like to keep it that way."

Kinza saw Zaid passing by the back hall again. He was getting antsy, so she needed to hurry this up, but she felt her heart sinking at the turn in the conversation.

"To be fair," he continued. "Tahir has been a steady presence in Rhapta for a long time. He may have made a few unsavory decisions, but he has kept the city from falling apart as well. You, on the other hand, only discovered Anunnaki existed a few weeks ago." He gave her a pitying look. "I know you mean well, but is that enough? You don't have any experience and hardly any plan when it comes to helping the city."

Kinza was about to speak, but he signaled to one of his security guards nearby, indicating he was about ready to leave. "Looking at the facts, we've never been in this scenario before," he said, turning back to her. "But I'm not about to make the risky move here. I don't know if I'm ready to swear allegiance to anyone, and I know I am doing my part by making a difference in the world with the way I've been doing things. There's no reason for me to change that." He sighed. "It was a pleasure to meet you, and I'll be keeping tabs on how things turn out for you. I wish you all the best of luck."

"Making a difference?" Kinza's tone had him pausing as he made to stand. "Who do you think you're making a difference for?" She looked around the restaurant. "These people? You're certainly not making a difference for the people who matter."

He regarded her with caution but didn't speak, so she continued. "Did you even notice that there is a line of homeless people just down the street? People who have nowhere to go, who are sick and tired and lost, are sitting out in the cold while you and I eat oysters. My grandma worked her whole life and still can barely afford the upkeep on her house. There are drug epidemics, poor education, and mental illnesses that bring humanity down, and that's just in the United States."

She looked him over. The crisp suit and neat hair were deplorable to her now. "You think you are helping, but you are not. If you don't swear allegiance to Rhapta, I hope that you will at least do better to those you think you are caring for. Thank you for lunch."

Without waiting for an answer, she stood and strode to the front door and out into the cold.

ZAID WAS ABOUT to pretend to be a staff member to go in and get Kinza when she stepped out onto the sidewalk. She was scowling so hard he thought the sidewalk would crack. He was only the slightest bit pleased that look wasn't turned on him for once.

"How'd it go?" he asked, already knowing the answer. On his third pass around the room, he had caught snippets of the conversation and the expression on their faces. Mr. Clark had seemed just like every other rich man in America and had no intention of aligning with a young woman like Kinza, despite the fact that was his job. He had too much power now. What could Rhapta do? Fire him?

"He's a lost cause," she said, crossing her arms. The drizzle had stopped, but the chill seeped through his jacket. While she had been warm inside, he waited out here as long as he could. It had gotten much darker from the clouds and looked later than it was.

Zaid clenched his teeth. "Should we head back? Try to regroup?" Behind them, voices were rising. They turned to find two valets struggling to usher a man away from the doors of the restaurant. He looked like he came from the group of people outside the homeless shelter and was asking for food, his voice shouting in confusion.

The scowl melted from Kinza's face, and she walked over to them. Zaid couldn't hear what she said, but the valet backed away, and she pulled some money out of her pocket and placed it in the shouting man's hand. She spoke softly, and eventually he calmed down before they turned, and she walked a few steps back down the street. The man nodded and kept walking, and Kinza came back to Zaid.

"Okay, we can go now," she said and headed toward the car.

"What did you say to him?" Zaid asked.

"I think he had some sort of disability, but he said he goes to the homeless shelter every night at five. He got confused because it's so dark out and thought it wasn't open. I told him that it's only one-thirty and gave him some money to get something to eat. That was all."

Zaid couldn't help but smile. When he didn't say anything, Kinza turned to him. "What?" she asked. "Was that funny?"

"No, Kinza," he said, looking at her. "I just think that you'll make a great queen." It was true. Even if she had no idea what she was doing, she always tried to help. She seemed to have a larger capacity for compassion than anyone else he had ever met.

She gave a warped little half-smile as they got in the car. "Assuming I ever figure out this coronation thing. Mr. Clark said that he wasn't going to align with either of us. He said that I had no experience and I didn't have a plan, and he's not wrong." She stared at the ceiling of the car. "Why can't they just ditch the whole 'passing of the barrier' from one monarch to another tradition and just decide that I'm queen?"

Traffic was lighter now as Zaid pulled onto the freeway. "Probably because we still need to deal with the barrier regardless. It won't matter who's in charge if it falls." He grimaced at the idea of the Tanzanian government finding an entire city just appearing. The nauseated look on her face had him changing his tone. "There has to be a way to deal with the barrier. We'll figure something out. Or at least the Elders and scholars will. There's no point in worrying about it now. Let's just focus on one thing at a time."

She nodded but seemed distracted. "For future reference, I think I hate oysters."

Zaid smiled. "Noted."

When they got back to the house, Grams, Mitra, and Haris were in the living room watching some old rom-com that Haris seemed to think was hilarious. Kinza had texted Mitra about what happened, and she looked appropriately glum.

"Well?" Grams said, turning around and looking at them over the back of the couch. "What happened?"

Kinza flopped face-first onto the other couch. "He doesn't care about anything but his stupid money," she said into the cushions. "He preached about how he was doing so much good, and there was no reason for him to align with me, Tahir, or Rhapta. I chewed him out about it, but I don't think he cared."

"What happens now?" Mitra asked, looking between Zaid and Kinza.

"We might need to head over to Paris to see if we can convince Vivienne Moreau," Zaid said, leaning against the wall.

"Is that another one of those important people?" Mitra asked.

Kinza nodded, finally sitting up. "If we can at least get one of them to swear allegiance to Rhapta or me, that would be better than nothing. It would really suck if I went back with nothing to show for it."

"These people are powerful," Grams said, muting the TV. "You can't be expected to pop in and just convince them to do what you say. Can you?"

"Apparently I am," Kinza replied before looking to Zaid. "Maybe we can try to contact Balasi. It'd be nice to talk to

Mikah and Eta and see if they have made any progress on the barrier. Assuming it's still up."

Ice crept through Zaid's veins at the mention of Mikah. It was clear Kinza had a certain fondness for the guy, but it didn't mean he had to like it. "It would be difficult unless we knew where Laiq was. Haris, any word from the network?"

Haris had his eyes focused on the TV but dragged them back to Zaid. "Huh? Oh, nothing today other than a potential tip off about Basma. One of the Ummanu down in Kentucky thought he spotted her there."

"Really?" Zaid said. "Was anyone assigned to her?"

Haris shrugged and rocked in the armchair. "No idea, but there apparently hadn't been any venari through. I'm worried they'll lose her again before someone is sent to capture her."

Kinza chewed at a fingernail and said, "We should let Savar know when we get back."

Zaid sighed. "It might be too late. We'll probably lose her again, but there is nothing we can do. I think we should head back up to Haris's place so we can get to France before Tahir and his other Elders."

"Ugh," Kinza said. "I forgot that a few of them escaped with him."

"This man is truthfully like a cancer, isn't he?" Grams said, shaking her head. "Spreading corruption wherever he goes."

"I still can't get over that you can just pop on over to France whenever you please," Mitra said, scrolling through her phone. "So if I wanted to go to Costa Rica for a weekend…"

"As much as I would love to show you my humble abode," Haris said, "Ummanu aren't supposed to use the portals." Haris pulled out his own phone and started tapping on the screen.

"Not supposed to or can't?" Mitra said, drawing a laugh from Kinza.

Grams gasped suddenly. "Oh my word..." she said, pointing toward the TV. The show had turned to a breaking news commercial. She dug around in the couch cushions, frantically looking for the remote. When she finally found it and turned the sound back on, the news anchor was detailing a massive mudslide on the southern coast of France, nearly demolishing a small town. According to the anchor, the odd thing was that it was in an area where mudslides had never occurred. In fact, that region was in a drought, and there shouldn't have been any mud at all. A few of the town's residents mentioned seeing two men up on a nearby cliff, but otherwise, nothing else unusual.

Kinza turned to Zaid. "What abilities did the other Elders have?" she asked slowly.

He crossed his arms, thinking. "Harran's ability is only that he needs to eat and sleep less. But Minesh's is knowing the faults in the earth, where the weak points are in the ground. That would create a mudslide unless..." He groaned.

"What is it?" Haris asked.

"Minesh's apprentice, Kiaan. That idiot's ability is turning stone to mud. I could have sworn that he could only do a small amount at a time, but clearly, that's not true," Zaid said.

The scowl had returned to Kinza's face. "So Tahir's people have beat us to France and are already causing chaos." She waved an arm toward the TV. "How can Mr. Clark watch this and not care?!"

Haris's phone beeped. "Actually, I think you might have done a good job chewing him out," he said, eyes scanning the screen.

"Why?" she asked. "Has he said something?" She went and tried to read over his shoulder, but Haris waved her off.

"Louis Reddington emailed me again. It seems you have made an impression on Edmund Clark. Apparently he 'saw what you did outside the restaurant' and is willing to give you another chance. He wants to hear more specifics about your plans for Rhapta's future."

"Another chance?" Kinza scoffed. "I should be giving him another chance. When can we meet?"

"Tomorrow," Haris said and looked up at her with a grin. "He's invited you to a charity gala."

Mitra clapped her hands together. "A gala! Please tell me we all get to go!"

Haris shook his head. "The invitation is for Kinza and her plus one. I wonder why he is letting someone else come this time."

"Probably because Zaid was the most conspicuous body-guard known to man today," Kinza said, eyeing Zaid. He was going to send a retort back, but he felt strongly warm and tingly that she automatically assumed it would be him that would accompany her. "So, like fancy clothes?" she asked.

"Yep," Haris said before eyeing her. "Someone needs to deal with your appearance. And you probably need to come up with a detailed plan for the future government of Rhapta with projected timelines and everything before tomorrow night."

"Shopping!" Mitra said. "I have no idea about that second part, but ooh, I know where we can get you a dress."

Kinza's smile turned wicked as she turned to Zaid. "That means you, sir, will have to wear something else for once in your life. Like a tux. And not dirty boots."

Zaid probably would have worn a potato sack if that's what kept her safe. "Not a chance," was all he said.

CHAPTER 10

NIGHTMARES TO REALITY

Eta hurried up the side streets, hoping she wouldn't be late. She had found a note and a stack of files on her desk this morning and had gotten caught up reading them. Mikah said that he had looked through Tahir's office for anything regarding the ink but had come up with nothing. The most extensive research he had was on the quarries. Seeing as Mikah had read through it three times, he lent it to Eta to look through.

She had spent the last hour before dawn reading through the material. There were logs on who worked in the quarries, who entered and when, which sections of Aurastone were excavated and where new deposits had been found. There was also a separate stack detailing specific studies Tahir had done on his own. Most of them were related to how far Aurastone could be taken from the city before it cracked and became Deathstone.

It seemed that Tahir had truly spent decades studying the stone. The scholars still had not the slightest clue as to how Tahir was able to create a camp outside the city, and the overseer in the quarries had conveniently died in the battle, and none of the other workers were to be found. It was clear Tahir had extensive secrets, but where would he hide them? Out in the open like this? In files in his desk? Eta tried to think about where she would hide something so important and realized she wouldn't have kept it written at all. Just long enough to memorize, and then she would have burned the evidence. Is that what Tahir had done?

If she could just *see,* this would be so much easier, but her mind had been a jumble of stone and wings and honey when she woke up this morning. A string of nonsense.

Badr was waiting outside the house of the venari when she arrived. He was leaning against the wall half-asleep, but at the sound of Eta's footsteps, he perked right up. She wished she could sleep that easily. *There you are,* he said. *I was getting worried. What's that?* He nodded toward the stack of files she carried under her arm. Of course he would have noticed right away.

The reason I was late. I'll show you after. Let's not make Savar wait on us. She knocked on the heavy door just as it was opening, and Savar stepped out. He didn't look surprised. In fact, Eta couldn't picture any emotion on his face other than disdain or disappointment. Had this man *ever* smiled?

Just in time, he said, pulling the door closed behind him. *I was just about to leave. Ready? This will be a bit of a walk.* He set off down the street, not waiting to see if they followed.

The two of them nodded and trailed him through the city. The sun was just coming up over the horizon as they made their way down to the south quarter. Eta hadn't been down here in years, since she was still living at the orphanage. Before her visions started, she was a rather rambunctious child, running wild in the streets with the other children. They used to play games out there, pretending they were kings and queens and magical creatures. Eta had always been small for her age, so she was usually forced to be a baby or a gnome. She didn't mind, though; the other children took care of her.

That was probably the last time she had friends, now that she thought about it. Once she was taken in by Hakim, people started looking at her with reverence. Like she was a holy, distant thing to be respected but never touched. Other children would look at her with wide eyes as she followed behind Hakim, fingers clutching the robes of the most powerful man in Rhapta. Eta wished she were still small sometimes, playing in the empty fountains of the abandoned plazas.

More people were here now since there had been so much damage to the center of the city. Families made makeshift homes out here in the ruins while the repairs continued day after day. Even though the Anunnaki had abilities beyond imagination, it didn't mean they didn't have hardship. She didn't need to be a seer to know that people grieved for the loved ones they would never see again and feared that they would follow in their footsteps soon if the barrier fell.

Once they got to the southern wall that separated the city from the quarries, Savar turned left, and they eventually came to a gate that he unlocked with a key he pulled from his pocket. It was no bigger than a door to a house, nothing like the massive central gates in the four sides of the city. This one was cleverly hidden, but not too secret. They stepped out right into a patch of tall grass.

Sorry, Savar said. *We'll need to climb through this a little ways, but it opens up again.* Eta didn't mind; she just hiked her robes higher and followed behind Badr. This side of the city was all fields to the left. If they went far enough north, they would run into the outskirts and the dwellings there. Instead, Savar turned to the right, following a makeshift fence that ran along what Eta assumed were the quarries on the other side.

She had only seen the quarries a couple of times, as all children did, but had found them boring and hard to get to. They were usually guarded, and she was never allowed to climb down them and look for Aurastones herself. Her teachers would say that there was always a risk of an Aurastone cracking and becoming Deathstone, and she didn't want to be subject to that, did she? Besides, she'd *seen* so many things in her life; what need was there to see some rocks?

The grass did eventually level out, and she could just make out the forest in the distance. She realized that this might've been the farthest she had ever been from the city. They hadn't gone too far, but the only time she really ever left was for funerals out in the fields, or when Hakim used to walk through the outskirts a few times a year. She had never gotten close enough to see the forest. It made her heart beat a little faster to think that humans might be just within the tree line, not realizing that there was a secret city on the other side. Even though the thought of humans scared her, seeing *them* would be far more interesting than the Aurastones in the quarries.

She had a hard time imagining that there was an entire world out there. She had seen much of it in her visions, but it felt far away and disconnected from her. Like humanity was just a story parents read to their children at night, not real but an interesting concept. She was a little jealous of venari at times, how they got to leave the city and go to faraway places that she could only dream about. But based on their grim demeanor, she supposed maybe it wasn't that great out there after all.

They started to round the edge of the quarry to the forest which was to their left now. *The flowers grow up here, almost the entire length of the quarry. Be careful, the fence is missing in some parts on this side, and you wouldn't want to fall in. It's a long way down,* Savar said.

They walked for a few more minutes when Eta realized what he meant. The fence ended abruptly, as if it was whipped away in a storm, and no one bothered to repair it. Realistically, no one was going to come out this far unless they knew what they were looking for. Most Anunnaki were afraid of accidentally crossing the barrier, even though you could only cross at certain points. And even though the barrier was guarded, it was mostly for safety. There was nothing to actually steal here unless someone wanted to vandalize the Aurastone, and that wasn't to anyone's benefit.

Eta didn't dare get close to the quarry's edge as she could see it went down further than she could see from here. Badr kept his distance as well, looking like he might pass out from the height. Up ahead, Eta could see a multitude of dark purple flowers growing. To distract Badr from the height, she asked, *So which ones do you pick?* There were so many flowers that grew in and around Rhapta; why were these special?

Savar slowed his pace and carefully walked through the violets, bending over to look at a few and inspect others. *It's difficult to say, but look here,* he pointed to one with three petals instead of five. *This one is missing petals, but I have a feeling it will be a good one.* He plucked it before moving to another. *This one has an even coloring all the way around, so I'm going to skip this one.*

You only go for the ugly ones? Badr asked. Eta could already see his mind working.

Not exactly, Savar replied. *See here? This one is also perfect, but it lacks any marks from insects, meaning that they wouldn't eat it. So I'll take this one.*

You're only taking the mutated ones, Eta realized.

Savar bobbed his head back and forth. *Sort of.*

Badr pointed to one further away. *What about this one?* he asked, pointing to one with a discolored stem.

Savar shook his head. *It's too far from the quarry.*

So it needs to be close to the quarry? Badr asked, puzzled. Eta had to agree that she didn't see the connection.

Savar sighed, looking like he regretted inviting them out here. *Generally yes, but only certain parts of the quarry. Other areas don't matter.*

Can you show me where? Badr asked. Savar nodded and pointed along the edge to where the different areas were, causing Badr to look like he was going to vomit. As soon as Savar was done explaining, Badr nodded and hurried back.

What do you think? Eta asked him as Savar went to pick more, just out of earshot.

There is definitely a pattern here, Badr replied, looking around them. *But we need to connect it to the ink and Tahir. What about the flowers is so special?*

I'm not sure. And there's nothing else out here besides the quarry. Maybe we can find some answers in this, she said, tapping the files under her arm. She hadn't seen anything that stood out to her this morning, but maybe Badr's abilities would help them find something.

She didn't know if they were going to be able to figure this out in time, but she wanted to have at least something to show Kinza when she got back. She had no idea when that would be, but the longer she was not coronated and holding the barrier, the longer they would be in danger. Eta almost offered her services to those who were painstakingly going over every detail of the Rhaptan monarchy's history but thought better of it. She didn't want to overwork herself, and she didn't think she would actually be of any use anyway.

Badr looked confused. *Tahir's research on the quarries,* Eta explained.

*Ah, yes. That could be useful. I think I have enough here to work with. I'll see if Savar will give me a sample flower, and we can go *over the files as well.* His brows knit together, already thinking over the possibilities. Kinza had had faith in him that he might be able to help, so Eta trusted her. She had to; if she didn't trust Kinza, then she would be right back where she started. So far, Badr seemed as intelligent as any scholar, but his methods were wild and erratic. Maybe this was his process? She would go with it for now.

Great, she said. *Let's head back.*

BACK IN BADR'S chaotic office, Eta sat on the only chair as Badr flipped through the files she had brought. Savar had let them keep one of the flowers he had picked, which Eta now twirled between her fingers. Its scent was faint but pleasant.

What if there is a certain parasite that leaves a residue on some of the plants? she mused.

I don't think so, Badr said, not looking up from the files. He had been devouring the information like a starved animal for the last fifteen minutes. When they had returned to the central plaza, Savar had pointedly said he would be busy the rest of the week and that he wished them luck on their investigation.

Maybe it's just extra petals that allow the tattoo to stay forever? She was trying to be helpful but admittedly was not very good at piecing things together. Just like her visions, she saw snippets but not where they came from or where they led to.

She hadn't had another intense vision like the one the night before. She wasn't trying to either. Just like the flowers, she had no idea what it had meant. Were visions more important the more all-consuming they were? Hakim had never told her since she hadn't ever had one like that. His approach had always been an informal one. Instruction would come as it was needed, never before its time. Now that he was gone, there would be no more instruction. *She* was the most knowledgeable seer in the city.

A few of the more unsavory Elders had been looking into the other seers, claiming it was just for research purposes. She knew that they were looking for an alternative to her or Kinza. She *also* knew that they wouldn't find anyone. Hakim may have been a somewhat relaxed teacher, but he was thorough in documenting the seers after what happened to Eta's mother. No one had nearly the level of visions Eta did, and she wasn't even close to what Hakim had been.

No, I don't think it's that either, Badr said, finally looking up. *It might take me some time to read through this, but I think there might be something here. I feel like I have almost all of the pieces. We are very close. How about I check in with you later?*

Eta knew she was being dismissed, but it was probably for the best, she had a meeting soon, and her visions were coming a little faster today. They appeared as broken fragments behind her eyes that she gently but firmly nudged away. *All right. I have a few meetings this afternoon, but I'll be in my office until evening. Let me know if you find anything.*

You too, he said, head already back in the papers.

Eta made her way downstairs, avoiding the construction, and stepped out into the central plaza. The midday rush was just starting as she hurried up to the Grand Hall and into its cool walkways. Many people smiled or greeted her politely as she hurried to her meeting, but she was lost in her thoughts. She had stopped trying to make friends long ago, knowing that most people were only nice to her to gain favor with Hakim. It was no different now that she was working with Kinza, and she had no intention of creating false friendships, regardless of how lonely she got at times.

As she turned the hall toward Ishar's office, she heard shouting.

—can't confirm that!

We should at least—

—only if we have a solid plan!

Eta knocked on the door as she entered the office, seeing Ishar and Ekbal turn toward her and sag with relief when they realized it was her. *Did anyone hear us?* Ekbal asked quickly, looking out into the hallway.

It was just me out there, Eta said as Ekbal closed the door and Ishar took a seat, looking defeated. *What is going on?* Eta asked, looking between them. This meeting was just supposed to be a status update. She was still only an apprentice, but had taken on a larger role than what would usually be allowed due to her ability and closeness with Hakim.

Ekbal came back and gave her a look that said to prepare herself. Most people wouldn't realize it, but Ekbal looked a lot like Hakim, same nose, ears, and hands. After Hakim had taken Eta under her wing, his nephew had become something of an uncle to her, keeping her in confidence. It seemed that because Hakim had trusted her completely, so did Ekbal. It didn't feel exactly like family, but she was glad to have someone who didn't see her only as the future "Grand Elder."

I've seen nothing, so tell me, she said. Her visions practically showed her everything except something useful. How many times had she tried looking for something related to Tahir or the future of Rhapta? Each time she was met with a wall of nonsense. Random images that told her nothing. The most useful thing she saw this week was that a prime member of the Grand Hall's investors was going to be pregnant soon. None of that would matter if they couldn't keep the city standing.

Ishar pursed his lips, always serious. *Humans have been poking around outside the barrier the last few days, with dogs.*

What!? Eta exclaimed. *Have they seen us?* That was not what she had expected. The barrier had dropped a couple times a day for the last few days, but never more than a few seconds. How could they see them so fast?

It's very possible their technology has been picking us up every time the barrier drops. So we sent a few of our warriors out there disguised as humans... Ishar said, taking a deep breath as if trying to realize that this was really happening.

And?! Eta was on the edge of her seat, emotions anything but under control at the moment.

Ishar and Ekbal exchanged a look. *One of the warriors we sent has the ability to see the true identity of anyone, including their intentions. They posed as hikers, and the humans ran into them, pretending to be the same. It was a lie, though, the humans were government officials, and they were definitely looking for something.*

Probably us, Ekbal muttered as he paced the room. He passed the window that looked out onto the city that was in shambles. It was a mockery compared to what the humans would do if they found them. The Anunnaki wanted to help humanity, but humans were like cornered animals. Fearful and aggressive toward anything that was different from them. There was constant proof of this in the way they treated each other.

Are we going to do anything? Eta asked, calming her mind and her racing heart. She wouldn't let this rile her. She wouldn't lose herself so easily and so quickly after Hakim's passing. He would be disappointed in her for crumbling so easily.

There's nothing we can do at the moment. Even if we use abilities to erase their memories or turn them away, their superiors are going to be waiting for a report, and then they will definitely know something is going on, Ekbal said. *No, we have to just sit here. Like ducks.* He hadn't sounded this bitter in a long time. He looked toward Ishar. *Go ahead, tell her the rest.*

The rest? Eta said, trying not to moan. Images of running feet flashed through her mind.

Ishar almost looked apologetic that he had to tell her. *It's Tahir. We have a few people who have abilities to pick up signals from human technology as long as they are standing just outside the barrier. It's taken a while to decipher, but we've picked up a frequency that sounded like gibberish at first.*

A code? Eta guessed.

Ishar nodded. *It talked about a city. A hidden city. The details of which were given by an unnamed informant. It was definitely a government channel as well, but we aren't sure which.*

Eta put her head in her hands, unable to speak. This was bad. This was really bad. Even more so due to the fact they didn't have a stable government at the moment. It was a wonder there wasn't a power vacuum. Many powerful Anunnaki families have voiced their disapproval of the government in the past, but that was nothing new. Now that they were weak, it felt like Rhapta's stability was balancing on the edge of the knife.

What is he trying to do? she finally mustered the courage to ask.

Ekbal answered this time. *He's leading them right to us. Eta, it's the worst possible scenario. The barrier is falling, and that scoundrel is serving us up on a platter!* He looked like he was going to burst a blood vessel. Ekbal had always despised Tahir. From the very start, he had tried to tell Hakim that something was off, but Hakim had called for peace and trust, always the beacon of light. But Tahir had snuffed that light out, and Ekbal was muttering disparities in the dark. Maybe Ekbal was more of a seer than Eta was.

Shh! Ishar said. *We cannot let anyone know of this. The only thing that could make this worse is mass hysteria.* He looked between the two of them. *Until we have some sort of answer, no one can know about this conversation. I've already sworn my men to secrecy. I trust you can do the same?*

Eta nodded, feeling numb. The bedtime stories were turning into nightmares now. Without another word, Ekbal and Eta left Ishar's office and went their separate ways. She was supposed to have another meeting but stopped one of the attendants to have them run a message that she would need to cancel. She needed to be alone for a moment to gather her thoughts. They swirled around in her head with the different possibilities.

Each day felt like a battle for her now. Every second was a possibility that they could be found or attacked, or a new civil war would start. Sometimes she wished she were born in the early days of Rhapta's existence, when the Anunnaki were known and worshipped. At least she would see the enemies coming if they decided to attack. Now she didn't know where they were coming from, and she had no way to stop them. They were all trapped in the city they revered, dead if they left it.

Halfway down the hall and still absorbed in her own head, the barrier snapped out of existence. She inhaled a breath along with the other people in the hall going about their business. She hadn't gotten used to it yet, and now knowing that humans could be watching them from their satellites at that moment, had her trembling. The city seemed to freeze as she waited for the barrier to snap back into place. When it didn't, people around her started screaming and crying. It was slow at first, but as the minutes ticked by, people started to panic.

Steady, Eta hushed the people around her in a calming voice. *It will come back. It will.* She didn't know if she believed herself, but her heart was galloping until, after three long minutes, the barrier returned, settling into place around the city. A sigh of relief escaped from her chest, but there was a frenzied energy in the hall that wouldn't calm.

When she was sure the barrier wouldn't fall again, Eta hurried to her office, shoes clicking on the marble floors with her nervous steps. While she had tried to emit an aura of serenity, her mind was a chaotic mess of thoughts and emotions. She entered her office, closed the door, and practically fell into her chair behind her desk. They had been minutes from being discovered. After thousands of years, they had been that close.

Resting her elbows on the desk, she dropped her head into her hands and was immediately consumed by a vision that felt as if she had been transported to another time.

It was the desert again, stretching all around her—or them. She was someone, a small someone packing mud together, palm slapping against the block she made. The mud was cool against her burning skin. She looked up to glare at the raging daystar. When she was done, she took the block and walked past tens of others doing the same to place it at the end of a long line, to bake in the heat. Around them was nothing. No—it looked like the start of a house. She walked toward the house and to the other side and saw a familiar river. She had swum in it so many times now; it always made her feel better after she did.

Wait. That wasn't right. Eta had never been here before. The someone *had though, and they had swum in the cool water. She remembered how it soothed the burns from the daystar.*

Eta.

On the other side of the river, people waived to her as they hauled buckets of the water up the bank to mix it with the dry earth. They were making similar blocks on their side, smiling as they worked. Their faces were indistinct, like they were hidden behind frosted glass. She needed to tell them to run, but she didn't know why.

Eta.

Everything was getting hazy as she tried to look up and down the river. The people had disappeared, and only the houses remained. Where had everyone gone?

The houses disappeared, and only the drying blocks remained. Was she going back in time, or forward?

Everything was gone now. The river dried up, and the earth cracked. There was no water here. The earth had been sucked dry, and machines soared high above her head. Lights shone down upon her, and her heart beat wildly as they came down and—

Eta!

Reality crashed back into place, and Eta found herself sitting at her desk, soaked in sweat and gasping for breath. She still felt the coolness of the mud on her palms. She looked down but only saw a layer of sweat, so she rubbed them on her thighs.

Creator, you scared the life out of me. Are you all right? Eta looked up to find the annoyingly symmetrical face of Mikah. He was bent over, peering into her face. *You're not going to die on me, are you?* he asked and plopped back into the chair on the other side of her desk. *I really don't have time to bury a body today, so if you could pull yourself together, that would be most welcome.* His words were dripping with disdain, but his eyes looked at her like she was going to collapse.

She gulped a breath and ran her hands over her face, wiping away the cold sweat that had formed there. *I'm fine,* she snapped. *Some visions are more intense than others.*

Anything interesting? he asked, picking at a piece of lint on his robes.

I got your note, she said in response. *Thank you for the files as well; they were helpful.*

Were they? Mikah asked curiously. *I thought them nothing more than junk.*

We are looking over them, so yes, they are helpful. Now, what do you want? She desperately needed to go lay down and just wanted him to leave. Her mind was still reeling from the vision, trying not to lose a single detail. One of Hakim's first lessons had been to write down her visions. Back when she was younger and the visions so infrequent, this was easy enough for her to do. But now, when she could easily have seen a hundred images in her mind a day, it was nearly impossible to write them all down. She would still chronicle the larger ones, though she had never had anything like this.

Had this one been worse than the night before? It was almost like she had been stuck in a dream and couldn't get out. It was definitely related to the first somehow, but were they even relevant? In the first vision, she had no idea the time period, whether it be past, present, or future. But in this one, it looked as if it were a rudimentary group of people making clay bricks in the desert. Was that not an early form of housing? Making bricks from mud and river water. But then the river was gone, and machines tried to attack her. What did any of it mean?

Eta inhaled another breath and realized Mikah had been talking and looked at her pointedly. *I'm sorry, say that again.*

He scoffed. *Figures. Your problems must be much more impor-tant than the rest of us. Tell me, was your vision of what I'll be having for dinner tonight? I could save you the headache and tell you—*

Just tell me what you want and leave, she said as calmly as she could. It took all of her effort not to haul him out herself.

What I was saying *is I came to see if you found anything inter-esting about the ink, seeing as you were so invested in it.* The way he lounged in the chair made it look like it was his office and she was here reporting to *him*.

It's none of your concern, she said stiffly. *Kinza assigned this to me and one other person. Not you.*

Funny thing, it seems like you need me though. So, in reality, I am part of this little bit of research you are doing. Besides, my job is terribly boring but somehow seems to have some use to you. He tilted his head back as if daring her to say no. Fortunately, Eta refused to bow to self-important men who thought they were entitled to a woman's time.

I have all the information I need from you, she said evenly. *There is no need to share any additional information—*

Mikah barked a laugh. *And who's to say you didn't steal it? It would look more than a little suspicious that you took Tahir's research for an unofficial investigation.*

Was he being serious? They both knew that wouldn't hold up for a second. She narrowed her eyes in confusion.

He leaned forward and rested his elbows on his knees, giving her one of those charming smiles he threw around town like calling cards. *You see, Eta. I get what I want in the end. Might as well just work with me here.*

Do you ever drop that charade? she asked, ignoring his threats. *Does anyone ever see the real you? You walk around like a preening warrior in red paint, but no one knows what you look like under all that. It's an ugly mask you wear, Mikah.*

The smile melted from his face, and she wondered if she got to see who Mikah really was as he stormed out of her office, letting the door slam behind him. It wasn't that she had found anything of note in her and Badr's research so far. The point was he was sticking his nose in her business and demanding that she divulge everything as if she owed it to him. The audacity that he expected her to bat her eyelashes at him and do any and everything he asked just because he gave her a pretty smile set her teeth on edge.

The stress of the day was starting to wear on her, and her head spun as she stood. She would need to take a nap to make it through the remainder of the afternoon and pray that the barrier didn't fall as she was asleep.

<h1 style="text-align:center">CHAPTER 11
THE GALA</h1>

Kinza and Mitra fell into the living room amid a mound of shopping bags.

"I'm so tired," Mitra mumbled into the carpet.

"And hungry," Kinza replied.

"Baby, what do you need all this for?" Grams exclaimed as she came in from the kitchen. "You needed what? One dress? Some shoes?" She waved her arms around at the bags. "Did you need a new wardrobe?"

"Okay," Mitra said, rolling over. "But she needed options. Gotta dazzle, right?" she said.

Kinza sat up. "Where are Zaid and Haris?"

Grams sunk into an armchair. "They went to run a few errands this morning. Said they needed to 'scope the place out' or something like that. Zaid thinks the gala is a trap."

Kinza snorted. "How does he figure that?" she said, fiddling with a curl.

"He thinks Tahir has already gotten to Edmund Clark, and they are going to kidnap you." Grams pointed a finger at her. "To be fair, it *is* a possibility. Why would he invite you back after he already said no? Zaid may be worse than a mother hen, but I'd rather not have you disappear again. Even if it was his fault the first time."

"Grams. It was a huge misunderstanding the first time," Kinza said. "But I see your point." She sighed. "Hopefully he gets something to wear while they are out. I doubt they'll let us in if he's in ripped cargo pants and dirty shoes."

"I'm sure he'd find a way in," Mitra mumbled. "Maybe he can sneak us in too. I want to go to the fancy party," she groaned. "I would look so good."

"You and Haris will be just down the street," she reminded her. Last night Zaid had decided that Haris and Mitra would be at a bar just a block away with their phones on and the car close by just in case. Mitra had wanted to pretend to be another one of Kinza's bodyguards so she could see the gala.

"Yes, I suppose I'll still look good there too." Mitra huffed. "Okay! Let's go try on the dresses again."

"There's baked mac and cheese in the kitchen," Grams said nonchalantly.

"Let's try on dresses *after* we eat," Mitra amended, and Kinza was pretty sure she felt drool coming out of her mouth.

Half an hour later, Kinza was standing in front of a mirror in her bedroom, holding up two dresses, side by side. "I really can't decide. I feel like the black one matches the theme better, and it's fancier, but the other one is just so... I don't know. What if I get cold?" She held up the sparkly black, floor-length gown again.

"It's inside, right? What does it matter then?" Mitra said, sorting through a pile of jewelry and makeup on the floor. "You just need to look regal. Edmund Clark is expecting a queen, not a girl going to prom."

"You're right," Kinza said, hanging the dresses on the mirror. She started mussing her hair, adjusting the curls.

"What happens if it actually is a trap?" Mitra asked, flicking her braid over her shoulder. "I know Haris and I will have the car, but are you going to be able to get out?"

"I'll know if I'm in danger," Kinza said. "It's one of my abilities. The back of my neck tingles when there is a threat close by."

"Oh right," Mitra said, picking out a necklace and holding it up. "I keep forgetting you have all of these super-big powers and all that."

Kinza stared at her reflection and tried to feel what Mitra was feeling. How would she react if it had been Mitra who was kidnapped and came back practically a new person? Kinza would have flipped. Her mind had been so preoccupied with how to save Rhapta and the Anunnaki that she forgot Mitra's world was a lot smaller and Kinza was a huge part of it.

"Maybe once you are queen," Mitra said, poking at the carpet now, "we could talk once in a while. I know you can't use cell phones there really, but maybe you could pop out to get a signal a couple times a year. Or I could meet you in Tanzania. I could tell my parents I'm visiting you at college or something. They might pay for it..." Mitra's voice started to waver, and Kinza turned to find tears lining her eyes as she ran her fingers over the carpet.

"Mitra, you are not about to cry right now," Kinza said, tears welling in her own eyes. She knelt down, and Mitra immediately gathered her into a hug.

"I'm not crying," Mitra said with a sniffle. "I think I'm just going to miss you a lot." Kinza had gained so many new people in her life over the last few weeks, but that didn't make up for the fact she would be losing one of the most steadying presences in her life. Sure, they could try to stay in touch, but she wasn't deluding herself into thinking it would stay like that forever. Kinza would have a civilization to run, and her duties would be demanding. Mitra had her own life here, and over time, they would lose contact.

Kinza couldn't tell if she was angrier at the Anunnaki or at humanity. If they had just gotten along in the first place, there would have been no need for a barrier. Mitra could call anytime she wanted or even come visit. Instead, they had to keep the city as much a secret as possible. Maybe one day, it would be possible to keep Mitra in her life somehow. Kinza wanted to ask Eta if she saw Mitra in her future. The woman would probably tell her she couldn't see anything that specific, but it was worth a shot.

Kinza kept hugging Mitra as she thought about the seer. Her eyes landed on the two dresses hanging on the mirror when she suddenly had a realization and a profound hope in Eta's abilities. "I know which dress I'm going to wear."

"Good," Mitra said, pulling back and wiping her eyes. "Because we need to fix this hair." She stood up, leaving Kinza in her thoughts. "Have you come up with a governmental plan to show Edmund Clark?"

Thoughts of Eta and Mikah and the Elders swam around in Kinza's mind. "I actually think I have."

Zaid was rarely afraid for his life, but with Haris driving, he was reminded that he should probably have a will made up sooner or later.

"I might actually vomit if you don't keep the car in a straight line," he said.

Haris just turned up the radio and yelled, "No, you won't! You haven't eaten in two days!" Zaid cranked the sound back down and gave Haris one of his deadliest glares when he made to touch the radio. "Fine, fine..." Haris said but made no effort to keep the car steady. "You big baby. So, are you satisfied now that we looked around at every exit, entrance, bathroom, and inch of that place?"

They just spent the last few hours overlooking the event center that the gala was to be at later that night. There were far too many ins and outs for Zaid to watch alone, so he would just need to stay by Kinza's side the entire night. If there was an attack, he would just need to grab her and make a run for it. Hopefully the humans would just think a stiff breeze went by.

"It's as good as it's going to get. You know where you'll be?"

"Yeah," Haris replied. "There's a nice little hole-in-the-wall restaurant down the street with excellent pizza. Do you think Mitra likes pizza? She looks like she likes pizza."

"Oh my god, just ask her out and save us all the misery," Zaid snapped.

Haris replied with a garbled scoff. "Do you want me to remind you—"

"No."

"Oh, so you are well aware that—"

"Yes."

"So are you going to—"

"Haris!" Zaid exclaimed. But Haris was grinning as usual, barely able to contain his own laughter.

"*Anyway,* did you want me to keep tabs on Basma still?" Haris asked. "As of last night, she was moving into other Ummanu territory, so I'm losing her soon."

Zaid rubbed his face. "If you can, yeah. I'd hate to let her go. She was crafty and slipped through your fingers like water. I mentioned her to Savar when I got back, and he was trying to find out if she still had family in Rhapta. Maybe we can find out more about her."

"I wish there were a way I could get her so you didn't have to. There are thousands of Ummanu and so few venari."

"Yeah, that'd be nice," Zaid said. "Where are we going?" Haris had taken the wrong exit off the freeway and was turning away from Grams' house.

"We need new clothes. We both have dates tonight," Haris said, turning into a parking lot of a large mall.

"We aren't—there are no dates tonight, Haris," Zaid said as they parked.

"Come on," Haris said, slapping Zaid on the chest. "We want Kinza focusing on you instead of anyone else at the gala." He got out of the car without waiting. Zaid wasn't sure if he wanted to hug Haris or bury him in Grams' backyard.

Two hours later, they stepped into Grams' house and were immediately assaulted by the delicious smell of her cooking. Haris had gotten a sandwich at the mall but still groaned at the smell of fried okra and rice.

"I feel like I haven't eaten in a hundred years," Haris said and went off to the kitchen.

Zaid made his way down the hall to Kinza's bedroom and knocked on the open door. He let out a low whistle when he saw the inside. It looked like a junkyard with piles of things in random corners. One side had a mound of blankets and pillows where she and Mitra had slept, but the rest of the room was semi-organized into clothes, jewelry, hair products, and just *things*.

"Don't judge," Kinza said from the middle of it. She looked like she was going through pieces of paper, discarding or saving them for various reasons. "And yes, I know I was the one who made this mess in the first place, but I inconveniently haven't been here to help Grams go through my things." Even though she was half-joking, Zaid could see the lowered brows and clenching of her jaw. She was trying to distract herself from the bigger problems by solving these little ones.

He raised his hands in mock defense and leaned against the doorjamb. "No judgment here," he said. "We just got back, but I wanted to let you know we need to leave in an hour to be there on time."

"All right," she said, turning back to her piles. "I'll be ready."

Zaid was about to leave but instead said in her mind, *You okay?*

Yeah. I think I'm just nervous. She crumpled a piece of paper and threw it in an overflowing trashcan.

You'll do just fine, he said. *No one in their right mind would choose Tahir over you. Just do your best.*

She gave him a small smile that almost reached her eyes. *Thanks. I'll get dressed in a minute here.*

Okay. He left her to go find Haris.

Another hour later and Zaid was standing in the living room with Haris and Grams before him. One of them had their arms crossed, and the other's eyebrows were up to their hairline.

"I have to say," Grams said. "You do clean up pretty well, kid."

"Something is off, though," Haris said, looking Zaid over. "Ah! Button the jacket." Zaid was wearing a simple tux he had found at the mall. The problem was none of them fit him right off the rack, so they had to get it tailored on the spot, which wasn't cheap.

Zaid tried buttoning the jacket and immediately undid it and pulled the tie off so he could unbutton the collar. "No way. I can't move, let alone breathe. I need to do both of those things to do my job."

"Well, you're going to stand out," Grams said, curling her lip.

"He's not the only one," Haris said, turning around to see Kinza step into the living room. Zaid was glad he took the tie off because he suddenly was unable to get a breath down. Heat ran up his spine as he watched Kinza walk up to Grams, twirl around, and ask, "What do you think? Fancy enough?"

She was wearing a simple one-shoulder dress that came almost to her ankles. The scarlet color was so vibrant it looked like she was draped in spun rubies that matched some of the beads in her hair. The dress hugged her curves like water flowing over her skin. The strappy black heels had her standing a few inches taller than her grandmother, who was cooing over how good she looked.

Zaid wanted to say he agreed but physically could not make his vocal cords work. When Kinza looked to him for approval, he had a desperate need to be in a different room. He didn't fail to notice the crestfallen look on her face as he strode into the kitchen, grabbed a glass, filled it with water, and drank deep. As soon as he finished one, he downed another.

Haris appeared in the doorway, looking smug. "You know, if you just—"

"Shut it."

This was going to be a long night.

KINZA LOOKED up at the massive event center that sat close to Lake Michigan. It looked something like a museum with wide staircases leading up to rows of doors set between Grecian columns. Lines of beautifully dressed people made their way up to the doors to get checked in.

"I supposed we just waltz in then," Kinza said. Zaid was looking everywhere except her as he scanned the crowd, noting the doors and security. He had been like this the last hour, and Kinza wondered if the outfit was the wrong choice.

Eta had been so vaguely clever, telling Kinza to "pick the red one", and at the time, she had no idea what it meant. But things weren't going as well as she had hoped. In contrast, Kinza had a hard time not looking at Zaid. She had never denied he looked good; he looked like an off-duty high-end fragrance model. The suit cut perfectly against his broad shoulders, and she had the distinct urge to reach up and fix his collar, but she kept her hands to herself.

"I suppose so," he said and gestured for her to head up the stairs. Kinza couldn't remember the last time she had worn heels, but she forgot how powerful they made her feel. That was until she had to walk faster than a mile an hour. She focused hard on not tumbling down the steps as she hurried up to the warmth of the building.

Haris and Mitra had dropped them off and said they would be at a restaurant just down the street and to call if anything felt off. Kinza had decided to leave her jacket in the car and was debating if she could release just a smidgen of her fire without being noticed.

"Names, please," the door attendant said.

"Kinza Solace and my plus one."

The attendant looked down at his tablet and said, "Thank you. Have a great evening, Miss Solace."

She and Zaid stepped into the short lobby and headed straight back in the direction everyone else was headed. Kinza's jaw dropped once they were fully inside. The main ballroom of the event center was massive. Giant golden chandeliers hung from the ceiling over the people. The gala had some sort of black and white theme, and there were elegant decorations everywhere. Vases of white lilies, black-liveried waiters moving around with appetizers, and flutes of champagne with tiny black or white bows on the stems. The back of the room had a wall of glass doors that led out onto the terrace that overlooked the lake.

"Wow," Kinza said. "This is wild. Maybe I *should* have worn the black dress," she said, looking down at herself.

Zaid grunted in response. "It'll be easier for me to keep an eye on you this way." He still wasn't looking at her. "Let's start looking for Edmund Clark. The faster we can talk with him, the sooner we can leave, and I can get out of this stupid suit." He tugged at his collar and gestured toward the crowd for her to pick a direction.

"All work, no play," she mumbled and started circling the room. To one side, a band in white suits started up with elegant music. People paired up and started dancing, sparkling or voluminous dresses swishing across the dance floor. At the far ends of the room were additional areas with more food and quieter conversation but the majority of the revelry was in the main area.

Kinza tried to keep her focus on looking for Edmund Clark, but she kept getting distracted by the beauty of the room. Zaid stayed closed behind her and gave her the occasional reminder that they were there for a reason. She didn't see any reason not to partake in the appetizers while they were searching.

After nearly half an hour of searching, they still hadn't found him. "Is he even here?" she asked.

"He has to be," Zaid said, watching the ends of the room where people were coming and going. Kinza wondered if he noticed the gaggle of women that giggled and sent him sultry glances as they walked by.

Kinza just smirked. "Let's do another pass around the room then."

They meandered a little longer as one song bled into the next. They were passing by the band when a man in a black-on-black suit came up to her. He was gloriously handsome with golden hair and piercing green eyes.

"I hate to say this," he said. "But I've watched you circle the room too many times without being asked to dance. I would be honored if you would do me the pleasure?" He held out his hand with a smile.

"Oh, I..." she looked around, and Zaid was nowhere to be found. He had been right there.

"Just one dance?" the man asked.

One dance wouldn't cause a fuss, right? Zaid had clearly found something to do, and they hadn't had any luck finding Edmund Clark. Might as well enjoy the night. "Okay, sure," she said, placing her hand in his. The next moment she found herself swept onto the dance floor. She didn't have the slightest clue how to ballroom dance, but her partner seemed to guide her around effortlessly. As soon as they got into the flow of the song, Kinza found herself smiling.

The man was tall enough that she needed to crane her neck to see his face. So she ended up staring at his chest instead. It didn't matter, though; they were whirling around the room with everyone else as the tempo of the song increased. Kinza's heart felt like it was beating in tandem with the song, and she wanted to laugh with joy. When was the last time she and Mitra had gone out dancing? When was the last time she had done something carefree like this? It felt like an eternity ago.

Strong arms lifted her up and dipped her low when the song called for it, and by the time it ended, she was breathless. "Za—" she started to say before she remembered who she was dancing with.

The man gave her a curious smile. "Thank you, I needed that," she said and hurried off into the crowd before he could respond. Kinza tried to spy Zaid, but she still couldn't find him. She headed out toward the terrace to see if he went looking out there.

It was cold outside as she shut the glass door behind her, but there were heaters set at intervals along the long length of the terrace. A few other groups of people were out here as well, taking in the view of Lake Michigan at night. She didn't immediately see Zaid, though.

She walked a little ways down, hand grazing the banister when a voice rumbled behind her. "Did you enjoy your dance?"

Kinza whirled to find Zaid standing behind her, eyes out to the water. His posture was relaxed, with hands in his pockets, but a muscle twitched in his jaw. "Where have you been?!" Kinza complained. "I've been looking for you forever."

"I was looking for Edmund Clark. And you should be able to have seen my Aura anyway," he replied.

"Your Aura? It's not out, though."

"We can work on sensing other Anunnaki's Auras later. I was close by, though, and you seemed to be having the time of your life." He had the same tone after the situation with Mikah a few nights ago.

"So I'm not allowed to enjoy myself while we are here?" she bristled.

"No, you are more than welcome to," he said. "I'll gladly go track Blondie down for you if that's what you want."

Kinza massaged her forehead with her fingertips. "*Why* are you being like this? You are doing the same thing you did when I was hanging out with Mikah."

He shook his head but kept his eyes on the water as if it were the most interesting thing in the world. "I told you, I don't care what you do. Come on, we should—"

"I think you do," she said before he could change the subject. "I think you do care what I do. So tell me why it matters so much." She crossed her arms and tried to be firm even though her resolve was shaking. She desperately wanted to keep Zaid's friendship, but it seemed like it was a dying thing with every day that went by.

He had leaned his forearms on the railing and looked like he was fighting something. Finally, he dragged his eyes over to her face, and her stomach turned molten. He didn't say anything as he turned to her, looking like he was still fighting the same fight in his head. Like he had one foot here and the other foot somewhere else.

As if in a dream, he reached out and trailed a hand down her arm. That resolve of hers threatened to collapse completely.

We're friends. We're friends. We're friends, she repeated in her head like a mantra while holding her breath, waiting for him to say something. Something that mattered.

The dream that Zaid walked through seemed to collapse as he snatched his hand back with a frustrated growl before turning back to the water with a shake of his head. "You're wrong, Kinza. I don't care what you do. I don't care that you want Blondie or Mikah—"

"You idiot," Kinza said so softly that Zaid's eyes snapped to hers in alarm. She could feel the heat on her arm where he had touched her. "I don't want Blondie. I don't want Mikah. I want—"

Glass shattered as two people fell through the French doors and ended up in a brawling heap on the terrace. Fists were flying, and men sheltered their partners from the shards that bounced across the ground. It looked like two of the musicians were locked in a vicious fight.

"Wait here," Zaid said and ran over. Several other people went as well, trying to break the two men apart.

Kinza crossed her arms over herself, heart pounding with

what she had been about to say. She was too warm now and made to move away from the heater. Suddenly a hand clamped over Kinza's mouth, and everything went dark as a hood was pulled over her head.

THE HOOD WAS YANKED from Kinza's head, and she looked around wildly to see that she was in some sort of large study or library. She was seated in a deep leather armchair and heard the door click behind her as someone left.

"That's much better. Don't you think?"

Kinza whirled back around to find Edmund Clark seated across from her in a clean-cut suit. A little further behind him were two large windows, and she could see Lake Michigan. That's when she heard the faint music coming from within the building.

"We're still in the event center," she said by way of greeting. "You could have just asked me to come upstairs. There was no reason to kidnap me." This meeting was already not going well.

Edmund Clark ran a finger around the rim of his wine glass. "I wanted to speak with you and know that your words were not influenced by anyone, including that rather persistent bodyguard of yours." He looked up at her. "I'm no fool. I know what he does for a living. We've got about five minutes before he comes busting in through that door. So talk fast."

"You're the one who invited me back," Kinza reminded him as she relaxed back into the chair. "Why did you change your mind?"

"Did you know that while many people say they want to help, when presented with beggars on the street, most people will ignore them? I found it touching that you cared enough to help that man."

"Let's cut the crap, Edmund," Kinza said. His do-gooder charade was starting to irritate her. "You don't do things because they are touching."

He smirked at that. "I did also see the mudslide that happened in France yesterday. Tahir's plans might not be the greatest for business. But before I swear allegiance to anyone, I want to know what your plan is. *How* exactly do you plan on running Rhapta? There hasn't been a monarchy in quite some time, and from what I hear, the city is already in chaos with no clear leadership."

This was it. Kinza had spent the last twenty-four hours racking her brain on how she was going to pull this off. She needed to be convincing enough that *not* siding with her seemed a bad idea. Her heart pounded a little harder now that the pressure was on.

Edmund watched her, and when she didn't immediately speak, a disappointed look crossed his face.

"I plan on returning the Rhaptan monarchy to a similar structure of what it used to be." She took a breath and continued. "The Elders that want to will stay on as my personal advisers. The others will need to find new ways to be useful."

"How are you going to continue helping humanity without Hakim?" Edmund asked. "That seemed to be your focus," he pointed out. He was all seriousness now, no more mega-watt smiles and distractions.

"Since you are so out of touch," Kinza said, resting her arms on the armrests, "Hakim had an apprentice; a seer who is becoming more powerful than he ever was." Just a tiny white lie won't hurt. "She has already sworn herself to me, and her visions will allow us to continue aiding humanity from the shadows, but in a less conservative manner. We have not been doing enough, and I believe with Eta's visions, we will be able to do more good in the world."

Edmund nodded for her to continue. He didn't look convinced yet.

"The warriors will be repurposed. They have been nothing more than a glorified tradition for thousands of years, and their abilities are wasted. Some will stay on as city guards, but I intend to make most of them venari. The ubir population is out of control, and venari numbers have dwindled."

"What about—"

"I also plan on using the allies that we already have. There are thousands of Ummanu who are ready to help us at a moment's notice. They are given no recognition yet devote their lives to watching *our* portals and never get to use them. I intend on changing that."

"What about the barrier?" Geez, this man left no stone unturned.

"I have a team of scholars working on it at the moment. I just spoke with them yesterday, and they believe they have figured out a way to keep the barrier standing without me." Two white lies wouldn't kill her.

"And if it falls?" A light twinkled in his eyes as if he thought he had her cornered. That she wouldn't have an answer.

She raised her chin. "*If* it falls, I'll deal with that too. You may have forgotten how powerful Anunnaki abilities are. One of my closest allies can wipe memories. We have others who now have abilities to hack into any human technology"—Edmund seemed interested at that—"erase satellite images, and even turn humans away from the city." One lie and three were all the same, right? It wouldn't matter as long as she kept the barrier from falling.

Edmund gave a shallow nod, thinking. He still looked dubious, though. It wasn't enough.

"Might I remind you," she added. "Tahir wants to expose the Anunnaki regardless. I, at least, am trying to prevent that. If Rhapta falls, you won't receive those handy little tips anymore. I'm sure you will survive; you have enough wealth amassed. But for how long?"

Edmund's eyes turned dark as he rubbed his chin, still watching her. She waited patiently until suddenly they brightened again. "There's something else, isn't there?" he asked. "Something big you're not telling me."

Kinza kept her breath steady, but her mind was filled with African violets. "Of course. But it's not wise to give you *all* of my cards, now, is it?"

A shout came from outside the door. Edmund continued watching her, and she was careful not to crumble. She wouldn't, not when so many lives were at stake.

"All right." That was it. He stood and walked over to her before kneeling to grasp one of her hands. Had she done it?

"I, Edmund Donovan Clark, swear absolute fealty and allegiance to Kinza Solace, future queen of the Anunnaki, and only to her. Long may she reign." After an intense pause, he added darkly, "Do not lead us astray."

The door exploded inward, and a moaning body tumbled inside, followed by Zaid, suit jacket fanning out behind him. A look of gut-wrenching relief crossed his face at the sight of her.

"Just in time!" Edmund said, standing, all smiles again. "Did either of you try the champagne?"

CHAPTER 12
GOODBYE AND BONJOUR

Kinza let Zaid steer her across the ballroom and toward the front doors. He had one hand on her bicep and the other shoving his phone to his ear. He was barking at Haris to meet them right away. He seemed upset, but Kinza couldn't care less.

She had done it! One of the three most powerful people in the world just swore their absolute fealty to her. *Her.* She couldn't help but think how preposterous that she was the one in charge. A giggle escaped from her lips, and Zaid looked at her like she had lost her mind.

The cool night air was nice while she was still riding on the high of the last few minutes. She didn't even care that she had been kidnapped; again.

"You sure he's on our side?" Zaid asked. None of the liquid fire intensity of earlier remained. Just calm, cool direction as he jogged down the front steps, Kinza doing her best to keep up.

"I mean, he got down on one knee and officially swore an oath. I would say that counts," she said. The air was quickly cooling her skin, and she shivered against the breeze coming in off the lake.

Zaid slowed his steps only enough to notice she was starting to shiver. He sighed in exasperation and took off his jacket. "Here. I hate the stupid thing anyway."

Kinza hated mushy chivalry but didn't think twice as she shoved her arms in, relishing the heat. The silence was awkward as they hurried down the sidewalk. "We don't need to run. I don't think we are going to be attacked anymore."

"I'd rather not risk it," he said. "Let's just get back to the car." Kinza hadn't forgotten their conversation earlier, but she didn't dare bring it up. The moment had passed, and they were back to whatever it was they usually were.

Haris and Mitra were coming up the sidewalk, and Kinza noticed Mitra giving Haris a curious look as he smiled and waved to them. "Congratulations, Your Highness!" Haris said. "You've got your first official follower. How does it feel?"

"Fantastic," she said with a mock curtsy. "Let's head home; it's freezing."

"Agreed," Mitra said, still eyeing Haris.

"While you two were enjoying yourselves, I tracked down Laiq," Haris said, pulling out into traffic.

"Where is he?" Zaid asked. He sat in the front, pointedly away from Kinza.

"Russia the last time anyone saw him, which was two days ago. He's supposed to be headed back there tomorrow, so I figured I could get a message to him if you wanted," Haris said.

Kinza nudged Mitra. *What happened with you two?* she mouthed.

Mitra gave a shrug and a nonchalant shake of her head. A very un-Mitra-like response.

"Not a bad idea," Zaid was saying. "See if he can get a

message to Balasi. He has a cell phone in the city. Have him tell them we got Edmund Clark."

"Sure," Haris said with a nod. They got back to Gram's relatively quickly, and Kinza wasn't surprised to see the light on when they arrived. They all piled into the living room and found Grams watching one of her shows.

"About time," she said, getting up. "This episode is terrible, and I need a little excitement in my life. Let me get some cookies."

Kinza giggled, and ten minutes later, they lounged on the array of couches, cookies in hand. Despite the fact that she was supposed to be queen, she had the distinct impression that Grams was some sort of elderly general who held war councils with tea and sweets as they were debriefed. Kinza and Zaid were still in their finery, but no one made a move to go change.

"He actually got down on one knee?" Grams asked after Kinza finished telling what happened.

"Yep," Kinza said, picking crumbs off her dress. "Apparently, I made a pretty convincing speech."

"Do you still need to go to France then?" Mitra asked. She was leaning against Kinza as if aware that she would be leaving soon.

"Tahir's people are already there, though, aren't they?" Grams said.

"Yes," Zaid said from across the room. "But I think we should still try. Haris will try to get a word to Rhapta for us, but it's relatively easy to get to Paris. We can at least check to see if Vivienne Moreau is aligned with anyone or not."

"I agree," Kinza said. "For all we know, she's realized that Tahir is a lunatic and wants nothing to do with him. Edmund thought the mudslide situation was pretty bad, and if he thinks it's bad, we should attempt to push back against Tahir if we can."

"Okay," Haris said, tilting his head against the back of the couch. "Head back up to my place in the morning, then?"

"Yes," Zaid said. "The earlier, the better."

"I'm coming!" Mitra interjected. Everyone turned to look at her. "I want to say goodbye. And besides, who is going to drive Grams' car back down?"

"Good point," Grams said. "All right, to bed with all of you. It's been a long day."

While everyone headed to their respective sleeping locations, Kinza followed Grams into the kitchen to make a cup of tea.

"Why don't you take some with you?" Grams suggested, indicating the jars of tea she kept.

"I'm pretty sure they have tea in Rhapta, Grams. Actually, they do have this spicy tea that I think you would like," she replied, getting out a mug.

"You'll have to bring me some back then." They made their tea in silence as the house slowly quieted down. When they were done, Grams motioned Kinza out the back door, and they sat on the back stoop. Grams had grabbed a blanket from inside the door and draped it over their legs as they warmed their hands on their mugs.

"Take lots of pictures too," Grams said. "I want to see what it looks like when you come back. The food too, I want to see what they eat. I've heard so many stories from my grandfather, but they feel so much more vibrant now that I know they are real."

"I'm not sure when I'm coming back," Kinza said, staring intently into her mug.

"I know, sweetie. But I'll be here when you do." It wasn't true, though. Grams was getting older, and every time that Kinza came back was a chance that Grams might not be here.

Who knows how much time she would have to travel? Once a month? Once a year?

"Sure thing. I'll take lots," she said, trying to control her breathing. Mitra would at least have her family, but Grams had no one else. The thought of her living out the rest of her life alone had tears welling in her eyes. How could she do this to her own family? Grams seemed over the moon on Kinza's behalf, but Kinza felt like she was sentencing her to life in prison. Who would care for her when she was too old to walk or bathe? Who would take her to the doctor or make sure she had eaten?

Kinza tried sipping her tea to distract her thoughts but found it scalding. She set it on the step beside her and huffed a breath. Grams seemed more than happy to look at the back-yard with the dead grass and wrought iron fence. The little garden in the corner had already wilted in the chill, but Grams would replant it next spring.

"I'll visit once a month," Kinza decided.

"That'd be nice," Grams said.

"For a whole weekend."

"Are you sure you are going to have—"

"I'll make it work." Grams gave her a sympathetic look; she wasn't fooled. That's when the dam broke, and Kinza found herself sobbing.

"Oh, baby," Grams hushed her and folded her into her arms. "It'll be okay." Grams held her for a long time as Kinza cried. She felt like a little girl again, back when she realized her parents were truly never coming back and Grams was the only person she had left in the world.

When she was pretty sure she had expelled all the water in her body, Kinza's sobs subsided. "Need I remind you," Grams said, "that this is the best thing I could have hoped for you. You will be provided for, you will get to fulfill your dreams of helping others, and knowing that moody hunk in there, you will be protected for the rest of your life."

"Ugh," Kinza said, making a noise. "Stop that." She sat up and rubbed at her puffy face, trying to wipe off the remnants of the night's mascara. "You'll just make me cry again. And who knows? I may very well fail the Anunnaki, the barrier will fall, and humans will stick us in cages."

"Edmund Clark seemed to have faith in you and your plan."

"That's because I may have fibbed a little bit."

"Kinza!" Grams exclaimed with a laugh. "No, I shouldn't admonish you for playing their game. We all know those people with vast wealth and power didn't get there from being saints. You are doing what you need to protect your people. I couldn't be more proud."

Kinza sipped her tea now that it had cooled and rested her head on her grandmother's shoulder. "Thanks, Grams."

"All right, off to bed with you. You have an early start."

"Night," Kinza said before heading to her room and snuggling into her makeshift bed next to her best friend for the last time.

"Now you listen here," Grams said to Zaid as he was about to walk out the front door. "I'll make you a deal."

Zaid arched an eyebrow that Ekaja would have smacked him for. "All right, what deal?"

Grams pointed around at the damaged house. "I will forgive you for all of this, *and* I won't bill you for a new pan as long as you promise to protect my baby. Is that a yes?"

Zaid softened. Kinza, Mitra, and Haris were already out in

the car and out of earshot. He couldn't help but overhear Kinza's tearful goodbye last night on his way back to the living room. His chest hurt at the thought of her upset, and he knew that her grandmother was only doing what she could to protect her family. "Of course I will," he said.

"I don't mean for the next year. I mean *forever.*" She gave him an imploring look to make sure he understood, but he knew what she meant. There was no use lying to her even if he attempted to lie to himself every day.

"I know," he said. "I meant forever too."

Grams nodded as if satisfied and gave a single pat on his shoulder. "Now get out of my house."

Zaid grinned and stepped out the front door and down to the car. Haris and Mitra were already in the front seat, leaving him to get in the back with Kinza, who was waving at Grams. "Okay, time to go," he said. "I want to get there before noon."

"It's not even light out yet," Mitra moaned from the front seat.

"By the time we get to the portal, it'll be much later in France, and I want to use the daylight while we have it."

They all waved to Grams as Haris pulled away, and they headed up north. Even though Zaid had promised to protect Kinza, he still had a hard time looking at her. He had almost slipped last night and told her everything. He would have put every inch of his heart out there for her to trample in those pretty black heels. He hadn't been paying much attention, but he could have sworn her heart had been beating as fast as his. And what had she been going to say? She said that she didn't want Mikah, but then that stupid brawl happened. He didn't dare let himself think let she was going to say she wanted *him.*

He looked out the window now and tried not to vomit at Haris's driving. They were all quiet for a good twenty minutes, but it seemed Kinza needed a distraction because she turned to him. "Will you show me the Aura thing now? I need to focus on something else," she said, pointedly eyeing the driver's seat.

"Hey!" Haris said.

Zaid ignored him. "Yeah, sure," he said, turning to her. "It's not hard, but you should be able to sense the Auras of nearby Anunnaki. It's why I thought you *weren't* one, because I couldn't find yours. But you're just an oddball, I guess."

"I'll take that as a compliment, but I feel like this would be handy in case we are ambushed by assassins again," she said with a half-smile. She was attempting to find some neutral ground after their argument last night, but he still found it hard to be so close to her. He tried his hardest to focus on his venari training and the lessons Savar had ground into him, and instructor-mode took over.

"First, close your eyes." She complied immediately, long lashes resting on her cheekbones. "Okay now, just feel my Aura with your mind."

"Umm…" She sounded less than understanding. "I think we skipped a few steps." Haris swerved around a car, causing them all to jostle in their seats. Mitra, who was fast asleep already, fell against the door and remained there, snoring softly.

"It's very simple," Zaid said, reaching out with his mind to sense hers and finding none. He wasn't sure if it was due to her Aura-controlling ability or if all Rhaptan royalty had hidden Auras. "Reach out as if we were going to speak, mind-to-mind, but less specific. Just sense *me* without trying to get into my head."

Still, with her eyes closed, she said, "Am I supposed to be seeing something?"

"No, it's more of a presence."

She opened her eyes. "I don't think this is going to work

because I already know you're right here. I think we need to practice with you hiding or something."

"Ooh, fun," Haris said. "Magical hide and seek."

"Just try again," Zaid said patiently. "It should be much easier since I'm close by, and there aren't a lot of people around."

"So it *would* have been hard to find you last night, even with your Aura!" she said, crossing her arms. He allowed himself the slightest pleasure that she was angry he had left her for even a few minutes.

"Not for me," he said with a grin. "Come on, just try again."

"Okay, fine," she said and closed her eyes again. She was silent for about a minute when a white light suddenly flared throughout the car, causing Haris to shout and swerve.

"Kinza!" Haris yelled.

Her eyes flew open, and her Aura diminished. "Oops, sorry."

"What happened?" Mitra said, finally waking up and rubbing her eyes.

"Kinza found the wrong Aura," Zaid said, gripping the door handle. "Maybe we should practice when we are on stable ground."

"Might be a good idea," she said, a little chagrined. "So you're saying that I shouldn't practice my fire right now either?"

"No!" everyone shouted simultaneously.

The rest of the drive was relatively mellow. Mitra and Kinza both fell back asleep, and the sun had barely risen in the sky by the time they reached the little town of Charlevoix that sat on the eastern side of Lake Michigan. This time of year still attracted a lot of tourists for the season change. The surrounding forests changed their leaves from green to vibrant oranges, reds, and yellows. It was calm and peaceful here, one of the few places Zaid found relaxing. Many of his assignments took him to the outskirts of cities, some even right in the middle, but few places actually reminded him that there were people who lived like this their whole lives. They didn't have to hunt ubir, or worry that they would be discovered by the rest of humanity, and they weren't shunned by the rest of the town. Well, he didn't know about that last part; everyone's business was their own.

He sometimes wondered what he would have been like if he had grown up here, human. Would he have been this closed off, angry thing all the time? Would he have asked a pretty girl to be his girlfriend without wondering if she would reject him entirely? Would his brother be alive? Maybe, once this was all over and the city was saved and the ubir under control, he would take a long vacation. He had earned it, not that venari ever actually got to do such things. He would deal with Savar somehow, but he could spend a month on a beach somewhere or in a cool forest by the lake, alone and at peace for once.

Haris pulled into the parking lot of the inn and drove around back to his house that sat within the tree line. Both girls woke up when the car stopped.

"I'm surprised you two were able to sleep through that," Zaid said as he got out.

"Next time, you can drive since you have so many opinions," Haris said. They followed him up to his house, and Zaid did a quick check to listen for any heartbeats inside. There were none, so he didn't say anything as Haris unlocked the door and let them in.

"How about we eat a quick breakfast before we go?" Kinza said. He knew she was stalling, but he didn't say no. She and Mitra were rather subdued as they cooked a quick meal with what Haris had in his fridge. He was in his usual chipper mood, and Zaid made a mental note to pay him back somehow at some point.

Despite how annoying he was, Haris had been a great friend to him over the last few years. Putting up with Zaid's moods was no easy task, and Haris had only ever helped him without question. He forgot that Haris had even less family than he did since his mom passed away.

As they sat down to eat, Haris mentioned, "I got a message to Laiq last night. I let him know what happened with Edmund and to see if he can have Balasi reach out to you if he can."

"Perfect," Zaid said, shoving a forkful of eggs into his mouth. "Updates on Basma?"

"Still in Kentucky," Haris said. "Once you leave, I'll head down there and keep an eye on her."

"Don't try anything," Zaid warned. "The longer they run free, the more wild and out of control they get."

Kinza looked between them. "Haris is going after Basma? Isn't that dangerous?"

"I'll be fine, cupcake," Haris said with a saccharine smile. "I took karate when I was seven."

Kinza leveled Zaid a look. "You can't seriously want him to follow her. If she finds out, she'll kill him."

"He'll be okay," Zaid said, taking another bite of eggs.

Kinza narrowed her eyes. "Did you forget that she took you out in two seconds flat?"

Haris snickered, but Mitra piped up. "I'll come with." Everyone turned to look at her. This was the second time she had offered to come with. The first time made sense because she got to spend more time with Kinza. But offering to go with Haris didn't make sense, unless...

She crossed her arms in annoyance. "I can shoot."

Haris gave her a dubious look, but Kinza was smiling. "It's true," Kinza said. "She goes hunting with her family. She's got a good eye." She gave Mitra finger guns, and Mitra turned Haris a haughty eye.

Haris's face changed so fast that Zaid thought he had imagined it. "So I get to go on a quest to find an evil demon only to be protected by a beautiful knight along the way? I'm in."

Mitra rolled her eyes. "I mean, I *do* look good."

"All right, fine," Zaid said, shaking his head. "You ready?" he asked Kinza.

"Yeah, I suppose. On to the next one," she said.

Before long, they were all piled into the basement, and Haris was gathering crystals to lay them out. "I notified Chloe to let her know you are coming," he said, laying the crystals across the floor.

"Chloe?" Kinza asked.

"The Parisian Ummanu," Zaid said. "She gets a lot of traffic being a major city. She won't yell at us, at least." Unlike Bahati, who thought he was the bane of her existence.

It didn't take Haris long to get the portal up and running. Mitra gasped when she saw it, and Zaid caught the smile Haris tried to hide.

"I'll call you as soon as I can, but..." Kinza started.

"I know," Mitra said, pulling her in for a hug. Zaid decided then that he would do whatever it took to make sure that Kinza got to see her friends and family as much as possible. It was clear that they were a stable presence in her life and would only help her become a better queen in the long run.

"Okay, I'm ready," Kinza said, turning to him.

Haris saluted them and said, "I'll reach out as soon as we get sight of Basma."

"Sounds good. Don't do anything stupid," Zaid said sternly.

"I second that," Kinza said pointedly to Mitra. Without

another breath, Zaid and Kinza stepped through the portal and into the heart of Paris.

"ABOUT TIME," a voice said in heavily accented English as Kinza stepped into a beautifully decorated living room. "I thought you were coming an hour ago."

"Needed breakfast," Zaid said. "Chloe, this is Kinza. Kinza, this is Chloe. Now we all know each other."

Kinza smiled at the beautiful woman sitting on the windowsill. The late afternoon light created a halo around her dark, curly hair. "Nice to meet you," Kinza said.

"You as well," she said with a nod. "Okay, children, out of my house. You are here now; I've done my part." She ushered them through the tiny apartment and into the hall.

"Thanks again," Zaid said, not at all bothered by her brusqueness. "I'll keep in touch when we need to come back."

"Yes, yes," she said with a flip of her hand. "I'll be here."

Kinza followed Zaid down a steep staircase and out on the streets of Paris and was immediately assaulted by noise. They must have been in the busiest part of the city, and she didn't know how she hadn't heard it before. Cars were everywhere, and people were walking by, most of them looking like tourists.

"Do you remember where Vivienne's office is?" Kinza asked.

"I think so," he said, looking around. "Let's go this way." Kinza was pretty sure he had no idea where he was going, but she followed him anyway. She was glad she had her sneakers on instead of the sandals she got used to wearing in Rhapta. The city was huge, and the roads were rarely flat. She was almost tripping as much as when they were coming down the forest.

The beautiful views and historic buildings made up for it. It was true that Paris was a beautiful city but still with a certain level of grit that came with any big city. She even caught a glimpse of the tip of the Eiffel Tower over the tops of a few buildings before they headed in the opposite direction. Her Anunnaki strength kept her from getting too tired. She more or less had a major case of jet lag. She had gone from Tanzania, to the United States, to France in a matter of days. How did Zaid do this all the time? Maybe it was something you got used to with time.

Not caring that she looked like a tourist, she snapped a few photos, intent on keeping her promise to Grams. When Zaid wasn't looking, she even got one of him as well. It felt like they had been walking for hours, and she pointedly didn't question his directional skill in case his pride was feeling fragile. But she was about to cave when he slowed down and said, "It's right up here around the corner."

"Perfect," she said, mentally apologizing to her poor feet. The area they had entered was one of high-end shops and galleries inside beautiful buildings, none of which were over two stories high. The people walking up and down the street looked like they came out of a fashion magazine, and Kinza wasn't surprised that a few people stared at them as they walked past. They probably stood out like sore thumbs with their plain jackets and dirty shoes.

When they turned the corner onto a similar street, Zaid pointed up ahead to a narrow building crammed between several others up on the other side of the road. "That's it; I can see the sign." As they walked toward the building, a black car pulled up in front, and two men got out. They were dressed in simple but clearly expensive clothing.

Zaid froze, Kinza stopping with him.

The two men walked up the short steps to the front door and rang the bell. One of them turned and looked in their direction. Kinza found herself being yanked into a nearby alley faster than she could scream, which was probably for the best because Zaid immediately shushed her.

"Is that...?" she asked as he peeked around the corner. When he looked back at her, she already knew the answer.

He nodded. "It's Minesh and Kiaan. Tahir beat us here."

CHAPTER 13
A SLIPPERY SLOPE

Kinza paced around the small hotel room she and Zaid had found on the other side of town. Zaid had insisted on choosing the shadiest place possible in hopes that Minesh and Kiaan wouldn't be staying nearby. Zaid didn't want to run the risk of the exiled Anunnaki detecting *their* Auras either, but Kinza thought he was being a little over-cautious. There were two dilapidated twin beds, a single window looking out onto an alley, and she was pretty sure she had seen a rat in the bathroom earlier.

"Anything good?" she asked, peering over his shoulder. He had convinced the hotel staff—which was just a middle-aged man smoking a cigarette outside of the building—to let him use his laptop. Zaid was trying to find any information what-soever on the building Vivienne's office was in and whether there was any additional news about the mudslide in southern France.

"I might've found the original blueprints of the building, but there is no way of knowing if they have renovated. I just want to know where all the exits are before we go traipsing in there," he said, looking at a blurry floor plan image.

Kinza resumed her pacing. "Why don't we just go bright and early in the morning? Maybe Minesh and Kiaan won't be there, and we can talk to Vivienne."

Zaid turned to look at her over his shoulder. "But what if Harran is there? Or even Tahir? We don't know that we aren't walking right into a battle or a trap." He turned back to the laptop. "If I can just find a good vantage point, we can watch her office for a day before we make contact."

Kinza went over to the window and, after wrestling with the latch, shoved it open to let in the fresh air. The room was stifling despite the time of year.

"We don't have a day, Zaid," she said, letting the evening breeze caress her face. "She could have already fallen into Tahir's smarmy hands."

"Smarmy?" he asked with a chuckle.

She shrugged. "I think it fits," she said and leaned against the open window. "You know I'm right, though. If we are going to do this, I don't think we can wait. Rhapta might now be doing well, and every second we delay is another Tahir could be filling her with lies. I think we should go to her right away."

Zaid twisted to look at her fully. "You think we should go to her house—tonight?" he asked seriously.

She nodded, and Zaid sat there for a moment, looking her over while deep in thought. It didn't mean anything, but it still sent tingles through her stomach.

He nodded, "Okay, it actually might not be a bad idea. I doubt Minesh and Kiaan would be at her house, so we would get a chance to talk to her alone. The problem would be getting access to her. I'll bet she has a ton of security." He stood and went looking for his phone.

Kinza was pleased he liked her idea. Zaid was always the one coming up with the plan, and she felt like she was always whisked along. It was nice that she could participate for a change.

"If we go, we should go now," he said. "I think I saw that her office closes soon."

Kinza was already grabbing her jacket. It may have been warm in the room, but who knew how long they would be waiting for Vivienne?

THIRTY MINUTES LATER, they were sitting on a park bench down the street from Vivienne's office. The bench was in clear view of the front door but still far enough away—and tucked behind a tree—for Zaid to approve they could wait here. It was already dark, but still early in the evening. The sounds of the city had not died down. If anything, it seemed busier than it had earlier. Kinza had a hard time taking her eyes off the door and tapped her heel against the ground in annoyance.

"Stop staring," Zaid said. He was sitting next to her, arms resting on the back of the bench. "You look suspicious."

"*You* look suspicious," she grumbled before looking over at him. "And why are you so relaxed? Shouldn't we be ready to run the moment she comes out?"

"Honestly?" he said. "This is probably one of the more relaxing assignments I've been on."

"This is relaxing for you?" she asked, perplexed.

He shrugged. "More than usual, yeah. When I'm hunting for ubir, the moment I get my eye on them, I can't let them out of my sight. And the more time I wait to capture them, the more likely they'll kill someone. I wouldn't be sitting around like this." He closed his eyes and did, in fact, look like he was enjoying the moment.

"Need I remind you that Minesh and Kiaan aren't exactly good Samaritans," Kinza replied, scrutinizing the building again from her vantage point.

"Yes, but they aren't dumb enough to attack Vivienne—or anyone else—in broad daylight. Actually…" he opened his eyes and looked down the street suspiciously a moment before closing them again. "Yeah, no. They're not that dumb. Either way, you're watching, so it's fine."

Kinza almost forgot that Zaid had spent the last seven years alone the majority of the time. Venari didn't have partners and worked by themselves, and were almost *always* on an assignment. She started to feel a bit warm and fuzzy at the thought that Zaid trusted her enough to relax, even for a moment.

Taking her duty very seriously now, she looked back toward the office and nearly yelped. "There they are!" she whispered, ducking down. Zaid shot up in a heartbeat, and they both peered around the protection of the tree to see Minesh and Kiaan walk down the front steps in the light of the lamppost and get into a waiting car. "I assume the younger one is Kiaan and the short one is Minesh?" she asked.

"Yeah," Zaid said, still watching. "Kiaan is probably only seventeen, but Minesh is around Tahir's age, I think."

"Seventeen?" Kinza asked incredulously. "He's huge for a seventeen-year-old."

Zaid shrugged. "He may be big for his age, but there's not a lot going on in his head. I don't see Vivienne yet. Let's wait a bit longer."

They watched the car pull away, and it was only five more minutes before two women came out as well, one of them locking the front door. They waved to each other and went opposite ways down the street. Kinza could see from where she was that the one walking toward them was Vivienne. She was an elegantly dressed woman who appeared to be in her late forties, and her voluminous hair was piled on her head in a way that made it look only semi-intentional but entirely in style.

Vivienne only walked about halfway down the street before a car pulled up, and she got into the back seat.

"Should we steal a car?" Kinza asked as the vehicle moved away from them.

"Into criminal activities now, are we?" Zaid said, standing up and waving his arm wildly at a cab that was driving by. It screeched to a stop, and they climbed in the back, Kinza shaking her head. Zaid was pointing to the black car at the other end of the street and speaking a sorry excuse for broken French, trying to get him to tail the other car. The cab driver was shaking his head, and it didn't look like things were going well.

Vivienne was getting away, so Kinza shoved her hand into Zaid's jacket pocket—earning a protest from him—and grabbed a handful of cash that he had taken out earlier. She stuck her hand out to the driver and said, "Allez!" while pointing toward Vivienne's car.

The driver must have understood because he slammed his foot on the gas, sending Kinza toppling in the back seat. Zaid yanked her upright and deposited the cash up front for their driver, and he sped through the streets of Paris. Kinza thought they had waited too long at that Vivienne was out of sight, but the driver seemed as if he had been waiting for this his whole life, or he did this daily. The car wove left and right at terrifying speeds, taking back streets and narrowly avoiding pedestrians and other vehicles until they caught sight of Vivienne's car again just a few ahead of them. The driver slowed as if understanding they didn't want to be seen, or maybe he noticed Zaid and Kinza ducking down in the back seat.

They followed Vivienne to another quieter part of town with ancient two-story townhomes along the Seine. Just as Zaid suspected, they all had tall gates out front, and she assumed cameras at every corner. Vivienne's car slowed, and she got out at one of the more expensive-looking homes. Their driver slowed to a stop further down the street and questioned something in French.

Zaid replied and ushered Kinza to get out. The driver muttered something, so Zaid rolled his eyes and deposited a second handful of cash that had the man nodding in approval. When they finally got out and the driver had left, Zaid said, "I didn't know you spoke French."

"I don't," Kinza replied, adjusting her hair. "But I've watched TV before," she said with a smile that had Zaid chuckling.

"All right, well, you got us here. Good job. Now you wait here while I—"

"Not a fat chance," Kinza said, crossing her arms. No way was he leaving her here. "This is a *team* effort, and you aren't leaving the *team* behind," she said firmly, pointing to herself.

Zaid shifted his weight. "Kinza, it would just be easier if—"

"I'm the one who needs to talk to Vivienne. So let's get going," she said, heading toward Vivienne's house.

Zaid sighed. "Fine. But we need to go through the back, which is *this* way," he said, turning the opposite way.

Kinza just grinned at having won the conversation and hurried to follow him, quickly erasing all traces of the smile when he glanced at her.

The backs of all the townhouses on this street faced the river, and there was a narrow, yet restricted, walkway just along it. Zaid scooped her up and hopped the fence faster than the security camera on the corner could catch them before setting her down again. They stayed along a line of hedges, watching for more security cameras posted outside the homes. It took less than a minute to find Vivienne's home, and they could see the light on in one of the lower rooms.

"Okay, how do you want to do this?" Zaid asked. "Knock on the door?"

"Do you think she'd answer?" Kinza said. "We came back here for a reason. I think we are just going to have to pop in?" She gave a chagrined smile.

Zaid groaned. "I'm second-guessing this idea. All right, there are at least four cameras on the ground, but I don't see any on the house itself. I'm going to get us both up to that balcony up there," he said, pointing to the terrace that sat on the upper floor. "I'm assuming she turned off the security in the house."

"Okay, I'm ready," Kinza said with a thumbs up.

This was going to go terribly.

Zaid took a steadying breath and picked her up. After one glance, they were moving fast. She didn't even know how he managed to climb a nearby tree while holding her, jumping into the small yard, and then climbing up the woodwork along the side of the balcony. The whole thing was less than four seconds, but Kinza was the one breathing hard out of fear.

Zaid put her on her feet, looking around as if waiting for the alarms to go off. Kinza looked over the edge of the terrace, but none of the security flood lights had come on. She let out a long breath, resting her hands on her knees. "That could've been bad," she said and then patted Zaid on the arm. "Good job, Spidey. Now the hard part."

"Stop messing around; let's try this door," he said, moving to the French doors that led out onto the terrace. "I don't think the security is on, but this door is a little stuck," he said, struggling with the handle.

"Well, here, let me try," Kinza said, grabbing for the handle and yanking down firmly. It did feel stuck as she tried to wiggle it with Zaid.

"No, I think I can—" the handle finally gave, and the door swung inward. Kinza and Zaid stumbled inside just as the door was opened on the other side of the room, and the lights flew on.

Kinza and Zaid froze halfway in the doorway as Vivienne stood opposite them, absolutely shell-shocked at the intruders for the half-second before she let out an ear-shattering scream.

KINZA DIDN'T NEED to know French to understand the string of expletives that came out of Vivienne. She also understood very well what it meant when someone hurled a vase at your head.

While Kinza was ducking and shouting, "Wait! Let us explain!" and throwing her hands up, Zaid sped over to the door and closed it so she couldn't run away. The shock of Zaid suddenly "appearing" on the other side of the room and closing them in had another scream coming out of Vivienne.

Zaid tried to ward her off gently as she swung a standing lamp in his direction. It looked like they were in some kind of office, decorated with rich and stylish furniture that Vivienne was trying to use as a barricade to put space between herself and her intruders. Kinza tried looking as unthreatening as possible, but Vivienne's enraged and terrified eyes were on Zaid as he tried to speak to her in French. Just like with the cab driver, it wasn't going well.

It seemed that Vivienne was too afraid to realize that they

were Anunnaki, despite the fact Zaid just moved at the speed of sound. At a sudden ingenious thought, Kinza lifted her shirt up high enough that her tattoo was visible, pointing to it wildly with her other hand and giving a non-threatening smile—hopefully.

Vivienne stopped screaming once she saw the tattoo but didn't drop the lamp and was still glaring at them with confusion and suspicion. Zaid spoke to her again, and Kinza heard the word "Anunnaki" before he pulled his collar aside to show the top of his tattoo on one side of his chest. Vivienne calmed a little more but started shouting at Zaid in French, probably wanting to know what they were doing breaking into her house.

Vivienne's eyes swung to Kinza at something Zaid said. "*What* do you *want?*" she asked furiously.

Kinza cleared her throat, hands still up. "My name is Kinza So—"

"I don't care who you are," Vivienne spat, setting the lamp down finally. "What is so important that you needed to break into my house? There are *protocols...*"

"I know," Kinza said, speaking quickly. "And I'm sorry. But we needed to make sure Minesh and Kiaan weren't with you."

"Ugh!" Vivienne said, running hands over her hair, trying to gather herself. "If you are with those two imbeciles—"

"We're not!" Kinza cried. "We are trying to warn you. I'm not sure how much they told you, but the Elder Tahir is trying to destroy Rhapta or at least regain some sort of power. To do that, he is trying to sway you and the other two human-Anunnaki who live in human society."

"Oui, oui, they've already given me their little spiel and tried to get me to sign their contract," she said, waving her hands as if not wanting to even deal with them.

"Contract?" Zaid said. He had moved a healthy distance away from Vivienne.

"Yes, they want my help and my influence. It sounds like Rhapta is already destroyed. I haven't been there since I was very young, but I have no interest in this mess if this is what it has come to."

"That's why we are here," Kinza pleaded. "I'm the heir to the throne—"

"*You?*" Vivienne asked. She looked Kinza over once and burst out into a haughty sort of laugh. "They did mention the monarchy had returned, but I didn't think in the form of a child. And one who doesn't understand basic decorum."

Kinza ignored the jab. "If you would just listen to me—"

"No," Vivienne said, holding a hand up. "You've said enough. I want nothing to do with Rhapta or these exiled Elders until they can display some semblance of composure. Now get out."

"But, if you just—"

"*OUT!*" Vivienne shouted, pointing to the door.

Kinza knew when she had lost. She and Zaid didn't speak a word, just scowled as they walked through the beautiful townhouse and out onto the street. The door was slammed firmly behind them, and she could hear the lock click.

Kinza groaned and rubbed her face vigorously. "That impossible woman! If she had just let me explain..."

"I know," Zaid said, looking back at the house. "I mean, we did scare her quite a bit, but I felt like she already had her mind made up regardless of how we showed up."

Kinza let out a long breath and found her resolve again. "Okay... to her office tomorrow then?"

"Seriously?" Zaid replied, giving her a skeptical look. "After all that?" He glanced back at the house again as if Vivienne were watching them.

"Yep," she said and turned him around to head down the street. "I've decided we give it one more shot. Maybe she'll feel better after some beauty rest." She yawned. "And maybe I'll feel better too."

Half an hour later, they were trudging back up the stairs to their hotel room. Kinza immediately headed for the bathroom to brush her teeth. They had stopped at a convenience store to buy her a toothbrush because, impending doom or not, she would not be caught dead going to bed without clean teeth.

Looking in the tiny mirror after she was done, she tried to see what Vivienne saw. Honestly, it wasn't difficult. She did look like a child. It wasn't surprising Edmund had rejected her right off the bat too. She looked like she had school in the morning and soccer practice in the afternoon instead of the weight of a civilization—or two—on her shoulders. The Anunnaki healing did quite a bit to maintain her basic health, but she could see the weariness under her eyes and in the stiffness of her jaw hidden behind the youthfulness of her face.

"Are you done in there?" Zaid said, pounding on the door.

Kinza pulled the door open to find Zaid with one arm propped against the doorjamb, but he didn't immediately move out of the way. "I am a queen, you know?" she said drily. "I can take as long as I want in the bathroom."

They were standing rather close in the small confines of the bathroom doorway, and for a moment, Kinza found her eyes locked with Zaid's, and she felt like they were back at the gala on the terrace. She could have sworn he looked right down to her soul, to that weariness she carried, but the moment was gone when he shifted to the side to let her pass.

"I didn't realize queens had larger bladders. My apologies," he said, rolling his eyes. "Move along now," he said, waving her past.

To get by, she still had to brush her shoulder against his

chest, but it only lasted a second, and he had closed the door behind him.

What is wrong with me? Kinza thought, putting her hands to her heated cheeks. She shook herself to snap out of it and hurried into one of the beds, fully clothed. The last thing she should be focusing on right now was a guy. If she couldn't walk by someone without swooning, how was she supposed to be the fearless leader of a magical race?

With a good night's sleep, she berated herself and closed her eyes firmly. Thankfully, she was fast asleep by the time Zaid came out of the bathroom.

"I HAVE TO SAY, I'm not entirely mad we had to come to Paris," Kinza said, taking another huge bite of her chocolate croissant.

They had gotten up super early, or late morning by Zaid's standards, to make sure they got to Vivienne's office early. They had no idea if Minesh and Kiaan were going to come back, but it sounded like Vivienne had already rejected Tahir. Kinza felt she needed to try one more time to really feel like she had pushed enough. It had taken Edmund until his second interaction with her to accept her as queen; maybe Vivienne would too. They hadn't heard from Haris again, nor Rhapta. It would take little time for them to go talk to Vivienne, and she would either accept or reject them. Either way, they would head to Rhapta right after. The silence from them made Kinza feel a little uneasy despite the fact they had said they might not be able to communicate. She hated not knowing what was going on, and there hadn't been any more displays from Tahir.

Hopefully, this meeting would be quick.

"I'm glad you're enjoying yourself," Zaid said as they

turned the corner onto Vivienne's street. He had his head on a swivel and was striding at a pace that Kinza almost had to jog to keep up with. Apparently he didn't share the same love of the city she did and wanted to get this day over with.

Kinza shoved the last bite of her croissant in her mouth as the office came into view. It was a bright, sunny morning, and people were already going about their day, making the sidewalks somewhat busy. "All right, if she lets me speak this time, I'm just going to give her the same plan I gave Edmund."

"What plan *did* you give Edmund?" Zaid asked, looking at her out of the corner of his eye.

"Oh, just that I am going to—" Kinza had a sudden thought that made her halt, forcing Zaid to stop with her. He looked at her questioningly, but she realized that she hadn't even told him what she planned on doing to help Rhapta. In fact, she hadn't shared any of her thoughts with him on how she was going to run their government, yet he was standing right there, in full confidence and support of her.

"Zaid, why are you helping me?" she asked.

His eyebrows went up. "Um, what? You might need to elaborate on that one."

"I mean, having the Elders continue as the government is still a plausible option; even having Eta as the Grand Elder wouldn't be a bad idea. And I never did give you a logical reason to accept me as your queen. Why are you choosing to?"

Zaid looked at her a second before coming over and placing both hands on her shoulders and ducking his head a little to look at her. "Are you getting cold feet?" he asked. "Of course I'd accept you." He shook his head. "You've done more for Rhapta in a matter of weeks than the Elders had for centuries. I'm sure the remaining Elders—and Eta—are much better than Tahir, but I've seen first-hand what you'll do for people you care about."

He gave her a pat on her cheek and straightened. "Now stop being ridiculous, and let's go." He turned and started back down the sidewalk without another word.

Well, that's that then, Kinza thought, and with renewed courage, strode after him.

She was still thinking about what Zaid said when they arrived at Vivienne's office and went up the steps. Kinza pushed the buzzer on the side of the building, and a moment later, a young woman's voice came on over the intercom.

"Bonjour?" she trilled and said something else in French.

"Hello!" Kinza said. "We're here to see Vivienne Moreau?"

A few moments went by. "Ah... she is..." the line cut to static for a moment. "Oui—uh, yes, yes, you can—" it cut off again, but the door buzzed, and they were let in.

"That was odd," Kinza said, looking at Zaid.

"A bit, yeah. It looks like her office is on the main floor," he said, pointing to a gold plaque on the wall with the office numbers. The main hall was large and spacious, with only one door on the left, a set of elevators, and a staircase further down. Two security guards stood by the elevators, and people were coming up and down the staircase, working an early morning. On the right, in the middle of the hall, was a set of double doors that must've been Vivienne's office. There were fashion ads and posters on either side of her door displaying different brands and a few fragrances.

One of the double doors was open, and they heard voices coming from within, so they strode over to them.

Zaid grabbed Kinza's arm right as they reached the door, but it was too late; she had already turned the corner and saw who was inside. The voices in the room stopped talking to look at them, and Kinza realized two things.

One, Minesh and Kiaan were as persistent as Kinza and Zaid were.

And two, this was not going to be a quick meeting.

Zaid shoved Kinza to the ground as a pair of scissors came whizzing by as fast as a dagger. Shouts erupted, and suddenly Zaid and Kiaan were fighting. Kiaan and Minesh must have arrived shortly before them, seeing as Vivienne's office had just opened. On the far right of the room were a set of bay windows with seating in front. A group of people who were seated screamed as the fight broke out.

On the left side of the room sat a large desk where Vivienne and, presumably her employee, huddled behind it. Behind them were several doors and a hallway leading further in the back. The entire office was displayed like a massive, fancy dressing room with large mirrors, plush couches, and stacks of magazines that Kiaan and Zaid crashed into.

Vivienne screamed something in French, and the two security guards in the hallway came bursting inside moments later, shouting at the two people grappling. It had only been a few seconds, but it suddenly went downhill.

Literally.

Behind where Zaid was standing his ground, the floor started to shake, rattling the whole building and chandeliers shaking as the ground below the building quickly turned to mud. The tiled floors on one side of the room cracked and started to cave in, destruction rippling across the office. The people sitting by the window clung to each other—still screaming—and tried to run out of the room amid the chaos. The security guards yelled, not understanding what was going on.

Kinza looked over to see Vivienne shove her employee toward the door. She, at least, had some sense to try to escape, but barely made it a few steps before Minesh took a large book and whacked her over the head, knocking her unconscious.

Vivienne gasped and started spitting enraged words at

Minesh, who was now coming toward her. The odd thing was that he was holding a stack of papers and a pen. She tried to turn and run, but Minesh grabbed her arm.

Kinza scrambled to her feet and dashed across the room toward Vivienne. The office was shaking, and one of the chandeliers finally gave way and shattered onto the floor, sending crystals and shards of glass scattering throughout the room. The security guards were doing their best to break up Zaid and Kiaan. Kinza wondered why the fight was lasting so long because Zaid was clearly a better trained fighter, but she noticed he was moving at a normal speed as well as fending off the guards at the same time. The humans didn't realize Kiaan was the one turning the foundation of the building to mud, but they would notice if someone started moving insanely fast.

Kinza got to the door Minesh had shoved Vivienne into, and she could hear her angered shouting inside. She had said that they had asked for her influence as well as signing some sort of contract. She banged on the door, mentally shoving the tingling on the back of her neck out of her mind.

She heard a crash behind her and saw a security guard had hit Zaid with a baton while he was holding Kiaan in a head-lock. It caused him to let go just enough that Kiaan got free and shoved Zaid hard. The security guards descended on Zaid, distracting him while Kiaan dashed the other way.

Where was he going? The tingling on Kinza's neck was practically screaming as she watched Kiaan scramble across the room and grab something under a broken coffee table. When she saw what it was, a familiar boiling heat started pulsing in her abdomen, and she started to run toward him.

"No!" she screamed as Kiaan turned back toward Zaid, who had just thrown a security guard off him. Zaid turned back toward Kiaan and saw what he had in his hand, eyes widening marginally.

Kiaan's arm had already come back, ready to throw the twelve-inch shard of broken mirror, but he would never get a chance to release it. Kinza didn't fight it as a white light suddenly filled the room, followed quickly by a deafening blast that sent everyone to the ground and the outer wall tumbling into the street.

This meeting really wasn't going well.

CHAPTER 14

MADNESS AND TRUTH

Eta woke to her nightmares slowly becoming a reality. It was just before dawn, and noise was coming in through her window. She ran to find the barrier had fallen for nearly ten minutes. Over the course of the morning, it would drop several more times, some longer than that

She fought through chaotic visions as she hurried to get dressed. Prairies burned in her mind, followed by children's toys in the sand, forgotten and discarded. She tried to focus, but the tension in the city was getting to her. Before she even made it downstairs, she knew today was different from yesterday. It *felt* different. They were getting close to the time when the barrier would drop and not come back.

She stepped outside the Great Hall's back doors. People were running across the streets, eyes fixed on the sky and terror on their faces. There was nothing they could do, though. They had to just hope it wouldn't fall and the humans wouldn't find them. Eta saw attendants dispatched from the Great Hall to go through the city, calling for people to prepare themselves just in case, gather their food and belongings in their homes, keep track of their loved ones, and not to panic.

Eta sat in the audience at a piano recital. She had never seen a piano in real life, only in her visions. Those were human things. Tears fell from eyes that weren't hers as the melody reached its peak and—

She shook herself, releasing herself from the vision but found she was shivering, palms already clammy. Wiping them on her robes, she went back inside the Great Hall. She barely made it a few steps inside when she stumbled as a new vision took hold.

She was freefalling, the clouds racing past her as the ground came up. The person that she was inhabiting screamed with delight at the drop in their stomach. Eta's mind scrambled to grasp the situation. The person tugged something on their vest and was violently ripped upward as a giant canopy spread out above them, slowing their descent. The terrifying drop became almost pleasant until a hole tore in the fabric, and she started to plummet—

Eta inhaled a gasp, grabbing onto the wall. She hadn't eaten anything today, thankfully; otherwise, it would have been all over the floor. Instead, she wiped away the thin sheen of sweat on her brow and hurried her steps to the office she had spent as much time in lately as her own.

The walk to Ekbal's side of the Great Hall had her more drained than usual. Attendants and Elders were hurrying up and down the hall, and she knocked on the third door on the left.

Come in, a strained voice said. She opened the door to find the familiar face of Elder Ekbal hunched over his desk, head in his hands. In her mind, a school of fish swam by, and she blinked to clear it. *Please tell me you are not here with bad news,* Ekbal said wearily.

No, I just woke up. I was hoping you had some news for me, she said, bringing her shaking legs to a chair. What was wrong with her? She'd had a barrage of visions before, but the past week had been nonstop, and today was even worse.

I'm sure you've heard the attendants we sent out? he said.

Yes, I saw them. And the barrier.

At some point in the night, it dropped for thirty minutes. Eta gasped, and he continued. *It's been up and down since then. I won't lie to you, Eta. A small group of humans saw the city just about an hour ago.*

Ice flooded her veins despite the warmth of the coming morning. She gripped the arms of the chair to keep them from shaking. *What happened?*

Hikers, we think. One of the warriors we posted at the wall saw them. They stood at the edge of the forest for no more than twenty seconds before turning around and running away. We didn't catch them.

A lightning storm struck in Eta's mind, and a whale breached the surface of the ocean. *What's going to happen?* Her voice was quiet in their heads, controlled yet terrified.

I don't know, Ekbal said, running his hands over his face. *We tripled the warriors on the walls and have started to move people toward the center of the city if possible. All farmers, field workers, and miners in the quarry were brought in too, just in case.*

Ekbal looked defeated. Face slack, staring at his desk. There was a good chance this was the end for them. Very soon, their home could be invaded by humans. They could be forced to leave, which would turn them human and make them forget their home. Their Aurastone would be taken and studied. Cracked and possibly turned to Deathstone.

Ekbal continued, *A few more humans have wandered in, but since the increase in the wall guard, we've captured them, had Mikah wipe their recent memory and let them go. He's been working all morning.* Eta didn't mention it wasn't even morning yet, really. Ekbal glanced up at her. *He mentioned you were doing research for Kinza?*

Eta tensed. If Mikah had ratted her out and made her look like she was disobeying rules…

Kinza asked me to look into a few things before she left. She said they might be important but couldn't say why.

Ekbal nodded vaguely. *Mikah said you were doing important work and to leave you be. I still wanted to check on you, though. I don't have the slightest bit of advice, so anything you can come up with to help us is better than what I am doing.*

Eta was slightly surprised but held it in. Mikah defended her? It sounded like he was planning something.

No progress on the barrier or Kinza's coronation then? Eta asked, already knowing the answer.

Ekbal gave a dry laugh, leaning back in his chair. The breeze coming in the window even felt tense, carrying the promise of ruin. *Everything that we find on the barrier points to using the monarchy to hold it up. Everything that we find on establishing the next monarch says they will 'carry on their backs the weight of river' and that they will coronate themselves when it's time.*

Something in the back of Eta's mind was confused. Her visions were knocking like an insistent visitor, one that, unless answered, would only demand louder that they be let in. Images of streets and rocks and Aurastones pressed themselves into her vision, and an overwhelming need to leave Ekbal's office spread through her like an ache. She wiped at the sweat on her brow again.

Well, she said, standing. *It seems nothing has changed, so I will go back to work.* She made for the door, gripping the back of the chair so she wouldn't fall.

Ekbal looked up from his desk at her with concern. *Eta—*

She was already out in the hall on shaky legs. Maybe she just needed to eat. It had been several days since she had a proper meal. No one paid any attention to her as she left the Grand Hall and out into the plaza. People were too preoccupied with keeping busy and minding the barrier. Vendors only opened their stalls halfway, as if ready to run. Schools were not in session as parents kept their children close. No one talked to each other except to ask for news. Several times an hour, the barrier would drop. Sometimes it would be as long as twenty minutes; other times, it was shorter. It was only a matter of time until they were found.

Eta tracked down one of her favorite vendors, who was already packing up. Despite the flurry of activity in the plaza, no one was hungry. Eta convinced him to make her something to take with, and he agreed. Ten minutes later, he handed her a large waxy leaf rolled up into a cone. It was filled with steaming rice, spiced vegetables and drizzled with a rich sauce. It was normally Eta's favorite meal, but today she was eating for functionality, not enjoyment.

After thanking the vendor and forcing herself to eat, she went to find Badr. She had to go back across to the other side of the plaza, passing by a group of angry people having a conversation. Pretending to pause to adjust her shoe, she listened in. One woman was saying how disgraceful it was to have "them" in the city. A man agreed. A second woman said there was more than enough room. Eta discovered that one of the prominent healers in the outskirts had started ushering everyone outside the wall into the city, leading them into some of the abandoned sectors.

That healer's head is too big, in my opinion, the first woman said. *What an upstart, thinking he can make these kinds of decisions. Who gave him the authority?*

What are they supposed to do, Uzima? the second woman

said. *If the humans come, the poor people living out there are practically lamb for the slaughter.*

As long as they stay in the south quarter, I supposed it's okay for now, the man replied. *But after this is over, I want them gone.*

Eta had heard enough. She kept walking toward the library. If the people living in the outskirts were being brought in as well, then it was truly bad. But the second woman had been right; their shacks outside the city walls were nothing but matchsticks. When she was younger, Eta had wished she were an apprentice to one of the Elders in city planning. She never understood why people had to live outside of the wall when there were so many empty homes inside. More than they could fill.

She remembered back before her visions, when she was still in the orphanage. Her teacher and caretaker had found her playing with a group of children the lived outside the wall. She had been scolded for playing with them. When she asked why she couldn't play with them, her teacher told her that they were not good people. That they had chosen to live a life of poverty. Over the next several years of her life, Eta figured out how wrong she had been.

THE WALK to the library didn't take too long, but as she stepped inside the building, the nervous energy that pervaded the city made her feel sluggish, like she was walking through silt. The library was as chaotic as ever, but the tasks had changed today. Instead of working on rebuilding, it looked like they were taking it apart. Nearly a hundred scholars and librarians were working to collect books and scrolls and precious artifacts and were carting them to the lower chambers of the building where the Apostles of Truth hideout used to be. Even some of the Apostles themselves were helping lead the efforts.

Eta listened to their conversations a little to help distract herself from the frantic visions in her mind. The knowledge in this library dated back thousands of years, containing information that could change the course of human history. The scholars had decided it was too important to leave out in case the barrier did drop and humans invaded. They couldn't afford to have this information shared. They were sending the books and scrolls down below and planned on sealing up the wall and hiding it.

There were silent tears in the eyes of many scholars as they worked. Eta could feel the grief. Their city had practically been destroyed mere weeks ago and wasn't healing. Instead, they were hiding away their possessions, possibly to never be seen again.

Frayed blankets, defiled paintings, and vultures swam in her vision. Underneath it all, the urge to leave that had sprung up while she was in Ekbal's office made her bones ache. She thought she was just feeling the anxiety of the day, but it was starting to become unbearable. What was this? She patted away the sweat on her neck and, with shaky legs, ascended the stairs to the second floor. Eta was out of breath by the time she got to the top, several people looking at her strangely. She wondered vaguely if the stress from her visions would kill her in the end. It was a morbid thought and even impractical, as Hakim would say.

As she approached Badr's office, she saw people angrily skirting the room. The door was wide open like last time, but papers and books had somehow drifted out into the hallway surrounding the room. It seemed Badr's theories were too big for the room he was given.

Exhausted, Eta leaned against the doorjamb and

surveyed the room. Truthfully, she couldn't see any section of wall, floor, or desk with the amount of paper Badr had attached to the surfaces. The young man himself was muttering and pacing back and forth in the confined space, his long legs only needing two steps before he was forced to turn around.

How is it going? Eta asked when Badr didn't notice her.

Great! he said without looking up. When he did, he blinked as if not realizing he had spoken. *Wait, what?*

Eta gave him an encouraging smile. *It's going well?* she reminded him. *Have you found anything on the ink?*

Oh, yes! I think so, Badr said, resuming his pacing. He picked up another piece of paper while glancing at a third in the opposite corner of the room. *There are coinciding events here, here, and here. They follow a similar pattern to this one over—* he strode quickly and flipped to the back of a book on the desk — *here. And the extract of the petals versus the stem was quick promising, although I'm still waiting on...* he trailed off, as if he forgot he had company.

The sensation of cool water running over her feet had Eta straining to hold off another vision. The insistent need to leave was pushing over her senses like gathering storm clouds, threatening to rain.

Badr, I'm not sure I understood that, Eta said, rubbing her temples. She felt dizzy just standing there and desperately wanted to get outside into the fresh air.

Oh, right, sorry, he said, remembering she was there. *Yes, I'm—I'm really close, Eta. Kinza was right. There is definitely something related to the ink, and I think I can figure out how it works. It's right here,* he said, gesturing around him wildly. *I just need to sort the pieces to find the answer. A little more time.*

Okay, she said. *I'll check on you later.* She took a deep breath, wiping her face and pushing away from the doorjamb.

Badr looked over at the tone in her voice. *Eta, are you okay?* he asked, stepping toward her.

Eta waved him off. *I'm fine, just a little tired. I need to check on something anyway. I'll see you later.*

She left the confused look on Badr's face and made her way down the stairs, relying heavily on the handrail. Her feet carried her out onto the street even as her mind was swarmed by visions she had kept at bay the last few minutes. They were unrelated and had no apparent meaning, but they kept coming. When she got outside, she gulped in several lungfuls of air, tilting her head up to the sky to allow the breeze to cool her already-clammy skin.

The barrier dropped then, and Eta hardly noticed for the vision that swam around her. She vaguely heard people screaming about the barrier as *the tide lapped against the beach, soft sand tickling her toes. The sun was setting, and all along the water, people relaxed, reclining on beach towels or walking hand in hand along the shoreline. Suddenly the water receded away from the beach. A few people whispered to each other about low tide, but the water just kept on receding. People started shouting then to get off the beach. Eta watched, unmoving, as far out in the distance, the horizon itself gently rose higher. It looked like nothing at all as people rushed inland, and Eta saw the wall of water descend—*

She didn't know how long she had been standing in front of the library, but people were no longer screaming. They still glanced fearfully at the sky but had moved on about their day. Had it been two minutes? Ten? Thirty? She couldn't tell. Her mind was still filled with a cloudiness, and the urge to leave had changed to something else.

Eta stood thinking for a moment, remembering the papers on Badr's wall. There were two whole walls in his office dedicated to the quarries. Most of those papers had been Tahir's. He had been the representative of the quarries, so why didn't she feel foolish wondering why he spent so much effort on them? They only mined the Aurastones that they worshipped. Why did they matter?

She realized that in her and Badr's research, they hadn't actually gone down there. They had skirted the rim, looking at the violets, but hadn't actually gone to see where the stones were mined.

The urge to leave turned into an urge to move; south. She let her feet choose their course because it took all her effort to stay standing. Droplets of cold sweat trickled down her back, and the dizziness made the sky wobble, but she kept her course. The visions were starting to come faster now, and a few people tried to ask her if she was all right, but soon enough, she was out of the central part of the city and entering the southern quarter.

She fought to keep her mind in reality, mentally shoving away the visions that whipped like fabric caught in the wind, demanding her attention. Somewhere in the back of her mind, she realized the barrier had dropped again. She was too far away from people to hear anyone scream this time, and she had no idea how long it lasted for. When had she left the Grand Hall? Hadn't it been just barely dawn? The sun was at its highest point now, and Eta was shaking from the cold. Why was she cold? She couldn't remember, but her feet walked through snow, and icy wind cramped her fingers.

At some point, she vomited her breakfast up onto a street corner, heaving until there was nothing left. The urging in her mind screamed at her to keep walking, but she held it down long enough to stumble over to an abandoned fountain and splash some water on her face.

The tattoo on her back was throbbing, she realized. Could Anunnaki get sick? She knew that those who dwelled outside the city walls slowly lost some of their abilities—like healing

—over time. That's why most of the healers spent more time out there; it's where they were needed. But Eta had been living in the Grand Hall since she was a child. What was happening to her?

She blinked and found she had walked further, catching sight of the southern wall up ahead. Visions of country roads, gaggles of children, and weeping mothers danced across her eyes. Most never saw her, but a few did, pleading for her help, coaxing her to dance.

Eta, remember everything Hakim taught you! she screamed into her own mind. She tried to conjure up the memories with Hakim, but they were drowned by the tide that was coming in.

Weak and delirious, she made it to the wall and found her feet going to the right instead of left like Savar had. About halfway down the wall, she found a door, or a small gate, really. She could see through the bars to the other side, and the edge of the quarries was only about twenty feet away. Looking to the side of the gate, she reached for the lever to raise it up.

What do you think you're doing?

Eta looked for the voice through the haze in her mind. She found it in the form of a young warrior standing up on the wall. Tilting her head up caused another wave of dizziness. *I need to get inside,* was all she could manage to say. Fighting the visions sapped her strength.

Not a chance, the warrior said. *The gate is closed unless you have orders directly from the Elders. We're under high alert right now.*

I am an Apprentice... she said.

Doesn't matter, the warrior said stoically. *Unless you have direct orders, I'm going to need you to turn around and head back toward the center of the city.*

Eta couldn't deal with this right now. How was she supposed to explain who she was *and* wrestle the visions at the same time? This was precisely the reason she never wanted to be Grand Elder. Her regular visions were hard enough, but whatever was afflicting her now was a leviathan she had never dealt with before. She couldn't fight a battle on two fronts.

Please... she whispered, placing her fingers on the gate. She was so tired, but the urging wanted her to move.

She heard the warrior's voice raise and then cut off. Another smooth voice entered the conversation coming from the other side of the gate. The words were lost to her, but she recognized Mikah's lean body stand from where he was sitting near the edge of the quarries. She could see his lips move and hear the sound but couldn't make sense of the words. She was too distracted and needed to get inside.

She must have said the last part out loud because Mikah spoke to the warrior with those honeyed words of his, and the gate rose up. On the other side, Mikah's face turned from one of confusion to one of thinly veiled concern. He spoke to her, but she couldn't form words; the need to descend into the pit was too great.

There was a path that zig-zagged back and forth, down through the several tiers of the quarry. She wiped the sweat out of her eyes and followed it downward. It would be a long way to walk, but she couldn't feel her legs anyway. Something was at the bottom that needed her.

Now that she was on her way again, the relentless need eased a little, as if satiated by her progress. She was able to see through the myriad of visions and noticed footsteps close by. Looking around, she noticed Mikah was following her, hands in his pockets like he was out for an afternoon stroll.

Why are you following me? she asked, picking her way carefully down the path. There were the occasional loose rocks and pickaxes left lying around.

So somebody knows where you are when you pass out, he

replied. Eta felt like he was invading her space, her life, over the past few days. He had tried to involve himself in her research, involved himself with Ekbal, and now he was following her. It may have been the visions she fought or how wretched she felt right now, but anger heated her clammy skin.

She turned back toward him, *I don't know what you are trying to do, but I won't let you manipulate me like you do everyone else.* She turned back down the path and kept walking; the need to move wouldn't let her stop.

I wouldn't dare assume to manipulate you of all people, Mikah said evenly. His voice rang of truth, but how could she be so sure? The visions picked up their pace again, swirling like water coming up from a drain.

Eta's muscles ached like she had been walking for years, and her mouth was as parched as desert sand. She had to slow down when the path got steep, holding on to the side, but it was hard to see past the visions. At one point, she stumbled, nearly going headfirst down into the pit, but Mikah was at her elbow. She stopped and immediately pushed him away, not knowing if he was real or if the visions were.

I'm just trying to help you, he said quietly, staying where she pushed him. She glared at him, not saying a word, trying to get air into her lungs. The sky was tilting above them, and she held onto the wall tighter. When she didn't move—or stop glaring—Mikah sighed and shrugged his shoulders.

You were right, he said finally. At her puzzled face, he continued. *I do wear a mask. All the time and with everyone. I have my reasons, but regardless, it doesn't work with you, so I'm not trying to force it.*

Eta looked him over. He was just standing there, waiting for her to respond. She shivered against the rock. He didn't have his usual charming smile, his eyes were tired, and his shoulders curled slightly inward. Once she thought about it, ironically, her visions had warned her about everything *except* Mikah. Now was not the time to debate whether or not she trusted the man standing in front of her, but she fought back the visions long enough to give a nod of her head.

A truce, if only in the slightest.

Unfortunately, her moment of silence had allowed him to look her over too, and his face had creased with concern. *Eta, you look like you are going to drop dead. What's going on?* he asked, looking into her face.

She shook her head once, trying not to scream at the over-whelming visions. *Down,* she said desperately, looking behind him toward the bottom of the pit.

Mikah nodded, not understanding but not questioning her either. He moved to help her, letting her hold onto one arm and wrapping the other around her waist. On the legs of a newborn colt, she started back down the path. It took a painstakingly long time to make it to the bottom. She did feel like this might kill her if she didn't get to her destination soon. Where was her destination? She had no idea, but the urging in her mind kept her going.

Mikah didn't say a word until they stopped on the bottom level. *Now where?* he asked, looking around. The rim of the quarry was high above them, and the lowest level was only thirty or so feet wide. On the other side of the path, she spotted a cave that the workers had been focused on. She started toward it, Mikah helping her along.

He didn't speak again as they entered the dark cave. The temperature dropped once they were inside, and Eta was shivering violently, barely able to stay upright. The tattoo on her back burned like the sun.

There was only one way down, and they followed that path into the dark. Before they truly couldn't see, Mikah grabbed one of the torches that had been left by the workers and lit it, but Eta could have found her way in the dark. She had a feeling now of where they were going and what they would find. Like a memory long forgotten, it came bubbling up to the surface.

They finally turned the corner and found the end of the cave, the back wall a few feet in front of them. The barrage of visions finally stopped, but she knew what she had to do. In the corner of the small area down by the floor was a crevice with a tiny stream of water flowing out, only to wind down a few feet away and disappear under the wall again.

Eta dropped to her knees, dipped her fingers into the water, and let herself be consumed by the vision that was waiting.

It was the first vision she had of the river. She was someone who was not herself, and the river was a blissful relief against the relentless heat of the desert. The people arrived, falling into the water like it was the greatest gift they could have received.

The heat from the desert rose up, and a mirage spread out before her, turning the river and sand into a white city. It was familiar, but not. She saw it from above, feeling the currents of the air under her wings. The river still wound its course, but it was smaller. Glowing blue stones had been found in the river and were placed in locations of honor. Crops were planted along the river to feed the people in the city. A wall was built.

The city changed again; the river even smaller as the city grew larger. Trees dotted the horizon; the desert was slowly becoming a forest.

The trees moved in closer, converging toward the city. The river was gone, cracked earth where it used to lie. Wide boulevards were paved over the riverbed, and the walls got higher. The walls kept growing, higher and higher, until they reached the clouds. Eta could only see inside through the eyes of a bird. As she drifted over, she could see the people inside were trapped in the beautiful city of their own making.

She tilted her wings, flying over the land further from the city. The earth grew hot again, slowly. Other cities burned, oceans turned black with sludge, and smog filled the sky. It was horrible. She didn't like this future, so she turned back to the white city, but it had fallen apart like sand and drifted away in the wind. There was nowhere to go now.

Somewhere in her mind, Eta heard her name being called, gently coaxing her back to the surface. She wanted to follow the voice and go back to a place that didn't burn her eyes and sear her lungs, but something pulled her deeper. Something else far away called to her.

The scene changed, and Eta was not Eta again. She walked along a metal hallway, familiar gray robes getting caught in her feet. Along the hallway were walls of windows on both sides, looking out into the massive city. The rainstorm shrouded most of it, but Eta-not-Eta knew it was a city of the future, filled with skyscrapers, flashing lights, and vehicles that flew by her on the twenty-seventh floor.

She was ushered along in line with many others in gray robes like her own into a large circular room crowded with people. Floor-to-ceiling windows wrapped all the way around, allowing them to see more of the dark, rainy city. Inside was warm, though. Humans and Anunnaki alike waited in anticipation, facing something in front of the room. Since she was a child, she was moved to the front of the room with the others, and they got to see what everyone was looking at.

A human king stood smiling before a throne at the back of the room, holding out a wreath of peace as they did every year. The man shifted, and Eta-not-Eta could see a beautiful and wise old queen take the wreath. On both sides of the throne were others in white robes, and only one black-clad figure, standing to the right of her throne.

As the old queen took the wreath, people in the room cheered; for both her and the human king. Anunnaki and humans held hands as they did on this day every year, marking another turn around the sun in peace.

It was another future. A different one. Not set in stone, but still a possibility. Eta clung to this one as hard as she could, refusing to let go. But as the cheering grew louder, the scene turned blurry, and she fell back into reality.

The urging had finally stopped when Eta opened her eyes. She looked up and found she was lying in Mikah's lap, fear and trust both set on his face.

Eta looked up at him and smiled. *I know how we came to be.*

CHAPTER 15
INTO THE FIRE

This is the bad kind of déjà vu, Kinza thought, looking at the dust settling over the rubble that was Vivienne Moreau's office. Most of the front wall had collapsed out into the street, as well as part of the wall leading into the hallway of the building.

Kinza stood from a crouch, trying to pick Zaid out from the mess. Thankfully the two security guards looked fine as they pulled themselves up from the dust, but there was a lot of screaming coming from outside. Sirens wailed in the distance.

The moment she spotted Zaid on the far side of the room, he gave her a look that said, *Seriously?* She threw an apologetic smile and went to find Vivienne, who was still locked in the back room with Minesh. She heard shouting again behind her and found Kiaan turning part of the rubble to mud again and Zaid trying to get to him without moving at the speed of sound.

They needed to get out of there before the police showed up.

The door was locked, and Kinza tried banging on it again,

wishing she had some sort of strength ability at the moment. They had minutes before the police arrived, and Kinza didn't have time to mess around. A little further down the wall, she found a fire extinguisher, smashed the case open, and started bludgeoning the door handle with it. On the fourth swing, the door flung open.

A waiting fist collided with Kinza's face, sending her back to the ground outside the door. She gasped at the sudden pain and dizziness. Above her, Vivienne was beating Minesh over the head with a keyboard—or trying to. Minesh may have not been tall, but there was still considerable weight to him, and he shoved Vivienne away easily. The papers he had tried to get her to sign were scattered all over the room as if she had thrown them.

From her spot on the ground, Kinza could just make out the flashing lights from the police who had just arrived outside the building and were shouting, presumably for them to put their hands in the air. From the sound of it, there was a helicopter flying above them as well.

The heat was still burning in Kinza's stomach, and she had to use all of her focus not to erupt into a human fireball, another explosion, or anything else unnatural. The situation was bad enough, but if the humans caught their abilities on camera, it would only hurt Rhapta.

Vivienne managed to get past Minesh and ran by Kinza into the crumbling hallway and out toward the police. Kinza saw that Kiaan had blood running down one side of his face, and teeth bared at Zaid. They were both standing close to the fallen wall, and the police had the building surrounded just outside, guns pointed in their direction.

This was really, really bad.

Kinza turned to find Minesh coming toward her, hate on his face. She scrambled backward, trying to get to her feet. She caught sight of Zaid, who saw Minesh coming for her, and he moved to help her.

"Don't!" Kinza screamed at Zaid, eyeing the police who were now coming into the building. It looked like they had gone so far as to bring in some sort of SWAT team, barking orders at them, guns pointed. In all fairness, it did look like they had blown up a building in the middle of Paris. That was more than a petty crime.

As Minesh came out of the room, he finally saw the police as well. Zaid looked like he wanted to sprint over to her, but they had all frozen now that the authorities had arrived. With a single glance at his apprentice, Minesh backed away and fled down the side hallway.

The police swarmed the building then, and the three of them that were remaining put their hands in the air. They weren't getting out of this one. Kinza didn't understand a word that was yelled at her as a police officer forced her to the ground, face down and hands behind her back as she was handcuffed. She couldn't see Zaid or Kiaan but assumed they were doing the same.

Don't say anything. I'll figure a way out, Zaid's voice came in her mind.

What was I going to say? she said back to him. *I have magic powers that are hard to control sometimes, and I accidentally blew up the building. Oops, sorry?*

Kinza, now is not the time for— Zaid's exasperated voice in her mind cut out, and she turned her head to see he was hauled to his feet by two men and shoved toward a waiting van. Kinza didn't see where they took Kiaan or if they captured Minesh, but she was soon taken to a similar van as Zaid, shoved inside, and left in the dark as the door was shut.

Kinza decided that Vivienne was most likely not going to help them.

ZAID HAD ALWAYS WONDERED what the inside of a jail looked like. He had never been caught, of course; way too fast for humans to catch. He quickly decided he hated every second of it. No windows. Locked doors. Cold steel and hard chairs. Not his cup of tea.

He had let them handcuff him and take him to an unmarked building that was probably a special location for special prisoners. He was thrown inside a damp cell, but it didn't last for long before they transferred him to an interrogation room, cuffed him to a table that was bolted to the floor, and left him there. The only other things in the room were two cameras in the corners and a one-way mirror. It was laughable that they thought any of this could hold him. He could've snapped the handcuffs at any time; the problem was that he was being watched. Other than the two cameras, he could hear three heartbeats on the other side of the mirror. He could hear several other heartbeats in the building but didn't sense Kinza's Aura close by. He needed to find a way to get out, get her, and leave without being seen.

After fifteen minutes, one of the heartbeats behind the glass left and then entered the interrogation room in the form of a man with a smiling face and a very shiny, bald head. He had a badge clipped to his immaculate gray suit with a picture of his face on it.

"Hello," the man said, taking a seat across from Zaid. "You speak English, yes?"

Zaid didn't speak, nor was he going to.

The man pursed his lips a little. "My name is Detective Lemaire. Can I get your name?" After a moment of continued silence, he opened a folder he had brought with him. "I see you didn't have any identification on you either. You can give me any name you'd like," Detective Lemaire said.

Zaid wasn't falling for it. Regardless, venari training had included what to do if, for some reason, you were captured by humans. Basically, say nothing and hope for the best. Anything that could potentially link you to Rhapta would be very bad.

Detective Lemaire glanced up, giving Zaid a long assessing look, and cocked his head slightly. When Zaid didn't answer, he closed the folder and laced his fingers over the file. "I'm just here to help you," he said. "You're not in any kind of trouble. We are just trying to find out what happened to the building and why there was a brawl."

Lies. Zaid knew he was a suspect, and any information would only add to that.

"How about we start with something easy," the detective said with a calming smile. "What were you doing this morning?"

Silence. The heartbeats behind the mirror shifted, as if anxious.

"All right, I see that wasn't easy," Detective Lemaire said with a chuckle. "How about you tell me about your two companions," he said, opening the file back up. "The young man and that *woman*?" He said the last word with a distasteful look on his face.

Zaid wanted to shake the man for addressing Kinza like that, but the anger was quickly replaced by pride. If they didn't mention her name and seemed so annoyed with her, that meant she hadn't said anything. She was being difficult for them instead of giving in.

Detective Lemaire winced at the silence. "I really do want to help you," he said. "But if you aren't going to meet me halfway, then things might get a little difficult for you around here, if you know what I mean." He raised his bushy eyebrows.

Zaid just looked at him and settled more comfortably into his chair.

The detective's eyes hardened. "I'll tell you what I think happened. I think you and your accomplices staged an attack on a very prominent woman in France, but something went awry. You and the other guy got into a fight, and the girl went after Ms. Moreau. That's when the local police force arrived. That's correct, isn't it?" he asked, total confidence in his theory.

It didn't matter what he believed. Zaid was going to be out of here before morning.

"I thought so," Detective Lemaire said, nodding. "The part we are having trouble figuring out is, we didn't find any evidence of explosives, or a faulty gas line, or any chemical substances. If you can just let me know what you used, I can help you shorten your sentence." He gave off an encouraging youth counselor type of persona, and Zaid couldn't stand it.

He wanted to laugh at the man. If he knew what had caused the explosion, his eyes would fall out of their sockets in disbelief. He could tell the man that woman they had was a living bomb day and night, that she could level this entire building if she really wanted to... but that wouldn't help their situation at all.

The detective sat in silence then, staring at Zaid for several minutes before he nodded, picked up his folder, and left. Shortly after the door clicked shut, Zaid sensed his heartbeat walk around to the room behind the glass where the other two people were. They watched him for another twenty minutes before two of them left.

Several other investigators came over the next few hours. Some were playing the good cop, and others played the bad cop. One of them even threatened that he was a national security risk and could be looking at twenty-five to life in a federal prison. Zaid never said a word. Every time they came and left,

Zaid would look out into the hallway, gathering as much information as he could. There were definitely ID scanners at every door in this building, and he was sure there were cameras everywhere.

The only part that really bothered him was that they took his fingerprints and a picture of his face. He assumed they would run his prints against a national database, but now that meant he was in a system, and that could make his job as a venari in the future very difficult. He would need to talk to Laiq and see if this were something he could deal with later.

The building had extremely tight security, that was for sure. The heartbeats always went left when they exited the room, meaning that had to be the way out, or at least to common areas. That meant that one of the few heartbeats to his right would have to be Kinza's, assuming they actually brought her here. Other than that, the only way for him to go unseen was to kill the cameras or the lights somehow. The alternative was that he waited until they brought him somewhere else, but human prisons weren't co-ed, so he and Kinza would be separated sooner or later.

He couldn't let that happen, so he was going to have to go on half a plan.

Hours had gone by since the last person had come into the room. It must have been night by now, having spent all day here. They hadn't given him any food, water, or let him use the bathroom, not that he needed any of that. They were probably trying to starve him out, see if he would break once he got uncomfortable. The thought almost made him laugh.

It must have been another few hours later when Detective Lemaire came back with an artificially apologetic look on his face. Did he seriously think Zaid would believe this charade?

"Sorry about the long wait," he said, sitting down. No

folder this time, just a Styrofoam cup of coffee. "We'll get you some pretzels soon, hopefully."

Hopefully meaning that he might not get to eat soon. A scare tactic. *You are clever and cruel, Lemaire,* Zaid thought to himself. It wouldn't matter; he would be gone soon. Now was as good a time as any.

"Remind me what your name is again?" Detective Lemaire asked.

"Zaid."

The detective's head came up, reigning in the surprise that Zaid had spoken. He shifted in his seat, excited at the breakthrough. "Zaid. Thank you. I just had a few more questions for you, if you don't mind?"

"Not at all."

The detective looked at him carefully. "I never asked if you knew the other young man. Did you know him prior to today?"

"Somewhat."

"Care to elaborate?"

"No."

"Mhmm." The detective made some notes in his files. Zaid sensed the two heartbeats behind the mirror, picking up their pace at his words.

"And what were you doing at Vivienne Moreau's office?"

"Business."

"And tell me about the explosion."

"It happened."

"Do you speak French?"

"A little."

Detective Lemaire thought for a moment. "Where are you from, by the way? I'm not familiar with your accent."

"Africa."

"That's a whole continent. Could you narrow it down?"

"No."

Lemaire leaned back, taking a gulp of his coffee. He seemed to be getting a little annoyed. "Do you have any family?"

"Yes."

"And the young girl. Tell me about her."

"She's—" Zaid hesitated, thinking carefully.

"Yes?" Lemaire said, leaning forward.

"She knows how the explosion happened." The heartbeats behind the mirror and Lemaire's own were beating faster now. Zaid had thrown them a bone.

"Did she now? Can you tell me more?"

"No."

Lemaire looked him over and seemed to realize that Zaid wasn't going to tell him much more. "All right, thank you for your cooperation. You'll be transferred to a holding cell for now, but you and I will talk again soon, Zaid. Have a good night."

The heartbeats behind the glass had left the moment he mentioned Kinza, and there was only one other out in the hall, probably a guard. Lemaire stood, grabbed his empty coffee cup, and headed to the door. The moment he scanned his badge, Zaid moved.

Zaid snapped his wrists up with a strength the handcuffs weren't meant to hold. The chain holding the cuffs together broke, and he was already away from the table. Lemaire didn't have time to turn around before Zaid smashed the cameras and the light, throwing them into the dark. He threw one solid punch at the man, and he dropped like a sack of potatoes.

Zaid only waited for two breaths; one to make sure Lemaire was breathing and the other to prepare himself because he needed to be very fast.

On the exhale of the second breath, he opened the door and burst into the hall.

KINZA GLARED at the sole camera in the room as she had been for the past thirty minutes. That was the last time anyone had come to check on her. And it had been hours before that.

They had brought her to one of the interrogation rooms, and a few of their detectives had come in, but it didn't take them long to realize they weren't getting anything out of her. She sat with her arms crossed and zero expression on her face. In reality, she was concentrating *very* hard not to turn into a fireball. They had brought up the explosion several times, asking her what had happened or if she had done it. Thankfully they hadn't whipped out the lie-detector machine yet. Otherwise, she would have been toast with that one.

Her neck had been tingling all day and had only let up a little when they had left her alone for a while. That didn't mean she was safe, though. She was trapped in a French correctional system with no ID, no idea where Zaid was, and no way out. She was acutely aware that any number of things could be happening in Rhapta or with Tahir, and she would have no idea.

After they had put her in the van, she hadn't seen Zaid or Kiaan, so there was a chance Zaid wasn't even in the same building she was in. They also hadn't told her if they caught Minesh... not that she gave them any names. Even though she despised the Elder and his apprentice, giving names would only come back to bite her later.

All in all, she had absolutely no idea where she was, no idea where Zaid was, no idea what time it was, and no idea how to get out. This whole plan of "just showing up" at Vivienne's had been her stupid idea as well. If she had just gone with Zaid's plan to scope the place out for a few days, they wouldn't be in this position. *Good job, Kinza.*

She mulled over how to get herself out first, but every plan she came up with was ruined by the fact there were cameras everywhere. She thought about asking to be moved to a different location, but that would only sound suspicious. They would probably move her eventually—to jail—since they weren't getting any information out of her. What was taking so long?

Kinza was in a foul mood for the next hour as she sat in the small room. She was mentally discarding her seventeenth escape plan when she heard voices outside the door. It sounded like someone was coming down the hall, maybe two people. She steeled herself for another lengthy interrogation.

She heard the ID scanner beep just outside the door when the lights went out. The confused voices outside the door stopped as well.

"Um, hello?" Kinza said out loud, hoping the cameras could at least pick up sound. They wouldn't leave her in the dark, would they?

The door opened, but no light from the hallway spilled in, and no one spoke. The tingling on the back of Kinza's neck started up full throttle, and her heart followed suit. It's not that she was afraid of the dark; it's just—

Something grabbed onto her arm.

Out of reflex, Kinza inhaled to scream but found a hand clamping over her mouth. She struggled, and the chain connecting her handcuffs snapped. Whoever it was moved to wrap their arms around her and lift her off her feet, leaving her mouth exposed. She went to scream again when a voice popped into her head.

Kinza, don't! Zaid said. *We have to be quiet.*

She stopped struggling, and he put her down. *Zaid?!* She

couldn't see a thing but spun around and looked in his general direction. *I thought we agreed no more kidnapping?!* she mentally hissed at him. *You nearly scared me into my grave. Ugh!* She tugged her shirt back into place and tried to calm her frantic heart.

We cannot make a sound, he said. *I killed the lights, but they might have a backup generator to turn on. We need to go.* He moved toward the door.

Do you know how to get out? Kinza asked.

Vaguely. We are just going to have to hope for the best. Don't blow anything else up.

I'll try, she said. He then picked her up and was out the door running. The moment they were out in the hall, Kinza realized the alarms were blaring and flashing lights every few seconds, lighting up the corridor.

What about the cameras? she asked.

I disabled as many as I could before coming to get you. Zaid turned a corner and immediately turned around, running the other way. It was eerily quiet.

How did *you find me?* Kinza asked. The building was much smaller than she had thought it was, but trying to find the way out was like trying to escape a hedge maze in the dark while someone was screaming at you, and monsters could appear at any moment. She saw the occasional prone body lying on the ground and assumed those were the people Zaid knocked out.

I may have told the detectives that you blew up the building.

You what?!

I figured they would head straight back to you, so I followed their heartbeats.

Kinza had to admit that was clever... but not out loud. At least Zaid could use his abilities to get them out of this situation. All Kinza's would do is destroy everything around her, and she hadn't practiced with her Aura enough to do much else with it, even though Jabari had said she should be able to use it in many ways.

They heard shouting coming from the direction they were headed and turned to go a different way. Zaid exhaled in frustration. *That's the way out.*

Is there a back way in? Kinza suggested. It was the most she could do since Zaid was doing all the work. *Like a service entrance?*

Maybe...

A few seconds later, Zaid stopped before an unmarked door that looked different from the ones outside the interrogation rooms. He set her down and tried the handle. Of course it was locked. *There's no ID scanner.*

Can't you just bust it open? Kinza asked, looking around to make sure no one was sneaking up on them. It was hard to see between the flashing lights of the alarms, but it looked clear.

Zaid backed up and rammed the door with his shoulder.

Nothing.

He tried again, but the noise was making Kinza nervous. Someone was going to hear it and come looking for them. *I think this might be a security door. They're reinforced with iron bars inside when the alarms are triggered. It's kind of like a fire door,* she said. *Look, it even has a special keypad on the door. Do you know the code?*

Zaid sighed and looked around. *No. Come one, let's try somewhere else.*

No, let me try quick, Kinza said. If they kept running through the halls in circles, someone was bound to show up eventually, and they would have to explain how they managed to escape. Not to mention the charges for incapacitating an entire floor's worth of state officials are probably not great.

Kinza stepped up to the door and took a deep breath. *Might as well try to be useful. The worst that could happen is we get out faster.* She put her hands over the lock and concentrated first on the tingling in her neck, slowly moving to the heat that sat in her abdomen under her tattoo. She coaxed it gently, like luring a feral cat out of a cage that could turn on you at any second and swipe. It didn't betray her, though. Kinza's Aura flared gently around her body before descending only to her hands over the lock.

Zaid put a hand on her shoulder. *Kinza, what are you—*

The lock popped, and the keypad fizzled. They heard iron bars slide back, and the door opened slightly.

It worked!

Okay, I'm a little impressed, Zaid said as she grinned up at him in the flashing lights. On the other side of the door was a stairwell that led down. The same alarms were going off here as well, and there were no voices, as opposed to the ones that were now getting louder in the opposite direction down the hall.

Time to go, Zaid said, scooping her up and dashing down the stairs. The rest of the way through the building moved like a blur. The stairwell did indeed go down two floors to the ground, which led down a short hallway and out into the night. The first thing they noticed was that none of the alarms could be heard outside; the chaos was only happening within the building. It definitely looked like the middle of the night, though, so it wouldn't be surprising if they only had a skeleton crew right now.

Zaid didn't put her down and kept running. They seemed to still be in the city, just on an unfamiliar side of it. Kinza didn't complain as Zaid ran for a long time, making them nothing more than a dark wind whipping through the city at night. It was better to put some distance between them and the police.

He finally stopped by an alley in a silent part of town. The area must have been only small businesses because no one was walking around, and no lights were on in the nearby buildings. Zaid and Kinza were both trying to catch their breath.

"Why are you tired?" Zaid asked.

"I'm not," Kinza replied. "That was just scary."

Zaid snorted. "Let's not get arrested again."

"Agreed one-hundred percent with you on that one," she said. "Back to the hotel?"

Zaid shook his head. "I think we should leave; get out of the city as fast as we can. And no vacations here in the near future."

"Yeah, I actually wanted to come back next weekend." Zaid shoved her playfully, and they started walking to Chloe's apartment.

It took them almost thirty minutes to find it in the dark, and by then, there were sirens on the other side of Paris. Kinza was acutely aware the police were out looking for them. Zaid had said he got the cameras, but what if he missed one? What would they have seen? A man moving at ridiculous speeds? A woman who started glowing and opened a locked door with her hands? Hopefully, they saw nothing at all.

They rang the buzzer four times before Chloe stuck her head out of the window three floors up. "Do you have any idea what time it is?" she said, still in her pajamas. Without waiting for an answer, she pulled back in, and the door buzzed open.

They climbed the narrow staircase to Chloe's floor. She already had the door open and ushered them inside. Once they were in the tiny living room, she turned to look at them standing in the middle of her apartment.

"*What have you done?*"

Kɪɴᴢᴀ ʟᴇᴛ Zaid fill Chloe in, who chewed him out in French. She didn't need to speak the language to know getting caught was very bad. Hopefully Savar and Balasi wouldn't skin them alive when they returned to Rhapta for the mess they caused. They didn't even have anything to show for it either. All they had was Edmund, and that would have to do.

The rest of the night happened in a blur for Kinza. Chloe opened the portal to Moshi, the town just outside of Mount Kilimanjaro, and Bahati was waiting for them, looking just as displeased as Chloe was about the time of night. It was only an hour ahead and still dark out. Zaid said a few weary words to Bahati, and they left.

Kinza followed Zaid through the little town to a hotel that happened to be open all night for tourists. Zaid probably could have just run them all the way to the city from here, but he looked drained, and Kinza was dead on her feet from the lack of sleep. They booked a room for one night and climbed the stairs.

"We can go in the morning. I just need a few hours of sleep," Zaid said, heading right for one of the beds.

"If you wake me up before eight, you're carrying me," she replied. That would only give her a few hours of sleep, but even that much felt like a dream right now. It had been a strenuously long day, and tomorrow was going to be hard as well. Somehow she had to explain that she only got one of the two remaining human-Anunnaki to side with them and that they happened to get arrested. Oh, and that she blew up a building in Paris.

At the very least, it would have been nice if they had apprehended Kiaan or Minesh. Unfortunately, Kiaan was still with the French police, and who knew what kind of information they would get out of him? She had no idea what happened to

Minesh either, so both he, Tahir, and one other Elder were out in the world.

This was a disaster.

She only hoped that the Elders and apprentices had come up with some way to deal with the barrier. If not, she would be their only option, and she hadn't made any headway with that either.

As Kinza lay on the other bed, her mind wouldn't stop running; like a hamster on a wheel, it turned and turned despite how tired she was. People were counting on her and expected her to take care of them, even though she was the one who left her life behind to help them. Her tiredness was more than just a lack of sleep. It went bone-deep, and the fear of failing so many people kept her awake for longer than she should have been.

For the next few hours, as Zaid slept, Kinza stared at the ceiling, turning ideas over and over, trying to find a way to get all of them through this.

CHAPTER 16

IN THE SHADOW OF THE MOUNTAIN

Kinza woke to the sound of a truck rolling by her window. She peeled her eyes open to find Zaid awake, dressed, and pulling the curtain back to look out the window.

"What time is it?" she mumbled into the pillow.

"Get up," he said. "We need to hurry."

"Yes, I'm aware. That's why—"

"No," Zaid said, interjecting her, voice hard as steel. "Tahir is here."

Kinza flew out of bed, stumbling toward the window. All traces of sleep were slipping away as she looked outside. Her heart started pounding at the sight of at least five massive military vehicles driving by their window. People were crowding the street corners, also watching the trucks. Kinza swore she heard a helicopter somewhere as well.

Zaid laid a hand on her shoulder, and the hammering in her chest eased only slightly. "What's going on?" she whispered.

"Remember how Tahir is a sore loser?" Zaid said bitterly. "Well, this is him flipping the board after he lost a match."

Kinza couldn't help the clenching of her jaw. She left the window and went into the bathroom to splash water on her face. There were little complimentary toothbrushes that she used to scrub her teeth hard enough that her gums started to bleed, and her tongue felt raw. The taste of blood was a terrible omen for the day to come.

When she went back out into the main room, Zaid was ready to go with a grim look on his face. They waited until there were no trucks nearby before stepping outside. The morning was already warm as they checked out and started walking down the street. Zaid kept them hidden in the crowd, going as far as finding them both new clothes, hats, and sunglasses to change into. The new clothes made her feel slightly fresher, but an oily feeling wouldn't leave her stomach.

Zaid's phone rang as they were weaving in and out of throngs of people walking down the road. It was busier than the last few times Kinza had been here, and they kept finding more military vehicles parked around corners as if waiting for something.

Zaid talked on the phone for a few minutes, stopping at a street corner out of the way. He didn't look much happier when he hung up.

"Who was that?" Kinza asked.

"Haris," Zaid replied. "He and Mitra had to follow Basma all the way down to Louisiana. They think Basma knows she is being followed."

"Wow, that's quite the trip," Kinza said.

"Yeah. Haris talked with a few other Ummanu around the world. Sounds like some of the portals have been acting up recently, like in the last few days."

"Acting up how?"

He shrugged. "Haris said it was hard to say, but some of them not connecting to other portals correctly, or sending people to the wrong location. Apparently one of them shut down altogether."

"That sounds bad," Kinza said, biting a fingernail and keeping an eye on one of the trucks that had just circled the block. It didn't look like they were looking for anyone, though, just killing time.

"Yeah," Zaid said with a sigh.

They walked to the edge of the little town toward the larger bus station. Normally there were buses going in and out all day, most of which were taking tourists on day tours toward the mountain or shuttling hikers back and forth. Right now, nearly every stall was full, and the buses were out of service. Zaid looked frustrated, and Kinza followed him around the other side of the station into the parking lot to get a glimpse of the mountain. The sight sent white-hot fear through Kinza's chest.

A long train of military vehicles trailed along the highway toward the mountain as far as her eye could see.

"Terrible day for business, eh?" Kinza and Zaid pulled out of their horrified state to find a wisp of a man standing next to them. He looked like he had spent every day of his life in the sun and chewed on a toothpick while looking in the same direction as they were.

"Ah, yeah, I guess," Kinza said. "Do you know what's going on?" she asked.

The man spit before saying, "Not really. Just that all tours stopped yesterday, and then these people showed up, covering every inch of Moshi and roped off entrances to the mountain. A friend of mine said they found something, but he's not the most truthful, you see."

"So they won't let people up the mountain at all?" Zaid asked.

The man shook his head. "No, and I would know. I'm a tour guide. I told them I don't get paid days off... they didn't care. I just hope they leave soon." He spit again.

"And if someone *really* wanted to get up the mountain?" Zaid asked slowly.

The man turned, took the toothpick out of his mouth, and looked Zaid over with a squint in one eye. "If someone *really* wanted to go up, I'm sure there's a trail... somewhere. It's probably hidden, though." He turned away from them.

Zaid pulled a couple of bills out of his pocket and handed them over. "I'm sure the trail is less hidden than you think it is."

The man chuckled and looked them over again before pulling a folded-up pamphlet out of the back of his pocket. It was the kind you gave to tourists with all the local must-see spots. He unfolded it to the map inside and grabbed a pen that was wedged behind his ear.

"The is the main entrance that everyone takes here," he said, pointing to a familiar road on the map. "But there *might* be a smaller, less known path a few more miles down the road. I've heard here and there that it's for the adrenaline junkies because it's so steep, even while traveling through the forest to *get* to the mountain itself. It would take at least a week to get to the top from there."

They weren't trying to get to the top, though. The entrance to the barrier around Rhapta was in the forest surrounding the mountain and only a mile or two up. This route would just take them further east than they needed to be, but they could cut across from there. The hard part would be finding their way back west with no trail, but the man didn't need to know that.

The man drew a line from the entrance to the top of the

mountain. "This isn't the gentle slope that the main entrance has. It's a very steep, rocky incline and requires a lot of stamina. I suppose you look like a mountain goat, though," he said, looking at Zaid's biceps.

Zaid moved to take the map, but the man snatched it away. "I've lost enough money today already."

Pulling a few more bills out of his pocket had the man shoving the map into Zaid's hands. "Like I said, it's *possible* there is a trail there, but you didn't hear it from me. And of course, the military isn't allowing anyone to go up today."

"Of course," Zaid said. "Have a good one."

The man tipped his head in their direction and sauntered off, counting the bills.

"You think we can make it up from there?" Kinza asked. "Isn't there another door we can take?"

"There are other entrances, but I've honestly never used them," Zaid said as they walked back around the bus station. "Regardless, I think we need to give this a shot. Cutting across the forest will be the hardest part without knowing exactly where we are, but the alternative is to wait until they leave. *If* they leave."

Kinza scowled. "That's not an option," she said firmly. After everything she had been through, leaving Rhapta to defend themselves against the humans was the last thing she would do. She would be with them for better or for worse. "We need to get going then if we are going to beat them. Can you run?"

Zaid shook his head. "I'd get too tired going straight up the mountain, especially carrying someone. And I don't know where I'm going for the second half. All right, let's find a car and go right away. I don't want to wait any longer."

FORTY-FIVE MINUTES LATER, they were driving down the highway in a borrowed pickup truck, keeping their eyes out in case there were any military checkpoints. It would be rather awkward when they found out neither of them had any ID nor owned the truck.

The ride was tense, and Kinza waited for something bad to happen. She kept the local radio on low, nearly expecting to hear the host cut in with breaking news about a hidden city found near Mount Kilimanjaro. Or maybe there would be sirens or fireworks. Maybe they'd cut down the entire forest, looking for anything else that was hidden.

They took the exit off the highway to the frontage road that ran closest to the base of the mountain. There were several exits to their left for hikers, but all were blocked off. There were very few cars on this road that weren't military, and all along the left side were parked military trucks, cars, and vans. The road wound east, and they passed the exit they took last time, driving for another mile or so. The road itself narrowed, and traffic dwindled until they came to a stop at the last stoplight before they truly moved away from the towns.

There was another camp of military vehicles on the left side of the road here, and Kinza's heart hammered, expecting them to notice them and make them stop. The light had been red for a while, and no other civilian cars were around when Kinza glanced to the left, past Zaid. She watched as two people stepped out of the back of one of the vans, speaking to each other. When the second person came into view, she thought her heart would burst from fear.

Tahir.

On pure adrenaline, Kinza leaned over and slammed her

foot down on the gas, lurching the truck forward a half-second before the light turned green.

"Kinza, what are you—!" Zaid shouted.

"Drive!" Kinza screamed, and thankfully Zaid listened, going top speed down the road, around a bend, and kept going for two more minutes before slowing down.

Kinza was breathing hard, head between her knees, when the truck slowed to a normal speed.

"You want to tell me what that was about?" Zaid said, glancing in the rearview mirror.

Kinza twisted around to look out the back window. When she was satisfied they weren't being followed, she turned off the radio just in case and said, "It was Tahir. He was with them."

"What?!" Zaid said. Now it was his turn to panic, glancing at the side mirrors every two seconds. "Are you sure? I didn't sense any Auras."

"Were you looking for them? And yes, it was definitely him." She kept looking out the back, but there was no one else on the road. Even the military vehicles hadn't come this far.

Zaid's face hardened. "So it was him who did this. He brought these people to Rhapta."

"He seriously would bring humanity to Rhapta's doorstep?" Kinza said, more to herself. She knew that was what he was doing, but truly seeing it was more of a shock. He really wanted to see the city destroyed if he couldn't have it.

They reached the spot on the map shortly and parked the truck off the road in a copse of trees. There weren't many around, and if they had kept driving, it would have turned into more of a rocky landscape; they were right at the eastern edge of the forest.

Getting out of the truck, Kinza noticed the air was slightly cooler here, but they would need it. After looking over the map, they realized the path in front of them wasn't really a path. It was a near-vertical incline up rocks and boulders. They didn't have to go far, maybe half a mile, but a half-mile near-vertical climb very well might be the death of her. They just had to follow the line of the forest on their left and deviate from the path on the map part of the way up.

It was mid-morning already, so they wasted no time talking about it before starting on their way up. Kinza didn't last five minutes before she was panting. Despite the cool air, without the shade of the forest, the sun was free to beat down on their backs and necks.

How long do you think until they get to the doorway? Kinza asked, not wasting her precious breath to speak.

Not sure, Zaid replied. *They'll be slow for sure, even with Tahir guiding them. They'll want to be methodical about it, and they don't have Anunnaki strength or endurance.*

Kinza was wondering if she did either as she hauled herself up onto a boulder jutting out of the hill. She added rock climbing to the list of outdoorsy things she hated. Each step required full concentration now so she wouldn't slip on the loose rocks and fall and crack her skull. Her tank top was soaked through, and she had tied her hair up to keep it off her neck, but she refused to stop. Every time she thought she was too tired to continue, she imagined Tahir and the military convoy breaking down Rhapta's wall, destroying homes, and capturing its people. It gave her renewed strength every time, an anger that boiled in her blood at the thought of someone taking that sense of peace and security from her people.

Kinza could tell Zaid felt the same because he didn't stop either, not even for a slight break. They were racing Tahir and the humans to get to Rhapta first. Not that they had a plan on how to defend them, but at least they would be there. Kinza became more energized as she climbed, caring less about the scrapes and scratches and bruises she got from the stones. They healed as they went, leaving dirt and bits of dried blood behind.

They didn't speak again until Zaid stopped almost two hours later. Kinza's body felt like it was pushed to the point of exhaustion, but she didn't dare sit down.

Okay, west now, Zaid said. *This is going to be the hard part.*

Kinza just followed him, trusting he would guide them in the right direction. Walking along horizontally through the forest wasn't easy by any means, but it practically felt like a beach vacation compared to the climb up. Kinza was quickly swarmed by the mosquitos she loved so much, and her skin felt like it was wearing a warm, wet towel from the humidity. She was pretty sure without the Anunnaki endurance, she would have collapsed long ago.

Kinza tried to walk faster several times, nearly jogging through the forest to get to Rhapta, but was forced to slow down. The trees grew erratically, and vines and roots came out of nowhere. She didn't even bother pulling the cobwebs from her hair and focused instead on keeping her eyes between her feet and Zaid's back. A few times, Zaid slowed to recalculate where they were. Too bad neither of them could fly so they could at least see where they were on the map. There was no cell reception here either, so they could only rely on the forest and the sun to know how far they had gone.

After an hour of walking, Zaid stopped. *We're getting close, but that means the convoy might be close as well. Keep your eyes and ears alert.*

Never turned them off, Kinza said, wiping sweat off her neck.

Zaid rolled his eyes at her. *Then try sensing for Auras as well. Maybe you can locate the city better than I can.*

Doubtful, she replied but followed him more carefully, listening to the sounds of the forest. Every movement made her heart stutter, imagining it was a hidden soldier or Tahir waiting for her behind a tree. They went slower this time, which made Kinza even more anxious. What if they beat them there?

Zaid stopped suddenly, putting a hand up. She didn't hear anything at first until the thundering beat of a helicopter came whooshing overhead. On instinct, they ducked down to the ground as it flew by. They wouldn't be able to see them with the dense canopy. Kinza was about to speak when Zaid tensed up again.

What is it? she asked.

I think there are people close by, Zaid said, looking around through the trees. *We need to hurry. I think we are close, but I'm not one-hundred percent sure.*

Kinza nodded and followed him again in more of an upward direction. Zaid changed his course several times and backtracked once or twice.

Suddenly he dropped to the ground, pulling Kinza with him. He nodded slightly south of the direction they were headed. Kinza didn't see anything at first, but she heard it. An unusual rustling in the leaves. It was coming from a couple locations.

Then she heard voices.

Before they could get any closer, the two of them shuffled back the way they came, only to freeze again a few feet later. More people were coming now from that direction. They hadn't yet noticed them, but Kinza knew that if she could see them, they could see her.

Which way do we go? Kinza asked in a panic.

I'm not sure, Zaid said, looking around. They couldn't move without being seen, and the people were getting closer. Kinza tried to control her breathing, but eventually, they got close enough that she could see they were military personnel.

You're going to need to run, Kinza said finally.

I'm not leaving you! Zaid said incredulously.

Well, of course not. You have to carry me, Kinza said, mildly exasperated.

I don't know which way to go. The door is close, but I've never come from this way. I could find it, but not with the military swarming the forest, Zaid replied, keeping very still.

Just get us away from them, and we can regroup. Zaid, we have to go now.

Okay, he said.

Oh, also, she added, *don't you dare trip.*

Zaid didn't say anything else, and Kinza felt the breath snatched out of her as Zaid hauled her up and sprinted as fast as he could through the forest. All the military would notice was that a strong wind came barreling through, but Kinza could have sworn one of them shouted, "Ghost!"

Despite her warning, Kinza was amazed at how fast Zaid could move through the trees, over roots, and under branches without colliding face-first into something. He ran for several minutes, trying to get away from the military's notice and to find a safe hiding spot. Kinza didn't think it was far enough when he did stop, but they needed to get to the doorway.

They were silent for a few minutes as Zaid panted, looking around to see if they were followed. They heard the helicopter in the far distance but no shouting or odd rustling in the trees. *Now we don't know where we are,* he said.

If Zaid was lost, then so was she. She had a general sense of where they were based on the slope of the mountain, but not how far from the doorway. Instead of feeling sorry for herself, she decided to at least *try* to sense the city.

Kinza closed her eyes and did as Zaid had taught her, mentally looking for a subtle glow in her mind, but attached to someone else. She had to tamp down on her own Aura this time; it was like a dangerous flaming kitten that wanted to come out and play, but now wasn't the time. She was about to give up hope when she mentally saw something to her left. It didn't feel like an Aura to her, though. Instead, it was more like the sky was brighter in that direction... in her mind.

The feeling was odd, and she wasn't sure what it was, but it was worth a shot. *There is something that way,* she said, pointing to their left, up the hill a little. *I don't know if it's an Aura, though.*

Zaid looked in that direction and frowned. *I don't sense anything. What did you see?*

Kinza shrugged but only made it halfway; even her shoulders were weary. *No idea, but that should be the general direction, right?*

Zaid looked displeased. *I suppose, but that's also back the way we came. We could be running into the military.* He looked at her crouched in the bushes, sweat running down his face. Kinza had the sudden feeling that she was very glad she was here with him. Not that she was glad she was *here,* but that it was *him* that was here and not anyone else.

It's try or leave, Kinza said.

Leaving isn't an option, he said, picking her up. She swore she would pay to get him a professional arm massage after this. How he still had arms was beyond her.

Zaid moved slightly slower through the forest, watching his surroundings more that time while still going in the direction she pointed. They didn't have to go far until Zaid picked up the pace, and Kinza knew they had found it. He didn't stop running until the too-thin weight of the barrier passed over them, and he put her down. They didn't walk through, and he grabbed her hand as they jogged through the remainder of the trees and out into the field surrounding Rhapta.

A wave of relief swept through her upon seeing the city

standing and no military trucks in sight. But something still felt off; it was eerily quiet. As they ran toward the wall, the barrier dropped for several seconds before snapping back into place. Up ahead, Kinza could make out the warriors on the wall. There were usually very few of them up there, but she could see at least seven who all spotted her.

They pointed obsidian-tipped arrows at her and Zaid, and two of them came running out of the main gate, obsidian spears pointed at them. As they got close, they saw who it was and immediately let their guard down. Just before they reached the warriors, a sound that would haunt Kinza's nightmares started overhead.

The thundering of the helicopter beat in time with her heart as it flew right above them, seeming to hover just above where they were out in the field, totally exposed. Kinza didn't know much about the Anunnaki Creator they believed in, but she prayed as hard as she could that the barrier stayed up. If it dropped now, it would all be over.

None of them dared breathe as the helicopter circled them once, then twice. The warrior's eyes were like saucers, never having seen something of the like before. It seemed Kinza's prayers were answered because it flew back south again.

In a frantic hurry, they all ran back into the city.

IF THE CITY WAS QUIET, the noise in the main receiving chamber was deafening. Elders, apprentices, scholars, and a few other officials were panicking. Kinza and Zaid had been led, still sweating and exhausted, into the chamber.

The walk through the city had been almost as bad as the night of the battle a few weeks ago. The city was silent again.

People hid in their homes, trying not to make noise or be seen by the helicopter and the occasional drone that flew overhead. It was like they were trying to will themselves out of existence.

The outskirts had been devoid of life; apparently, Khalil had ditched Anunnaki upper-class protocol and herded everyone inside. Kinza could have kissed him. Even the central plaza was practically empty; the only remaining people hurried as if their lives depended on it.

In the Great Hall, someone handed Kinza water and something to eat. She inhaled it like her life depended on it as she listened to the dozens of people demanding her attention. Some people were clamoring for information from her, and others wanted to give her information on their research. Others wanted to know what the plan was when they got captured. It seemed that when she had left, her queenship had still been up in the air, still in question. Now that everything was truly falling apart and no one had any ideas, they looked to her for guidance.

She saw Eta come up to her, leaning heavily against Mikah. It was an odd sight since the last time she saw them in a room together, it looked like Rhapta was about to freeze over.

Kinza, I need to speak with you— Eta said, but an Elder pushed forward.

What news of help from outside? they asked.

Kinza replied. *We do have help from Edmund—*

And what of the others?

What about the humans? someone else asked. *They are outside our doors!*

Yes, I saw them, Kinza said. *And Tahir—*

The room audibly gasped, and the energy became more frantic. The mental weight of all of their voices was becoming tiring. She didn't know how to move forward, and she needed to *think.*

Eta pushed her way forward again. *Kinza, I really need to—*

Do we have help from two of the three human-Anunnaki? a scholar asked loudly. Kinza saw the Apostles of Truth were here as well, and Nim was standing to the side as their representative. He looked as tense and tired as the rest of them. Had only the Elder listened to him and the Apostles, they might not have been in this mess.

No, Kinza replied. *Not the French—*More voices towered over hers, some asking for help, others saying she is a sorry excuse for a queen. Zaid stood by her side through it, refusing to leave, but there wasn't much he could do to help her either. This was her battle to fight.

Elder Balasi came up and pulled her to the side. *How bad is it?* he asked quietly.

Kinza gulped. *We may have gotten arrested in France.*

Balasi looked momentarily stunned at her admission. He quickly recovered, and the part of him that was good at his job took over. She could see the wheels turning in his mind on how to fix this.

Zaid was behind them, talking with Savar, and others had broken out into arguments. Kinza wanted to hear all of them, but this wasn't the way to do it.

"Quiet!" an angry voice boomed out loud, something that was rarely heard with the Anunnaki. Kinza turned to find Mikah, still supporting Eta. Kinza realized that the young woman looked like she had just come from her death bed, which was almost as startling as Mikah's face. It was the same unmasked, frigid anger he had when he stopped Tahir from killing her. It made her uneasy to see Mikah without his usual charming smiles and smooth words.

"The queen will be making a statement in ten minnutes in the main receiving *auditorium.* This is the main receiving *cham-*

ber. Please see yourselves out and down the hall where the queen will join you shortly."

Everyone looked to Kinza for confirmation, and she quickly nodded as if she had planned that all along. As people started to file out, Eta and Mikah came up to her, and Kinza gave him a questioning look.

Eta needs to speak with you, Mikah said, quieter this time.

Suddenly, the tall, lanky form of Badr burst into the room in a cloud of papers, some in his hands and others trailing behind him wildly. There was a barely contained delight in his eyes that could only be found in the eyes of a scientist who had just discovered something groundbreaking. *As do I!*

ZAID LISTENED WITH KINZA, Badr, and Mikah as Eta detailed the events of a vision so profound that he was almost hesitant to believe it. The details made little sense to him, but he thought he understood their meaning. They didn't have much time before people would come back looking for Kinza, so Eta spoke quickly.

He hadn't known that Kinza was having Eta and Badr do research for her, and he looked at her in a new light. This queen of his was becoming very clever indeed.

When Eta was done speaking, the only person who didn't look at her like she had three heads was Mikah.

I don't think I fully understand, said Kinza. *You had a vision that we were both destroyed but also lived in peace.*

No, not that, Eta said, taking a deep breath. *The part about the city being destroyed is what could happen, and what is on our doorstep.*

I think we figured out that much, Zaid said.

But the part about us in the future, living peacefully with humans... Eta's eyes were wide with amazement. *The fact I had that vision meant it was still a possibility. I know everything looks hopeless right now, but there is still a way to get there. It* can *happen.*

Okay, but how? Kinza said, in all seriousness. *The Elders couldn't figure out how to deal with the barrier or make me queen.*

That's the part that's complicated, Eta said. *I'm not sure how, but somehow our history ties into it. What the vision did tell me was how we came to be. Long ago, a group of humans traveling through the desert came upon a river. The river was filled with what we know as Aurastones today. Over the next several thousand years, that group of people built a city—our city—over that river. They drank from it, used it for their crops, built their homes with it, hunted by it, and we kept it contained. The entire time, the Aurastones eroded and mixed with the sediment in the river. Since we relied so much on the river...*

Kinza's eyes widened. *We ingested the Aurastone over thousands of years... changing our DNA.*

Eta nodded. *The Aurastone deposits in our blood showed up in the form of tattoos, and some of us ingested more, giving us larger tattoos.*

Kinza looked as confused as Zaid felt. *But the ink and the violets...* she said. *Also, there is no river here.*

Yes! Badr said, jumping in. *Only certain violets work because only some of them are mutated by the river, because the river is still filled with Aurastone deposits.*

*But there is no—*Zaid started to say.

It's beneath the quarries, Eta said, light in her eyes. *Yes, we used most of it up, so our population stopped expanding over time, but some of it still seeps into the aquifers under the city that we use for drinking water. It also feeds the plants outside the quarry.*

But wait, Kinza said. *How did Tahir make his tattoo perma-*

nent? We know the violets only make a temporary ink. If the Aurastone literally needs to be in our skin, do we just crush it up? I thought breaking Aurastones creates Deathstones?

Yes, and sort of yes, Badr said. *Only if you break an Aurastone with an act of defilement would it turn to Deathstone, but if you do it right, it could be turned into an ink that could be used to add to the Aurastone deposits already in our skin.*

Zaid was dizzy listening to this. This information was... it would be life-changing for the Anunnaki. *So... we can leave?*

Badr shrugged. *Honestly, I'm not sure what the long-term effects are. There has never been an Anunnaki who lived outside of Rhapta outside of the monarchs. We could be fine, or we could fade away.*

Zaid remembered what Kinza's grandmother told her about Prince Malik's descendants. Some of them never had the Anunnaki tattoo, and possibly no abilities either until Kinza came along.

The five of them stood in silence. The news rocked them to their cores. Finally, Kinza asked, *Badr, do you think you could recreate that ink?*

Possibly, he said quietly. *Would need a few rounds of experiments and help from Savar probably.*

Kinza nodded. Zaid could see the wheels turning behind her eyes, and right then, she looked more like a monarch than ever. He waited for his queen's command.

This information does not leave this room, she said. *Understood?*

They all nodded without question. While it was joyous news, it would only cause more chaos right now and would help in dealing with the humans.

Good, she said, lifting her chin. *Now I have a speech to make.*

CHAPTER 17
THE BARRIER

Kinza strode into the auditorium, and the frenzied conversation died down to a whisper. She wasn't timid or uncertain as she went to the front of the room and turned to face the people. Her people. She felt like she was dreaming, like she had so many times during her first few days in Rhapta. None of it felt real, but it did feel right.

Eta's revelation, despite how shocking it was, gave her hope. If there was a chance they could make it out of this safely, then Kinza would find it. She would use what abilities she did have, and if that wasn't enough and they were captured, she would do everything she could to free her people. She wouldn't stop until her last breath was gone. A certain resolve filled her, and even though she was still scared witless, she wasn't without hope.

She wasn't alone in this either. Looking out into the small crowd, she saw the faces of those who would stand by her and fight for their city. They looked frightened, but they were counting on her and willing to stand by her. Even those who claimed she wasn't fit to be queen were looking to her now for answers. She didn't know if she had the right ones, but she would try.

Just before she spoke, the drumming sound of the helicopter came in through the windows. Everyone started to cower as it came low enough to kick up sand outside and blow it into the auditorium. Kinza didn't hide, though. Even as the sound of the helicopter moved further away, even as the barrier dropped and fear beat in her heart, she didn't move. She just waited for several minutes until the barrier had returned again, the helicopter was further away, and it was quiet enough for her to speak. She didn't know if the humans saw the city, but she couldn't control that, so she didn't worry about it.

The Elders, apprentices, and scholars in the room must have noticed how she didn't flinch at the sound of the helicopter in the distance, because as they watched her, they straightened up and stood tall, even if they were still afraid of the humans that stood outside their city.

Kinza had a sudden realization that they *were* humans. The Anunnaki always referenced humanity as if they were something separate and the Anunnaki were godlike. But it wasn't true. They were human, too, just affected by the properties of the Aurastone, but still human all the same. The only difference was that the Anunnaki held a power that was a tool to help the rest of them. They shouldn't be hiding here, scared of the rest of the world. They should be out there, guiding and healing and helping. It was something Kinza was determined to change.

She took a steadying breath.

I know you are afraid, she started quietly. *I know the sounds of the machines above our heads are not natural to you. I know the thought of humans at our doorstep is frightening. But they are just as afraid of us as we are of them. To them, we are the terrors in the night, the frightening monsters in the forest and in the dark places of the world. This is just another loop in the cycle we have been repeating for thousands of years. We become afraid and pull away from the world we promised to protect, deeper and deeper behind our barrier until we start dying out. If we keep pulling away like this, we will vanish from history.*

Kinza paused to look around again, hoping that her words reached them in some way. She didn't have a grand plan, so she resorted to the truth. She couldn't fake their way out of this, nor could she just pretend to be queen. She had to *be* the queen for them to lean on.

We have to stop fearing them, Kinza insisted. *This cycle won't stop until we remind ourselves that it's our job to take care of them. They have the capacity to do both good and bad, just as we are able to do both good and bad. I know how wonderful they can be; trust me, I lived with them my whole life.*

The small crowd was watching her intently now. Some of them looked like they believed her; others were still skeptical. She could see they still wanted to know what her plan was even as they listened to the sound of the helicopter in the distance and waited for humans to knock down their walls.

Kinza took another breath. *I'm not Hakim,* she stated. *I can't see the future. I'm definitely not Tahir; I will not deceive you, nor do I think I am some type of deity. I don't have years of experience, strength, or speed. So I am going to use what I do have... light. There isn't any master plan to get us out of this, and I'm not going to blow the forest to pieces. I also have no idea if this is going to do anything, but it helped before. And now I think I may need your help to do it again. I won't command it of you; I won't be that kind of queen. I will do what I can, and seeing as this is our last shot, I hope that you will join me.*

Without another word, Kinza strode straight through the crowd, past the confused and hopeful faces, to the door. She didn't need to look to know Zaid was right behind her, and Eta, Mikah, and Badr all followed after. Eventually, she heard the shuffling of footsteps of the larger group of people and hoped they were following her as well.

Kinza walked through the Grand Hall, down the front steps, and toward the giant Aurastone that sat in the middle of the central plaza. She had placed her hand on it once before and found it to be warm and oddly humming. She felt that energy now as she stopped before it, but the moment she did, the barrier dropped again.

People gasped, and Kinza looked up into the clear blue sky. It was terrifying, knowing that the sound of the helicopter could come back at any moment and there was nothing there to hide them. They were standing out in the open and could be seen as plain as day. It took too long for comfort until the barrier struggled back into place. At any moment, it was going to drop again and would never go back up.

Kinza looked around to see the Elders, apprentices, and scholars had followed her out to the plaza, still unsure of what she would do. Before she had the chance to show them, they heard shouts coming from the opposite side of the plaza. Kinza and everyone else turned to find three warriors sprinting like death was nipping at their heels, headed straight toward her, yelling.

My Queen!

They are here!

Just outside the doorway! the last one said, coming to a halt before her. Elders gathered around, demanding to know what the warrior had seen. The frantic looks on the warriors' faces spread fear again through the group.

The first warrior finally spoke, eyes wide with terror. *The humans. We saw them! They are less than two hundred yards from the doorway. They will find us momentarily. There is nothing else we can do!*

Cries of outrage and dismay swept through the group surrounding Kinza, even as her own heart beat wildly. Thankfully, Zaid was the only one who would ever know how scared she was. Instead, she kept the same resolve thrumming through her as she did in the auditorium. She would not give up now. If anything, she had to try harder.

She placed a hand on the first warrior's shoulder and gave him a gentle smile. *It'll be all right,* she said. *You three don't need to go back to your post. You may stay here with us.* The warrior looked at her like she hadn't heard what he said, like she had lost her mind. She knew he doubted how she could stay so calm at a time like this, but he would understand soon enough.

Again, without another word, Kinza turned toward the Aurastone before there could be any further interruptions. She stood before it and closed her eyes. She had gotten really good at this part—connecting with her Aura. She knew it flared immediately like a fallen star when the gasps whispered through the group. The hard part would be getting everyone else to participate. She waited a few breaths, and a warm hand slipped into hers. She could've cried at that moment because, without needing to look, she knew it was Zaid at her side once again.

A moment later, another hand held her empty one, and then she heard footsteps and the rustle of clothing. She didn't open her eyes, though; she kept focusing on her Aura and looking for the others. It wasn't hard this time. Suddenly in her mind, Aura after Aura started to flare like bright, colorful lights. Sapphire, emerald, charcoal, scarlet, lavender; more and more kept coming, and Kinza knew that they had surrounded the Aurastone. More Auras trickled in from the other side of the plaza, coming to stand by the others.

Kinza couldn't help but peek her eyes open, just a bit. The center of the plaza was filled with people from the Grand Hall and surrounding buildings. The group was small compared to the entire Anunnaki population, but the rainbow of lights was by far the most beautiful thing she had ever seen. No one was bickering or arguing. No one was fighting or screaming. They were just... glowing.

Just before she closed her eyes again, she caught sight of Zaid's Aura and realized she had never seen it before. She wanted to laugh. Of course his Aura was the polar opposite of hers. The midnight black glow pulsed around him like the night sky, the edges mingling with her dazzling white one. She just smiled and closed her eyes, squeezing his hand a little tighter.

Kinza was starting to feel the psychic energy of so many people thrumming around her. In her mind, the large Aurastone pulsed in the center, as if the stone itself wanted to beat in tandem with them. She wanted to bask in the feeling but remembered why they were doing this. The sound of the helicopter wasn't far off.

Regaining her focus, Kinza's mind swam among the lights and drifted out over the city. She saw the thousands of other Auras huddled together in their homes, and she felt their fear. Without thinking too much about it, she *pushed* some of her massive Aura toward them, making them glow a little brighter. She didn't pause long, though, and kept her mind moving over the city.

The feeling of the collective Aura was making her skin tingle, and her heart beat faster. It tasted like electricity in her mouth and a rising wave under her feet. Alone, her Aura was huge and brilliant, but mixed with everyone's was something else entirely. It felt like a net was cast across all of them, tying them together. In some places, that net was weak or dim, so she would push a little more of her own Aura into it, trying to bring it back to life. It started to become more solid and the threads binding them together became tighter. It was then that Kinza understood it wasn't a net at all.

It was the barrier.

Joy and relief sparked through her. The barrier! Her own Aura pushed at the edges of her skin and streaked around the plaza with her excitement. She had found the barrier and was able to grab onto it, following it out to its outer rim. It ended just where it was supposed to, about a quarter-mile outside the city in every direction like a dome. Now that she understood what she was looking at, she wanted to open her eyes and tell Zaid, but they couldn't waste any more time. She could see how the Auras of the people and the energy from the Aurastones were numerous, but they weren't bright enough to hold the barrier. It was like a lamp too small for the room. She just needed to make it a little brighter.

As her excited mind wandered along the rim of the barrier, it passed over the doorway. It felt more like a small, feeble curtain, and just outside it, her mind sensed another Aura. This one was cold, very cold. Tahir was here, ushering the humans toward the door. Anger boiled through her veins, and Kinza could feel the sharp heat building in her abdomen. Her Aura—and the fire—wanted to come out and set the forest alight.

She pushed it into the barrier instead.

Like waking up from a long sleep, it drank her Aura like the first glass of water in ages. Kinza didn't hold back and let her light flare brighter; she had a lot to give. The anger was still there, but she didn't let it get out of control. Now was not the time for explosions. Her body felt far away as she focused on feeding the barrier, but faintly she could feel the Anunnaki—as one—jolt in surprise. They could sense the barrier too and felt it getting stronger, and just like when Kinza had let her Aura out a few weeks ago, the people got stronger too. Their Aura shone more brilliantly across the city.

Kinza? Zaid's voice came in her mind. *What's happening?*

Kinza couldn't keep her attention on Zaid, or the others, so she gripped his hand in response. The barrier took all her focus now as it was regaining its strength. It used her Aura to fill in the gaps, seal the cracks, and solidify itself all around the city. It was no longer like a net, but more like an invisible iron wall surrounding Rhapta and locking the doorways so the humans, and Tahir, could not enter.

It felt like an eternity, but eventually, the flow of Kinza's Aura slowed to a steady trickle, never quite shutting off. She knew the barrier was as tight as it had ever been and that they were safe. Slowly, she drifted back to her body while keeping a small awareness in her mind attached to the barrier so the flow of psychic energy wouldn't stop.

As she came back down, she looked at the Auras again across the city. They were vibrant and beautiful, not one of them dim anymore. She opened her eyes and looked out through her white light. The people who had held her hands and surrounded the Aurastone had opened their eyes as well, slowly pulling their own Auras back in. The large Aurastone was humming happily, but the people looked at her differently than they had before.

All around her, not a single person said a word. Elders, apprentices, scholars, warriors, parents, and healers all just looked at her until she too dimmed her Aura. Kinza was about to speak when Eta let go of her hand. She had tears and relief in her eyes and smiled before slowly kneeling down before her, head bowed.

Kinza was too overwhelmed by what had happened to say anything. Before she had a chance to speak, like a wave, everyone else followed suit, kneeling down one by one. Even those who had spoken out against her said not a single word as the entire plaza knelt before her. Kinza turned in a slow circle, tears welling in her own eyes, realizing what she had just done, and she looked at her people that she had saved. And they truly were *her* people now. She had somehow managed to get ahold of the barrier and strengthen it like all the monarchs in Rhaptan history had. This was what the scholars had been searching for.

She was now the queen.

CHAPTER 18
MONSTERS IN THE FOREST

Tahir hated the feeling of human clothes. The seams were irregular, and the fabric was cheap. Everything was made in a factory and not by hand like in Rhapta, where the old ways were still prevalent. There were other things Rhapta did better as well. Things like food that grew naturally, houses that stayed cool in the heat without the use of machines, and even unpolluted water for every citizen.

It was a shame the city had to fall.

He loved the city; he always had. But like a spoiled pet, it grew to no longer recognize its master and needed to be put down. The Anunnaki had slowly been losing their senses as the population dwindled. Tahir had tried in every way that he could to return them to greatness, but they had strayed too far. He would admit that it was his own mistakes that had led them this far. Maybe he hadn't planned meticulously enough. Maybe he should have been the one to kill the outsider from the prophecy instead of sending useless assassins. Maybe he should have prepared better. Either way, the mistakes were his, and he needed to deal with the monster he had created. They couldn't be allowed to continue.

To his great pleasure, nothing else had gone awry since his departure from the city. It had been a long, arduous journey around the world and back home, but here he was, climbing back through the forest with the army he had marshaled behind him. It moved like a giant, slow creature across the forest floor. They were many in number, but their machines and technology slowed them down. That, and an officiousness that even tired Tahir.

The army suddenly stopped, and a crackle of conversation came on from over the radio attached to the nearest sergeant's vest. The man, in his thirties, was as nondescript as they came, and Tahir had a hard time remembering his name. The sergeant responded back before coming over to Tahir.

"We are pausing for fifteen minutes," he said and mumbled something else into his radio.

"For what?" Tahir replied. Speaking aloud had been an adjustment for him. He had to remind himself that they couldn't hear his words in their head and used their ears instead. It was tedious, but he got used to it. "We've already stopped several times. We need to hurry."

The sergeant gave him a bored look. "To catalog each square meter. In case there are monsters." The sergeant flicked his eyebrows at Tahir and walked away, earning a laugh from some of the men nearby.

Tahir restrained the urge to let out the ice that snapped at his fingertips. Only a select handful of the military operation here actually knew the full details as to why they were here. Some of the lower grunts were told it was a research expedition—albeit an overly extensive one that required shutting off all access to the mountain without full explanation. Some of the men gathered were looking for something at Tahir's behest and thought him a madman that had seen shadows in the forest.

He wouldn't have to wait long until the look was wiped from their faces.

To be fair, convincing the humans that an entire invisible city existed near a well-known mountain based on little evidence was difficult, to say the least. After he had left Rhapta mere weeks ago, he and his most loyal followers had endured a grueling time traveling through human society. That may have been one of the things he hadn't prepared enough on. In all his life, he only left the city once in his younger days, close to fifty years ago. He hadn't traveled far, only to a nearby town and back in the same day. Things had changed drastically since then.

He knew immediately that they had needed to get to one of the three human-Anunnaki. It was the only way they would survive out in the world without any money, ID, or connections. Tahir had the foresight long ago to keep tabs on the three and knew that the one in China would be his best bet. Tahir and the three others that had departed the city with him had made it as far as Ethiopia before they finally found an Ummanu. Tahir had known where most of the portals were in the world, or at least how to find them. The Ummanu there was out in the middle of nowhere and rarely had any visitors. It didn't take long for him to submit to Tahir's needs.

With the Ummanu's help, they were able to get ahold of Wang Hàorán, who found a way to secure passage for him to Sichuan, China.

Tahir had sent the others on separate errands, though. Elder Minesh and his Apprentice Kiaan he had sent to France to sway Vivienne Moreau to his leadership. Elder Harran he sent to Peru for something else. He knew he wouldn't hear from Harran for quite some time, but that was to be expected. Tahir was a long range planner, and there was something in Peru that he would need in the future if things went his way. Unfortunately, Tahir hadn't heard from Minesh and Kiaan either. He hadn't told any of the humans about the other Anunnaki that were with him, and he didn't plan to.

Looking around now, he was glad he hadn't. The humans that traveled with him were skittish creatures, afraid of everything and trusting nothing. They had reacted with fear and astonishment when Tahir had proven his words with his abilities. How would they react if they knew that Anunnaki walked among them on a regular basis? The venari moved through their cities unchecked, tracking down the escaped ubir. If they knew there were crazed beings with devastating power running rampant throughout the world, they would fall quickly into hysteria. Tahir didn't care for hysteria.

Tahir watched as several of the military men and their analysts walked over every square meter in this section of the forest. He wasn't sure what they were recording, but they had an extensive arsenal of technological devices to measure everything unseen; the air, the particles in the ground, the magnetic field, and even light in wavelengths humans couldn't see.

The sergeant that had spoken to him earlier was only a minor cog in the wheel. Most people of actual importance were not here in the dirt. Only one of them was; the man Tahir remembered as the director. Tahir turned around and looked further down the path they were creating and spotted the white-haired man surrounded by several analysts who were reporting their findings as they went.

Tahir waited far too long in the sweltering humidity, freezing bugs when no one was looking, and attempting to keep himself cool without raising suspicion. There were too many of those military men around, and they seemed too jumpy for his taste despite the jokes they cracked at Tahir's expense. In truth, none of the local military really knew why they were here. All they knew was that the government had lent them out to an international research organization known as SPE. The director was in charge of this particular project, and his analysts were like bees swarming around the hive, collecting information to bring back to him.

One of the analysts, a young woman in a tan vest, came over to Tahir with a tablet in her hands. Her fingers tapped wildly over the screen, recording something she had seen.

"Hi, Tahir?" she said when she reached him. She was scrawny and wouldn't have spoken to him so brazenly had she been Anunnaki. Being one of the director's analysts, she probably knew why they were really there and who Tahir really was, but she didn't seem to care.

"Yes," he replied, hoping they were ready to leave.

"The director wanted you to take a look at this," she said, turning her tablet around to show him a visual of what looked like an aerial view of their location. "He wanted to make sure we were going in the right direction."

Tahir rolled his eyes to the sky. "Of course I know where I'm going. I don't need a map to get there, you foolish child."

Now the young woman did look a bit nervous, but for the wrong reasons. She shifted on her feet and said, "Will you please just take a look?" she asked, glancing back down the path. "The director is a very orderly man. He doesn't like things to be missed, and I could get fired for not insisting you verify we are in the correct location."

Ice crept under Tahir's arm and down his leg underneath his clothes. No one could see it, but he could turn this section of forest into a deep northern winter if he didn't keep his anger in check. This woman was afraid of the director and not him? He kept his breathing even and reminded himself he wouldn't need to tolerate this idiocy for much longer.

He made a show of looking over the tablet before nodding. "We are in the correct location. Now, may we continue?"

"Thank you very much," the woman said, looking relieved. "I will update the director." She hurried off before he got a chance to ask another question.

Despite the fact that he was the one leading them to Rhapta, he had little authority in how and when they got there. When he had finally gotten in contact with Hàorán, Tahir had quickly talked some sense into the man. He explained how the Anunnaki had been twisted by a prophecy Hakim had told over centuries, and now a young woman had bewitched the people. He explained how he had tried to save them, but the woman was too powerful, and only Tahir had escaped. They would need to eradicate the city to make sure Kinza Solace didn't use the Anunnaki against humanity. Hàorán agreed with Tahir's words but, like any man in his position, didn't want to give up the power he had. That was understandable.

Tahir and Hàorán had come to a sort of alliance, and through Hàorán's connections, Tahir learned of SPE. The research organization was exactly what it said it was and studied many things across the globe in the realms of medicine, geology, space, genetics, and weaponry. No one really knew how extensive they were, though. While the company reported most of its research and investments, many things were kept under the table. Tahir was never told this explicitly, but it was clear that the rich and powerful put a lot of money into the organization and did all they could to keep some of the projects a little more... discreet.

It was so discreet that Tahir had needed to be a bit dramatic to gain their attention. It was at Hàorán's advice that

Tahir had publicly used his abilities in a small town in rural China. It was quickly dismissed as the powers of technology, but within twenty-four hours, Tahir had found himself seated before the man he now knew as the director.

A crackle of static over the nearby radios pulled Tahir from his thoughts. He looked up and found the military men and their analytic counterparts picking up their equipment again, ready to move. The sergeant came back to Tahir, picking his way through ferns and roots that covered the ground.

"We're ready to go," he said and pointed up the hill before saying, "that way."

"Yes," Tahir muttered as he got to his feet, the stiff boots biting at his ankles. "I know the way home."

THEY WALKED for another half an hour, slowly moving upward at a gentle incline. At this rate, it would take them hours to reach the doorway. Before this expedition started, Tahir had given them a relative location but never the exact spot. He also told the humans that they wouldn't be able to access the doorway without him. He didn't mention that the barrier would most likely be down before they even got there.

In the decades leading up to recent events, Tahir had known that the Anunnaki population was dwindling and what it meant for the barrier. There was extensive research on the barrier over many years that was led by him, and he had a fairly good idea of what kept it going. The recent deaths in the city and the hopelessness that had spread would only weaken it to dust.

But he wasn't going to mention any of that either.

Tahir knew his position at the moment was tenuous at

best. His usefulness was currently outweighing his usage as a specimen in a lab, but if he gave away too much, he would find himself under the bright lights and scalpels of the SPE's underground facilities. He had already spent more time there than he would like and had no intention of returning.

Tahir ducked under a low branch while keeping an eye on their location.

His first meeting with the director had been anything but promising. In fact, he had thought he might've made a grave error. They had taken him to a plain white building after traveling for close to a day by both plane and car. The building had a shiny sign out front that indicated it was SPE Research Facility, but Tahir was taken down an elevator deep into the earth. It required two separate badges and three passcodes to get to the final room. The underground portion of the facility looked vastly different from the pleasant, airy upper floors. It was clear this part of the building wasn't public nor known by many. The rooms underground were cold and dark, and everything was made of metal. There was no sunlight down there, and Tahir had been placed in a room that felt like a cage. Four walls and a table and chairs.

Eventually, the director had come in. He was a solidly built man in his sixties. Stark white hair kept short and neat. Everything about him was efficient and precise, a man of few words and high expectations. He explained that he oversaw several projects at the organization and was told Tahir was trying to get his attention. Well, he had it.

I can respect this man, Tahir remembered thinking. This was a man that was in control. His employees ran to do as he commanded with extreme precision. Not one of them ever questioned his word, and everything: movements, changes, and updates were run by him first. It was like a well-oiled machine, and Tahir had calculated that bluntness was his best course of action.

The small room with him and the director had frosted over like early winter. The man had shown no reaction, only listening while Tahir had detailed a dangerous group of people living in an invisible city in Tanzania. After he was finished, the director didn't speak. He left the room quietly, and three men entered the room. Before Tahir could realize what was happening, something sharp pierced his neck, and his vision went dark. He had woken inside a cell with an iron door a foot thick and spent the next two days there without food or water or contact.

"We found something!" a voice shouted, bringing Tahir back to the present.

Found something? Tahir thought. *What could they have possibly found? We aren't even close yet.*

Several of the men hurried over to where one of them had pointed to. A couple of the analysts shouting not to touch it pushed their way through the small crowd. Tahir stood off to the side, waiting for them to show what exactly they were so excited about in the dirt. Crossing his arms, he waited patiently next to a twisted tree.

They buzzed around the thing, and Tahir noticed, not for the first time, that humans reminded him a lot of insects. They were many in number, and it was their size that was formidable. But on their own, they weren't very smart. The evidence sat before him as one of the men pulled out what they had found and presented it in the air.

A boot.

Tahir heaved an irritated sigh and leaned against the tree, careful not to frost the bark over. He watched their mood change to shades of disdain and disappointment. They slowly trudged back to their positions and recorded the nonevent on their tablets. The analysts scolded the men about using common sense before alerting the entire group.

Out of the corner of his eye, a figure stepped up next to Tahir, watching the mishap. He stood still as a statue, his eyes watching every movement his employees made.

"Are you sure you know the way?" the director finally said, displeasure written across his face.

Despite the man's skepticism, Tahir was not swayed. Of course he knew where Rhapta was. The sooner they got there, the sooner Tahir wouldn't have to deal with the doubt that surrounded him as of late. "Yes, and we would get there faster if we didn't keep stopping for every rock and leaf along the way."

The director turned on him with threatening eyes, sunlight from above the canopy dappling his face. "You had better not be lying. I don't like people who waste both my time and my money."

Tahir wanted to laugh in his face. If only he knew who he had been in Rhapta, or the things he had done in his long life. He knew that laughing would be the wrong card to play here, though. Instead, he watched the men move back into position and announce they were ready to move again.

"By the end of the day, you and I will both have what we want."

The director nodded and walked off to talk with his analysts. It was a fine line that Tahir was walking right now, and the director liked to remind him of that. After Tahir had spent those two days in a cell, men came and took him again— not without jabbing him with a needle first—to the same room he had met with the director in before. It was the longest that he had gone without sunlight in his entire life. He didn't realize how the weather and movement of the celestial bodies affected him so much until they were gone. He had no idea what time it was or even what day unless they told him how much time had passed.

The director had come again, but instead of wanting Tahir to demonstrate his abilities again like he assumed, the man wanted to know what Tahir wanted. It was a fair question. He said he wanted to warn humanity because the Anunnaki could destroy the world if they weren't stopped. The man had asked him for the coordinates, and that's when Tahir had stopped him. He knew the moment he handed over all of the information, he would be put back into the cell, or worse. He said that he would show them where it was, and once he was proved right, he only wanted to live out the rest of his life in the human world in peace.

The director understood what he meant: Tahir wanted immunity. He wanted to make sure that when the hammer came down, he would not be the target, now or ever. Of course, Tahir never mentioned that he had other plans for humanity in the future, but that was another thing the director didn't need to know.

He spent another few hours in the cell with only rage for company. No one came to tell him what was going on or even what time it was. When they did finally come to bring Tahir back, he had half a mind to shove the needle into the nearest man's thigh. He let them prick his skin again though, and woke up in the metal room.

The director looked displeased when he entered but told Tahir they would be going to Tanzania with him in the lead. It was clear that the director was not the one to make the final decision, so who was really in charge?

Tahir had asked what convinced them.

"Your ice is... unusual," he had said. "That, and you survived a concentrated tranquilizer that is eight times the dosage for a horse, four times at that. You should have died the first time."

Red hot anger had flashed through Tahir. They had intended to kill him! Without a single thought, they would have buried his body in some nondescript location had he not survived through the night. He would need to be more careful about how he approached the situation. The humans were fearful and rash, even if they didn't immediately show it.

Tahir only nodded, and the director went on to tell him there were additional stipulations to the agreement. Tahir would need to divulge additional information, essentially becoming something of a consultant to SPE. In return, he would be exempt from their research on the Anunnaki and would consider Tahir an ally of sorts.

They had very little trust in him, though. And the trust they did have was on very thin ice. At any moment, it could break and send Tahir drowning. So he played their game and agreed to lead them on this "research expedition." It was agonizingly slow, but they got the job done. At first, he was surprised how easily SPE acquired the use of the Tanzanian military. He didn't even know which country SPE originated from. He was never told where the facility he went to was located, and the people had varying accents, but even if they did all have the same accent, Tahir wouldn't know which country it was from. The lack of information was frustrating when the level of power SPE had was so apparent. How could this organization be so secretive yet have so much influence?

He kept quiet and continued leading them through the forest. He craved the open space of a boulevard and the sky clear above him even though the heat of the sun beat down on the tops of the trees. It started to get a little cooler as they went up, but not enough. He forgot how feeble humans were. They needed breaks quite frequently and had to stop for water and food; otherwise, they would collapse. The pace they were at was grueling for them, but with Tahir's Anunnaki strength and stamina, he could've gone the whole way without stopping even though he was in his middling years.

Finally, after hours of picking their way through the vines and roots, Tahir noticed a cluster of familiar trees. He pulled one of the analysts aside and said they were close. Not much longer now until he was home. Unfortunately, once they arrived, it would be his last view of the ancient city before humanity swarmed its walls for the first time in history.

THEIR PACE HAD QUICKENED NOW that they knew their goal was within range. They stopped for fewer breaks, and the director pushed them to eat and drink as they walked. It was close to afternoon now, and they had started early morning.

"What was that!?" a man shouted, and Tahir noticed too late that he was mocking him. "A ghost? Oooo!" the man said, laughing with his buddies. The director was too far behind them with his analysts to hear the remark; otherwise, the man would've been sent home immediately and relieved from his position.

"These are no ghosts," Tahir said, stepping over a large root. The man behind him missed it and stumbled, nearly grabbing onto Tahir. He just turned to glare at the man.

"Aliens, then?" another man joked.

"No," Tahir replied. "They are from Earth. But they should be treated as such. They have gotten out of control."

"Riiiight," the man said, nudging the person next to him. "World domination, yes?"

"I'm not sure of their usurper queen's intentions, but she

is bent on having her way, whatever that may be." Tahir only saw Kinza Solace for a few short minutes, but that was more than he needed. It was worse than he had thought. Through all of Hakim's visions over the years, he had gathered as much information as he could about the outside from the prophecy and felt he knew much about her. He knew she would know nothing of them and would be young and inexperienced. Seeing that she was practically a child was infuriating to him. How could any of the Anunnaki truly believe she was the best option to lead them? Even over Hakim's apprentice?

It was only proof of how far the Anunnaki had fallen that they would trust this outsider over one of their own. The hilarious part was that she had been inclined to agree, kneeling down to accept her death blow.

Until Mikah.

Disgust and self-loathing filled Tahir, things he rarely felt about himself. He had kept the young man by his side for years, teaching, exemplifying, and molding him into a future Elder. It was Tahir's own fault for not paying more attention to how rotted his apprentice had become. He should have dealt with him years ago instead of letting him turn into this defiant, rebellious welp that he had become. He could have done it in the Great Hall, too. Mikah's abilities were nothing compared to Tahir's ice, and Tahir could have frozen him solid on the spot.

And Zaid. Poor Zaid. Tahir did feel the slightest bit of remorse for what had happened to him. Zaid had always had the obedience that Mikah lacked, but apparently, that only went so far. He just *had* to go snooping around. Tahir was never disillusioned that Zaid would truly understand the difficult things that needed to be done to care for a city. So of course he would be angry that Tahir had started a war. Tahir would mourn for what Zaid could have been if that *woman* hadn't entered his life. But that was Tahir's own fault too, for sending him to retrieve her in the first place.

"A queen of monsters?" one of the men asked as they hacked away at branches and stomped over leaves.

Tahir looked up, having forgotten they were there. "Yes," he said wistfully. "A queen of monsters, indeed."

"Well, you let me deal with her," the man said, puffing out his chest. "I'm a professional monster-hunter, you know." This only made the nearby men cackle with mirth. Tahir would relish the moment they realized he wasn't insane.

"By all means," Tahir said, humoring him. "You can have the first shot." The men continued to laugh and joke among themselves, and Tahir tuned them out. They were so close he swore he could feel the barrier from here, but he could be imagining it.

The director had also commissioned a helicopter and several drones—things he quickly learned were fast and efficient and could travel long distances via flight. They had been sent up ahead to scout for the city. Each report came back empty-handed, and the director became tenser and tenser each time. Tahir reassured him that it was to be expected. How could the helicopters be expected to see an invisible city?

Tahir did wonder if the barrier would completely drop at some point, revealing the city to the army in the sky before the men on the ground had a chance to get there. Tahir hoped it didn't. He wanted to be the one to open the door, to watch the humans' faces as the great city of Rhapta sat before them.

They climbed through the trees and ferns for another hour until excitement started humming through Tahir. He marched quicker, ahead of the others now. When he caught sight of the two trees up ahead, he signaled the group to stop.

The director came up to him. "What is it?" he said, displeased that the group was no longer marching.

"We're here," Tahir said with a smile. He felt like he had been away for so long. Traveling through the countryside, through planes and cars, through cities, and now back again. The last few weeks had been the longest in his life, but he was so close to a new chapter. He could feel it, how things would change soon. The world was going to be a very different place, and Tahir would be at the center of it.

The director looked around, unimpressed. "Where is 'here'? There is nothing but more trees. If you're wasting my time..."

Tahir sighed dramatically. "It's just up ahead," he said, taking a step forward. The director's hand stopped him, and he signaled for two of his men to go ahead in front of them.

"My men will scout the area first," he said before one of his analysts came scurrying up to him with a new report.

Tahir watched two armed men walk ahead toward the two trees and beyond as he listened to the analyst's report. It was nothing special, just more reading on the usual heat signatures in the forest and what the aerial team had seen or not seen. Tahir crossed his arms and waited an agonizingly long twenty-five minutes until the two men came strolling back.

They gave the director a detailed report of what they saw— which was just more trees. "I thought you said we were here?" the director said menacingly to Tahir.

"I did," Tahir replied. "You didn't honestly think you could just walk right in, did you? You're human; you won't be able to find the doorway. Only the Anunnaki can find it, so I have to go in first."

"Fine," the director growled. "You can—"

He was cut off by one of the analysts, who hurried over with a concerned look on her face. "Director! You need to see this," she said and handed him her tablet.

Tahir peered over their shoulders, and all he saw was a bunch of wobbling graphs that he couldn't make sense of.

"The readings suddenly started fluctuating a few minutes ago," the analyst said quickly, pointing out specific markers on the screen.

"Which ones?" the director asked.

"All of them, sir," she said, looking at him for an explanation. "Everything started going haywire, and we have no idea what could have caused it."

"Is a change in the earth's magnetic field possible? Or a reaction from a solar flare?" the director asked.

"Well, yes… I suppose," the analyst said meekly.

"Then let's get some real proof before you start alerting the media." The director turned toward Tahir. "I'm giving you clearance to go ahead, but stay in sight."

Tahir reigned in his retort that nobody gave *him* approval, and instead started walking forward with the group a few meters behind him.

The two trees loomed before him, and his heart beat in excitement. This was it! He would finally be rid of that wretched woman. Just past the trees, he paused and brushed aside a vine heavy with thick leaves. The analysts and men behind him gasped when he revealed a wooden pole staked into the ground. On top of it was a skull with beads and feathers strung around it.

Tahir glanced back, keeping his grin in check at the director's angered look toward the two men who had missed seeing the pole when they were scouting. The analysts started snapping photos and making notes, but Tahir moved ahead.

Finally, he could feel the barrier up ahead in his mind. He could no longer suppress his laugh as he stepped forward, eager to push through. One step, and then two.

Tahir breathed a sigh of relief just before he stepped across the barrier. One more step, and another, and another, and another, and...

Tahir looked around. He was still within the trees. The sounds of birds far above his head and other animals croaking in the distance. The two men were behind him, looking confused, and the analysts were still snapping pictures.

The director's expression darkened.

"Wait a moment," Tahir said, walking a little further. Was the door not where he had thought it was? No, that couldn't be. It was always just past the pole.

Tahir ran back to the pole, shoving the analysts aside, and inspected the base of it, but it didn't look like it had been moved. He turned and ran back to where the doorway should have been and fully expected to pass through to Rhapta, but...

Nothing. He felt that the barrier was there, but not there. He just couldn't find the door.

"It's here," he muttered, starting to panic. "Just a moment, it's here..."

He ran back and forth, feeling the air for the doorway that had stood for thousands of years. It was never just *not there*. Whether or not the barrier was strong or weak, the doorway would remain, but he couldn't find it.

One of the men scoffed.

"It's here! It's always been here!" Tahir started to shout, shoving branches aside and looking through the trees. The analysts were looking around, not sure what they should have been doing.

No, no, no, no, this cannot be happening! Panic flooded through Tahir's mind. He felt like he was drowning. This was real!

Even colder fear crept through him as the director sighed and looked down. "This is an unfortunate waste." When he looked up, Tahir knew the ice had broken, and he would drown.

"No, please!" Tahir said, now letting his own ice out to the horror of the two men and the military further behind them. Frost crumbled the leaves around them, and branches turned as white as snow. One of the men shouted in his own language.

The director was unmoving. He made a signal to one of his men, and a dart came flying, piercing Tahir's neck.

The world darkened as he screamed. "It's here! The city is here! It has always been here! NO!" His vision slowly went dark until the last thing he saw was boots crunching over the frozen ground.

As the unconscious form of Tahir was being hauled away, the director turned to his most trusted analyst. The young woman was small and looked timid, but he knew beneath the exterior was a viper beneath. He waited until the armed men were out of earshot.

"Keep an eye on this place," he said to her.

She nodded obediently. "You still think there is something here, sir?" she said, tapping on her tablet.

"I think something is going on, yes." He looked around at the frosted trees, already melting in the heavy heat. It was silent in the forest now. No birds or monkeys or rustling of leaves.

"What of the men?" she asked. "They already saw the ice."

"I'll deal with them," he said. The woman nodded and went back to the group as they rounded up their supplies and made to head back down the mountain. The official report would show that nothing was found here today, and this research expedition failed. Once the surrounding populations had calmed from the military activity, SPE would start on their real work. There was enough evidence here to know that *something* was hidden in this forest.

The director took one more look around, waiting for his eyes to catch on something that was missed. When nothing came to him, he turned and followed his analysts down the mountain. He would be back soon enough.

CHAPTER 19
AS THICK AS IRON

Kinza somehow found herself back in the Grand Hall receiving chamber amid a flurry of activity. Thankfully, the mood was lighter than an hour ago. Tears streamed down relieved faces, and cries of joy echoed throughout the large room as people came up to Kinza left and right, trying to grip her hand or thank her or just look at her.

Those closest to her and the largest Aurastone had understood what had happened. Kinza had taken hold of the barrier and was now fueling it like a massive generator. The rest of the population, however, was still confused. Kinza had instructed several warriors to go out to the barrier and make sure they were safe and that humans—or Tahir—had not made it through. In the meantime, she was still reeling from how drastically their situation had changed in only a matter of minutes.

Her skin still tingled faintly from the hum of energy that had coursed through her while every Aura in the city could be seen. She did feel tired, though, as if she had just come back from a long trip and desperately needed sleep. Sadly, the queen was needed.

The Elders wasted no time in bringing forth matters they had been unable to settle. They shoved documents, scrolls, and books at her, wanting her to read, sign, or approve them. Others demanded an immediate coronation to solidify her rule. Not surprisingly, the Anunnaki were very fond of their traditions, and a coronation was *always* done when a new monarch ascended the throne.

Kinza looked around and noticed Mikah and Eta were gone. She hadn't gotten a chance to ask Eta if she was all right and couldn't imagine what kind of toll had been taken on her in trying to use her Aura when she was already so clearly drained. Zaid was ever-present and was trying to fend off a few of the more aggressive congratulators and well-wishers.

Suddenly the door to the chamber banged open, and a woman came running inside, skirt hiked up so she could move her legs. Two attendants came yelling after her, shouting that she wasn't allowed inside. When Ekaja caught sight of Kinza and Zaid amid the throng of people, she made a beeline for them, only to be blocked by a few warriors.

Let her through, Kinza said gently to the warriors. They stepped aside, and Ekaja hardly noticed them as she flung her arms around both Kinza and Zaid. Many Elders and attendants gasped, and the lack of proper protocol around the queen, but Kinza just hugged Ekaja back.

I didn't even know you two were back, and then suddenly the barrier was down, and then the city was glowing, and then the barrier was up, and people were shouting that we have a queen! Ekaja said angrily. She smacked Zaid's arm. *Why didn't you come straight home?*

Zaid gave her an exasperated look. *We've been a little... busy?* he said, gesturing to Kinza, who just laughed. Ekaja just hugged them again. Over Ekaja's shoulder, Zaid smiled at Kinza, and Kinza smiled back.

It took way too long for Kinza to deal with the gaggle of people all wanting to talk to her or demanding her attention. She called for a few attendants to find Mikah and Eta and then collected a few others before retreating into a separate, smaller room. She hated that she felt like she was hiding, but nothing was going to be accomplished if she was stuck inside a human whirlpool all day.

The room looked more like a spare office with a desk, a few chairs, and an empty bookcase. They waited for about ten minutes until Mikah and Eta came in. Eta looked slightly better than she did before but would probably need to rest soon after.

Kinza surveyed the group she had gathered. Elders Ekbal, Ishar, Balasi, and Hija. There were also Apprentices Mikah and Eta, and Badr standing awkwardly to the side. Zaid, of course, was in the room, but no one questioned why he was there anymore.

So, Kinza started, looking around. *Just to confirm, I am the queen now, right?*

A few of the Elders looked at each other before Ekbal turned to her. *I thought that was apparent, but for the most part, yes. You are the queen in all the ways that are important.*

Great, Kinza said, clapping her hands together. *We need to make some changes.*

Some of them looked a little bit nervous, and Badr asked, *Like what?*

To start, I want all of you to be my closest advisers. In fact, let's just make that a new title. Adviser. Kinza wasn't sure if that was how it worked, but she had put a lot of thought into it and felt it was right.

Do you mean to do away with all the Elders, then? Hija asked from her chair.

Kinza thought about it a moment. *No... I don't think so. But I do need a small group of people who I trust who can advise me on certain matters as we move forward. The Council of Elders was the best decision that was available during the time the monarchy was gone, but there are too many Elders, and not enough decisions are being made while everyone is arguing. I think a smaller council of advisers to the queen would be best, and we can worry about restructuring the Elders later.*

Kinza didn't mention that she thought many of the current Elders treated their positions like a part-time summer job where the implications of their actions didn't matter. Some of them never took their roles seriously and only used the position they had gained for power and prestige. Many of them even had overlapping duties, and things still didn't get done.

Too many cooks in the kitchen? Badr asked wryly.

Yes, exactly, Kinza said. Before she could continue, Mikah raised a finger.

I'm not complaining, and I think you have made exemplary choices in your council of advisers, but Eta and I are only apprentices. Also, isn't he an apprentice scholar to a rebel organization? he said, pointing to Badr. Badr looked like he wanted to whack Mikah over the head with a book.

The Apostles of Truth are allies, Kinza said before a brawl could start. *And I'm promoting you and Eta to advisers now. You both have been invaluable to me, and I hope to have you with me in the future. As for Badr,* she said, turning toward the younger man. *Your Apprenticeship is up to the Apostles and Jabari. But I would like to also name you the personal scholar to the queen... which of course would be a position on the council of advisers.*

Badr's eyes lit up like twin suns. He inhaled a sharp breath, and instead of letting out a long stream of excitement, he bowed deeply. When he rose, he said, *I would be honored, My Queen.*

Eta nodded, her large eyes both tired and serene. *As would I.*

Kinza was coming to believe that Eta was like stepping in a puddle and discovering it was as deep as the ocean. This was the woman who would have led Rhapta had Kinza not come along—and if Tahir hadn't tried to overthrow her. She knew that Eta would be as vital to the Anunnaki's survival as Hakim had been for the past two hundred years. Kinza would make sure she kept Eta close.

Mikah nodded. *As would I, Your Royal Highness.* Despite the usage of her title, Mikah's face was as serious as ever, and Kinza knew he meant it.

Ekbal, Ishar, and Balasi all agreed as well. When Kinza finally turned to Hija, the old woman had a sad smile on her face. Her hands were resting on the cane between her knees, but she looked far more regal than Kinza did.

Sorry, dear, Hija said. *I want to retire. I'm old, almost as old as Hakim was. I don't want to spend the rest of my life dealing with a political mishmash. I want to play cards and listen to music. I want to lie naked in a field!*

Elder Ekbal rubbed his temples.

That doesn't mean I don't support you to the fullest, Hija said to Kinza. *But I have to decline your offer.*

Kinza, understanding, smiled and nodded. *Then I wish you a happy retirement, and you are relieved of your duties, so you can, uh, go do whatever you were planning on doing.*

Kinza then looked around at the six remaining people. Badr, Eta, Mikah, Ekbal, Ishar, and Balasi. These would be her council of advisers. *Good, it's settled then.*

I hate to be a snake in the ditch, Mikah said, using a phrase Kinza would need to ask about later. *But you are still going to need a coronation. The people won't be satisfied until they see you crowned.*

Then I hear by delegate that job to you, Kinza said with a cheeky smile. *You can make the arrangements.*

Mikah sighed and gave one of his bows. *As you wish, My Queen.*

The people will be getting anxious right about now, Balasi said. He stood quietly to one side, glancing out the window. Kinza knew he was thinking about how the changes would affect their relationship with the humans and the human-Anunnaki. Kinza had secured the allegiance of one of the three, but it would be difficult to have an impact on the world without the other two. That was something she needed to deal with very soon.

*You're right; we need to—*Kinza was cut off by a knock at the door.

The door opened, and a warrior poked his head in. Upon seeing Kinza, he bent into a deep bow before rising. The concern on his face told Kinza everything she needed to know. *I'm sorry for interrupting, but we've just returned from the edge of the barrier.*

Everyone in the room turned toward the warrior. *Great,* Kinza said. *How does it look? What of the humans?*

The warrior looked a little nervous. *Well, thankfully, the humans didn't get in, but neither did Tahir, and we think it's because the barrier is locked.*

Locked?! Zaid said, finally speaking. *What do you mean locked?*

The warrior's throat bobbed. *We scouted the edges, and well... we can't get out. Not even for a moment to check to see if the humans are outside. The barrier is solid through and through.*

Now everyone turned to look at Kinza. *Did you mean to do that?* Ishar asked her.

She shook her head.

That's not the worst part, the warrior said. *Somehow the news is spreading throughout the city that we are locked in, and people are getting worried. They want to know if the venari are locked out and if any future ubir are locked in.*

Now they care? Zaid scoffed.

Thank you, Kinza said to the warrior. *We'll be out in a moment to give a statement. If you see anyone else asking about the barrier, you can assure them we are just fine.*

The warrior nodded and left.

Well, that's not good, Mikah said.

Kinza turned to Eta. *Can you see anything regarding the barrier or even Tahir?*

The woman shook her head. *I'm sorry, I'm too tired, and most of my visions are nonsense at the moment.* She did look about ready to fall asleep as she leaned heavily against the desk.

That's okay, Kinza said. *Ekbal and Ishar, would you be able to organize time for me to give a speech to everyone today? Maybe in the central plaza?*

I'm sure that could be arranged, Ekbal said. *It might take until later today to get word around the city, but we could do that.*

Kinza nodded. *Thank you. In the meantime, the rest of us will go and check out the barrier and the doorways and see what can be done. But before you all leave, I think it's only fair we fill you in on a few things that we recently discovered.*

What kind of things? Balasi asked, looking wary.

Things about Rhapta's history and the ink the venari use, Kinza said. She figured that if these were going to be her closest advisers, they would need to know the truth of things. So Kinza detailed Eta's vision and Badr's research. She told the Elders about how the Anunnaki came to be and how the venari ink could potentially be modified to become permanent. The shocked looks on their faces were identical to the ones Kinza and Zaid had that morning. She knew this piece of information was like dropping a bomb into their hands.

You mean... we can leave? Ekbal asked, almost confused.

Kinza nodded slowly. *We think so. Actually, it has to be true since Tahir found a way to do it; we just need to experiment with it a little before we test it. I've already asked Badr to look into this for me.*

The Elders looked lost, and Kinza felt sorry for them. They were older than the rest of the group, especially Hija, and lived their entire lives thinking they would have to stay in the city forever or lose themselves. She imagined they were thinking of all the possible futures Rhapta and the Anunnaki had now that leaving was no longer a mythical concept.

This needs to be kept secret, Ishar said finally. *I'm afraid of what would happen if people found out about this.*

Kinza nodded. She hated the thought of lying about it. It made her feel like she was doing exactly what Tahir had done, but was this not the best course of action? She didn't want to cause more panic.

They all agreed to keep quiet about it for the moment. Ekbal and Ishar went to arrange the speech for Kinza. Mikah took Eta, presumably to her room so she could sleep. Badr went back to the Apostles to talk to Jabari. Hija bid her good-byes, leaving only Kinza, Zaid, and Balasi.

All right, Kinza said. *Let's go see what I did to the barrier.*

Zaid was used to feeling dirty. He spent days out in human society without access to a shower sometimes. During venari training, Savar would make them camp out in the fields surrounding the city with nothing but the clothes on their backs so they would understand what it meant to be uncomfortable. But today, he felt like a walking corpse.

Maybe it was the emotional exhaustion from trying to beat

Tahir here that morning, or that they had been terrifyingly close to getting caught, or maybe it was because he and Kinza had hiked part of a mountain in the sweltering heat, ran through the forest, and were still covered in grime. Either way, he hated the feeling of sweat running down his back again as he and the others walked through the fields toward the edge of the barrier.

He technically could have just run out there and come back with a report, but Kinza wanted to see it for herself, and Zaid was dead tired. The only thing keeping him going was the sheer elation that Kinza—*his* Kinza—had managed to save an entire city all on her own. She kept saying that it wouldn't have been possible without the other people standing beside her in the plaza, but she was the one now channeling her Aura into the barrier. She did it without breaking a sweat, either. It was like a switch flipped, and she became the queen because they needed one. He wondered if that was what being a parent was like. He would have to ask his mother.

Regardless, he was in awe of the woman that walked next to him.

He, Kinza, and Balasi walked through the city as discreetly as possible, trying to avoid anyone who "needed" Kinza's immediate attention. They made it out to the fields, but Balasi steered them toward a different doorway than Zaid was familiar with. He said it was just in case the humans were still camped outside the barrier; they didn't want to get caught if Kinza did manage to reopen the door.

They finally got to the tree line near the north quarter. This was where the path to Tahir's camp had led. He would have to remind Kinza that the camp was still there and technically could be used if they needed it. He assumed the barrier would hold out there as well.

A few meters into the tree line, Kinza paused. Zaid felt the mental presence of the barrier inside his head, but he assumed it felt different for Kinza and assumed she could "see" it better.

I think there is supposed to be a doorway just ahead, she said.

Balasi nodded. *Yes, there should be one right... here.* He had walked forward and reached his hand out, only to be met with an invisible wall. *But the warriors look to be correct. It should allow us through, but it won't.* He pushed against the invisible wall between the trees to no avail.

Kinza tried as well, pushing her hand against the wall, but it wouldn't budge. Zaid thought about all his fellow venari out there in the world. Would they come back with ubir in tow only to never find the doorway? He couldn't imagine what kind of chaos that would create. On the flip side, it would actually be easier to hunt the ubir down if they couldn't get very far. Even though the Unfettered were mostly captured—and still rotting in cells—after the battle a few weeks ago, they weren't eradicated by any means. There were always going to be dissenters and anarchists who wanted their freedom more than they wanted the safety of others.

Kinza, can you try easing off the barrier? Just around the doorway? Zaid asked.

I can try, she said. For a moment, she stood there, concentrating on the place between the trees. After a few seconds, she walked forward toward the doorway and reached her hand out. When it didn't connect with anything solid, she stepped forward and suddenly disappeared. A moment later, she came stepping back through the door.

Looks like it worked, she said. But when Balasi tried, he was met with a solid wall again. Kinza gave a chagrined expression. *Sorry, it's... heavy. Like lifting an iron door every time. I'm not sure if I could hold it open all the time so people could pass through.*

Hmm, Balasi hummed, deep in thought. *So it seems we will need to come up with a system so you can let the venari in and out.*

Kinza shrugged. *At least for the time being. I don't like the idea of doing that forever.*

Neither do I, Zaid said, thinking about how tedious it would be for future assignments. *But at least we are safe, and no one can get in without you letting them in.*

Right, she agreed.

I will see if I can find a way to get ahold of the venari that are on assignment right now, so they know what is happening. I will probably need to speak with Savar.

Kinza nodded. *Good idea, thank you.*

Zaid peered toward the forest and the barrier. *Well, at least we aren't stuck in here.*

KINZA SPENT the next few hours back at the Grand Hall again, trying to deal with as many matters as she could. Ekbal and Balasi had set out a message that the queen would give a speech in the afternoon. She still had a hard time comprehending that they meant *her* every time someone mentioned the queen.

She spent a good deal of time thinking about what she would say to her people in her first real speech as queen. Things like this were supposed to be like the initial handshake when meeting someone. It would set the stage for the rest of her reign, however long that was. Seeing as things had started out on a really bad foot, she needed to instill in the Anunnaki a sense of trust. They had been deceived so recently; she could only imagine how skeptical they would all be at a new leader, regardless of the fact she was keeping them safe.

The central plaza filled with people in the late afternoon sun. There was no way the entire population was going to fit, but she would send out messengers later into the smaller plazas to relay her words. The people had a mixture of emotions on their faces and looked around, somewhat confused. Some of them smiled and laughed, a sound Kinza would strive to hear more of. She figured the best indicator of how well she was doing as queen would be how much people laughed. It was hard to fake a good laugh.

Kinza hadn't had time to bathe or look for something queenly to put on, so she stepped out of the Grand Hall in her dirty clothes from that morning, covered in dirt, sweat, and a little dried blood from the cuts on her scramble up the mountain. The best thing about her attire was that it couldn't get any worse. She tried to squash aggressive butterflies in her stomach but found them persistent.

She stopped at the top of the steps and looked around. To the left and right of her, the Elders and apprentices stood around the pillars of the building. She could make out the Apostles of Truth in the crowd to the left, and she was pretty sure she saw Khalil to the right. There was one person that was missing, though...

Not getting nervous now, are you?

Kinza turned and was relieved to find Zaid to her left, leaning against one of the pillars. He stood out between the white robes of the Elders, looking like a shadow against the wall.

Maybe just a little, she replied.

You'll do fine, he said, looking almost bored watching the people fill the plaza. His calmness was like a balm to her, and the butterflies in her stomach died down.

A sudden pang ran through Kinza as she looked at Zaid. There were thousands of people around her waiting for her to speak, she had just become queen, and the only person she looked for amid the masses was Zaid. For a moment, she felt like she had something of Eta's gift and imagined a possible future where she never told him how she felt. In that future, he stayed by her side as he promised, but only as her subject. He would go on to marry another woman and have a family with her. He would start to look at that woman like he used to look at Kinza. They would live in one of the beautiful houses in the city, and Kinza would see him less and less as she spent her days surrounded by Elders and advisers but somehow still alone.

She couldn't let that happen.

Standing on top of the stairs, she made the decision to tell him how she felt as soon as possible after her speech. Turning back to the crowd, she exhaled a breath she hadn't realized she had been holding. The butterflies had come back, but now she almost felt giddy at the prospect of the conversation to come.

Focus, Kinza, she admonished herself.

The crowd had quieted as she stepped forward. Just before she was about to speak, a woman stepped up beside her and held out her hand.

Let me help you, she said with a smile. *Just place your hand in mine when you speak.*

Kinza was a little confused but nodded and placed her hand in the woman's. When she spoke, she realized why.

I know many of you know who I am, but we've never been formally introduced, she started. *My name is Kinza Solace.* Her voice echoed throughout the plaza like she had a megaphone attached to her vocal cords and the people looked toward her.

The first thing I want to say is that you are safe. She let the sentiment settle in their minds before continuing. She wanted to calm their fears. *The second thing I want to say is that, yes, I am holding the barrier right now.*

She took a breath and continued. *I want you to know that as long as I live, you will never need to worry about that barrier drop-*

ping or invaders coming over our walls. Yes, OUR walls. As many of you know, I grew up thinking I was human. Only recently did I discover who I really was and adopted Rhapta as my home. I want you to know that I do consider it my home and will defend it as such. I vow to never let you feel the fear you felt the night the city was attacked ever again. I will never let you worry that you will be taken or captured by humans. I will spend every single day of the rest of my life making sure we don't disappear from existence. You have my word.

Kinza wasn't sure if that even meant anything to them, but it was the truth. Just before she spoke again, a sound started all throughout the crowd. She didn't know what it was at first, but soon she saw the looks on the people's faces and knew.

They were cheering. For her.

It went on and on, getting louder by the second. Fists raised in the air as people waved and cried toward her. The reaction shocked her, and she felt tears welling in her own eyes. After all the hatred and fear these people had been through over the last few weeks at her expense, she hadn't truly believed they would be *happy* she was queen. She could only muster a tight-lipped smile as she focused very hard on not sobbing in front of thousands of people.

When the sound died down, and Kinza had regained her composure, she thought about what she would say next. These people were starting to trust her, and she knew this moment was a sort of crossroads for her. One path was safer, but the actions followed too closely in Tahir's footsteps. The other path was much riskier, but she would be able to sleep at night. Kinza glanced once at her new council of advisers and knew which path she would take.

The third thing I want to say is that I will never lie to you. You have been lied to too many times, and I won't be like that. She took a deep breath.

Are you sure? Zaid asked in her head. She could tell he hadn't expected this from her and was a little concerned.

I'm sure, she said back and meant it.

I want to tell you something that will change the course of the Anunnaki's future, Kinza said to her people. She told them about the research they had done and that soon they may have ink that could be used to extend the tattoos of anyone who wanted to leave the city. Shock rippled through the crowd, and for a moment, Kinza wondered if telling them had been a mistake. But the talking eventually quieted as the people looked at her again, and Kinza knew she had made the right choice.

The last thing I wanted to say to you today is that I know change is hard. You have lived with the same rules and traditions for thousands of years. But as queen, there are many things I think it's time to change, particularly about our future, and that means we need to start making those changes now.

Rhapta has been too far removed from the world for too long, and it's time we reconnect with our human neighbors. Not now, but soon. There is a lot of work we need to do first before it's time to reintroduce ourselves. You are not alone in this, though, as I will be with you every step of the way.

Kinza looked around and took one more breath. *Thank you.*

This time the people cheered even louder, calling her name as the late afternoon sun cast a golden glow against the white limestone buildings and the tops of the baobab trees. Kinza's smile was wide as she waved to her people, not bothering to hide the few tears that trickled down.

CHAPTER 20
TIME NEVER HALTS

"There has to be a better system than this," Kinza said to herself.

Did you say something, Your Highness? one of the four attendants in Kinza's spacious office asked.

No, it's nothing, Kinza replied. It was, in fact, not nothing. She had been given the largest office in the Grand Hall temporarily for her personal use. It seemed gigantic when her advisers had presented it to her, but it quickly filled with mounds of papers, proposals, books, and scrolls that had been put on hold. Now that Kinza was queen, it was her duty to take care of these things. The problem was there was no organization to anything. She didn't know what needed to be done first and didn't know what half of them even meant.

Actually, Kinza said. *Would you be able to find another bookshelf, please? I think we should be able to fit one more.* Her attendants had been running around collecting spare furniture for the room, and she hated asking them for more.

Of course, the woman said. *We will return shortly.* The other three attendants followed her out of the room, each bowing before they left. That was something Kinza had a hard time getting used to, and had even thought about abolishing the need to bow anytime someone saw her.

She tried tackling the chaos again in an attempt to get *something* done today. Only five blissful minutes of silence went by before someone knocked on her door.

Come in, she said.

The door opened, and Mikah stepped inside. *Good afternoon, Your Most Royalness,* he said with a grin. He looked as perfect as ever, not a hair out of place.

Hi Mikah. You know you don't need to call me that, she chided, looking back down at her mess of papers.

Yes, but I actually enjoy it, he said, looking around. She realized she had hardly had a chance to have a real conversation with him since the awkward night they had almost kissed outside of her house. Since her return to the city, every waking moment of her days have been filled with making changes, delegating projects, and dealing with overall queenly issues.

Remembering she had dealt Mikah quite a load of projects as one of her new advisers, she said, *How are things coming along? I didn't overwhelm you, did I?* She set her papers down to look at him, and he wandered around her office, looking at things.

I will admit that it's a lot, but nothing I can't handle, he said. *How is your palace?*

Kinza snorted. Mikah knew full well that she had been given additional rooms in the Grand Hall as her residence, but that wasn't saying much. Sure, they were larger than anyone else's, but she would have much preferred to go back to her little house in the abandoned sector of the city. Her advisers, however, would not hear of it. Mikah and Ishar had scolded her, saying that queens can't live in run-down homes and that she must stay in the Grand Hall. Somewhere in her chaotic office, there was a proposition to turn the Grand Hall back into a true palace. Apparently, it had been converted to its current state after the change in government a few hundred years ago. Despite her lackluster rooms, Kinza didn't know how she felt about making that change.

I'm surviving, she said to Mikah as he stopped before her desk.

She earned a wide smile from him at her joke. *I'm glad you saw reason in our sentiments. Some of the Elders had suggested more extreme measures like having everyone else move out so you can have the Grand Hall to yourself.*

Thankfully, they are not in charge, Kinza said with a laugh. After her public speech, she had a smaller meeting with the Elders, letting them know that their positions might be changing soon. She introduced her new council of advisers as well, making some of the more traditional Elders a bit affronted at her choices. Kinza hoped any negative comments she received about the changes she made were just growing pains and not sparks of future dissent. For now, the Elders were going along with her new orders.

Indeed, Mikah said, glancing around again. *Where is your shadow? I feel like I haven't seen him lurking about.*

Kinza hid her expression by reaching down to grab another stack of proposals. *I'm not sure, but he's probably doing something with Savar. They are still dealing with the changes from the barrier.*

In truth, Kinza had hardly seen Zaid since the day of her speech, and that was a week ago. She was still resolute in her decision to tell him how she felt, but there just hadn't been the right moment. They were never alone because she had people demanding her attention at all hours of the day. She would only get to see Zaid for brief moments before he was pushed to the side, and then she wouldn't be able to find him again after. The nervousness in her stomach was there, and she knew it wouldn't go away until she talked to him, but finding a way to do that was becoming difficult.

Ah, I see, Mikah said, seeming to understand. He peered at her over her stack of papers. *And how are you doing?* he asked, a bit quieter.

She looked up to find him staring at her intently. It wasn't lost on her that they never really talked about their relationship or what had—or had not—happened between them in her first weeks in the city. *I think I'm doing okay. Everything is... a lot, obviously,* she said, using his own choice of words. *But that's to be expected, and once things are a bit more settled, I think I'll feel better.* She paused, looking down at her lap. She needed to set something straight but didn't know how to say it, so she went with the truth.

Looking back up at him, she said, *I do really appreciate your friendship, Mikah. I'll be honest, I think my first few days here would have been much harder if you hadn't been there. Not to mention you actually saved my life,* she said, chuckling. *I think I just wanted to say thank you, for everything. And I'm glad you agreed to be one of my advisers.*

He gave her an understanding nod and a soft smile. Thankfully Mikah was someone who understood the subtleties of communication, and she didn't have to say it outright. She meant every word she said to him, that she was thankful for his friendship, and that was all.

Of course, Your Highness, he said. *Anything I can do to help.*

Trying to change the subject, Kinza perked up a little. *And how is Eta? She looked a little better yesterday, but I haven't seen her today at all.*

She is much better, Mikah said. *I think she just needed a few days of rest after such a... monumental vision. But she'll be all right.* Kinza reflected on the change between him and Eta. The first few times she had seen them, it looked like fighting cats and dogs, but over the last week, Mikah seemed different when Eta was around.

Good, good, she said, trying not to comment and then failing. *Are you and Eta...*

Mikah looked at her under lowered brows. *Now, Your Highness, you must know it's rude to pry. Even for a queen.*

Kinza couldn't help but smile. *Fine, fine, I won't ask.*

All right, he said, *I assume you are drowning in coronation preparations, so I'll leave you to it before you decide to give me more to do.* He gave her a deep bow and a charming smile at the door.

See you later, Mikah, she said, laughing and shaking her head as the door clicked shut.

He was right, though. Mikah had done an excellent job setting up and organizing a coronation ceremony for her, which for him meant delegating those tasks to other "qualified" individuals. It was to be tonight at sunset, which left her only a few more hours to finish up her work and get ready.

Taking one more look at the horrendous stacks of proposals, Kinza got up and left her office to see if she could find Zaid.

ZAID PUSHED OPEN the door to the house of the venari. The sounds of the city were muffled as he stepped inside, but he could still hear the construction that was ongoing throughout the central plaza. Despite the fact that Rhapta had gone through several traumatic events recently, the mood of its people had been surprisingly bright over the last week. It was probably due to the fact the city had a new queen, and she was keeping them safe.

Zaid ascended the rickety staircase up to the gloom of the

upper floor. He was pretty sure he was the only person *not* in a good mood this week. He needed something to do, something to distract him. So here he was, knocking on Savar's door.

Enter, came the voice from the other side. Zaid went in to find Savar in discussion with Tejas, another venari and somewhat of a friend to Zaid. Savar was explaining the new barrier system since Tejas had returned the night before. For the time being, Kinza only opened the doorway to the barrier twice a day. The venari would need to calculate their arrival and departure based on those times until they came up with a new place. It was tedious, but it wouldn't stop them from working. The venari that had come and gone in the past several weeks each had a rude awakening. Each time they would return to news that either the city had been attacked, or that they had a new queen. Such was the life of the venari, though; one foot in Rhapta, one foot in the rest of the world.

Tejas nodded to Zaid on his way out, probably directly to another assignment. Zaid had already earned himself a few dirty looks from several venari due to his "extended time off." Zaid would be ending that hiatus today, though.

I'm ready for another assignment, he said, stepping up to Savar's desk.

The older man leaned back with shrewd eyes, assessing Zaid far too long for comfort. He sucked on a tooth and nodded, reaching for a file that sat on the side of his desk and plopped it in front of Zaid.

Two ubir were spotted by an Ummanu in Thailand. They are relatively new, so there's a chance they could be healed. It was noted to bring them back alive.

Zaid nodded. *I'll leave tonight after the coronation, and it shouldn't take me more than a week.* He reached to grab the file, but Savar smacked his hand down on top of it.

You're not going to ask me for more time here in the city? Savar questioned.

Zaid couldn't look him in the eye. *No. You were right.*

He hated saying the words; they cut at him like blunt knives. Over the past week, Zaid realized those words had been true. When Zaid had seen Kinza and Mikah back before they left for the United States, it had felt like a sharp pain in his chest that it was possible Kinza could fall in love with someone else. But ever since she truly became queen, he saw what Savar had really meant.

Kinza had a totally different life now. Her days were filled with official meetings and events, and she was surrounded by advisers, Elders, and other important people. She never had time for him, and he wasn't complaining about that either. He was so proud of the woman she was becoming in the short time he had known her. She had pulled his people out of the darkness they had been in the past two hundred years and continued to make their lives brighter every day.

Zaid, on the other hand, was a venari and had no place in that. He lived in harsh conditions, fighting ubir, all entirely alone. In the same breath the people used to praise their queen, they spewed insults at him. What use did a queen have for him if he wasn't doing his job? The best way he could help her was to deal with as many ubir as possible.

Savar looked him over again, and something like sadness crossed his face. *Okay,* he said finally, back to business.

Zaid turned to leave.

Also...

Zaid turned back around expectantly. Maybe Savar had another case for him.

The head of the venari leaned back in his chair. *I've been thinking about finally taking on an apprentice. I wanted to offer the position to you first, if you're interested.*

Zaid was stunned but did his best not to show it. This was definitely not what he had expected. As far as Zaid knew, Savar had never taken on an apprentice, one that would take his place eventually.

Why? Zaid said, confused.

Savar shrugged, but he knew the man was anything but nonchalant. *I'm not getting any younger, and there will be a time when I need to pass the torch. It would mean taking on a lot more responsibility, handling training, selecting new venari, handing out assignments, that sort of thing.*

Zaid didn't know what to say.

It would also mean you'd spend a lot more time in the city and less on assignments. Zaid knew there was more to Savar's reasoning for choosing him as his apprentice, but that particular benefit was a gesture of kindness, something rarely seen in the house of venari.

Did Zaid really want to spend more time in the city watching Kinza from afar? The thought didn't seem appealing, but the idea of being the head of venari one day lit a sort of fire in him. There were so many changes that could be made, especially now that Kinza was reorganizing the city. He could lead a larger effort to try to control the ubir population.

Can I give you my answer when I get back? Zaid asked.

Savar nodded. *If I don't have it by then, I'll need to ask someone else.*

Understood.

Zaid left and closed the door behind him. As he stepped outside, thoughts of what his future would look like swirled around him. He had thought the rest of his life would be on assignment until the day he was too old to work or he died. It was almost funny thinking back to when he was a child. All he had wanted was to become a warrior and have everyone look at him in awe and hope. Now there was a good chance he would end up being the head of the most shunned group of people in the city.

Life really does hit you with a curveball sometimes.

The coronation was in a couple hours, and Zaid wanted to talk to Khalil before he left. He hadn't had a chance to talk with his oldest friend in almost two weeks and thought he had seen him walking toward the library earlier.

Zaid made his way down the small street that opened up to a larger boulevard. The city was starting to look much better, almost better than it had before the night of the attack. New stones were placed in the roads, soot stains removed from buildings, and new roofs put up. It also meant more business for vendors when hungry workers stopped for their midday meal. People still avoided Zaid on the street like he was carrying a plague, but it wasn't bad as it used to be.

He entered the central plaza and headed toward the library. On his way up the stairs, he ran into a face that had always sparked a bitter rage in him—until recently.

Zaid! Hunar said, pushing up his glasses. The man had on his scholar's robes and was carrying a handful of books out. *I haven't seen you in some time. Here to accuse me of anything else?* He said it with a smile, but Zaid thought he deserved it. For years, Zaid had blamed what happened to Amir on Hunar's influence. He, of course, knew that was all wrong now and that everything that happened with Amir was Tahir's doing.

No, Zaid said. *I'm here to see a friend of mine, actually.*

You have friends that read? Hunar asked, scrunching up his face.

Yes, I suppose. Actually, Hunar, I wanted to talk to you, so I'm glad I caught you. I wanted to say that... I'm sorry. For blaming you after Amir... I'm just sorry. If I had listened to you or Amir back then, there's a chance none of this would have happened. Zaid already felt better getting that off his chest.

The man looked up at him with surprise, his eyebrows halfway to his hairline. *Well, don't regret the past. If things had been different, you wouldn't have met a particularly beautiful queen,* he said with a wink.

Zaid winced and rubbed his neck. *Actually, it's not what you think. I just got a new assignment,* he said, holding up the file Savar had given him. *I'll be back on regular duty again.*

Hunar looked confused. *Did the queen order—*

Zaid shook his head. *I chose this. It's for the best.*

Hunar pursed his lips. *Well, it's a terrible decision,* he said bluntly, moving past Zaid to be on his way. Zaid didn't know how to argue that, but Hunar turned around again. *If you ever want to know more about what Amir and I were studying, come find me. There is much that your brother discovered before Tahir did what he did. I still have his notes if you want them.*

Zaid hadn't known there was more to Amir's research. His brother had talked about all sorts of things every time he came home, but Zaid had understood none of it at the time. *I'd like that,* he said.

Hunar smiled before leaving Zaid standing outside the library.

Zaid found Khalil in one of the large back rooms used for storage. The library was still undergoing construction as well, and many of the undocumented materials were piled in rooms for sorting later. Khalil was knee-deep in crates and boxes of items, muttering to himself about the mess. As soon as he saw Zaid, he handed him the box he was holding.

Here, be useful, Khalil said.

Hello to you too, Zaid replied, looking at the mess. *What are you looking for?*

Several healing scrolls from the 16th century. They are priceless, and I need them to teach a few methods to some of the apprentice healers. But I don't know how I'm ever going to find anything in this disaster! Khalil said, grabbing at his hair. The curls immediately stuck straight out, but Zaid dared not laugh.

There was a new wave of healers that entered into Apprenticeship recently, and I was asked to teach a few classes, but without the proper materials. Khalil sighed heavily, digging through a crate. *I'm also in the middle of writing a proposal to keep those from the outskirts who want to stay inside the city. That needed to be done yesterday, but I've spent the last three days looking for those ridiculous scrolls!*

I'm sure you'll find them, Zaid said, but he wasn't actually sure at all based on the state of the room. *And I know Kinza wouldn't have a problem with the people staying inside the city if they wanted. There are more than enough empty houses.*

Khalil suddenly straightened from the crate and looked at Zaid. *Why are you here, by the way? Aren't you supposed to be with her? She's in the middle of transferring governments. I'm sure that is stressful.*

Zaid avoided looking at him the same way he avoided Savar. *Not really. She doesn't actually need me with her that much. I'm leaving on an assignment after the coronation, and I'll be busy for a while, so I wanted to stop by.*

Khalil groaned and went back to his crate, tossing out several tomes. *Back to making poor decisions, are we?*

What's that supposed to mean?

You know exactly what it means, Khalil said, arching a brow at him.

Zaid was no longer in the mood to discuss his life choices today. He'd already done that enough. *I'll be back briefly in about a week. Let's talk then, all right?*

Khalil stood up and looked at him again, hair awry and an annoyingly knowing look on his face. Zaid had been friends with him for so long that he sometimes forgot that Khalil knew how Zaid was feeling regardless of whether he wanted him to or not.

Of course. Just don't die, Khalil said and went back to digging through the mess.

That's the idea. Zaid left Khalil to his work, silently vowing that he would be in a better mood the next time he talked to his friend.

He paused outside the library for a moment. The sun was on its downward arc, and there wasn't much time left until the ceremony. He decided to make one more trip to his mother's before he left.

ETA WALKED in the shadow of the baobab trees, relishing the relief from the sun. She had been wandering around the south quarter for a few hours, avoiding her responsibilities. It was unlike her, she never did anything like that, but she had needed a break when her visions started quickening again.

She had spent much of the last week resting and even had to insist Kinza give her something to do to get her out of bed. Her body had needed a little longer than she had anticipated for recovery. Hakim had never mentioned how the larger visions could take such a toll on her physical health, so she supposed that was something she would need to learn to navigate on her own.

Overall, her visions had mellowed out, and she hadn't seen anything more exciting than a possible rainstorm next week. She was glad there was some semblance of control in her life. Not that the visions would never be chaotic and terrifying ever again, but now she knew what to expect. That, mixed with the elation of Kinza's queenship, had made a remarkably wonderful week for Eta. At this evening's coronation, it would be official. Eta would finally no longer have to worry about leading the Anunnaki. Kinza miraculously was able to defend the city on her own, leaving Eta the time to focus on her visions. She could even see herself becoming true friends with the queen, something that she never truly had before.

Eta made her way back toward the Grand Hall to prepare for the coronation ceremony. Normally it would be led by the previous monarch or highest adviser in years past, but Eta offered to do it.

The plaza was bright in the late afternoon sun as she entered the hall. She thought about going back to her office to spend a little more time reading. Someone had left a stack of journals on her desk the day before with a note saying they were found in the rubble of the library. She had held back tears when she opened them. They were Hakim's personal journals when he was her age. Daily logs of visions he had; some even looked remarkably similar to one's Eta had. She wished she could thank whoever found them because the journals were the only link she had to the man who practically raised her.

Eta made her way to her rooms, passing by frenzied attendants preparing for the ceremony in a few hours. Just as she turned down the hallway to her room, a familiar feeling crept through her. Something in her mind urged her to turn around and go back the way she came.

Oh no... she groaned. It was the same feeling, that urging that she got leading up to the vision she had in the quarries. Not knowing if her body could handle that again so soon, she immediately obeyed the feeling and went back down the hall.

It took her back through the Grand Hall but to the opposite side, past offices and meeting rooms, before she finally stopped before a closed door.

The urging suddenly stopped, as if satisfied.

It was the door to Mikah's office. Eta closed her eyes and tilted her head back, letting out a breath. Why of all places did it take her here? She already knew the answer to that of course, so she went ahead and knocked.

Come in.

Eta entered to find Mikah looking uncharacteristically stressed, staring down at a stack of papers. She was sure many people in the hall looked like that right now, but it was odd to see on Mikah, who normally looked so unbothered. Eta knew Kinza had given them both a mountain of work, so he was probably just trying to deal with it the same as she was.

He looked up, and she realized she hadn't said anything. *Hi,* she said awkwardly. Mikah had helped her several times over the last week, making sure she had time to sleep and eat through her recovery. They hadn't actually talked about their temporary truce, though, seeing as she only just got back to work. She remembered his admission in the quarries through the haze of her memory, about how he did wear a mask all the time, and she wondered if he kept it down around her now because of it.

Mikah hardly glanced at her and went back to his stack of papers, flipping through them aggressively. *Did you need something?* he asked, not unkindly.

No, not really, she replied, not really knowing what to say. She clenched her hands together within the sleeves of her robe.

I apologize if I was intruding, Mikah said, head bent over his desk. *I didn't read them. Just the first few pages before I realized what they were. I know you don't like people invading your work.*

I—what? Eta asked. She had no idea what he was talking about.

The journals, he said, absently waving a hand. *I left them on your desk. I assumed you got them.*

Eta stood there with her mouth open. Mikah had been the

one to leave them for her? She closed her mouth before she looked like a fool.

If you aren't feeling well, I can take some of your duties. Just leave them on the side table there. His brow was furrowed as he read over whatever report had him so engrossed. Eta remarked on how different the person before her was compared to the man who had introduced himself a few weeks ago. The man she had met gave her too-bright smiles and honeyed words. Every one of his actions had screamed *lies!* to Eta. But the man before her was honest and real, and even though he was drowning in responsibilities, he offered to take over some of her so she could *rest.*

Actually... I was wondering if you wanted any help.

Mikah finally looked at her again, standing there in the doorway, and set down the page in his hand. A crooked smile that Eta was sure no one else had ever seen spread across his face, and he stood up.

I would be honored, he said. So Eta closed the door, and they got to work.

CHAPTER 21

UNDER THE BAOBAB TREES

Kinza entered the chaos of the library. She could have sworn she saw Zaid come in just moments ago but lost him just as fast. She had been looking for him for hours and couldn't find him anywhere. She might as well look here too while she still had a little time left.

The progress the city was making made her very happy, and it seemed the people were a little happier as well. As she entered, people bowed to her left and right. Kinza tried and failed not to give an awkward smile every time. She asked a few people if they had seen a man dressed in all black, but everyone just shrugged or shook their heads.

The entrance down to the underground levels of the building was open again now that the city wasn't going to be invaded. Kinza descended the staircase while deftly avoiding workers coming up and down. She hadn't been to the former headquarters of the Apostles of Truth since the night of the battle. It looks relatively the same other than half of the library's contents had been hauled downstairs. She heard a few people mention making it an archive of sorts as she passed by.

She heard a familiar growling voice arguing with another more excited voice coming from one of the many multi-use rooms. Inside she found Nim and Badr locked in verbal warfare.

You would think that brain of yours had some sense! Nim shouted at the younger man. Since the death of the former Apostles leader, Sa'id, Nim had become a bit more somber compared to the jovial nature he had prior to the battle. Kinza hated to see the effects of the destruction Tahir wrought.

And that thick skull of yours isn't able to comprehend the nature of deduction, so leave the thinking to me! Badr shot back. He was holding an armload of scrolls and books that Nim was trying to take from him.

Ahem! Kinza said, trying not to laugh.

Both men saw her and bowed low. *Your Highness!* they said in unison.

What's going on here?

Nim sighed as if exasperated that he needed to explain. *This imbecile of an apprentice thinks he needs all of the records on Anunnaki healing properties. That over a hundred volumes and forty scrolls!* Nim shouted.

I need them! Badr said. *And need I remind you that I am an adviser to the queen!* Badr had taken his duties very seriously, immediately pulling together a small team to help him formulate the ink needed to extend the Anunnaki's tattoos. Kinza gave him leave to work on additional projects as well in his spare time, usually ones recommended by Eta. This must have been one of such projects.

Okay, that's enough, Kinza said, attempting to calm them down. *I apologize, Nim. I asked Badr to get those scrolls. Is that too much, or does he need to take them out individually?*

Badr looked like he was about to protest, but Kinza shot him a glare. Thankfully, Nim relented.

Not if it's on the queen's orders, Nim grumbled. *Ach! Fine, but don't bend the spines,* he said, shaking a finger at Badr. *And NO ripping pages out.*

Badr nodded quickly. *No pages in the books—I mean, no ripping pages in the books. Or out of them. Keep the pages in the books. Got it.*

Someone down the hall yelled for Nim. He sighed again. *I'm needed everywhere today. One might think I'm the queen,* he muttered, bowing to Kinza as he left.

Badr gave Kinza a sheepish look once Nim had left. *Thanks for taking the fall.*

Anytime, Kinza said. *Now take them quickly before he changes his mind.* Badr didn't waste a second and hurried out and up the stairs.

Across the hall, Kinza found the door to Jabari's office open, so she stepped inside.

Ah, he said, looking up from the ledger he was writing in. *My pupil returns after skipping several lessons.*

Kinza leaned against the door. *If you hadn't noticed, I've been a little busy.*

I supposed saving our lives is a forgivable excuse, he said with a smirk. *Especially seeing as you used my teachings to do so.* He looked up at her over the page of his book. *Just don't skip any more.* He flared the flame on the candle on his desk for emphasis.

Kinza smiled. *I'll make time for two lessons next week.* Jabari agreed to the deal with the exception that they were going to start training her fire abilities at the next lesson.

As she made her way back upstairs, she still didn't see Zaid anywhere, so she went back out to the plaza. The sun was heading down now, and she didn't have any more time to go looking for him. She needed to prepare for the ceremony.

The decorations were already mostly up in the plaza, but

Kinza wasn't really paying attention to them as she hurried to the Grand Hall and up the steps. She really had wanted to talk to Zaid before this evening, but that didn't look like it was going to happen. Was he avoiding her again?

Now she actually started to worry because the more she thought about it, the more she realized he was absent all the time now in the same way he had been before they left for the United States. He couldn't really still be mad at her, could he?

She made it up to her room only to find several people already inside. Several attendants and Ekbal were there as well as Ekaja with an armload of beads, paints, and clothing.

Didn't we talk about you keeping a retinue on you at all times? Ekbal said as she walked through the door.

She didn't mention his tone. *Yes, we talked about it, but I never agreed to it.* Kinza would fight to retain the smallest shred of privacy she had left.

Ekbal shook his head. *I'm going down to talk with Eta before the ceremony. This woman here says she will be getting you dressed.* He leaned in a little closer. *I think your attendants are a little upset.*

Kinza put on her queenly face and voice, thanking Ekbal and her attendants before letting them all know she would see them downstairs in an hour.

Let's get you ready, my dear, Ekaja said with a wide smile.

For the next hour, Kinza bathed at Ekaja's command before letting her primp, preen, lotion, braid, dress, and decorate her until she thought there was nothing left for the woman to do. Every time she thought she was done, Ekaja would shove her back down in her seat. It was a good distraction from Kinza's nervousness, and she even asked if Ekaja had seen Zaid. She said she had earlier briefly. Apparently he was going on another assignment tonight after the ceremony.

A sick feeling coiled in Kinza's stomach. He was leaving

again? He had said he would need to go back to his duty at some point, but why hadn't he told her? There must have been something wrong for him to avoid her this much.

When Ekaja was done, Kinza looked at her handiwork.

She had been dressed in scarlet robes, much the same shape as the Elder's and apprentice's. There hadn't been time to completely redo Kinza's hair, so Ekaja had adjusted the half braids and left the rest of her curls down. She had also added more lapis and turquoise beads for color. Kinza's arms and hands were painted in a variety of colors with markings she would learn later on. Finally, around her neck Ekaja placed necklace after necklace of colorful beads, so it looked like the top of the robes had a multicolored collar. Similar beads were draped over her hair as well.

Ishar and Badr had given Eta as much information about the ceremony as they could, but no one had actually been to one in hundreds of years. The monarchy never had a crown; only their white Aura was needed. The ceremony was also just that: a ceremony. It was more the beginning of a day-long celebration. All Kinza needed to do was kneel and say a few words and then light up her Aura right as the sun set. After that, there would be dancing and festivities all night and well into the next day.

Kinza was still nervous as she went with Ekaja through the Grand Hall, hardly thinking about the ceremony at all now. The sun had almost set, and the plaza and surrounding streets were filled with people. There were flowers everywhere, and people cheered the moment she was visible. Torches burned in anticipated for the evening. Just like with her speech, the advisers and Elders stood up by the pillars, but there was no Zaid this time. Had he already left?

Kinza did her best to smile and wave, and at the right time, a drum beat signaled the beginning of the ceremony. People quieted down as Kinza took one last glance around the crowd, hoping to find Zaid.

Eta stood to one side with an ancient tome in her hands. She was wearing a bright blue dress as opposed to her normal robes, making Kinza almost not recognize her. Her arms and face were painted with symbols like Kinza's, and she smiled and opened the book.

Kinza turned to face her like she was told to, trying to focus on the task at hand. The woman who helped Kinza amplify her voice at her speech came over as well and placed her hands on each of their shoulders.

Now, they were ready.

At Eta's indication, Kinza kneeled down, careful not to get caught in the voluminous robes. Eta held out an open tome written in Rhaptan, its pages yellowed and spine worn. Again, at Eta's nod, Kinza started to recite the vows on the page. She didn't actually need the book because she had already memorized them, but it was part of the ceremony.

The day before, Ishar and Eta had told her how the vows had come to be, and the story had touched her. All Rhaptan marriages had the same set of vows sworn before an Aurastone, but when the first Rhaptan king took the throne, he swore that Rhapta itself was his first love, and so he spoke similar words upon his coronation.

Rhapta, I vow to hold the barrier, even when you cannot.
Rhapta, I vow to light the way, even in your darkest moments.
Rhapta, I vow to protect you from your enemies, even if your enemy is yourself.
Rhapta, I vow to care for you, even if it means my death.
Rhapta, I vow to right your course, even when you go astray.
Rhapta, I vow to stand by your side, until the end of my days.
Rhapta, I, Kinza Solace, vow to love you.

Moments before the sun set, Kinza finished speaking and Eta helped her to her feet. They both turned toward the crowd, and Eta held Kinza's hand aloft, displaying the Anunnaki queen. Kinza took a moment to scan the crowd as best she could for Zaid.

All hail Kinza, Queen of the Anunnaki! Eta cried, and the people erupted into cheers. Kinza still couldn't find Zaid, though, even as the sun officially set.

Eta nudged her. *Kinza,* she said in her mind. *Your Aura!* Kinza was supposed to let her Aura out the moment the sun set.

Right at that moment, she spotted him. He was off to the side of the plaza, standing in the light of a few torches.

Kinza let her Aura out, the white light stretching across the plaza like a star, and the people cheered louder. Relief washed through her that he hadn't left, so she smiled at her people as they cheered for their queen.

THE MUSIC and dancing started immediately. Kinza barely made it down the stairs before she was swarmed for the umpteenth time that week. People bowed and congratulated her. Some cheered or wanted to hold her hand. After what felt like thirty minutes, Zaid appeared before Kinza.

All hail the queen, he said with a smile that almost looked sad. In an odd sense of formality from him, he bowed like the others had, hand over his chest.

If you do that again, I'll beat you up, Kinza replied. Despite her words, his presence meant a lot to her. Other people were already trying to push their way to her, but Zaid managed to hold his ground.

He laughed. *I have no doubt. I'm going to get out of the way before I get trampled. I'll catch you later?*

Yes, she said, nodding profusely. Before she knew it, he was gone, and she was the queen again. She felt a little better than she had earlier knowing that he would talk to her later. The problem was that time never came.

For the next hour, Kinza was herded around so people could speak to her and express their sentiments. It was expected that she be in the middle of everything as celebrations took place around the city. Many people lit up their Auras for the light, and the city reminded Kinza of a dance club in downtown Chicago. There was so much going on and so much happiness; she couldn't begrudge her people that.

So, she did what a good queen was supposed to and let her advisers tell her where to go and who to speak with. She caught Mikah sneaking glances at Eta in her blue dress and decided she would tease him later about it. Vendors came and gave her food to try, and she had to politely decline the mango beer that she couldn't stand.

Once the festivities had been in full swing for a while, Kinza finally managed to sneak away. It was immensely difficult, and she thought she should be awarded some sort of prize for managing it while in her current outfit. She kept her eyes out the whole time for Zaid again but never saw him. The longer she hung around the plaza, the higher the chance that someone would spot her.

Kinza finally gave up.

The walk back to her room was surprisingly lonely. Even though she had people around her all the time now, she felt a bit empty as she headed inside. When she got back to her room, she heard the voices of her attendants coming from inside, and she decided she wasn't quite ready to deal with others at the moment.

Relishing and hating the few moments of solitude, she walked back down the hall. At the very end, she normally would turn right to go to the main sector of the building. For some reason, she looked to the door on the left, at the end. She had never seen anyone use it and assumed it was some sort of broom closet.

Trying the handle, it opened easily. Inside, she found a dark staircase leading up.

Kinza felt a bit rebellious but reminded herself she was the queen now. Why wouldn't she be allowed to go up the creepy staircase? She stepped inside and made her way up. It went a lot further than she expected and ended with a sort of trap door above her head. Deciding she had already come this far, she turned the handle until it came unstuck and shoved upward.

It opened out onto the roof.

Kinza coughed at the cobwebs and inhaled the fresh air. The door was situated on the eastern side of the building on the flat roof. There was a low wall surrounding the entire top, but it was otherwise empty. She walked toward the vibrant lights on the southern edge, and when she got close, she could see the entire central plaza from her vantage point.

This was a secret place she would keep to herself, if only to get away every once in a while. She leaned on the wall, watching the people and thinking over how her life had changed so drastically in such a short time.

I'm pretty sure they are expecting you down there.

Kinza twisted to find Zaid's dark form coming toward her. He stepped up next to her and leaned against the wall too.

How did you find me? she asked with a slight smile.

Tracking is my job, remember? he said, resting his chin on his fist. Kinza had been looking for him all day—all week—and now that he was here, she found she couldn't speak. She had thought over and over about how she wanted to start her sentence and how she would convey her feelings. All those plans washed away, and they just stood there, looking out over the city. It was Zaid who finally spoke again. Maybe he felt the tension coming off her.

How has your first week as queen been? he asked.

Hmm, she thought. *Exhausting. I made a million and one changes, and I'm sure I have just as many things to deal with tomorrow.*

Zaid frowned at that and laced his fingers together. *I suppose you miss your grandma and Mitra too?*

Kinza nodded. *Actually, I talked with my advisers, and I think I might bring Grams here.* She smiled at the thought of her grandmother in Rhapta. Ekaja would probably demand she live with her.

Tell her to leave the pan at home, Zaid mumbled. Kinza snorted a laugh.

They watched the dancing a little longer, but it quickly turned into an awkward silence. *I talked to Haris again,* he said. *Portals are fixed, I guess. Even the bigger ones that have been down for centuries. They haven't caught Basma yet, though. Haris mentioned something about larger problems with the ubir.*

That didn't sound good. *Like what?* she asked. The soft wind rustled the beads in her hair, causing them to click together like wind chimes.

Zaid sighed, squinting in thought. *Not sure. He said he would update me when they had more information.*

Kinza nodded, and the awkward silence returned. She tapped her fingers on the wall, unsure of what to do with her hands. The butterflies were eating away at the lining of her stomach now. Eventually, she cracked.

Where have you been all week?! she demanded, whirling

toward him. *I've been looking for you everywhere, and you keep disappearing!*

Zaid raised his eyebrows at her outburst. *Well...* he said slowly. *You looked a little preoccupied, and I wanted to give you space.*

Well—not, no, not from—

I should also probably tell you I'm going on another assignment and will probably be back in a week or so. He looked so calm telling her this. Did he really not feel anything for her?

No. She didn't know why she said it, but it was too late to back down now.

What? Zaid asked, facing her. The light from the plaza danced across the side of his face, making his skin glow. Kinza had the sudden urge to ask him to see his Aura again.

I forbid it, she said, crossing her arms. She knew she was acting sullen, but she couldn't help it. This was not how this conversation was supposed to go. She was supposed to confess her feelings in an organized, non-confrontational way. Yet here she was.

Why are you being like this? Zaid had crossed his arms now too, and narrowed his eyes at her.

She heaved a breath. *You said you would stay by my side through all of... this,* she said, gesturing toward the city. Her heart was pounding now with what she was going to say. He could probably hear it too.

You clearly don't need me—

I do! she burst out, arms wide. *I do need you! Forever. By my side. There was no end date to that position.* Her chest was heaving at the pent-up emotion. There. She had said it. That was enough, wasn't it? Why was he being so dense? Maybe he didn't feel the same...

Zaid was a little wide-eyed now, looking at her. *Kinza, I don't think you actually want—*

Kinza had had enough. In a brief fit of madness, she flung her arms around his neck and planted her lips on his. He was tall enough that she really needed to reach to get to his lips. They were warm, but his body was rigid, and she immediately jumped back once she realized what she had done.

Kinza clapped a hand over her mouth. *Did I really just...* she thought to herself. Heat crept up her neck at her mortification. Zaid looked like he was in shock, not having moved. Was he even breathing?

I am so sorry, she said, closing her eyes. She couldn't handle looking at him... at the rejection on his face. This had been a terrible idea. *I would never order you to stay with me like that. I'm sorry.* Of course he didn't want any of that. How could she have been so stupid?

Warm hands suddenly grabbed the sides of her face, and Zaid was kissing her. It was Kinza's turn to be in shock. He pulled back, and she opened her eyes to find the most ridiculous grin she had ever seen plastered across his face. Never in her time with him had she seen the absolute joy that radiated off him now.

I accept, he said, still holding her face between his palms.

What? Her mind was reeling at what was happening.

I accept, he said again. *As long as you want me by your side, I will stay. Okay?*

Tears welled in Kinza's eyes and spilled over. Her heart was going a million miles an hour, and she felt like she was flying. Was this real? Did he truly mean it?

By the look on his face, Kinza had not a shadow of a doubt he had meant every word. She realized that she had gotten everything in life that she had ever wanted. There was an entire city for her to heal, a family who loved her, Grams would be cared for, and the man in front of her would never leave her side.

Kinza smiled through her tears. "Okay," she whispered.

Zaid kissed her forehead and tucked her into his chest under his chin. The silence was no longer awkward as they stood there watching the Auras across the city. In the coming days, there would be a million people pulling them in different directions with an endless list of work to be done. For now, they let the people enjoy their celebration under the baobab trees, and tomorrow they would start a new chapter.

EPILOGUE

 month later...

KINZA SIPPED ON HER TEA, letting the spiciness coat her mouth as she listened to Elder Urash present his official opinion. He was one of several people standing in a semicircle around Kinza's desk this morning but by far the most opinionated. She wasn't sure how he had so much to say this early in the day while she was still blinking sleep out of her eyes.

Ultimately, Urash said, lacing his fingers together, *I think it's a risk, but one we might need to consider taking to avoid further population decline.*

It's for a lot more than that! Khalil said, throwing his hands up. *The people living on the outskirts—the ones that don't want to be there—have no reason to be other than past political maneuvering to cater to the wealthy. They are sick! If we bring them into the city, say the south quarter, then we could keep all of our healers inside the walls, create a few of those... Kinza, what did you call them?*

Clinics? she offered, taking another sip of tea.

Yes, clinics! Khalil continued. *We add several of those throughout the city, and then we have a better way to regulate the use of healers and be more efficient while we are at it. I don't see what the problem is.*

Urash, currently still the representative of all healers in Rhapta, was intent on weighing all possible outcomes several times over before coming to a final decision. *We do need to consider the fact that if we bring those on the outskirts inside, that will force any lingering rebel groups to reside in the city as well. That may create more problems, though.*

I say we let the warriors worry about that, Ekbal said, massaging a temple. *The number of Unfettered has dropped drastically since the battle, and maybe keeping them in the city will force them out of hiding; it's easier for us to regulate what goes on inside the walls due to the warrior patrols.*

That is true, Ishar agreed.

Kinza stayed quiet a little longer while the advisers, Elder, and healer made their various points on the matter. She still didn't know why they continued to have this conversation, but apparently it was good form for one to think things through before they acted, or so Ishar and Ekbal said. Based on their expressions, there was a chance they were regretting their words. If Kinza had her way, she would have completed all of Khalil's suggestions a month ago.

This, along with the thousands of other proposals she had to sit through, did give her quite a bit of practice in her new position as queen. She quickly discovered that letting them get their entire opinion off their chest before responding was the best way to avoid a conflict. So, she let Urash speak his piece before responding.

All right, she said, *I think everyone has said their piece. Based on your opinions, I understand that there are risks to allowing those on the outskirts inside as well as creating clinics that may disrupt the natural flow and independence of the healers. On the other hand, I have to agree that the benefits outweigh the risks, so I am going to approve this proposal.*

Khalil looked pleased for once, and the others nodded their agreement. *Now, if you'll excuse me, I do need to check in with the venari on their progress.*

Urash thanked her, bowed, and left, leaving the door to her office open on his way out. Ekbal, Ishar, and Khalil stood as well, talking over the plans of implementation. Kinza made to leave but was stopped by a disapproving noise.

Ahem. She turned to find Ekbal and Ishar looking at her under half-lidded eyes. *I'm not as oblivious as I look,* Ekbal said.

Whatever could you mean? Kinza asked innocently, inching toward the door. She had hoped to leave without notice, but Ishar and Ekbal had been watching her like a hawk since taking on their new positions as advisers.

Your Highness, we are your advisers to give you advice. *This is one of those things you should heed,* Ishar said, his bushy white eyebrows going up.

Khalil, who had heard similar conversations of late, attempted to look like he wasn't paying attention, fiddling with something on Kinza's desk.

*I really have no idea what you're—*Kinza had inched further toward the door but bumped into someone who had just come in. She turned to find not one, but two men in the red paint of the warriors, looking at her with the same expression as Ishar and Ekbal.

Her guards.

Kinza sighed dramatically, turning back to her advisers. *And I, the queen, should be able to walk out of the most protected building in the city, into the busiest plaza in the city, to the building where the people who hunt ubir are literally trained. How am I not safe? This is ridiculous.*

Please, Your Highness? the shorter of the two guards asked. *It would make us feel much better. And useful.*

Yes, very useful, the second and taller of the two guards added. Kinza had slowly gotten used to seeing their faces following her around the city in rotation with a few others. Before long, she would know them better than her own grandmother. She rarely complained about her duties as queen, except to Zaid when they were alone, but the fact that she couldn't walk around the city by herself was practically embarrassing. She literally had an ability that alerted her of danger!

You know, I really don't think—she started but was saved by an actual angel.

A knock came at the open door, and the six of them turned to find Zaid leaning in the entryway. The two warriors looked mildly offended that he had managed to sneak up behind them. *I hope I'm not interrupting? I figured I would walk the queen to the house of the venari.*

It was Ekbal's turn to sigh dramatically as he pinched the bridge of his nose.

Not at all, Kinza said with a devilish grin. *We just finished up.* She knew she had won. While Zaid walking with her wasn't exactly walking alone, it was as close to personal space as she would get.

Your Highness... Ekbal pleaded. It seemed Ishar had given up, ushering the guards out with him.

I'll see you tomorrow morning, Ekbal, Kinza said with finality, heading toward the door. For good measure, she reached up and planted a kiss on Zaid's cheek on her way out, eliciting a gag from Khalil and a comment from Ekbal about decorum.

Zaid snorted. *You're not happy when we're not together, but you're not happy when we are,* he said to Khalil, shaking his head in mock annoyance before following Kinza out.

Kinza laughed as they walked down the hall, happy at her freedom. While she had made no official announcement that she and Zaid were together, she had made no attempt to hide it either, much to her advisers' disapproval. She had been lectured that past monarchs had only entered into a courtship with those of the highest birth and nobility in the city. Kinza would never have a king since royalty wasn't based on marriage. She could have a consort, however, and that was the highest position excluding hers. Her advisers had cautioned her against making any hasty or public decisions in that regard and advised she... look at all of her options.

Kinza would have none of it. Besides the fact that Zaid wasn't the most comfortable with overt public displays of affection, Kinza still made it very clear that they were together and that they came as a pair.

Kinza steered them down the hall toward the back exit of the Grand Hall, nodding and smiling to those who greeted her on the way out. She liked that the back way was less busy than the central plaza and would allow her and Zaid a moment's peace on the walk there.

Zaid playfully nudged her shoulder when they got down to the street. *So, how'd it go?* he asked.

Well... she said, thinking. *They argued for thirty minutes before coming to the same conclusion I recommended weeks ago.* There were still people out and about in the streets behind the Grand Hall, and many of them ogled at Kinza and Zaid as they walked by. She was still a bit uncomfortable with the attention she received from strangers, but this was her life now.

So you and Khalil both got what you wanted, he said, *just slowly?* He had his hands shoved in his pockets and watched the ground before them as they walked. Even though he seemed cool as a cucumber back in her office, she knew the stares got to him more than her. After years of people looking at him with disgust, as they did all venari, those looks only got more intense. Some people made comments as they walked by, but others started to become curious, wanting to know how this reclusive venari had garnered the attention of the queen.

Yep! she said brightly. *I'll take what I can get, especially since I've already done so much as queen in just a month. How is your new position as an apprentice going?* Kinza had been ecstatic when Zaid told her he was taking on a new position with Savar, meaning that he would be in the city instead of going on assignments regularly.

Zaid grunted. *That's what I was going to show you, but it's best we wait until we get there.*

They turned right onto a slightly quieter street, and Kinza walked a little closer to Zaid. *Oh, I forgot to tell you, we are supposed to go over to your mother's house for dinner tomorrow.*

I assume your grandmother will be there as well? he asked.

Kinza nodded, smiling. *Of course.* A weight was eased off her heart two weeks ago when she finally brought Grams to Rhapta. Well... Zaid was the one who went and got her. He refused to talk about how that trip had gone, citing that it was over and done with.

It hadn't taken much convincing to get her grandmother to want to move across the world. She said her house was full of old, sad memories that weren't doing her any good. They hadn't sold the house yet. Grams had grabbed her most important belongings and left with a single suitcase. They would need to go back and deal with everything sometime soon, though.

She had been in a permanent state of shock for the first two days after she arrived, looking at everything in wonder. Kinza had been almost thankful that Grams couldn't speak telepathically because she was sure that would have been too overwhelming. Ekaja had been there with open arms from the first moment, and the two had spent most hours together. Grams had even mentioned to Kinza that she had found a group of old ladies to play cards with, and she had a sinking suspicion of who she meant.

Kinza glanced over and saw Zaid's brows were furrowed. *What's wrong?* she asked.

Nothing, he said, shaking his head.

Still nothing from Haris?

Zaid sighed, running a hand over his head. *No, nothing at all. Radio silence, in fact.*

Dread pooled in Kinza's stomach. They hadn't heard from Haris or Mitra in over a week. It was still difficult to communicate with them due to the barrier, but Zaid should have been able to reach them if he left. Yet, every time he called—even attempting Mitra's cell—he only got a voice mail. Where were they?

Kinza pursed her lips. *I guess we'll need to make a trip back to the United States sooner than we thought then,* she said quietly.

The house of the venari came into view; the nondescript building wedged between others on a rather quiet street. Zaid steered her toward the back entrance of the building, where a few large bushes blocked the view of the door. He turned to her and said, *Hey, I didn't mean to start your day out so glum. I don't want to stress you out more than you are already.*

You, of all people, are the least stressful, Kinza said with a laugh. *In fact, I'd rather spend all day with you than listen to another silly proposal that should have been made weeks ago.*

Zaid stopped before going inside, looking around for

anyone that might walk by. *All day, huh?* he asked, wrapping an arm around her waist when the coast was clear and tugging her closer.

Kinza didn't care that he could hear her heart start to pound and grinned. *I mean, I might need to get* some *work done...* and she found herself kissing him. She vaguely remembered that they were in public, but she didn't particularly care as she reached up to twine her arms around his neck, allowing him to deepen the kiss. Kinza's brain emptied, and she forgot the rest of the world existed for a moment.

Then, right as he tightened his arms around her waist, the door slammed open.

Kinza and Zaid jumped apart as if they were electrocuted, putting a healthy distance between them to greet whoever had opened the door so aggressively. She was confused for a moment until she looked down and found a child with a wooden sword staring up at them. Kinza turned to Zaid, hoping for an explanation, but he seemed bewildered by the child's existence, as if a goblin were now guarding the house of the venari.

Who are you? Zaid asked, still dumbfounded.

Aryan, the kid said, looking up at them.

Um, what are you doing here? Zaid asked.

I'm Waqas' brother, he replied. *He said I could be here while you fight.* He waved his wooden sword as if remembering he held it.

You're who—ohhh no... Zaid groaned, stepping inside and pushing past the kid who scampered to the side. Kinza followed them in and down the short hallway that opened out to the training ring in the center of the building.

Her jaw dropped.

There were at least ten children in various states of chaos in the ring. Savar stood to the side, doing nothing but looking every shade of angry. This was confirmed when he started barking questions at Zaid about how and when they agreed to open a childcare center.

The children looked like they ranged from seven to fourteen years old, and all seemed to have impressive abilities. A stream of water shot by Kinza's face, and she backed up as two squealing boys ran by. Another girl was throwing daggers at a wooden target with startling accuracy... while another little boy held the target over his head, running back and forth for added difficulty. Two more kids were having a ridiculous battle with wooden swords, barely able to lift them. Another kid jumped from the upper floor balcony and landed with a thud in the sand.

Kinza was supposed to be checking in on the progress the venari were making in recruiting new members. This looked a bit more like an orphanage. She walked over to where Zaid was right as Savar stormed off, yelling at the girl throwing daggers.

Um, I don't mean to be a downer, but what is this? she asked hesitantly.

Zaid rubbed a hand over his face, looking like he wanted to pull his hair out. *I have no idea. I don't even know who half of these kids are! I only tapped four to become venari, and only two of them were actually old enough to start training!*

One of the taller boys shooting streams of water tried to run past Zaid, but he caught the boy and dragged him to the side. *Waqas, what is this?* Zaid asked incredulously.

The boy was panting and grinning, still exhilarated from his chase. *These are my friends. And two of my cousins,* he said happily.

Yes, but what are they doing here? Zaid asked.

They all want to be venari too! Waqas said.

They do? Zaid said, releasing the boy.

Yes!

The boy Waqas had been chasing had come back, out of breath but grinning just as hard. *We want to be like you!* The two kids having a swordfight heard their conversation and came running over, yelling their agreements, saying they wanted to learn how to fight and go on adventures.

Kinza tugged Zaid to the side. *What exactly did you say to them when you recruited them?* she said, leaning in.

Zaid shrugged, showing his palms. *I have no idea. I just did it differently than Savar used to. I just told them what venari do and that we travel to different places and hunt ubir.*

Kinza chuckled. *So you made it sound exciting? Like they could be adventurers?*

Fun? Zaid said, watching the two boys run off again, chasing each other around the training ring. *What about hunting ubir is fun? It's dangerous!*

Kinza started to giggle. This was the most expressive reaction she had seen from him probably ever.

How is this funny?! he cried, gesturing toward the kid who had just jumped off the balcony again. It only made Kinza laugh harder.

I can see you have your hands full, she said, touching his arm. *I'll leave you to it, then.*

Kinza, don't you dare leave—

She kissed his cheek. *I'll see you at dinner tomorrow,* she said and left him to his chaos. She was still laughing when she walked out the front door of the building and stepped out onto the street. Her smile died upon seeing two red-painted warriors waiting for her like they had all the time in the world.

Utterly relentless, she said sourly as one of the guards gave her a sheepish grin.

Sorry, Your Highness, but Ekbal said there was a good chance you would attempt to return alone.

Of course he did, she said with a sigh. *All right, well, I'm in a good mood, so I'll allow it.* Without waiting for them, she strode off down the street. *Let's go; I have a lot of proposals to read and a trip to plan!*

The guards hurried after their queen, never letting her out of their sight.

GLOSSARY OF TERMS

abilities *(ah bill it ees) n.* Powers that each Anunnaki has. The abilities vary per person and are supernatural in nature.

Anunnaki *(ahn new nock ee) n.* A species thought to have originated from Rhapta to guide humanity. They live longer than humans, can speak to each other telepathically, and have abilities. They reside only in Rhapta. If an Anunnaki leaves the city limits, their abilities fade and they slowly become human and forget Rhapta. Some live outside the city limits, but still within the psychic barrier. Their abilities are weakened and have developed a need for verbal speech.

Elder *(ell der) n.* One of the fifty leaders of Rhapta. One out of every fifty is a Grand Elder who leads in ceremony and prophecy.

guakal *(gwa kall) n.* A fist-sized, rigid-shelled, lime green fruit with miniature red spikes on its exterior; native to Rhapta.

laqueus *(la kwees) n.* A rope, silvery-gray in color, made by Anunnaki used to bind or dampen abilities. Mildly annoying to Anunnaki, physically painful to humans.

magalkan'a *(muh gal kahn uh) n.* Commonly known as Aurastone, believed to be the origin of Anunnaki abilities. Shades range from white to azure.

mark *(mar k) n.* The tribal tattoo that every Anunnaki is born with. Only *venari* and ubir have different tattoos. *Venari's* are larger and need to be reapplied monthly; it allows them to enter the human world while retaining their abilities for a short time. Ubir tattoos are similar but red and swollen, as if infected.

reykalkan'o *(ray kal kon oh) n.* Commonly known as Deathstone. It is cracked Aurastone. Created either by blood magic, or taking it from Rhapta. Its presence is extremely painful to Anunnaki, creating a high-pitched ringing. If the Anunnaki cannot hear it, it's unlikely to be harmful.

Rhapta *(rap tuh) n.* An ancient city located near Mt. Kilimanjaro. It is hidden behind a psychic barrier and unknown to humanity. Currently at half capacity due to its dwindling population.

ubir *(oo beer) n.* Anunnaki that have defected from Rhapta and turned to blood magic to exist outside of the city while retaining their abilities. They quickly become rabid and need to sacrifice humans to retain their abilities. Their Aura is chaotic and painful.

Ummanu *(oo mon oo) n.* Humans who are aware of Anunnaki existence and have allied with them. Most watch over the portals around the world.

venari *(venn are ee) n.* Anunnaki bounty hunters tasked with locating and returning ubir from human society. They are shunned within Rhapta due to their "dirty" work and closeness with human society.

DRAMATIS PERSONAE

Kinza's Family

Grams – Kinza's maternal human grandmother; is Ummanu
Sadia Solace – Kinza's mother, a descendant of Prince Malik; deceased
Jay Solace – Kinza's father; deceased
Prince Malik – Kinza's Anunnaki ancestor on her mother's side, former heir to the Rhaptan throne

Mitra Burman – Kinza's best friend in Chicago

Zaid's Family
Ekaja Hatem – Zaid's mother
Amir Hatem – Zaid's older brother; deceased

Khalil Sadek – Zaid's oldest friend, a healer who lives on the outskirts
Haris – Zaid's Ummanu friend who lives in northern Michigan

Elders and Apprentices

Grand Elder Hakim - Seer of Rhapta; deceased

Elder Tahir – Former representative of the quarries, currently on the run

Elder Ekbal – Representative of agriculture, Hakim's nephew

Elder Yuvaan – Representative of the warriors

Elder Ishar – Representative of the venari

Elder Minesh – Former representative of city planning; currently on the run with Tahir

Elder Utu – Representative of education

Elder Sumai – Representative of the south quarter

Elder Harran – Former representative of the north quarter; currently on the run with Tahir

Elder Urash – Representative of the healers

Elder Balasi – Representative of human relations

Elder Qirin – Representative of city cisterns

Elder Hija – Only other Anunnaki, besides Kinza, with four abilities

Apprentice Eta – Former apprentice of Grand Elder Hakim, current Seer of Rhapta

Apprentice Mikah Sultan – Former apprentice of Elder Tahir

Apprentice Urbarra – Apprentice of Elder Qirin

Apprentice Kiaan – Former apprentice of Elder Minesh; currently on the run with Tahir

Apprentice Riku – Apprentice of Elder Urash

Apostles of Truth

Sa'id – Former leader of the Apostles of Truth; deceased

Nimatullah – Current leader of the Apostles of Truth

Hunar – Former mentor to Amir Hatem and current scholar

Jabari – Scholar and Kinza's trainer for her abilities

Badr – A young scholar and apprentice to Jabari

Tammuz – An older scholar and former guard of the Apostles

The Venari

Savar Basu – Head of the venari and trainer, answers to Elder Ishar

Tejas – A young venari who trained with Zaid

Laiq – An older venari with a technology ability

Rafael- A venari

Tahir's Assassins

Yusuf – Collected orders from Tahir, deceased

Ghufran – An assassin; deceased

Aisha – A double agent, friend to Kinza and Ekaja

Jafar – Leader, killed Kinza's parents, deceased

Rafiq – An assassin; deceased

Warriors

Commander Kartik – Leader of the warriors, answers to Elder Yuvaan

Feroz – Young warrior, Zaid's childhood bully

Maheer – A warrior trainer

Parwez – A young warrior Zaid sparred with in his youth, deceased

Nazim – Older man and former beloved warrior trainer; a leader during the Rhaptan attacks

Tariq – One of Elder Tahir's former personal guards

Known Ubir

Ghassan Lahgari – Part of the northern Michigan pack, potentially assisted the Unfettered, deceased

Basma – Part of the northern Michigan pack; escaped/status unknown

Amir – Zaid's brother; deceased

The Human-Anunnaki

Edmund Clark – American billionaire and CEO
Vivienne Moreau – French fashion icon
Wang Hàorán – Chinese chairman of a conglomerate

Louis Reddington – An Ummanu in the employ of Edmund Clark

Others in Rhapta
Anjali – Rhaptan woman who spoke out against Kinza
Rayaan – Rhaptan man at Kinza's trial, spread the word about the results of the trial
Tiamat – Ekaja's friend and friend to Kinza
Zabu – An account scholar and Khalil's former friend; tried to kill Kinza out of fear
Zakariah – Upper member of the Unfettered, spread lies about Kinza
Ojasvat – Member of the Unfettered; status unknown after the battle in Rhapta
Walid – Former overseer of the quarries; deceased
Tashiq – Young boy living on the outskirts that Khalil healed

AUTHOR'S NOTE

Dear Beloved Reader,

Thank you so much for continuing to follow Kinza and Zaid in Infinite Magic! I hope you have enjoyed their story. If you enjoyed Infinite Magic, I would be grateful if you would consider leaving a review. Reviews help other readers find my stories, and each review is priceless to me.

Although this book completes the trilogy, you can continue to catch up with Kinza and Zaid in my next stand-alone book, Corrupt Magic, which will feature Mikah and Eta as well as Haris and Mitra. Keep turning the pages because as a bonus, I've included a sneak peek of chapter one!

In addition, I've published a new novella that is only available to those who sign up for my mailing list! Portal Magic: A Rhaptaverse Novella is a glimpse into my upcoming Rhaptaverse series which will show the new batch of venari as they go out into the human world to save humanity from the ubir. You absolutely don't want to miss it! Click here to download your copy today.

Visit my website (LilySkyy.com) and interact with me on social media. There's awesome merch available for each of my series. Also, make sure to sign up for my mailing list to be the first to know about new releases and special happenings such as previews and give-a-ways!

I love getting feedback from my readers, and if you'd like to stay in touch (or discuss my books), join me over at the Lily Skyy Readers' Group. I'd also love to connect with you on Instagram, TikTok, and Twitter! Feel free to reach out to me directly via email at social@lilyskyy.com. You may access all of my social media profiles by visiting: https://smartpa.ge/lilyskyy.

Again, I thank you for reading, and I can't wait to join you on the next adventure! Remember, chapter one of Corrupt Magic is on the next page!

Sincerely,

Lily Skyy

SNEAK PEEK OF CORRUPT MAGIC

CHAPTER 1
THE DEEP SOUTH

The flatness stretched on for miles in every direction. A sea of grass and corn stalks flowed in the late September breeze. It felt like there wasn't a single soul left in the world as Mitra stretched her cell phone high up toward the sun, trying to get better reception. When she glanced at it and noticed she still had no bars, she huffed in irritation.

The two-lane road was devoid of traffic, but she still glanced in both directions, hoping to see some sort of sign she might have missed. It was a futile effort though, because she never missed anything. Mitra was the sort of person who noticed things others didn't; rarely did a single detail escape her attention. She had been watching for a sign for miles, trying to find the way back to the main highway. This "shortcut" was anything but short, but Haris had assured her this way was faster. He was also sure they weren't going to run out of gas, but she had a feeling she would need to be a bit more firm on that one. She had no intention of walking miles to find another gas station.

Glaring at the empty road one more time, she walked back to the green, beat-up truck parked on the shoulder and climbed into the passenger side of the cab.

"Still nothing," she said over the blaring country music, yanking the door shut. "You actually like this stuff?" she asked. She had never been a fan of the twangy sounds of acoustic love songs.

"Hm?" Haris said, looking up from the map he had pulled out of the glove box. She had picked it up at the last stop, though Haris had promised he 'knew where he was going.' "This? I like to immerse myself in my environment. Be one with my surroundings," he said mystically, with a smile. He bent back down to the map and pointed. "I'm pretty sure we're on the right track. We just need to follow this road for...a few more miles, and we'll come back out to the highway. And then we should be in Tennessee tonight."

Mitra sighed, mentally preparing to walk down the highway in the dark when they got lost again and ran out of gas. "I hope so. I feel like we're wandering around in a massive corn maze."

Haris folded the map back up and tossed it in the back seat. He snorted. "That's Illinois for you," he said and put the truck back into gear before pulling onto the road again.

To Mitra's annoyance, he turned up the music.

They had only been traveling for a day and a half, even though it felt like much longer. They had left Haris's house in northern Michigan right after their friends Kinza and Zaid had gone through the portal in Haris's basement. The portal that would transport them to another portal on the other side of the planet so they could go to the magical hidden city in Tanzania.

Mitra still had a hard time remembering all that stuff was real. The last few weeks had been a nightmare for her. First her best friend went missing and her grandmother refused to say where she was. And then she later finds Kinza casually walking through Chicago with a man she'd never seen before. And *then* Kinza tells her she's the long-lost heir to a civilization of people with magical abilities and she had to go live in that hidden city for the rest of her life as their queen. If Mitra was being honest with herself, it still hadn't set in that she would never see her best friend again. In her mind, she would wake up tomorrow and they would both go to work, cleaning toilets for the fancy businesses in downtown Chicago.

Yet here she was, hunting a deranged monster with magic powers across the country with a sometimes equally deranged red-haired guy she met a few days ago. Seriously, was he ever in a bad mood? Mitra didn't understand how he could be so cheerful all the time.

She glanced over at Haris in the driver's seat. A pair of sunglasses sat over his eyes and his fingers tapped against the steering wheel out of time with the music. She didn't know how she felt about him yet. He had flirted with her relentlessly since they met at Kinza's house a few days ago, but he seemed to have a similar disposition with everyone. Always teasing or grinning, or cracking jokes at the worst times. She could have sworn he did it more with her, though...

Haris caught her looking and waggled his eyebrows over his glasses. "Want to take a picture? It'll last longer." Point in case.

Mitra crossed her arms and turned back to the road without answering, thankful she had on a pair of gigantic sunglasses that partially hid her blush. She refused to be embarrassed, though; she just wasn't that type of girl.

Literally nothing made him mad either. Mitra had tried for the first day, taking over the crackly stereo and pumping her most obnoxious songs through the speakers. Haris only bobbed his head along with the noise. She even went as far as to start backseat driving, telling him to slow down or use his blinker or speed up, but he only remarked on how *helpful* she was being. Maybe he had been sarcastic. Either way, she gave up on trying to push his buttons pretty quick seeing as it had little effect on him. They had a job to focus on anyway.

Kinza and Zaid had filled her in on the ubir that they were chasing. Apparently the Anunnaki—Kinza's people—weren't supposed to just leave their city, or they would lose their memories and powers. A group of rebellious Anunnaki discovered a way to leave while keeping their powers, but it required routine blood sacrifices that warped their minds over time. They turned into something very close to a monster from a children's nightmare, stealing people in the night. Similar to a drug addiction, the longer they practiced this ritual, the more broken their minds became, until they were killing people for pleasure.

The ubir normally moved throughout the world alone, but they would occasionally form small groups of twos or threes and cause that much more damage for the venari—the Anunnaki bounty hunters—to clean up. Kinza and Zaid had run into one of these packs a few weeks ago, killing two of them, but the third escaped. Basma was her name, and she was supposed to have some sort of agility power, like a zombie gymnast. Kinza had described her as more aware than the others. Maybe she had been practicing the blood rituals for less time. Either way, they couldn't let her go free, so Haris had offered to track her down for Zaid.

Mitra had immediately demanded to come along, but she wasn't ready to admit to herself why yet. Instead, she thought about how it had been a thousand times more boring than she expected monster-hunting to be.

"Remind me, why couldn't we just have used the portal at

your house to pop down to one of the others down south instead of driving the whole way?" she asked. The windows were cracked; the further south they got, the warmer it was, and Mitra relished the breeze whipping over her long braid.

"We aren't allowed to," Haris replied brightly. She could tell he didn't like that fact based on the slightly pained smile. "They're only for Anunnaki; venari specifically. No humans allowed."

"So you guard over the portal your whole life. You operate it so the venari can use it. And you keep it hidden from other humans. Yet Ummanu can't use it?" She was a bit skeptical of the rules between the Anunnaki and their Ummanu allies.

"Pretty much," Haris said. "But in all honesty, we don't really travel much. What we're doing right now is pretty unconventional. Ummanu don't keep tabs on ubir, let alone track them down. We have a few things to protect ourselves, but we try to keep off their radar. Which is what makes this so exciting!"

Mitra secretly had to agree. Despite the endless fields of corn and wheat, the thought of tracking down a rabid Anunnaki had her energized in a way she hadn't been in a long time. There was nothing in her life that had her springing out of bed in the morning as much as this.

Haris had started singing along to the music, and not quietly.

"Do you want me to drive?" Mitra asked.

"Not a chance!" Haris sang and kept on driving. "Either way, we shouldn't be far now. Look up where the motel is again on the map."

"Why do we have to stay in a grimy motel?" Mitra said, reaching in the backseat for the map.

"Do I look like I'm made of money to you?" he asked, making a face behind his glasses. "Portal-guarding doesn't exactly pay much. Nothing, in fact. I still have to have a human job to pay the bills."

"You do all that for free?" Mitra asked. She couldn't find anything on the map, so she pulled out her phone. Still no reception.

"Yup. I'm a good Samaritan," Haris said, running a hand over his hair.

Mitra checked her phone again and yelped. "I've got reception!" She quickly looked up their location and the distance to the motel. Haris was off by a few hours, though. She gave him the directions and screenshot them just in case.

"I think we should go over the evidence again," Mitra said as they pulled back onto the main highway.

"Well, there isn't much," Haris said. "We know Linda said a body was found by the local police a few miles outside of Jackson. They said the blood was drained and looked a bit ritualistic, which tends to be the ubir's trademark. But that was days ago. I got another hit from an Ummanu named Abe down in Louisiana, something about more murders that way too."

"I'm guessing we'll stop and check them both out if we don't find Basma here?" Mitra asked as they flew down the highway.

"Might as well."

"What do we do when we find her?"

Haris turned her a devilish grin. "Do you know how to fight?"

Mitra snorted and looked out the window, but deep down she could feel that thrum of excitement building.

"Sorry, kids, that's all I got."

Mitra and Haris stood dejectedly on Linda's white-painted porch. The two-story house sat in a picture-perfect suburban neighborhood in Memphis that looked like it could have come out of a magazine. The potted plants on her doorstep were immaculate, and her two kids played in the yard while mommy had a "business meeting."

The woman herself looked nothing short of a typical soccer mom. Short blond hair, expensive athleisure, and one eye on her kids at all times. Mitra was a little baffled that this woman had connections to the Anunnaki and even knew what the ubir were. She looked like she was about to attend the local PTA meeting after they were done before proceeding to the town bake sale, where she would present her "famous" snickerdoodle cookies just like last year. She didn't have time to ogle at the pretty house or smell what was baking in the oven before Linda had jumped into her story about the murders.

They had spent the night in the grimy motel Mitra had detested and gotten up early to get a head start, making it into town by late morning. Linda had invited them in and offered them sweet tea and some lemon bars, which Haris accepted enthusiastically. She had gone over the murder that had happened five days ago now, but was just as Haris described; a ritualistic murder of a young woman outside of Jackson. The body was found on the train tracks with the throat and wrists slit, something she couldn't have done herself. The police had found little signs of struggle and no suspect whatsoever.

When it was clear that Linda wouldn't have any helpful information, Mitra took the opportunity to drill the woman with questions about being Ummanu in plain sight, what her life was like, or if any of her family knew. Mitra wanted to take every opportunity to ask about the people who lived this lifestyle before she went back to her boring life with strict rules and expectations. Linda answered patiently, and when she had gone to check on her kids, Haris elbowed Mitra.

"This isn't an interrogation. I can tell you anything you want to know about being Ummanu," he said.

"I'm just curious," she replied. Mitra had always been a curious child, and a thorough student, to her parents' delight. She just wanted to know *more*. "A week ago, none of this stuff existed for me."

They had taken their leave, saying goodbye to Linda with a promise from Haris to connect more in the future.

"Well, now what?" Mitra said while jumping into the driver's seat. Haris didn't complain, only tossing her the keys.

"Just start driving," he said. "I'll see if I can give Abe a call."

Mitra navigated through busy Memphis and out to the highway again, heading south. Haris had a conversation with Abe, yet he had an odd facial expression the entire time and asked the man to repeat himself more than once.

"That was fun," Haris said, ending the call.

"What?"

"That's the thickest accent I've ever heard. He said they had two murders down that way, similar to the one Linda described. The last one was two days ago, though. I still think it's worth checking out." Haris leaned his head on the back of the seat, drumming his fingers on the door.

"Alright, Louisiana it is." It was quiet for a moment before Mitra asked, "So how *did* you get into this stuff?"

Haris rolled his head to look at her, brown eyes questioning.

"You said you would tell me whatever I wanted to know," she reminded him.

"Ah, right. Well, I—" he hesitated as if thinking "—was chosen on a game show as a child," he said with a totally straight face. "Something about my look screamed 'defender of portals, hunter of monsters, most attractive dude alive.' Or something like that."

Mitra shook her head, trying not to laugh. She had spent her fair share around guys, having had a string of boyfriends in high school that all wanted to impress her with their shiny cars, fancy clothes, and stoic demeanor. She couldn't help but compare Haris to the other guys she'd known, so she felt like she was stuck in a group project with the class jokester.

"Ha, ha, so you just happened to have your career chosen for you as a child. Must be rough."

"Yep," Haris said, leaning his seat back and placing his hand behind his head. "Unlike you. The world is your oyster."

"If only," Mitra grumbled to herself. She would've given anything to have the kind of freedom he did. Everything had been chosen for her since she was a child. Her career options, her extracurriculars, and even certain boys were pushed in her direction by her parents. They loved her dearly, but sometimes their love could be suffocating. She had managed to get them to let her take a year off before college, citing that all the wealthy kids did it. But in reality, she just wanted more time. More time before she had to start working toward a career and a life she didn't want. Every day she dreaded having to fill out the college applications to the nation's best medical schools while fending off her mother's constant prodding for her to go on a date with a friend's "perfect" son.

She didn't have to think about that right now, though. With the blue sky above her and the beat-up truck beneath her, she turned up the volume and let the obnoxious music Haris had chosen wash over her as they headed to the deep south of Louisiana.

THEY CHOSE to stay one more night in a motel, to Mitra's disgust. She could have sworn the bed had bugs, so she wrapped herself in a towel before lying on the floor to sleep. Haris had no such qualms and was tucked beneath the blankets on his bed and asleep within minutes.

Mitra had a hard time falling asleep, so she scrolled through her phone, looking at social media, the news, and old pictures of her and Kinza. She wondered what her friend was doing at that moment. Was she safely back in that magical city of hers, or was she fighting monsters just like Mitra? They had seen each other almost every day for years, so she had felt bereft this last week without her. It seemed that Kinza had her life all figured out now and Mitra was approaching...nothing.

As she did every night, Mitra sent a text to Kinza, knowing that she wouldn't receive it unless she left the city—no reception in magical lands. Mitra told her how her day was and what she and Haris were up to. She suggested that the two of them take a real road trip sometime soon, knowing it would never happen.

Mitra wiped a tear that had slipped out of the corner of her eye before shutting her phone off and attempting to sleep. Just before she drifted off, she had the rebellious thought that maybe that was why she wanted to come with Haris. While she was off monster hunting with him, it felt like she was still part of Kinza's world. But the moment it ended, her best friend would be beyond her reach.

IT DIDN'T TAKE them long the next morning to get down to Thibodaux. Abe lived just a few miles from there, seemingly out in the middle of nowhere. Mitra couldn't get over how humid it was, even in September. She was glad they had stopped to get clothes at a random store, but the t-shirt and cutoff shorts she had on still felt like a parka.

They drove down a single-lane county road, further south, following the directions Abe had given them. Apparently he had his own plot of land out here where the portal was. The further they got, the more trees and water they found. Houses and buildings disappeared behind them and they finally found the mark in the side of the road where the driveway was. It went on for another quarter mile through the trees, the truck bouncing along on the uneven road.

They pulled up to what Mitra thought was a literal junkyard.

"Are you sure this is it?" she asked.

Haris slowed down, "Um, not really..."

They looked around a lot filled with various old cars, tires, scrap material, a bathtub, and even a school bus. There were also scattered children's toys, piles of wood, dog crates, the three dogs themselves, and a broken kiddie pool. Mitra finally spotted the house beneath a curtain of wind chimes and wind fans. The single-story shack was actually relatively decent in size, if you actually made it to the door without tripping and harming yourself.

The dogs had little interest as Haris pulled up as far as he could and killed the engine. On the side of the makeshift driveway was an old sign that said "NO TRESPASSING."

"Maybe we should call again..." Mitra suggested as they got out and walked up to the door.

"I think it's a little late for that," Haris replied. There was a large porch across the front of the house and it looked like the short staircase had fallen in long ago. There was no way the owner would hear them coming with the army of windchimes blowing, but they went up and knocked on the screen door.

At first there was no answer, so Haris knocked again, harder this time. They heard movement from within and saw a shadow on the other side of the frosted glass of the inner door. The thumping of footsteps grew louder just as the shadow did as the person came to answer the knocking.

After what felt like a year, the door opened and on the other side of the screen, Mitra saw exactly what she had dreaded. An older man stood there, a little taller than herself, but three times as wide. Wild tufts of gray hair stuck out from underneath the straw hat, and she caught a glimpse of several missing teeth in the angry face of the man as he pushed open the screen door.

Mitra waited for him to yell at them for trespassing.

Then, in the thickest southern accent she had ever heard, "What took y'all so long?!"

WANT MORE CORRUPT MAGIC? Get your copy today!